PRAISE FOR THE NO[...]
GRACE TIFFA[...]

KT-194-493

WILL

"A moving story of love, loss, and the true cost of genius."

—India Edghill,
author of *Queenmaker*

"A plausible glimpse of young Shakespeare as a sympathetic figure, caught between the demands of purse and muse, ambition and family, word and deed."   —*The Charleston Post and Courier*

"Lively, boisterous."   —*Booklist*

"There can be no doubting Tiffany's comprehensive historical research, which flavors her elegant prose."   —*Library Journal*

MY FATHER HAD A DAUGHTER

"I was hopelessly hooked from the very first page. . . . Judith Shakespeare is a remarkable creation, as unforgettable as her famous father."   —Sharon Kay Penman, *New York Times*
bestselling author of *Prince of Darkness*

"A view of the life and psyche of the playwright that is unparalleled and fascinating. Her richly detailed portayal of Elizabethan England and a woman's place in it is enthralling."   —*Library Journal*

"A gem of a novel—wise and funny, romantic and heartbreaking."
—Herman Gollob, author of *Me and
Shakespeare: Adventures with the Bard*

"Judith Shakespeare is a daughter William Shakespeare himself might have imagined and set on stage . . . A wonderful novel."

—Carrie Brown,
author of *Confinement*

THE TURQUOISE RING

GRACE TIFFANY

B

BERKLEY BOOKS, NEW YORK

THE BERKLEY PUBLISHING GROUP
Published by the Penguin Group
Penguin Group (USA) Inc.
375 Hudson Street, New York, New York 10014, USA
Penguin Group (Canada), 10 Alcorn Avenue, Toronto, Ontario M4V 3B2, Canada
(a division of Pearson Penguin Canada Inc.)
Penguin Books Ltd, 80 Strand, London WC2R 0RL, England
Penguin Ireland, 25 St. Stephen's Green, Dublin 2, Ireland (a division of Penguin Books Ltd.)
Penguin Group (Australia), 250 Camberwell Road, Camberwell, Victoria 3124, Australia
(a division of Pearson Australia Group Pty. Ltd)
Penguin Books India Pvt. Ltd., 11 Community Centre, Panchsheel Park, New Delhi—110 017, India
Penguin Group (NZ), cnr Airborne and Rosedale Roads, Albany, Auckland 1310, New Zealand
(a division of Pearson New Zealand Ltd.)
Penguin Books (South Africa) (Pty.) Ltd., 24 Sturdee Avenue, Rosebank, Johannesburg 2196, South Africa

Penguin Books Ltd., Registered Offices: 80 Strand, London WC2R 0RL, England

This is a work of fiction. Names, characters, places, and incidents either are the product of the author's imagination or are used fictitiously, and any resemblance to actual persons, living or dead, business establishments, events, or locales is entirely coincidental.

Copyright © 2005 by Grace Tiffany
Cover design by Lesley Worrell
Cover illustration by Robin Davis
Book design by Kristin del Rosario

All rights reserved.
No part of this book may be reproduced, scanned, or distributed in any printed or electronic form without permission. Please do not participate in or encourage piracy of copyrighted materials in violation of the author's rights. Purchase only authorized editions.
BERKLEY is a registered trademark of Penguin Group (USA) Inc.
The "B" design is a trademark belonging to Penguin Group (USA) Inc.

PRINTING HISTORY
Berkley hardcover edition / May 2005
Berkley trade paperback edition / April 2006

Berkley trade paperback ISBN: 0-425-20666-1

The Library of Congress has catalogued the Berkeley hardcover edition as follows:

Tiffany, Grace, 1958–
    The turquoise ring / Grace Tiffany.—Berkley hardcover ed.
        p.   cm.
    ISBN 0-425-20248-8
    1. Venice (Italy)—History—1508–1797—Fiction.   2   Fathers and daughters—Fiction.   3. Refugees, Jewish—Fiction.   4. Jews—Italy—Fiction.   5. Rings—Fiction. I. Title.

PD3620.I45T87 2005
813'.54—dc22   2004065595

PRINTED IN THE UNITED STATES OF AMERICA

10 9 8 7 6 5 4 3 2 1

To Karen

ויש אהב דבק מאח

"It was my turquoise.
I had it of Leah, when I was a bachelor. . . ."

—William Shakespeare, *The Merchant of Venice*

THE TURQUOISE RING

Grace Tiffany

LEAH

Toledo, 1567

*"Who chooseth me must give and
hazard all he hath."*

ONE

THE RING LAY on the back corner of one of the swordmaker's shelves. The young woman was not interested in the swords of Señor Julian del Rei, and had only glanced at the small window underneath his signboard to show herself that her hair was still properly tucked beneath her veil after a sudden wind gust had knocked the fabric askew. But her eye was drawn beyond her own flawed image in the bubbled glass to the glint of blue on the shelf. The ring was the only colored thing among the wares near it—the iron and steel weapons, buffed to a mirrorlike sheen and suspended from nails on the rear wall; the silver and lead oddments set in front of the ring on the cedar plank.

Without thinking, Leah opened the door and went into the shop.

The room was empty of living beings save for herself, a little boy who swept dust from the floor, and a small, dark-eyed girl who sat in the rear at a worktable, counting silver coins. The boy looked at Leah quickly—a narrow, sidelong glance—and then left the room, clutching his broom. The little girl gazed at her as if in awe or fright, then shyly dropped her eyes and resumed her counting. Above the rhythmic clink of the coins Leah could hear the voices of men in a room behind, speaking of sword tempering and filing and weight.

She closed the door behind her. With one hand she again fixed her veil, and with another she touched the purse at her belt. "Good morrow," she said to the girl, who looked up again briefly and smiled.

Leah crossed the floor to the ring.

Its design was unusual. Its band was composed of five interlocking strands of silver woven into an intricate circle, crowned with a silver mount that held the tear-shaped turquoise. It was the stone that had drawn Leah, and she squinted at it, holding the ring up to the shaft of midmorning light that pierced the small, high window. The turquoise was as blue as the winter sky above La Mancha, though not as clear. Indeed, it was veined with a matrix of dark, spidery lines. But, perhaps by a trick of the mind, Leah saw light shifting, color changing, in the heart of the flawed stone.

The sound of dropping coins ceased behind her. She felt the child's eyes on her back. But when she turned it was to see a stooped, leather-aproned man standing in the doorway to the workroom behind, smiling at her slightly, in a manner that suggested inexplicable intimacy. "Señora." He bowed in a peculiar fashion, with his arms crossed over his bosom. She nodded, acutely aware that she was a woman alone; that she had left her house without her father's leave and with no servant trailing her steps. She replaced the ring on the shelf, and once more smoothed her veil.

The craftsman stood aside in the doorway to give passage from the workroom to a grand-looking man in a fur cloak and hat, who wore a red silk doublet lined with yellow. When the craftsman bowed to the man he did not cross his breast with his arms, and unlike Leah, the grand man did not return the craftsman's greeting; his gaze was absorbed by the yellow hair of a tiny girl whose hand he was tightly holding. She was all in cloth-of-gold, from her cap to her pointed shoes. She chattered merrily as she glanced about the shop. Her father—so he must be, Leah thought—spoke over the golden child's babble, in Spanish with an accent of north Italy. "The sword, then, Maestro del Rei," he said, "with the jeweled hilt. And the Spanish rapier."

"Both shall be delivered before your return to Venice, my señor," the craftsman said, bowing once more. He darted his eyes leftward at Leah.

The yellow-haired girl reached into her father's fur-lined pocket and extracted a handful of silver. This she offered to the dark girl at the rear worktable, who had begun coin-counting again. "Say *grazie!*" commanded the golden child, holding her hand out to the other girl, who only looked at her calmly. The gold-clad child's father brushed the silver from his daughter's hand back into his pocket, saying, "That is mine, my dear one. We will look about us; we will find other things to amuse you." To the craftsman he said, "You have new business. I will not delay you."

"My lord." The craftsman bowed again, and approached Leah. "And you, señora doncella," he said in a low voice. "I see you have an interest in that ring, but it is not for sale. You would do better to look at its sibling." He lifted a shining steel sword off the wall. "Do you see the hilt of this one? Inlaid with silver. And the blade is of the ice-brook's temper. In December I heated it at my forge outside the city wall, then plunged it into the Tagus to harden it. The cold numbed my hand, but now the sword is strong and sharp." He touched the filed steel lightly. "Deadly on both sides, though light. It will pierce any breast in battle."

Leah winced, and the man noticed. He said, "You are too tender in years to know anything of bloodshed."

"I am seventeen. I did not wish to look at the weapons."

He shrugged. "It is well. You could not have the sword either, even if you wanted it. This"—he tapped the sword blade with a bruised fingernail—"is spoken for, too, by a young man, a Morisco of Venice." The man replaced the blade on the wall. "I made that turquoise ring as I make all my oddments, from the ends of silver and gold and stone that I use for sword grips and hilts. Remnants. I convert them to jewelry, and to other things of interest, and why not? Why should they go to waste? I asked the young Moor if he would want such an oddment. I told him the silver strands bound the finest Turkish stone, from Constantinople. Of the kingdom of the infidel. He only laughed and said he was a soldier and never would wed, and what use could he have for a ring? But it is not for sale all the same, señora doncella, despite that young man's princely disdain. I keep it there on the shelf for my daughter." He gestured toward the seated girl, who nodded, her pursed lips silently counting. "She likes to look at it. It is a man's ring, and one day she will give it to her husband." He turned suddenly to his daughter and said, "Go! *Ameji!* It is time for the meal."

Obediently, the girl slid off her stool. She laid a last silver coin atop a stack, then disappeared into the back.

The man turned back to Leah. "See, again, the hilt." He pointed to the handle of the sword he'd replaced on the wall. Her eyes followed his finger and came to rest on a small graven emblem. "There is my sign, the same picture hung outside my shop, under *Julian del Rei, Fine Swords of Toledo.* Can you tell what it is?"

"Of course, señor," Leah said. "A dog."

The man laughed appreciatively. "Good! Most think it a fox. It is a dog because I am a Moor and they think *dog* when they look at us. Do you not find it so, lady?"

Leah narrowed her eyes at him. "Us?" she said. "But I am a Christian."

"But not a very old one, señora doncella."

Her skin felt hot. "My name is Elizabeta de la Cerda. My father is a hidalgo, a nobleman! His name is Sebastian de la Cerda."

"Ah. And your mother?"

Leah stared at him for a moment. "My mother is dead," she finally said.

"May she rest in peace, like all good Christians," the man said smoothly. "There was a time, a little more than a century ago, when the Christian ground where she doubtless lies buried was the Sinagoga del Tránsito. Toledo was a city of three faiths then. No longer. But the world may abide such harmony in a future time, yes? Things will recur. An old age sees itself repeated in a new one. God forges similitudes, as the Holy Book says."

"I do not know the saying," Leah said. Her heart beat quickly and she wondered why she did not now take her leave, but stayed, curiously bound by his tongue. "I do not know it," she repeated.

"You would not. 'Tis not in the Old Testament. Ah, forgive me. You do not call it that. It is not in the New Testament, either. Look you now," he said, before Leah could respond. He gestured at the brilliant swords and rapiers that lined his wall. Among them she noticed a heavy-looking jeweled scimitar, with a blade curved like a new moon. "When I sell these steel blades I convert them as by alchemy into silver coin. So I am a magician of sorts. But one day their sharp splendor will crumble to dust. The age of gunpowder is upon us. It is the sword and not the gun that proves a man's valor, but my swords are threatened in this year of Our Lord fifteen hundred and sixty-seven. I say fifteen hundred and sixty-seven, though to you, of course"— he glanced slyly at Leah— "the world is much older."

"I know not your meaning," Leah said nervously, thinking that she was not a man and had no interest in steel or gunpowder. Her eyes returned to the turquoise, and he saw them move. He picked up the ring.

The man's daughter reappeared at her counting table bearing a platter of fruit, a cloth, and a knife. She carefully pushed the stacks of coin to the side and then spread the cloth. At the same time the lordly Italian and his little girl, who had been looking at the shelves on the far side of the shop, returned to speak to the craftsman, and Leah stepped back. Seeing the turquoise ring in the craftsman's hand, the little gold-clad girl suddenly jumped forward and seized it, then dashed again to the little girl in the back. She handed her the ring. "Say *grazie!*" she demanded.

The other girl took it wordlessly and laid it next to her on the table. As the little one stood expectantly, awaiting her thanks, the craftsman walked to the back of the room, smiling wryly, and replaced the ring on his palm. "Shall she give thanks, small señora doncella, for what is her own?" The gold-haired child's face fell.

"These boxes," her father said quickly. He held out three small, neat caskets, each composed of a different metal. In one hand he grasped the two of gold and silver, and in the other he held a thicker one that seemed to be much heavier. Its color was leaden. "My daughter would like them." He placed the boxes carefully on the floor before him, then reached into his pocket. "What do you ask?"

"Ah, my señor, they are mere oddments. Already you pay me a fine price for the blades." The lord began to remove his hand from his pocket, but the craftsman hastily added, "Two hundred mar-avedís would be sufficient."

The man frowned slightly, but dug in his pocket for the silver, counted it, and handed it to the craftsman Señor del Rei, who with one hand dropped the coins into his apron. There was more bow-ing, and then the wealthy man and the child left the shop, the girl chattering, the man bearing the metal boxes. Before the door swung shut Leah saw the man hand the boxes to a manservant who stood outside.

The craftsman watched their exit, the turquoise ring still lying on his palm. When he turned back to Leah he saw her eyes on it, and closed his fist.

"The ring is not for you," he said, his voice suddenly blunt. "Go back to your synagogue and find a man to give you one."

In Leah's haste to leave the shop, she stumbled over the boy who had been sweeping the floor and who now sat hunched over a rind of cheese on the front stoop. She righted herself, but in her confusion failed to beg his pardon, and as she disappeared into the crowd of milling customers in the Plaza de Zocodover his dark eyes followed her angrily.

"She was the one," the boy told his master inside. "She came to the forbidden meal, on the Shabbat. I thought her beautiful. I spoke to her, but she would not look at me. Her eyes were fixed on a man."

"I care not, boy, for other people's worship," said the craftsman, readying his tools to go out to the forge. "Look to your work. Let her be a Jewess if she pleases. Let her believe in the one God. And you also may believe what you will."

The boy stared darkly into the plaza as though he could still see Leah's turned back. "Nothing," he said under his breath. "I believe in nothing."

The swordmaker's daughter hummed, on her perch in the rear of the shop, behind the frowning boy. Placidly, she sliced rings from a Sevillan orange for the noonday meal.

TWO

AFTER THAT DAY Leah went quickly past the shop of Señor Julian del Rei when she walked in the Plaza de Zocodover, and willed herself not to glance up at his small window. She feared if she did she would be greeted by the craftsman's shrewd, mocking stare, assaulting her through the bubbled glass. It startled her, then, when a week later, on Ash Wednesday, when all the shops in the plaza were closed, she heard a tap on del Rei's window; and, when she looked up involuntarily, saw Señor del Rei's face indeed peering down at her, but with an affable expression. His face was smudged with ash, though not from the holy day. It was mixed with grease in a smear on his cheek, and she guessed that, ignoring solemnity, he had been working with his tools. He beckoned her to the shop's front door. Again without knowing why, she walked toward the entrance. Her servant was with her that day, and she bade him wait outside.

"Here, señora doncella." The aproned craftsman held out the turquoise ring. They were alone in the front room of the shop on this day, and she dimly noted the place's emptiness with her ears. Her eyes were drawn by the ring's blueness. She took it from him, and only then looked at the maestro's face. "Why?" she asked.

He shrugged. "My daughter says it is yours. She is an odd one, and stubborn."

Clutching the ring with one hand, Leah opened her purse with the other. "What do you ask, señor?"

She saw regret in the craftsman's eyes as he looked at the bulging purse at her waist. He sighed and shook his head. "A gift. I made it for her, and she gives it to you."

"Well, maestro!" Leah closed her purse. "Please give her my thanks." She half-turned to go, then stopped and held the ring up with two fingers. "But one question, señor. The braided silver strands. I . . . like the look of them. But I think they will hurt the wearer's finger. Why did you fashion the ring that way?"

"As it usually happens I do not make rings, señora doncella. The wealthy buy here, and they wish their jewelry perfect. Yet a circle made by a craftsman should not be perfect."

"And why not?"

"Because perfection mocks great Creation." The shrewd look returned to his eyes. "Does not your own commandment against graven images suggest the same? My oddments, my designs, are twisted, abstract. What Allá has made is perfect. What men create is a broken maze."

Boldly, she held his gaze. After a moment she said, "You are not a Christian. Not even a New Christian. You are unconverted."

He said nothing, staring back at her with the half smile he had worn the day she first saw him standing in his workroom doorway.

"Why do you show me this much of yourself?" she asked.

He turned away then, straightening the objects on his shelves: a gold-plated cup, a statue of a dog made of iron or lead, a silver plate beautifully etched with geometrical patterns so intricate it dizzied her to look at them. As his hands arranged the objects he hummed softly.

She knew the melody. It was a Jewish wedding song, and had been taught her by her mother.

IN THE PLAZA she forced her way through the crowd of beggars and peasants and shop-folk surrounding the slow-walking penitents in their long dark robes. The penitents wore black masks with pointed hoods, and bore on their shoulders eight jeweled statues of the Virgin, each of which was clad in cloth-of-gold. One of the hooded figures hissed at Leah as she bumped against him. His eyes were baleful and dead as a shark's, and looked blankly at hers through the slits of his mask. Repelled, she fell back into the crowd, smelling garlic and incense and ashes. Children followed the procession, casting petals from the hothouse roses they had been given by the priests.

AT HOME SEBASTIAN de la Cerda ripped the veil from her head. "What, are there funeral processions?" he asked. "Or do you pretend to be a nun?"

"I have been to the mass, Father!" she replied angrily. "It is fitting for a woman to be veiled in the cathedral." She sat in a velvet-covered chair and stared at him defiantly.

He half-raised his hand, then dropped it as she flinched. "You lie to me, daughter. You went not to the mass, but to lurk about the old Jewish quarter, and then to enter a shop in the Plaza de

Zocodover. Nay, knit not thy brow. You should know by now that those who serve the Casa de la Cerda answer to me, not to you. Your follower betrayed you, Elizabeta."

"I am called Leah, my lord."

"Only by yourself!" de la Cerda yelled, red-faced, as he unstopped a crystal decanter.

THAT WAS NOT quite true, Leah thought, as she climbed the stairs to her room. When Leah was fifteen, in the last hours of her mother's life, as she lay dying of the blood lost in the birthing of her son—the son who had also died before breathing three breaths—she had gifted her daughter with the name. "My mother's, may she lie in peace," she had whispered. "She was dead before you were born. My marriage sped her death, or so it was said. But I would have liked to have remembered her in your naming, Leah."

"My father would not allow it," Leah guessed. Sebastian de la Cerda was then pacing with unsteady step in the carpeted hallway outside the room. In his grief he had drunk three bottles of muscatel.

Leah's mother laughed weakly. "*I* would not allow it. Not . . . allow myself to give you any other than a Christian name. Daughter, I could not bear the marks of the old faith then, from the time before I was Christian. It was not my faith, and I hated it then." She closed her eyes. "But you know all this. I have told you."

Discreetly, the Sister of Santa Catalina who had changed the bed linen now bundled the bloody sheets and left the room, with lowered gaze. The door closed softly behind the nun. Leah's mother opened her eyes and looked at her daughter, who was crying copiously. "Leah," she said tenderly.

"Why do you call me that now?" Leah sobbed, gripping her mother's hand. "What of my Christian name?"

Her mother smiled tiredly. "The new faith is as hollow as the old," she said. "It brought me only wealth and bitterness. Silver to cast at the beggars, and a husband who wanted forgiveness every night." She closed her eyes again. "Forgiveness, to keep on sinning."

AFTER THE DEATHS of her mother, Serafina, and her nameless infant brother, Leah's father had turned bitter and short-tempered. Though he still drank to excess, the wine no longer awoke his reveling spirit as it had in the past, when several nights in the week he had solaced himself with the witty courtesans in the House of Venus after his wife tired of his chatter. Eternally remorseful, Sebastian de la Cerda had sworn again and again to be virtuous; had confessed his sin to Father Bartolomeo and acquired the habit of saying penitential prayers. Leah's mother had been instructed by priests at the time of her marriage and knew it was a Christian's duty to forgive another Christian's failings. But she found it harder and harder to pardon her husband. She would have preferred that he honor the commandment forbidding adultery, as did she, and there an end to it.

Leah herself had been taught by the nuns of Santa Catalina, had taken her first communion and been confirmed as a Catholic. She knew her *Paternoster* and her catechism. She loved the hushed solemnity of the cavernous cathedral at the base of the Callejón de San Pedro. When her father had first taken her there, when she was four, the church's size had awed her. She and Sebastian de la Cerda had walked downhill on steep, twisting, crowded streets overhung by cobertizos, new-built dwelling places that blocked the light. They followed a procession that began wide, ten men abreast, in the Plaza Mayor, but gradually dwindled to a slow thread of single walkers because two could not walk side by side in the dark lanes. The images the men carried did not fit in the Callejón de San Pedro, and the procession took another way. Coming to the bottom of the hill alone, Leah and her father had passed through an enormous wooden door into the stone palace. Inside, she had stopped and stared in amazement—not at the spreading domes of the roof or at the massive columns and stone buttresses that supported it, but at the very air. There was so much of it! The inner cathedral was bigger than its outside. It was deeper, wider, and more open than any place in the walled city of Toledo—and outside Toledo's walls she had never been. She had not known there was so much space in the world.

As she grew, she came to understand from her mother's oblique complaints to her father that Serafina had once also thought the cathedral spacious. The cathedral and all it stood for had seemed bigger than anything her mother's old life promised. Serafina had sought the wide liberty she'd thought marriage to an Old Christian would give her, but had found only a new confinement. She herself had been a New Christian, from a family of Jews who had lived and practiced as Jews in Toledo since the seventh century of the Christian era. While other Jews moved south, to Granada, or fell from the faith, whose practice in Holy Christian Toledo grew more and more dangerous, Serafina's family stayed true. But by the end of the fifteenth century, when the spreading Moslem empire of the Ottoman Turks threatened Spain from the east, King Ferdinand and Queen Isabella had conquered all Spain, even to Granada. The Catholic monarchs had raised the flag of Christian Spain over the Alhambra and decreed that the kingdom belonged to Christ now, and that Spanish Moors, who were Moslem, and also all Spanish Jews must convert to the true way. Tens of thousands fled to Salonika, to Constantinople, to Jerusalem. Those who could not flee forged a compromise. The year was 1492 and the Catholic monarchs were giddy with victories at home and abroad, and with the prospects of New World silver and gold. Their era had begun, and Leah's mother's family had retreated into the shadows, waiting. They were the anusim, the "forced ones," though the New Christians called them an uglier name: *marranos,* which meant "swine." Outwardly the anusim conformed to the Christian faith. They submitted to baptism, attended mass, and received communion. Secretly, they kept kosher and Shabbat as best they could. They said the Kol Nidre, the prayer of atonement for Yom Kippur, asking that God disregard the Christian vows they had had to make.

For two generations, Leah's mother's family had lived this double life, among a small community of fellow secret Jews in Toledo. Some fell away and became true conversos, New Christians in fact as well as in name. The others said Kaddish for them. To them, the conversos were dead souls.

Leah's mother had been such a soul.

SHILOH WAS WAITING for Leah on the steps below the Moorish keyhole arch on the east side of the Plaza de Zocodover. Far below him stood the city wall, and beyond that, the shimmering river Tagus. Shiloh's eyes were shining like the river, with merriment rather than sunlight. He batted at Leah's hands as she pushed the corner of a prayer book, which stuck from his coat, deep inside his shirt. "I was reading my little Talmud!" he said, brushing at her fingers.

"So you expose yourself here, in the Puerta del Sol. Are you mad?" she said, evading his hands and persisting in her tucking until the small book was well out of sight.

"Yes, I am. Mad to be seen with a madwoman."

"I was only walking in the plaza." Leah adjusted her veil primly, as Shiloh watched her, amused. "I did not think you would be here."

Shiloh shrugged. "I said I would be here at three. I was here at three. Another five minutes and I wouldn't have been."

"You would not have waited?"

"I have work to do, fine lady. I have been a man since the age of thirteen."

"Seven whole years!"

"There is wool to be carded. A bargain is a bargain. You said three."

"I had to wait until my father fell asleep."

Shiloh took her arm and they descended the steps. "And why should the great Sebastian de la Cerda slumber in midafternoon? The estimable hidalgo. Son of something. Son of what?"

Leah giggled. "Son of a father who also slept the day away. They have lands and rents."

"Ah."

"They do no work, as you do, laborer."

"Money from nothing."

"But it looks well on your lady love, does it not?" Leah stopped to display her dark blue gown and her cheveril gloves. Her lace veil blew back, and a brown curl escaped.

This time Shiloh himself adjusted her veil, letting his fingers briefly touch the wayward curl. Regretfully, he said in a low voice, "Maidens may show their hair, Leah. It is when you are married that you may not. Then, only your husband must see your hair."

She looked at him boldly. "Will I have a husband, Shiloh ben Gozán?"

He held her gaze steadily, and both of them felt their cheeks grow hot. Behind them passed a man who said, "Good day, Benito," and Shiloh looked up at the sound of his Christian name. He bowed briefly. "Good day, Señor Casales." He turned Leah by the elbow and continued to guide her down the steep steps. "Beloved, that was a man with whom my family does business. We owe him woven wool. And he looked at you curiously."

"He cannot know who I am."

"Your dress is costly."

"Not as costly as my father would have it! He would have me in a three-piled farthingale and an orange gown with a deep neckline. *He* would have me show my hair and wear jewels!"

"The better to attract another son-of-something like himself," Shiloh said, laughing.

"He has thought of one already, but I do not like him."

"Leah." Shiloh's voice was tender as he spoke the two syllables of her new, old name. They had reached the city wall, and now halted in its shadow. "Leah," he said again. "Is this not a mere prank of thine, to defy thy father?"

"Is *what* a mere prank?" Leah said, stamping a foot. "My love for thee?"

"In that, I trust." Shiloh held up her fingers and kissed them. "But love is not everything, as you know."

"Yes, I know. There is also the Law."

He smiled at her then with such warmth that she knew her answer had unlocked his heart. Joyfully, she whispered, "Shiloh, I have a thing for you."

"What manner of thing?"

From the purse at her waist she took the ring and held it out to him. It lay, bright, on the flat of her palm. In silence he took the silver-bound stone. Squinting, he examined it carefully, as though he might buy it. "A turquoise. From Salonika, no doubt; or Constantinople. Where did you get it?"

"The stone is Turkish, but the setting of it was done here, in Toledo." She told him of the swordmaker's shop: of seeing the blue glint through the window, of the shining weapons on the walls and the strange things the craftsman had said to her. "He spoke as though he knew me for a Jewess."

Shiloh frowned. "How?"

"I know not how. But he seemed not to care what I was. He only wanted to speak of the ring and gunpowder and his crafts-manship. At first he denied me the ring. And then it was almost taken from him by a little girl from Italy, who had a rich father and bright yellow hair!" She told Shiloh of the antic girl in gold, and of the even odder older girl who had told her father to give Leah the ring. "And so a week later it was mine. I would not have expected the craftsman's daughter to give it to me; on my first visit to the shop she seemed to care for nothing but silver! She sat in a corner counting coin and smiling like Leonardo's Gioconda."

Shiloh looked blank at this, and Leah regretted her clever com-parison. He had never been inside one of the wealthy houses of Toledo, such as the mansion where Leah herself lived; had never seen a sketch of the famous Mona Lisa or an oil painting hung from a wall. He would have thought such an image frivolous, if not immoral. She fell silent.

He looked down at the ring, which now lay flat on his own palm. "What do you mean by it, Leah?"

She felt shyness descend on her, and suddenly could only stammer. "It . . . brought you to mind. The stone . . . it is like you. Or like something you will become."

He cupped her chin in his hand. "You speak like a mystic. Have you been practicing kabbalah, along with your other pursuits?"

At that she laughed, and ducked her head.

"Leah," he said. Again his rough voice caressed the syllables of her name. "Your gift is bold. I accept it. I will give this ring a meaning, since your talk is the merest babble." He held the silver circle before her. Taking it, she slipped it on his calloused finger, where it rested, at home. The stone sparkled in the sunlight. He smiled, his teeth white in his dark-bearded face. He said, "It means you will give me your heart."

THREE

Leah had known of her mother's Jewish blood as long as she could remember. When he was angry her father had kept it no secret from his daughter, or from any listening servants, that he had married twicefold beneath himself, first by taking to his breast a woman from a family of laborers, and second by wedding a New Christian, the liquid in whose veins had not yet been cleansed by the requisite passage of Christian generations according to the law of *limpieza de sangre,* purity of blood.

"I suppose, my sweet, you think *your* blood well cleansed by the eight hundred gallons of muscatel you have poured down your gullet," her mother would reply in a bored voice. "This week alone!"

Little Leah gave small credence to her father's sporadic rantings, but at every opportunity she plagued her mother with questions about her family, none of whom Leah had ever met. She learned that they were silk spinners and had lived in the old Jewish quarter of the city; that her religious grandmother, Serafina's mother, had died soon after Serafina's wedding; that her less religious grandfather, despite his attendance at Christian mass, had observed some of the Mosaic law. Her mother told her that Leah had an aunt, her own older sister, Astruga, who had married a shoemaker and now lived in the Calle de la Chapinería. She had not seen Astruga for years. As for Serafina's father . . . though he had himself drifted from his faith, often slighting its laws, still, a year after Serafina's marriage she had passed her father by inches in the Plaza Mayor and he had not looked at or spoken to her. Six months later she heard he had died of the plague.

These facts were painful to her mother to recall, Leah could see, and her own eyes clouded with tears as she listened. She knew her questions pricked her mother like a knife, but was driven to ask them all the same.

"Why did you leave them, Mama?"

Serafina laughed and held out her arms, not to hug Leah, but to display her two sleeves of rose-colored satin.

"I cannot believe it was only for money!" Leah's voice was indignant.

"Then you think better of me than I am, my dear." But her mother's face grew dark, and she added, "Yes, there was more to it. To be called *marrana*, pig, and *tornadiza*, 'turned one,' in the marketplace; to be spat on—when I was ten, the same age as you, dear girl, I saw my own father beaten and kicked just for walking past a church."

"And yet you wanted to go to one?"

"I *did* go to one. So did we all. There was no escaping that. The Holy Brotherhood seek every chance to make an accusation of Judaizing. They would have hunted us down for missing mass."

She laughed dryly. "The Old Christians miss them all the time. We must be more pious than they. Well, why all that piety and no payment for it? Only spitting and kicking in the marketplace? Yes, I wanted to live in a fine house. Who would not? And your father was gracious and witty and handsome when he came to the judería, scattering his gold and silver, on his way to the House of Venus. Yes, I guessed where he was bound the first time I saw him. My family had money enough. They were mere laborers, but they were skilled and thrifty. I had never seen a man let money run like water through his fingers until the day your father and his fine friends came striding through our courtyards, looking for a pretty Jewess to make them laugh. He found more than he bargained for. He saw me feeding my mother's chickens—"

"Daintily?" Leah said, laughing at the picture of her silk-clad mother scattering feed for squawking fowl.

"Oh, very daintily, sweet girl. And my eyes bought his heart. I made sure that they would, when I saw those gallants come singing down the street. I ran inside and lined my lids with kohl I had bought from an old hag of a beauty-peddler, to make the whites stand out!" She batted her eyes at Leah, who laughed. "My mother beat me later, but the purchase was worth it. A bruised backside for a hidalgo. The next day Sebastian de la Cerda brought me a diamond pendant. For a laborer's daughter whose name he did not yet know! He enjoyed defying his father in marrying me; he exulted in his wealth and his freedom—"

"Freedom?" Leah said. "Perhaps it is easy to feel free and throw money about when one has never had to earn it!"

Her mother looked at her sharply. "You sound like my own father when he spoke of Sebastian. How he despised him! But you, Elizabeta. Sebastian de la Cerda is *your* father, and you should show respect for him. Honor him."

"Pardon, Mama," Leah said sweetly, folding her hands in her lap and batting her eyes as her mother had.

Now Serafina laughed. "Ah, I teach you insolence, do I not? It is my fault. Gozán ben Eleazar, now—there was a man who earned his money. He might have commanded your respect."

"Who?"

"The man my father wished me to marry."

"Tell me of him!"

"I will tell you nothing of him. He bored me with his Talmud and Midrash."

"What are those?"

"Some writings of the Jews. Gozán ben Eleazar's views were peculiar. He found in the Midrash—the part of it that he owned, and kept in a wall as though it were treasure—a law that told him it was possible to be a good Jew while pretending to be Catholic. And he had odd views, such as that women should learn to speak pure Hebrew, and even to read it. I had less interest in learning Hebrew than in the look of a gold-trimmed farthingale I had seen a fine doña wearing in the carnival season. I wanted one like it, and I got one!"

"Ah, Mama, you are content with your lot."

"Elizabeta, I do not know what contentment is. I thought I would find new friends among the Old Christians, but they shy from me still. I miss my sister." Her voice faltered, then steadied. "I would like to have women friends," she said quietly, wiping her eyes.

"I am your friend."

Her mother smiled at her warmly. "Yes." Her voice resumed the silvery tone Leah knew hid a leaden heart. "I am content with my house, my clothes, and my daughter. And I hated the judería. I hated being treated as though I were a dirty dog, and did not belong in the church I was made to go to. And always there was the fear." She looked at Leah, suddenly serious. "One of my cousins was taken by the Inquisition, in Seville. Her crime? She bought chicken sausages instead of pork in the marketplace. They burned her with the pinga."

Leah's eyes were round with fearful wonder. "What is the pinga?"

"A dripping of hot olive oil on whatever part of the body pleases the Inquisitor." Her mother rose and crossed the room to sit at her mirror. She picked up a comb. "With her it was the chest."

Leah winced and covered her own chest involuntarily. Perhaps her mother saw her in the mirror, for she said in a voice that was both soothing and proud, "Such things do not happen to the women of the Casa de la Cerda."

WHENEVER LEAH ASKED what Jews believed in besides chicken sausage, Serafina only shrugged and said that she was a woman; she had never been taught the Law. But Leah knew her mother was lying when she claimed not to know Jewish law at all. She showed too many odd behaviors, not only the refusal to eat pork in any form, but the occasional habit—which became more frequent over time—of letting torches burn themselves out on Friday evenings rather than snuffing them. And she lit candles when it was no Christian holiday.

In the last year of her life, during her pregnancy, she began to say unintelligible prayers in the dark when she thought no one heard.

It was the prayers that made Leah most curious. They were in a language she did not know. When she asked her mother to teach her the words and tell her what they meant, her mother shushed her and bade her recite her catechism. "You are a Christian," her mother said. "Pray as a Christian."

Leah tried to pray as a Christian, but she did not know how to pray to three people at once. A strange notion! And the Holy Mother? Her own mother was married and pregnant. That was the natural way. It seemed the oddest of fantasies, that an unwed virgin might get pregnant and give birth to an edible god who was both Himself and His Father at once and also something called the Holy Spirit.

"These are mysteries," the nuns said, and whenever they said it, Leah thought, *They don't know.*

"Never," said Serafina, "never, *never* discover these thoughts to anyone else. Not a friend, not a servant, not your father, and above all, not a nun or a priest!"

"Then how may I be answered?" asked Leah. "Is it not right to ask questions?"

"In Toledo, it can get you into trouble."

AFTER HER MOTHER died trying to give birth to her father's long-awaited male heir, Leah fell to her knees in the hall outside her chamber and rent her bodice. Her father grabbed and shook her in his grief and rage and asked her where she had learned to do such a thing, and, crying, she had said she did not know; she could not remember. He dragged her into her room and told her to dress herself in Christian mourning, and she hated him, though she labored to forgive him because she knew his heart was as broken as hers.

Within the year his drunkenness was almost constant, but the drink more often sent him to sleep than it made him violent. At sixteen Leah took the opportunities his drowsing afforded her to wander the city, sometimes with a servant she thought she could trust, but more often alone. She found herself in the old judería, a region whose narrow cobbled streets were little different from those of the rest of Toledo, though the remains of an old wall divided them from the Old Christian city. She knew there was no official neighborhood for the Jews anymore, because there were no more official Jews. Still, she knew from her mother's stories that most of the anusim families lived in the areas where they had lived for centuries, since even before the Expulsion.

She looked for the streets she had heard her mother mention; spent hours treading twisted, mazy corridors and blind alleys where the cobertizos made day into night. She was looked at askance for walking alone, but none troubled her. She walked, hearing lively conversations in an odd tongue, a Spanish mixed with something else that reminded her of her mother's mumbled prayers. She smelled frying migas, bread crumbs mixed with garlic. She passed women in head scarves selling alheras, sausages of partridge and chicken. "No pig!" one of them assured Leah, nodding her plump face vigorously. "No impurities!" Leah bought migas and sausages and listened for the names she had heard her mother speak: Gozán, Maymó, and her mother's own family name, Selomó.

One day she was walking the narrow ribbon of the Calle de la Chapinería when the dark street suddenly curved into an open courtyard, where the sunlight reached the rose-colored sandstone of the low buildings and set the walls aglow. She had slipped from the sight of the servant her father had sent to go with her to mass, and now stood alone in the entrance to the courtyard, her eyes sweeping the uneven ring of dusty housefronts. In the midst of the yard two children were throwing a rag ball to a barking dog, and next to a cobbler's bench, set in front of a Moorish-domed dwelling, sat a tall, thin, wool-clad woman of late middle years who was craning her neck backwards to call to someone inside the house. The woman's hair was veiled. Among her Spanish phrases mixed with what Leah now thought was Hebrew, she heard "Selomó."

Without planning it, she approached the woman, begged her pardon, and asked if she was familiar with the family Selomó. The woman jumped to her feet and called for her children—"Aaron! Yehuda!"—and then asked, "Who are you, and why do you ask?" She grew suddenly still, and looked at Leah carefully.

Leah looked boldly into her eyes. "I am Leah," she said. "And I have seen your face mirrored in my mother's."

"Baruch Hashem," the woman said wonderingly. With one hand she hugged her two boys, who now clung to her side and looked at Leah curiously with large brown eyes. "Baruch Hashem," said the woman again. "Praise be to the Blessed One. You yourself are a mirror. I think you are my niece."

HER AUNT ASTRUGA sent her boys back to their play and took Leah inside, past her husband's shoe shop into a living area that looked into an inner courtyard. Against the wall by a window, on a table, stood a small plaster statue of Mary. Past the Virgin, Leah could see a well in the hidden, slate-paved courtyard, and a blossoming lemon tree.

Leah found herself crying in the presence of her aunt, who not only looked but sounded like her mother. Her aunt cried too at the story of her sister Serafina's death, though she had already heard of it from an Old Christian who bought boots from her husband. Her husband was a distant cousin, a childhood playmate who also bore the name Selomó. "He grieved for my sister, too," Astruga said, wiping her eyes with the corners of her apron. She called Serafina "Sarah," a name Serafina had kept secret from Leah, though she had told her daughter so much else. Leah stayed for a meal of lamb, roasted egg, and walnuts, and met her young cousins, though not her uncle, who was away from the city buying shoe leather.

"Eighteen years," Astruga kept repeating. "Eighteen years, and she came not to see us!"

"She said that she missed you," Leah said. "She was dead to your family. So she thought."

Astruga shook her head. "I know my sister better than you think. My father and mother would not have seen her. They no longer mentioned her name after her wedding. They died with no kind word for Sarah. But she might have come to me, had she willed it. A shoemaker's wife could not come calling at the house of the family de la Cerda, but she might have come to us. Sarah ben Selomó was not dead to me. No, she was dead to Serafina de la Cerda. She traded us all for a mansion and an Old Christian name."

Leah could not argue with that.

After that Leah came often to see her aunt. The two of them sat in the courtyard shelling nuts or mixing spices for the evening meal, or sorting clothes that the laundress had washed, and Leah asked her aunt as many questions as she had asked her mother. Astruga's answers were fuller than Serafina's, but still they were partial, fragments and remnants of things she said only the men knew fully. "Only the men," she said, "and the not-yet-existing daughters of someone like Gozán ben Eleazar the wool-weaver. He is a widower, but he swears that if he marries again and his new wife bears girls, he will make them all learn Hebrew and even study the Talmud!" She laughed at the notion, shooing a chicken who was pecking too close to the shelled filberts she had cast into a bowl by her side.

Astruga warned Leah to have a care and visit less frequently, and marveled at how each time she saw her, Leah was more plainly dressed. Her niece was clearly imitating, as closely as she could, the manner of dress of Astruga herself, as well as of the other women she saw in the old Jewish barrio. The colors of her garments became more muted, and she tucked all her hair behind a scarf like the married women of the quarter.

"You are your mother's daughter," Astruga chided. "After her marriage she wore outlandish ruffs and magenta-dyed satin and jewels in her hair to outrage our father when he saw her at a distance, and could do nothing about it. You go the other direction, but are you obedient? What good daughter wanders in the streets? You are your mother's, from head to toe."

"Ruffs are scratchy," Leah said.

Often Leah stayed for the evening meal, having told her father she was going to vespers. Usually food at the table Selomó was preceded by a Hebrew blessing, delivered by her swarthy uncle Reuben. Reuben was thick and muscular and an inch shorter than her tall, fair aunt, and one night when a visiting Old Christian tradesman from Madrid broke bread with them, Reuben was called Carlos, and prayed in Latin. "We will recite the Kol Nidre at Yom Kippur for that," Reuben said when the man had gone, and the whole family shrugged.

But Shabbat was a different matter.

"Here."

Leah stopped abruptly behind her aunt, uncle, and small cousins at the entrance to a narrow two-story building in the Calle del Ángel. The sun was setting, but the walls already cast the shadows of night over the narrow street. Smoke puffed from the roofs of half the sandstone houses in the row, but the other half, including this one, showed only candles glowing dimly in their windows.

"We enter here," said her uncle Reuben. They passed a doorpost that was carved into the shape of a Madonna. To Leah's surprise, each member of the family kissed the Madonna's foot upon entering the doorway. She did not understand why they did it, and so she refrained.

They mounted a narrow stair to an upper room. Nervously, Leah tagged behind the group, fixing her veil.

Laughter and voices sounded behind a door. Reuben knocked on it, and the voices quieted a little. The door opened a crack, and a man stuck his bearded, capped head through it. "Who is the fifth?" he asked Reuben.

"My niece," Astruga answered boldly, earning a frown of disapproval from the man.

"No strangers," said the man, beginning to shut the door. "Take her back!"

Reuben stuck his foot over the doorsill. "She is of our blood! She—"

"I know who your niece is. The daughter of the uncircumcised Don Sebastian de la Cerda, who worships the Nazarene."

"Her mother was Jewish!" Astruga said, while Reuben tried to shush her.

"*Was* is not *is*."

"*She* is. You must trust us."

"Trust!" The man laughed harshly. The room had grown silent behind him. Leah heard chairs scraped back; folk moving toward the walls; windows opening. "Trust is for Old Christians. We are not fools. Our lives and our families are at stake. The Holy Brotherhood has been known to send children to spy on us. Why should they not send women? We will have some better surety than mere *trust*."

"Here, then!" Grabbing Leah's arm, Astruga moved forward and peeled back the wool of the girl's sleeve. "Here is the bruise her father gave her for coming to us last week. Would you touch it? She came to learn a woman's duties according to the Law, though she told him she was going to mass."

In fact, on the day she earned the bruise Leah had come to play ball with her cousins Aaron and Yehuda, and had fallen on the hard ground of the courtyard before the house of the family Selomó. But now she played the role her aunt had fashioned her, holding out her hurt arm and assuming a suffering look. The blunt man softened, seeing her eyes. A rough voice behind him said, "Daniel, we were told to expect the visitor. The sun is setting. Let the family Selomó enter!"

As they came into the room, Leah saw that the rough-voiced man who had just spoken was young. He had risen from a crowded table to bow and greet her family in Hebrew. He was dark and bearded and tall, and from a pocket of his shirt peeped a prayer book. He had a hawk's profile, and his eyes were bright and amused. Behind him stood another tall man whose face was the same as the young man's except for its lines; and whose hair was gray and thinner, but who had the same dancing eyes. "These," Leah's uncle said to her, "are the family Gozán. Gozán ben Eleazar, the elder, and Shiloh, his son."

Gozán ben Eleazar. Leah's eyes widened. The learned one, who had been meant to marry her mother. It amazed her that the fellow actually resembled her father, Sebastian de la Cerda.

Shiloh, the younger man, arched a brow and bowed, holding his hands together as though in prayer. *"Shalom,"* he said, looking at Leah with interest.

THEY WERE FIFTEEN at table; both women and men, though the women spent some of their time serving lamb and lentil soup, and missed much of the talk. As a guest and something of a curiosity, Leah was excused from even the minimal labors the women performed at Shabbat—*"This* time," her aunt whispered to her meaningfully—and she sat wide-eyed, saying little, doing her best to follow the Ladino, the Spanish-Hebrew in which the group chattered, and laughing at the jests she understood.

They began, of course, with a prayer, not a jest. The woman of this particular house lit the candelabra that stood on the hearth, and the eldest male, who happened to be Daniel, the now affable man who had gruffly blocked their entry, said the prayer welcoming Shabbat, and blessed the challah, a braided bread ring woven from five ropes of dough. The bread lay on the white linen tablecloth on a curious ceramic plate that was round, uneven, and green-trimmed, and on whose center was painted the Hand of Fātimah (her uncle explained), a Star of David, and a cross. When, after the prayers and the ritual silence of hand-washing, and the blessings of children and wine and bread, she asked what those symbols were doing together, Reuben shrugged. "It's only a plate."

Gozán ben Eleazar heard Leah's question and gave a bark of a laugh. "A very well made plate. As sturdy as the Madonna's foot on the doorpost. A plate strong enough to hold a cross, a Moorish hand, and a Star of David. Just as a plaster Mary's foot is strong enough to hold a mezuzah!"

"So please you, what is a mez . . ."

The occupants of the table looked at Leah oddly, and she fell silent. Then Gozán said kindly, "'Do not bow to the gods of the peoples who are round about you.' 'Fear the Lord and keep His commandments.' So says Deuteronomy, the fifth book of Moses, and so says the scroll inside the box that is the mezuzah. 'And you shall write the laws on the doorposts of your house.'"

"It is better in Hebrew, Gozán," said another man, sipping soup.

"But perhaps our Hebrew is rusty," said Gozán. His son, Shiloh, who sat next to him, winked at Leah, or so she thought; the movement was so sudden she could not be sure. She smiled at him, then looked down, suddenly shy. The youth turned to say something to Daniel, who sat at his right, and Leah looked back at him covertly, admiring his sharp profile and the chestnut brown curls that fell down the back of his neck, almost to his shoulders. So struck was she by the thought that, had her mother married this young man's father, neither he nor she would exist, that she did not hear the soft voice of the young boy behind her who asked her if he might fill her plate. After a moment of waiting the boy frowned fleetingly, almost imperceptibly, and his shoulders stiffened. He moved down the table and placed a loaf of bread next to an older woman.

Leah's aunt nudged her and gestured toward the boy, whose back as he served was now to them, so that Leah could not see his face. "This you should know," Astruga whispered. "I have told you that even women work as little as may be during Shabbat, from sundown to sundown. That boy has been hired to do services we may not do—cook, relight the candles, sweep after we finish our meal. His name is Santiago Mendoza. Named for the apostle James, Santiago Matamoros, patron of Christian Spain, may his tongue turn to powder."

"But how is it lawful for that boy to do kitchen labor, if not for you?" asked Leah.

"He is a Christian of sorts, though he has been heard to mutter that he believes in nothing. His father was Jewish by blood. A muleteer from Ávila, or so his mother told him. She was a Christian zoná, a prostitute, not a fine one from the House of Venus, but a miserable woman from the streets outside the city wall. She beat Santiago when he was three and cast him from her when he was four and she thought him big enough to beg his own bread."

"Poor lad!" Leah said.

"Gozán saw him sleeping by the cathedral wall and took pity on him. No child should be fatherless, whate'er his blood, says Gozán ben Eleazar. He came to trust the boy for odd jobs like this one, and he is hired to sweep by other kind folk of the town. We trust him, as well. He has proved an honest lad, well-meaning, and devoted to us, though he does not house with Gozán. He is not a Jew, but his blood is part Jewish." Her voice turned sour. "Not *pure*, according to the king's laws. Because of that, he could not betray our gatherings to the Holy Brotherhood without betraying himself. How he lives from Friday to Friday I do not know."

How he lives. Leah wondered how everyone else in the gathering lived; whether the daily prayers and rituals of which she had learned something from the family Selomó were practiced identically by all who now sat at the Shabbat table. She hardly dared eat, watching the others, especially the women, to see what they did with their food.

"Do not worry so much!" murmured Astruga, watching her. "Drink some wine. You are learning. Next time you come to our house I will teach you about our holy days. Starting with Purim."

"What do we celebrate on that holiday?" Leah whispered.

"Not getting killed. As on most of them." Young Shiloh ben Gozán's dry voice made her jump. She dropped her spoon in surprise at being overheard, and glanced at him quickly, feeling flustered. But he was leaning behind his father to pass the wine bottle, and she could not see his eyes.

"We celebrate things other than that!" her aunt said in mock anger. But seeing that Leah only half-listened, she smiled, patted her niece's elbow, and turned to chat with her neighbor.

"They are burning Jews in Zaragoza," the man at Leah's left said companionably, as he sprinkled a heel of bread with olive oil. She stared at him.

Shiloh ben Gozán's short, rough laugh sounded from across the table, and Leah looked at him once more. His eyes were alight with merriment at something just said by a pink-faced man they called Hayim. Shiloh was resting one arm on the ledge of the curtained window behind him, holding a wineglass in his hand. His other hand lay quiet, cupped and empty, on the white linen cloth of the table. His fingers were hard and square.

Feeling her eyes, he suddenly turned his own toward her. She held his warm gaze for a moment, then, embarrassed, looked down at her plate.

"Father Hayim!" one of the men was calling from down the busy table. "May I come to you Sunday to confess that I just took communion?"

"Why not?" said Hayim. "But will the ten Ave Marias I give you clear your debt to God, or put you further in trouble?"

"We need Maimonides to answer that question," said Daniel. They all laughed, save Leah, who wondered whether Maimonides would be there the following Friday. "The Talmud permits a lie to save a life," Daniel added philosophically. "Praying to a Virgin you don't believe in is a kind of lie, but it does save a life. Yours."

"But Baruch is a bachelor, with no family at risk," Shiloh said laughingly. "Does the Talmudic law hold good when one lies only to save one's own life, Father Hayim?"

"Ah," said Hayim knowingly, wagging a finger. "Ah."

Can that man truly be a priest? Leah wondered. Seeing the confusion on her face, Daniel's wife, Rachel, said to Leah, "This is the *only* priest for Jews. They call him Lope, though in secret he is Hayim and one of the faithful."

"We should each have a priest in the family!" Gozán clapped his son on the shoulder.

"Not me," said Shiloh.

"If not you, who? A priest can hear our problems in the confessional and tell us what to do. And if he is fortunate to find a kind Old Christian friend like Father Bartolomeo, between the two of them they can see that the right one performs all the Jewish marriages."

"But how can Hayim marry Jews?" protested Daniel. "He is a priest, not a rabbi!"

Gozán shrugged. "And you garbled the prayers tonight! What sort of a 'shel-Shabbat' was that? I do not think you welcomed Shabbat properly; I think you told the Blessed One something about spilled olive oil and a broken axle! I can only hope the Most High forgives us for the botch we make of the rituals."

Shiloh smiled warmly at his father.

Gozán shook his head. "Yet what can we do, when our rabbis have all fled to Constantinople? One hundred synagogues there, and forty thousand Jews who greet Shabbat openly! Here a Jew keeps fragments and remnants of the Law on faded parchment hidden in his genizah, in a hiding place under the floor or below the tiles on a rooftop. As a priest anyway Hayim can find my learned son Hebrew prayer books, and study Hebrew texts in the cathedral—may it crumble to dust in our lifetime!"

"May it do so, and drop a gold monstrance on Bishop Quiroga's head," said Hayim the priest, munching challah placidly. "And may we train still more secret Jews to be priests. Grand Inquisitor Torquemada was a Jew—"

"A bad one."

"Admittedly. Yet there are faithful Jews even among the bishops! More and more enter the Church. Secret Jews are everywhere. They marry Old Christians, but, like us, they do not give up their observances. They keep the laws of kashrut. They give birth to more of the chosen. After three generations they become Old Christians and may serve in the councils of state—"

"Soon we will conquer Spain," said Shiloh.

"Yes!" Hayim shouted, pretending to take him seriously. "Yes! Toledo is the new Jerusalem."

"Because its buildings are made of the same-colored stone?" said Daniel the elder. "No. Toledo is like Spain, very Catholic. Fear it, Father Hayim, and take care to hide your Talmud well underneath your Christian gown. This new Inquisition is like nothing this country has ever seen."

Hayim was too Shabbat-happy to be sobered. "I trust in Hashem, the Most High," he said. "Toledo is my city, and I will not abandon it. Toledo is the beating heart of Spain, and Spain will be ours, and when we have Spain we will have the world!"

"Let us not lose our souls in the gaining of it," came the dry voice.

Hayim squinted at Shiloh. "Pardon me, young Shiloh ben Gozán, but is it a saying of the Nazarene that you preach to me now?"

Shiloh raised one brow. "And how would you know it, had you not read their Gospels yourself?"

"Of course I have read them! I'm a priest!"

"Then you know that the Nazarene was not such a fool. He was a Jew, after all. That saying of his is one I like. I heard it at a secret meeting of Luteranos in Valladolid."

That sent the table into an uproar, with Gozán ben Eleazar pounding the board and laughing helplessly. "My son! My son! Who else of the anusim would play the New Christian in a church of Luteranos? He would not be content to be caught and fried by the pinga for Judaizing. He wants also to be thought a secret Protestant!"

FOUR

LATE THAT NIGHT Leah's uncle walked her home, through streets as twisted as coiled blacksnakes. Reuben watched as she vanished, wraithlike, through a side portal into the magnificent de la Cerda mansion, then made his way back to the Calle de la Chapinería. It was past midnight and the torches at Leah's house had been doused. Her maid sat in the kitchen, dropping frijoles in water by candlelight, preparing them to soak. She was a New Christian Moor who years before had scrubbed off the chrism of her son's baptism, after the ceremony. Leah had seen her do it, in the courtyard garden. Now the woman looked up, nodded, and laid a finger to her lips, smiling at all their Spanish secrets.

Sebastian de la Cerda's snores sawed through the dry air of the passage that joined the upper galleries. Through the windows cut in Moorish arabesques, starlight entered fitfully, now and again, from between passing clouds. Dizzy from Shabbat wine, Leah bumped against the walls, as she'd heard her father do countless times. She was grateful for the soundness of his sleep, and glad her lightness kept her from thudding and crashing as *he* usually did, although in her mild drunkenness it was hard to tell just how much noise she was making. Once inside her chamber, she shut the door and leaned back against it for a moment in the dark. Behind her closed lids lights and colored streaks and mysterious Hebrew characters reeled and danced. Slowly she walked to her bed and lay upon it, fully dressed except for her veil, which she loosened, then dropped to the floor. She spread her curls over the pillow behind her, running her fingers through its tangles.

The mood of the gathering had defied all her expectations. She had desired and feared the Shabbat celebration: desired welcome among a gathering of Jews; feared that her ignorant missteps would mar their ritual. Yet in that upper room a rippling tide of merriment had buoyed the solemn prayers, and had eased her fears. She understood the laughter's source. The anusim jested to stay alive, or to make their lives bearable. Humor was the firelight that kept Old Christian wolves at bay.

This new Inquisition is like nothing this country has ever seen.

She tried to summon the chill the man Daniel's words had briefly put into her at that forbidden table. There they had sat, munching challah blithely, though when the fire died their smokeless chimney would announce to all of Toledo that they honored the forbidden Shabbat. But her heart floated on wine, and she could not stop smiling in the dark. For another voice drowned out Daniel's grim statement. That voice was dry, and merry, and belonged to a quiet young man with dark hair and clear brown eyes.

She folded her arms over her chest like a cross and hugged her shoulders, thinking of Shiloh ben Gozán's face.

———

THE NEXT FRIDAY she begged to go to vespers accompanied by the Moorish servant who had reversed her son's baptism. She knew the woman would part with her amiably at the Puerta del Mollete, under the arches that linked the cathedral to Bishop Quiroga's palace. There her aunt and uncle would be waiting among the thin, graceful Moorish columns of pink sandstone. Astruga and Reuben would take her to the Shabbat meal, not at Daniel's house this week but somewhere else, for secret Shabbat was a moveable feast. It danced through Toledo with unpredictable steps, just ahead of the grasping hands of the Holy Brotherhood.

But Sebastian de la Cerda suspected Leah's piety. He would not permit her to go to mass that evening, even under what he assumed was the watchful eye of her woman. In the Alcázar, where he talked with the city's rulers, he had heard rumors that his daughter had been seen walking the streets of the old Jewish quarter. Through the haze of his habitual drunkenness he feared and suspected something like the truth: that she missed Serafina; that in tracing the broken paths of the judería she was seeking the mother she had lost. In fact Leah's quest was impelled not only by her memories of her mother, but by a past that stood behind Serafina, behind *Sarah,* the name her mother had rejected. Leah did not think her mother had ever fully grasped the thing Leah now wanted. She sought the Jewishness her mother had cast from her, like a pearl whose value she had not guessed.

Her father saw only that he was losing his daughter, as he had begun to lose Serafina even before she died, when she began to turn from his kiss and to leave his bed cold while she sat by the wall, mumbling her prayers in Hebrew. Leah's wanderings in the judería enraged him. He would have her married to a hidalgo; would have her, Elizabeta de la Cerda, doubly marked with Old Christian names.

So he forbade her to go out. It was fitting that she should stay home, he said. After all, that night he was hosting a banquet.

Leah knew what he intended. Vainly she pled to be excused from the festivities. After a furious argument with her father in the salon—though the doors were closed, the bitter sound of it left the maids white-faced—Leah ascended to her chamber, from whence she emerged an hour later dressed in silks and a gloriously stiff, scratchy ruff, her dark hair dressed with diamonds. She descended the stairs to stand by her father's side, her back rigid, her dark eyes furious.

All that Friday morning the grooms and housemaids and cooks and pastry makers had busied themselves, and when seven of the clock arrived, the torches and the hearthfire were lit and the guests began to come. Among the attendees was a nobleman of the family de la Fuente. Twenty-five years old, languid and long-fingered, the younger son of a younger brother, he was entranced with the angry eyes of de la Cerda's daughter, and further besotted with the thought of the wealth her dowry promised. Leah danced the morisca with the young man, and smiled at her father's other guests. Then she returned to her room. She did not pass a word with anyone.

In her chamber she tore off her torturous ruff, which her woman picked up silently and hung in another room. Heavily she threw herself on her white linen sheets, where she wept with frustration, thinking of the Shabbat table and of Shiloh ben Gozán's hands.

TWO DAYS LATER Sebastian de la Cerda threw up *his* hands, for the nonce, at his daughter's stubbornness, and visited his farm in the countryside of La Mancha, taking with him a crossbow for hunting partridge. Leah thought in his bleariness he would be lucky to hit a sheep, but was glad to see him go. He left on horseback at midmorning, trailed by four servants on mules laden with pillows, sweetmeats, and casks of Manchegan wine. Two hours later, Leah was knocking at the gate to Astruga's courtyard.

It was opened by her twelve-year-old cousin, Aaron, whose hands were black with boot polish. "Keep away from me," Leah said gaily, edging in past him. "Did my woman bring a message yesterday saying I would visit today? Has your mother received it?"

"I gave it to her myself!" Aaron said behind her. But Leah was not listening. Her ear was attuned to a rough, dry laugh that drifted from the open window of her aunt's front rooms into the communal yard. For ten straight nights she had dreamed of that laugh, tossing on the sheets of her bed.

She crossed her arms nervously and stood where she was, watching her uncle Reuben, who sat on the bench before his house, repairing soles. "Christ, the sun beats down!" he muttered. He raised a hand briefly, then dropped it to steady the shoe on his wooden last and pound a nail into its heel. Chickens pecked near his feet.

Astruga appeared in the doorway. "Leah!" she said. "Don't stand there like a fool. A man has come to see you."

HER AUNT'S KITCHENS and inner courtyard were, after that day, only places where she could meet Shiloh. In the evenings, or in the siesta times of midday, when both of them could manage it, they sat at her aunt's broad cedar-planked table while Astruga, smiling, did her best to ignore them; or they leaned close to one another under the shade of the narrow-trunked lemon tree.

Once they met in the shadow of the cathedral, as Leah, crossing herself, emerged from an early mass. Shiloh stood under a flying buttress, squinting cynically at the bulk of the huge and holy structure.

"What have you done today?" she asked breathlessly, taking his hard hand.

"Woven woolen cloaks since dawn." Two Sisters of Santa Catalina passed them, looking like flying ravens in their breeze-blown habits. Shiloh lowered his voice and waved toward the postern gate of the church. "My father used to come there bearing a cartload of copes for the priests, and leave with a sackful of silver."

"Used to?"

"Before the bishop began to insist on the purity law. Our blood is not clean enough to allow us to serve the Church."

"Not to weave a cope?"

"Not to shape a wax candle. Not to melt ten pounds of gold into a chalice. No marriages with Old Christians among us." Shiloh's dry voice turned arid. "Money is lost us thereby."

The two passed a line of gaunt paupers gathered by the Puerta del Mollete. These shuffled quietly toward the church door for the daily bread distribution. Shiloh and Leah quickened their steps as the priest came to the door with his basket. A little farther on, in the Calle de Santa Isabel, they were passed by a Moorish girl of nine or so, who like them walked toward the market stalls in the Plaza de Ayuntamiento. She looked at them curiously, then smiled dazzlingly at them both. But so absorbed were Leah and Shiloh in one another, their heads together as they walked, that they did not note the daughter of the swordmaker Julian del Rei.

"But the priests think you pure enough to worship in the cathedral," Leah said, matching Shiloh's irony. "And to give your tithe."

"Yes, though to do both makes me *less* pure. Like eating food that is not kosher."

"Ah, the wrong meat. All must be drained of blood by your butcher, the—"

"The shohet, yes."

"No pork ever, and no tasty boiled crabs, and at your Passover, bread baked flat and tasteless so as not to sully your perfect stomachs! Jews think they are better than anyone else."

"We are. And so think you, else you would not haunt our Shabbat and try to hook a poor Levite with your eyes. Show me your flowing locks, *Elizabeta!* You need not wear that veil. You are a maiden, and half Gentile besides."

Laughing, Leah pushed her veil back slightly to expose her hairline, then pulled it forward again. "No! Only to a husband."

"Play your game! I'll never marry an Old Christian who was baptized in a silver font."

"I had no say in it! And so were you!"

"Nay!" Shiloh laughed. "Did I not tell you? My parents borrowed a Christian baby from a friend. He took my place. His parents thought two baptisms even better than one, and I escaped with none. And would that I could have avoided that place forever." He tilted his head back toward the cathedral. "When I come in of a Sunday and the first thing I see is a huge gold cross wearing the image of that poor bleeding Nazarene like a brooch—"

"Hush!"

"And the gold monstrous—"

"Monstrance!"

"As I said! The monstrous monstrance! Forty pound of gold and four hundred pound of silver, all studded with pagan images."

"Not pagan. They are depictions of the saints!" Leah said, for the pleasure of argument, though Shiloh was voicing thoughts she had often had herself. Yet only Shiloh, she thought, would have bothered to discover the exact weight of the Custodia de Arfe, the communion monstrance made (for the glory of God) with the first gold and silver brought to Spain from the Americas.

"The depictions are pagan. They are graven images. I would do better in Valladolid, with the Protestants, if I must go to a Nazarene church at all. Better to meet in a plain room with plain-clad Luteranos and hear scripture said, though not all of it be from Moses or the prophets."

"Shh!" Leah hushed his frightening blasphemy, though she could not keep from laughing at his absurdity. "But what kind of converso goes to church with the Luteranos?" she said in a low voice. "What kind of a secret Jew *are* you? It is as your father said. You will be twice arrested!"

Laughing with her, Shiloh shrugged. Now he lowered his voice to a whisper. "Here in Toledo the bishop can find nothing better to do with New World silver than to melt it into a vertical bread pan."

Leah giggled.

"And people call the bread 'flesh of Christ' and smack their lips over it. Ghouls!"

"Hush!"

"Four hundred pounds of silver from New Spain! It could feed those legless paupers for five years." Shiloh gestured behind them, though by now he and Leah were passing the busy stalls of the Plaza de Ayuntamiento, and the huddled poor had vanished from view. "Once I saw a ragged woman kneeling before a painted Virgin in one of the chapels. She wore a pearl corona and had a cross of gold on her breast."

"The beggar?"

"Ah, you laugh at the poor."

"No," Leah said quickly. "Only at you."

"Hear, then, how the poor cherish their state. I whispered to her that that single gold cross on the statue might buy her a cattle farm outside the city walls, if it were properly melted down by my cousin Hosea, who has a nice little forge in the Calle de Ave María—"

"You did not!"

"And she said to me, *Beef feeds my belly, but this feeds my soul*. And she pointed to that same gold crucifix on the Virgin's breast." Shiloh shrugged for the second time. "What can be done with someone like that?"

"Shiloh, you did not say those words to a Christian woman!"

Shiloh laughed. "Ah, she only thought me a Protestant."

LEAH KNEW SHILOH loved her. He had told her so. But she knew he doubted her seriousness, and that it was shrewd of him to do so. She was the daughter of wealth, brought up an Old Christian, not steeped in the tradition she was only now learning.

"If you do not know what it is to be a Jew, how can you know you want to be one?" Shiloh asked her one day under her aunt's lemon tree.

"You do not understand," she told him, leaning forward earnestly, touching his woolen sleeve. "I *am* one. I do not think I have a choice. I only want to know what I am."

He looked at her solemnly, and for the first time she had the joyful sense that she had turned a key in a lock inside him. She did not understand her own truth, but in speaking it, she had said something right.

"And I know I am not a real Christian," she said. "I have done what the nuns and priests told me, all of my life. But it is as you all say. My training was like your family's conversion, forced, and so nothing. Only the heart can choose."

He looked thoughtful, though troubled.

HE HAD TOLD her of the Law.

The Jews, he said, worshiped a blessed one whose name was too holy to know, and whose face too radiant to see, let alone to be shaped into a skinny, suffering mask and hung on two crossed bars on a wall. He recited to her in Hebrew from the Psalms, then told her in Spanish what the words meant: that delight lay in keeping the Law. That meant to keep from defiling the body and the sacred books, to care for one's brethren, and to worship only the Creator, Hashem, the Blessed One, the Most High. "These verses are in your Bible, too," he said. The ideas were not strange to her, but as for the verses, she had never read them.

She swallowed his words like new wine or manna, and he saw that she panted for them. Yet her family was Old Christian, and despite what she'd said of her choicelessness, it was hard for him not to believe she yet could choose in a way he never had: could choose her name, choose her faith, choose her husband. And she was young. Why should such a fortunate one hazard all she possessed for love? Did she truly know the risks? He felt he endangered his own heart, in daring to believe she would pick a double life— would agree to hover forever behind closed curtains at a secret Shabbat.

She knew he wanted to trust her, and wondered what token of hers could be precious enough to seal his faith. All that she had was given by her father's hand, and Shiloh wanted nothing from the Old Christian wealth of los de la Cerda, soft dons who reaped money from harvests brought in by the calloused hands of

Moriscos who tenanted their lands. No. Leah needed something of her own to give him.

And she saw it, on that cold February day, through the sword-maker's window.

The turquoise ring, its blue stone darkly streaked, spoke to her of Shiloh. Later, when the old craftsman gave it to her freely, the gift seemed a mystical sign. Perhaps, she'd mused, were she to place the ring on Shiloh's finger, she and he would thenceforth be one. He would think a woman bold enough to give a man a ring also bold enough to claim her mother's perilous hidden past. He would undertake to deliver her to herself. She desired that, craving her legacy.

Though mostly she wanted him.

FIVE

She did not lie to her father, though, weeping later on her bed, behind a door that was locked from the outside, she wished she had. When she told him she was betrothed to the New Christian known as Benito Gozán, a weaver and wool trader of Toledo, he struck her flat across the side of her face and closed her in her chamber without food or water for a day and a half. By now her Moorish woman had been suspected and dismissed, and while the house harbored servants of all hues and several faiths who sympathized with Leah, it contained none brave enough to bring her a pile of sheets sufficient in number to knot together and reach the courtyard garden, or to unlatch the gate that opened into the street, should she manage to reach the ground.

On the second night of her jailing, her father opened her door himself. She heard him jingling his keys with an unsteady hand,

and by the time he entered she was sitting, hungry and pale, but straight and angry, on a velvet settle by the window. He handed her a glass of water, which she knocked from his hand to the floor. He raised that hand to strike her again, then mastered himself and dropped his fist to his side. "Elizabeta," he said coldly.

"Leah!"

"Elizabeta Santa Leocadia de la Cerda, I will not keep you under lock and key. The corregidor of this city would not permit such slavery—"

"Of Old Christians."

Her father ignored this. "But I tell you that if you marry as you purpose, not only will you have nothing from me, not a maravedí, not a Turkish soltani—"

"I care not, sir."

"—but I will not raise this hand to help you if the Holy Brotherhood take you or your husband or your mongrel marrano children. Do you hear me?" He did lift his hand as he said this, not to strike, but to commit an oath to heaven, while Leah stared at him in silent fury, wondering by what cruel image of God he swore. His voice grew cold. "I will not betray you, Elizabeta. But if you leave this house without my blessing, you are no longer of my blood."

"Of *your* blood?" Leah spat. Her night and day of thirsty brooding had robbed her of pity for her grieving, dissolute father. All she saw were his broken vows to her mother and his cruelty, and she embraced his hate. "The thought of your blood shames me."

"And the thought of the blood of the Jewish dog you will marry inflames you!"

She rose to her feet, swayed slightly, and held on to the edge of the settle. "There is more difference between his blood and yours than there is between fine red wine and muscatel," she said firmly.

———

THEY STOOD UNDER the stretched chuppah, both clad in white linen kittels, the overgarments falling to their feet. Both her hair and her face were veiled, but underneath the veil her tresses lay washed clean by the mikvah, her purifying bath, in which she had thrice immersed herself. Her curly ringlets were woven and pinned into braids, a labor performed early that morning in her aunt's bedroom by Astruga and Reuben's laughing nieces. As they had woven her hair, they had sung the wedding song her mother had used to hum, so loud that their bell-like voices rang through the windows, and Astruga dashed up to shush them.

Leah wore a heavy belt of old gold sent her by Shiloh, and he wore one of silver, given Leah to give him by Reuben, who had received it from Astruga at their own wedding, but who had no daughters to give marriage belts to their grooms. On Shiloh's finger he wore the black-streaked turquoise, bound with silver. The stone and its band drew their guests' curious gaze. The ring Shiloh placed on Leah's finger was of pure gold, unornamented by any stone, though in place of one a small gold house stood, fused to the band. "The wise woman builds her house," he murmured to her, seeing that her head was bowed to look at it on her forefinger.

He could not see her eyes behind the veil. Worn for modesty's sake, it had been hung from Leah's brow so that, like Rebecca with Isaac, she should refrain from viewing her bridegroom until their marriage bond was complete. She kept her gaze averted when, eyes dancing, Shiloh lifted it to make sure he was not tricked with the wrong bride, as Isaac's son Jacob was with the first Leah. Yet after, nodding with mock gravity, he let the veil fall once more, she squinted and peeked through its gauzy fabric throughout the ceremony. She saw him watch raptly as Father Hayim, playing the rabbi, said the seven blessings, and she saw his look turn serious when he crushed the glass beneath his heel in reminder of the destruction of the Temple at Jerusalem. But when he said *"Mazel tov!"* his face changed entirely.

Then he wore the widest smile she had ever seen.

To Father Hayim's right stood a small, slight man who was as quiet as Hayim was exuberant. Though Hayim had discarded his clerical garb for this ceremony, this other man wore a priestly habit. He took no part in what was said, but after Shiloh broke the glass he gestured—covertly, it seemed to peeping Leah—toward the pair of them in blessing. Could he, she wondered, be yet another Jew who had trained as a priest, who dispensed communion wafers at mass and observed secret Shabbat? Yet at the dinner that followed, where he sat at the far end of the crowded board, she heard this man addressed by a Christian name.

"Bartolomeo!" Hayim called. "Is this pair married forever, according to you?"

Father Bartolomeo only smiled vaguely and waved his hand in a friendly way, as he chewed on a roasted egg.

The family sat in the courtyard behind the house of Reuben's brother in the old judería. The wedding had been done secretly, in the inner rooms, with few witnesses, and now for the open air Leah and Shiloh had discarded their kittels, and sat in their finest wear, doing their best to look like a Christian couple at their marriage feast. Leah's brow and eyes were now bare, though a scarf of gold-threaded white linen still hid her hair, for she would not concede this tradition. It was not time to free her curls yet. To veil her hair was a mitzvah, a good commandment. Shiloh had taught her that word.

"Now, Bartolomeo, let us discuss this thing," Hayim persisted. "Can Leah get rid of this tall, thin husband if he fails to satisfy her in any way?"

"There is no danger of that," Shiloh said, winking at Leah as he poured wine into her glass. Leah wished for her brow veil back, to hide her blush, which deepened as her cousins giggled. At her elbow appeared the young boy who had helped serve at the Shabbat table. Joyfully embarrassed by Shiloh's jest, she looked at the boy and saw his face fully. She recognized it, though she could not remember where else in the city she had seen him. For his part, on this day he only glanced at her with friendly blankness, set down a bowl, and turned away.

Astruga threw a piece of bread at Hayim. It bounced from his nose, and he grabbed it by the crust and ate it. "You know as well as anyone that if Leah wished to rid herself of Shiloh she would have to get the elders to grant *him* the right to put *her* off," Astruga said. "But do not talk of sad endings here!"

"What do the scriptures say, Father Bartolomeo?" asked Shiloh's father, Gozán.

"Which scriptures?" said the priest at the table end, in a quiet voice.

"Whichever you choose!" said Gozán.

"If *I* am to choose, the answer is simple," said Father Bartolomeo, placidly swallowing his egg. "They are one flesh til death does them part."

"AND SO THAT is the priest to whom my father confesses his failings," Leah said wonderingly, as she and Shiloh walked, hand in hand, up the stairs to his rooms in the Taller de Moro, near his father's workshop in a crowded section of the old judería. "He knows what I flee from as well as what I run to. His name was heard oft in our house, but I never before saw him."

"He is an Old Christian. A priest of some note. He is a vicar of the Church. Even Bishop Quiroga respects him, and Quiroga, who one day will be archbishop, is not to be sneezed at. Quiroga is a fanatic, zealous to straddle the earth for Christ. Six cities, two hundred and eighty-seven towns, four hundred and nineteen villages, one thousand two hundred and fifty-three benefices, one hundred sixty-four monasteries, five thousand persons, and two hundred thousand ducats a year to the archbishop—"

"But Father Bartolomeo! Tell me of him."

"He and Hayim study Hebrew together, as well as the Torah—though Bartolomeo does not call it that—and he keeps Hayim's secret. And all of ours."

"In conscience, as a true Christian priest, how can he?"

"He says in conscience as a true Christian priest he can do no other," Shiloh said, shrugging. "He's a curious Christian."

"And we trust him?"

Shiloh smiled warmly at her, noting the "we." "We must trust some of them," he said. "Like that boy, Santiago Mendoza, who douses embers and turns the spit and carries plates. He is faithless, and so, reliable."

Leah was silent, trying to recall the time before Shabbat when she had seen the boy.

"And like you," Shiloh said, pushing open the door to his small apartments. He kept no lock on his outside door, he had told her, because there was nothing to steal in his rooms. Everything he had of value—his pieces of holy writ, given him by his father; his silver—he kept in a *genizah*, a hidden space under the floor. That space was locked. In the rooms he kept only a table, two chairs, and a brand-new bed he had built himself.

She felt a blush rising again when she saw the bed, and her heart beat fast. "Like me," she said. "What can you mean by that, Shiloh ben Gozán?"

Shiloh lifted her as though she weighed no more than a cat. "You were an Old Christian once. Yet you have my trust."

As he kissed her he loosened her linen veil. It dropped to the clean-swept floor, taking with it the pins that had held her coiled tresses, and her hair fell down, covering her shoulders. He buried his face in its thickness, and said in her ear, *"Kol haneshama, t'hallel ya.* With every breath I praise God."

SIX

In THE WINTER of that year was held the first of the Toledo autos-da-fé.

Those arrested had all been conversos, and each one was taken alone, without witnesses, so that it seemed to his friends and family as though he had dropped from the face of the earth. Only gradually, through low-voiced conversations in the marketplaces and the courtyards of the old judería, was certainty arrived at. The Holy Brotherhood had seized and delivered the men to the Inquisitors of the Church. No official announcement had been made in Toledo of their arrests, much less of their whereabouts. But all five men were New Christians, and none was fond of pork. What had happened was clear.

Two weeks after the men's disappearances a bill in the cathedral and, for the benefit of the illiterate, a priestly homily announced at Sunday mass that a public tribunal, an auto-da-fé, would be held the next Saturday in the Plaza de Zocodover. The relatives of the taken looked at one another in hope and in dread.

On the appointed day, Bishop Gaspar de Quiroga of Toledo mounted his red throne on the top tier of a raised platform at the far end of the plaza, close to the keyhole arch that overlooked the River Tagus. He seated himself under a lemon-orange canopy, holding his crossed crook tightly in his right hand. On benches on each side of him sat the lesser clergy, a few clad in red robes and caps. Among the group were a tonsured monk and a black-gowned priest whom the others called Lope, though his true name was Hayim. That one looked sickly and green.

The wind was bitter, but the press of the people warmed the watchers. Like the Red Sea, the crowd of jostling Toledans parted to admit the passage of the dons of the city, the governing corregidor, the lower-ranking regidores, and last the caballeros, clad in ceremonial armor made of New World silver. They came past a new, mysterious, high thing hidden by an encircling canopy in the middle of the plaza.

Shiloh, watching with Leah from a hitching post near a southern archway, felt his wife stiffen, and followed her gaze as the knights and noblemen took their places below the clergy. On a bench lined with green velvet he saw Sebastian de la Cerda, his father-in-law, who had looked beyond him, unspeaking, on the three occasions since his marriage when their paths had crossed in the hated cathedral. He had looked beyond Leah, too. De la Cerda's gaze now was stern and set on something, or nothing, in the middle distance of the plaza. He looked dignified today, with his green silk finery and his black hat.

Shiloh patted his wife's shoulder.

Now the crowd murmured as the prisoners were led in. There were only four, and the anusim, the secret Jews who had scattered

themselves for safety among the crowd, craned their necks, looking anxiously to see which one of their number was not among
those who walked clad in sanbenitos, yellow robes embroidered
with the cross of Saint Andrew. The shackled prisoners' heads were
upright under tall yellow hats painted with flames and cartoonish
images of dancing devils. Behind the unlucky ones, on horseback,
rode the badge-wearing guards of the Holy Brotherhood, clutching
their long spears.

One by one the prisoners walked to the dusty ground before
the tribunal. One by one they were questioned by the Inquisitional
priest. *Do you believe that Christ is God? Do you believe that His mother
was a Virgin? Do you believe that the pope is God's supreme minister on
earth?* Each admitted that all of these things were true, and re-
canted his heresy. Each had his property confiscated and was ordered to wear the sanbenito for three years. The men's wives,
children, and parents fell upon them, crying, as they were led away,
two to exile, and two back to prison.

Shiloh knew them all, and whispered as much to Leah. Only
one of them was a true member of the anusim, a real secret Jew.
By means of Father Hayim (who now appeared close to fainting
on his high bench), word had slipped out that the other three had
been arrested on the merest suggestion of Judaizing: lighting candles
while it was still daylight on Friday evening; buying alheras instead
of good Spanish pork sausage in the market stalls.

The fifth prisoner was brought out. This one wore no sanbenito and no high-crowned hat, only a torn wool garment. His face
was bruised. The crowd's jeering rose in volume now; he was
called diablo, matacristo, killer of Christ! He put his face up to the
sky and laughed through a bloody mouth whose front teeth had
been knocked out. Leah knew him at once, and drew in her breath.
He was a man of her father's, the first servant who had led her

through the maze of the old judería without telling her how he knew it. She had never known his secret name.

Now she wondered who had given his Christian name to the Holy Brotherhood.

"He is a pertinace," a girl next to Leah said quietly. "He does not repent."

Looking to her side, she saw the small daughter of the Moorish craftsman, whose shop was three closed doors away from where they stood. The girl was standing on a box. She looked at Leah with warm dark eyes, then turned her glance pointedly to Shiloh's hand, which was gripping a pillar. The blue stone on his finger shone. She looked back at Leah and smiled.

Seized by the horror of the yelling crowd, Leah could only stare at her.

The loud speech of the bishop became a buzz in Leah's ears. Wresting her gaze from the Moorish girl's eyes, she watched, transfixed, while armed guards withdrew the white canopy that shrouded the thing in the center of the plaza. When its nakedness was revealed, the Toledans howled. It was an uneven, high-built pile of wood.

Following a signal from the corregidor, a black-hooded man approached the pile, knelt, and held a torch to its base. The dry faggots blazed upward instantly and the smoke rose straight to God, it seemed, while the black-hooded man seized the stubborn man, the pertinace, and, mercifully, quickly, strangled him with two giant hands. Then he mounted the rough-built wooden stair by the pyre and threw the corpse in like a ball of rags.

"They would not question him in public," Shiloh said at home. He had broken a chicken bone with his teeth and was sucking the marrow. "They did not wish the crowd to hear him say the Adonai Echad, the Lord Is One. None of that for the good Christians of Toledo."

Leah looked at him distastefully. "How can you eat?"

Shiloh shrugged. "I carded fifty pounds of wool in the shop before that travesty of religion and justice robbed my attention. I am hungry."

But Shiloh's appetite was less hearty three weeks later when he returned, late at night, from an encounter with a member of the Holy Brotherhood. He had been missing for hours, and Leah, frantic with worry, had just decided to brave the black streets to find his father, Gozán, when the door opened and her husband appeared. His clothes were torn and his face, while unbruised, was ashen. She fell on his chest, sobbing, and he held her gently by the elbows.

He told her what had happened. Two men of the Holy Brotherhood had appeared behind Gozán ben Eleazar's shop where Shiloh, alone, was stacking burlap bags of fleece for the morrow's carding. Night had already fallen, and in the dark, by the light of a single torch, they had taken him to a building next to the Church of San Vicente and had seated him on a stone bench and questioned him for hours.

"I gave the right answers to everything," he told her, stroking her hair.

"Please, husband," she said. Her ear was against his chest, and she heard the slowing beat of his heart. "Please. Tell me not that you spoke like a Luterano."

"No," he said. "I'm not a fool. I professed reverence for the pope, may baboons gnaw his testicles. They did not think me a good Christian, but I gave them no proof to the contrary. They took pleasure in making me think they would kill me. Or one of them did! He had a face like a monkey. He questioned me with a knife at my breast, the very point at my ribs. He told me he could cut out my heart and feel no remorse. I told him to slice and then eat it, if he would. He was playing, like a cat with a mouse. I knew he would do nothing."

Shiloh did not tell her the other thing the vile monkey had said, which was that he was tempted to cut Shiloh's breeches to ribbons and circumcise his prick, too, along with his Jewish heart. *Though I am no shohet!* he'd said, and laughed, pleased with himself for knowing the word. *Not trained to the task. It could be my knife will slip and cut something else.* He had moved his blade lower as if to plunge it into Shiloh's groin, and Shiloh had flinched without willing it, though he'd known the man would not cut. There were limits to the tricks the Holy Brotherhood were allowed to play, at least within the precincts of the city.

He said nothing to Leah of the crudest threats. She was already sitting rigid on his lap, staring at him with alarm, her face flushed. "Only a cat with a mouse," he said, patting her head.

She held a hand to his cheek and said, "Cats *kill* mice!"

"Then call him a monkey instead of a cat. An ape. I almost did call him so—"

"Shiloh!"

"—but his fellow was listening, and then the monkey would have *had* to cut me for shame. I decided I preferred to see you again."

"I thank you!"

"He wanted silver. He looked at the silver in my ring"—Shiloh turned his hand and held the turquoise to the light of the candle—"but he thought the stone ugly. In the end I gave him what was in my purse, and he let me go, 'of my holy charity!' he said. He pocketed the coin when the other left the room to piss in the alley, or perhaps to fetch his holy brother a banana." Shiloh shook his head in disgust. "Neither of them had a crumb of evidence against me."

"But something led them to you," Leah said in fear. "Could it have been me? That your wife walks veiled—"

Shiloh was shaking his head. "No. Many Old Christian women go veiled, too. The New Christians are *always* watched. This has happened before."

Leah stared. "To you?"

"To others. Once or twice a year the Holy Brotherhood try to frighten us this way. My father's cousin Asher was taken from his breakfast last winter and kept for a day in a room near the Alcázar—they blindfolded him, so he knew not truly where he was, but by the uphill walk to the place, he thought it was there."

"What did they do to him?"

"Slapped his face, pulled his beard. Called him a Christ-killer, then took him back down the hill and kicked him into the Plaza Mayor in time for Shabbat. They play with us, Leah. We give them nothing."

"The auto-da-fé was not play. Now four men are stripped of everything but the yellow sanbenito, and they will wear it three years for doing nothing. For eating chicken sausage, my love!"

Shiloh was silent. He kissed her neck. After a time he said, "It comes hard to me, this pretending. For Hayim and even my father Gozán it is a game—one they are forced to play, but one they delight in winning." He shrugged. "Each to his road. For me to say a thing I do not mean is . . ."

"A violation. I know thee, Shiloh. I know."

He tightened one fist. "The family ben Gozán have been Spaniards since before the Moors controlled Andalusia. Eight hundred years in La Mancha, and they call us aliens! Even decades after the Expulsion it seemed we could continue, but things are worsening. Tightening. Why? The Luteranos scare the bishops, perhaps. . . . They fear the Church may crumble into powder."

Leah looked at him worriedly. His eyes had gone very dark. She raised his fist to her chest, straightened his clenched fingers, and kissed his ring. He smiled at her a little. "Ah, Spain!" he said. "Dry air breeds fanatics. At times I think we should go eastward; you, my father, and I. Even out of Europe, or at least from Iberia. To Italy, perhaps."

"Where the *pope* lives?"

"Not Rome. Though Rome could be no worse than Toledo. No, farther north. There are parts of Italy where we might be suffered to exist. Places where the state disdains the pope's power, because it thwarts commerce." He brooded. "Places where the Inquisition is defied."

Italy. Into Leah's mind came a picture of a small gold-haired girl and her fur-robed father, buying blades and odd boxes from an old swordmaker, speaking in the accents of that country. She looked down at Shiloh's ring and touched it gently, remembering how the little girl, no doubt liking its bright blue color, had seized it, then generously handed it back to its owner.

She shook her head to bring her thoughts back to the urgent present. "But how Italy, or anywhere?" she asked Shiloh. "King Philip has forbidden conversos to leave Spain. He needs converso industry, converso—"

"Wealth," said Shiloh bitterly. "As the Church needs our tithes. So they send their monkey-faced ministers to terrify us into being good Christians. Fools!"

Leah shuddered then, imagining her husband with his shirt torn, a knife pointed at his breast by a sneering Holy Brother. "Ah, by Santiago—"

"Santiago? Is *he* our friend?"

Leah pinched Shiloh lightly. "Thanks be to Hashem you were not carrying your prayer book!"

"Yes," Shiloh said, sitting up straighter and pushing her off his lap. "What angel made me leave it home today? But Leah, they would be too stupid to know what Hebrew was if they saw it."

"Not all of them are stupid," she said, moving to the table and uncovering his plate of moros y cristianos, black beans and white rice.

"Not all," he conceded. "Some men of the Church are most clever." He frowned thoughtfully. "Those ones must be Jews."

SHE HEARD THE taunts at their backs as they bowed their heads in the cathedral. *Tornadizo. Jew. Marrano.*

"Marrano," muttered the pork butcher to Shiloh as they passed his stall in the Plaza de Ayuntamiento.

"I wonder," he said mildly, turning, "why you call me *pig* when I do not eat the stuff. You, on the other hand, do, and if the saying is true that one is what one puts in one's belly—"

"*Shh, shh—Benito!*" Leah whispered forcefully. "Have a care!"

"He is only angry," Shiloh told her as they walked on. "A dealer in swine, hurt in his purse. Trade-fallen, due to the habits of the chosen."

From the corner of her eye, Leah saw the butcher make the sign against the evil eye at their backs.

"THE MAN WAS a negativo," said Bishop Quiroga. "He revealed nothing." He brooded, drumming his long fingers. Then he said, "These forced conversions are not what we would wish. The constrained Christian believes with his lips but not with his heart. Jew, Mohammedan, or Luterano, each returns to his old faith like a dog to his vomit."

"If it is hopeless, *why* persist in the torture?" asked Father Bartolomeo, who was seated, hands folded, at the bishop's document-strewn table. The face of the small, quiet priest was aflame with anger. He looked at the bishop's miter, which stood on the table in front of him. In its shape he saw the tall, mocking hats of the accused heretics in the Plaza de Zocodover. He closed his eyes. "Why, my lord bishop?"

"To save their souls, or, failing that, to set an example for the rest." Quiroga threw up his hands. "They are a poison, these heresies! I myself saw the book that led to the burning of the Luteranos in Seville. *Image of the Antichrist*. A fine title. A book meant for a heretical priest, and delivered to a good Catholic one of the same name! Can you imagine his horror when he saw, on the frontispiece, an engraving of the pope kneeling to Satan?"

Bartolomeo gave a short laugh. "I wish I had seen his face, my divine señor."

The bishop regarded him with frustration. "You laugh!"

"I am sorry, divine señor." Bartolomeo looked only slightly chastened. "The image amused me. God sends absurdities to make us smile amid our pains and fears."

"God sends us this. God sends us that." The bishop slapped his table, and his papers bounced. "God sent us eyes to see that the Church is perishing. She will not survive this century if we fail to raise our hands to defend her." He leaned forward. "Are you blind, Bartolomeo? Spain is the vanguard. We are ringed by God's enemies! England's red-haired Protestant queen has refused our king's marriage suit, and begins to turn her guns against us. It is not eighty years since the Moslems were pushed from Granada, and not forty since the Turk raged at the very gates of Vienna! Even now the Moors mutter in Andalusia, pretending piety in public while they observe their secret sacrifices and spy for the Ottomites.

Sulemein the Second sends his corsairs to slaughter what Christian men he can capture off our coasts, and to sell our women into wretched slavery. And this today from the archbishop." He rattled a paper in Bartolomeo's face. "Moriscos from Spain go to France, pledging support for a Protestant Huguenot prince's invasion of Navarre! And your Jews? They are in Turkey, converting lead to gunstones for the sultan's cannon!"

"The ones you torment are the ones who *stayed*. And my señor, would any of our Jews be in Salonika or Constantinople, had we granted them safe harbor as the sultan does? Preached love on the hills, like Christ; and of His empty grave in the marketplace, as did the first apostles? They drew men not by chains, but by their hearts!"

"Very nicely said," the bishop snapped. "Do you like that cloud you dwell on? Is it soft and fluffy? I live in Spain. And I say that in your zeal to be like Christ, you would throw away His kingdom."

"That kingdom was not meant to be of this earth, divine señor."

"But *we* are on this earth!"

"To seek Him, and to set an example. Not to kill."

"It is the civil arm that orders executions. We only—"

"Persuade, yes." Bartolomeo said tiredly. "But not very well."

Quiroga looked at him warningly. "You were not present at the auto-da-fé last month. Your place on the bench was empty."

Father Bartolomeo shook his head sadly. "My lord bishop, I revere your office. But, as I have said, I find the questionings and the tortures and the burnings an abomination."

"The word is harsh."

"So is the pinga, my lord. I cannot be a priest in a manner that defies my conscience."

Bishop Quiroga rose, narrowing his eyes. "How long has your family been Christian?"

Bartolomeo rose also, and bowed. "Since Santiago died head-less in Galicia. The first century, that was. A notable Jew, was Santiago, who knew Our Lord personally when He yet walked this earth. My own ancestors met the Christ some decades after He ascended to the right hand of the Father. They were Celtic converts from northwest Spain, but they too came to know the love of the gentle Redeemer." He bowed again, touching the cross at his breast. "The love of the gentle Redeemer, your grace. Who Himself was beaten and hung on a—"

"I know what they did to Him," the bishop said curtly. "And I dismiss you." His parting words briefly stopped the small priest at the door. "For now."

SEVEN

WORD OF WHAT had been done to Shiloh spread quickly in the community of the anusim. The Jews walked more guardedly than before. Some fell away, began working on Shabbat, and slowly stopped keeping kosher. They bought forbidden food. Sometimes they only threw it on the fire, but sometimes they ate it. For some, it turned their stomachs. Others discovered a taste for roast pig, and began to break other laws. Prayers went unsaid, or were mumbled in greater haste and confusion in the darkness.

Though it pained them, Reuben and Astruga kept their sons from their secret Hebrew lessons with Father Hayim. "We will speak Ladino for another generation, watering our holy tongue with Spanish, and our prayers will sound ever fainter to Hashem's ears," Reuben said bitterly.

But Passover could not be avoided. It was the sixth millenium of the Covenant, and there were only so many duties the anusim could scant before the Blessed One abandoned them altogether.

So one evening Leah appeared, great-bellied, in the workshop of Gozán ben Eleazar bearing her plate of cilantro, lettuce, roasted lamb bone, and egg, and said to her husband, "It is time!"

Shiloh stood shirtless in the heat of the shop, sweating from the labor and the warmth of April. He had half-finished carding the new hanks of fleece that he and his father had brought that morning from a sheep farm across the Tagus, bending their backs to cart it up the high hill to the city. Now Shiloh stepped back from the loom and wiped his hands with a rag, smiling at Leah.

"Clean up!" she said, and turned awkwardly, steadying herself with one hand on the door handle.

"Soon you will not fit in this room!" Shiloh called after her.

THEY STOOD BY the table, which was spread with spotless linen to welcome the first night of Passover. The family Selomó had joined them with their boys, and now under a napkin Leah's aunt Astruga placed unleavened bread. Eight months with child, Leah had to stand back from the cloth, and everyone laughed and reached and patted her stomach joyfully.

A cup of silver sat, full of wine, at the far end of the board, awaiting the prophet Elijah. On a plate Leah had filled with lamb, egg, lettuce, and bitter herb, her father-in-law Gozán placed a smidgin of haroset. *"Zakhor,"* he said. "Remember. Thus we recall the mortar with which the Israelites built Egypt."

That was not so hard to keep in mind. Leah thought of the Jewish wool and silk makers of Toledo and their tithes, which bought stone for the cathedral.

Astruga lit candles. Expressionless, the boy Santiago Mendoza brought four glasses to the table, and set them there carefully before he retired to light a fire in the hearth. The sun had set, and the families ben Gozán and Selomó would not light the fire themselves at this holy time. But now they bade the boy do so, knowing that on this night of all nights the Holy Brotherhood would be seeking smokeless chimneys.

Gozán poured wine and began the prayer. In Ladino he blessed the wine, saying, "Blessed are Thou, O Lord, King of the Universe, creator of the fruit of the vine." The praise should have been loudly sung, but he kept his voice low. Combining their voices, all those assembled finished Gozán's prayer in Spanish. "Let all who are hungry come and eat. This year in Spain; next year in Jerusalem. This year we are slaves; next year, free."

Gozán then unrolled a page of the Haggadah, torn on its right side, but beautifully inscribed and illuminated with gold letters surrounded by geometrical and vegetable motifs. In faltering Hebrew, he read a portion of the story of the plagues that befell the pharoah and of the Jews' escape from Egypt, across the Red Sea. When he concluded his reading, he reverently rolled and bound the small scroll and replaced it within his shirt, close to his breast.

Before them lay lamb and matzoh and wine. This table was their Jerusalem.

"FIVE THOUSAND THREE hundred and twenty-eight," said Shiloh, calmly chewing.

"Five thousand three hundred and twenty-*seven,*" said Leah's cousin Yehuda.

"I have taught my son to make no errors with numbers," Gozán said. "It is the year five thousand three hundred and twenty-eight if he says it is."

Astruga shook her head. "We are in a bad way. We need a rabbi to instruct us."

Father Hayim, who had arrived puffing and habitless at the end of the prayer, looked wounded. "By my calculations, Shiloh is right," he said.

"The Christian world does no better with dates," said Reuben. "All expect their next pope to be Gregory, he who proposes the new calendar. The Protestant English, to defy him, already say they will keep another, even if all the nations of Europe go the other way! The English must always hang apart."

"Good for the English!" said Leah, laughing.

"But England is madder than Spain," said Astruga. "Since you speak of hanging. A few years ago they were burning their Protestants. Now they're hanging Catholics."

"Good," said Shiloh.

Father Hayim wagged his finger at him. "England is not a blessed country because it hangs Catholics. Do not think of going there. Do you know that England's King Edward the First only suffered Jews in his realm as long as they gave him their gold? When he ran out of money he took a venerable rabbi and pulled his teeth out, and said so it would be with the rest of the Jews unless they handed over their wealth. He bled them dry, then forced them out!"

Shiloh laughed. "And because one old English Jew got his teeth pulled out more than two centuries past, we should all stay in Spain and wear the sanbenito?" He pointed his knife playfully at Hayim's breast. "I'd sooner risk your teeth to a king than my chest to the pinga."

"Shh, Shiloh!" said Leah. "He is a priest."

"And despite that, we honor him," laughed Gozán, patting Hayim on the shoulder.

They drank more Passover wine and the minutes sped by. They told all the stories they could remember and then invented a few, and laughed harder than they had in a year. Such was their merriment that no one noticed that the boy Mendoza was no longer serving at table.

Or that the hearthfire in the kitchen had not been lit.

WHEN THE HOLY Brotherhood broke open the door, Leah jumped up without thinking and, shielding her belly, threw the blazing candelabra toward them. The flames streamed long in the air and then the candelabra struck one man in the sleeve, burning him with hot wax and setting his garments afire. He cried out, and a second Holy Brother dropped his sword and threw a rug over him. Shiloh stamped out the flames not for pity but to give them all darkness, then grabbed Leah's arm and pushed her toward the window. Reuben and Astruga and their sons had already forced open the shutters and dropped from one opening to the roof below, Yehuda and Aaron bringing up the rear and pulling the panting priest. Together Gozán and Shiloh half-pushed, half-pulled bulky Leah through the other window to the roof, just evading the hands of another of the holy brethren. Gozán's feet were outside before the armed man caught up to him but he could not evade the man's sword, which stabbed outward and sliced deep into his side. Gozán fell, and with Shiloh and Leah rolled on his own slippery blood off the roof and into the dusty courtyard eight feet below.

Leah was shielding her stomach as she dropped, and landed hard on her rear end. "Run, Leah! *Run!*" Shiloh rasped, holding his bleeding father. Gozán's vital organs were protruding through the slash in his side and his blood was everywhere. Shiloh dragged him into the shadows and kissed and blessed him as shouts came from above and a torch was lit and heavy, booted feet were heard on the slate roof.

Leah ran from the courtyard. Gozán rolled his eyes and went slack, and Shiloh, weeping, tossed his cloak over his father. He climbed over a stone wall and fell into the Calle del Ángel. Dimly, he heard Leah's running feet and sped after her, praying that she would find a hiding place. Fog had begun to rise, and he could see only the reddish glow of hearthfires beyond the courtyards he passed. He ran harder, though he could no longer hear Leah.

SHE COULD NOT go fast or far without wheezing and doubling over for lack of breath. Behind her she could hear the running steps and shouts of the Holy Brotherhood. She kicked off her shoes and ran blind, stumbling over stones, praying that the fog would hide her. Once she ran straight into the wall of a closed alley, stunning herself, bruising and scraping her face. She held her belly fearfully, and felt the baby kick. Dogs howled far and near and she imagined they chased her. The Passover wine she had drunk made her dizzy, and in the fog she thought she ran in a dream or nightmare. Names hammered in her thought: *Toledo, tornadizo, Toledo, tornadizo!* Finally, near collapse, she held on to the wall and slowly felt her way along the twisting streets, through the broken maze of the city. *Shiloh,* she thought. *I love Shiloh. Have they taken Shiloh?*

She came to a hill and walked upward, hoping in her weariness to reach the Plaza de Zocodover, imagining, she knew not why, that she might knock on the door of the shop of the swordmaker Julian del Rei and find refuge with him and his daughter. She would come to the Plaza de Zocodover, she thought, pulling herself along the wall up the hill, thinking she must almost be at the arch that gave way to the open space. But instead she came up against another wall at the end of the black street. When, sobbing, she turned to go back, she heard shouts coming closer and saw torches bobbing in the fog like balls of flame. She fell to her knees, and gloved hands grabbed her on both sides. She heard the fiery zeal in the voice of one of them, as he said, "Come on, Jew!"

EIGHT

A DEAD JEW was no use to the Holy Brotherhood, so they left Gozán lying on the ground by the wall where Shiloh had pulled him. His son found him there at dawn when he returned, white and drawn, from his fruitless search for Leah. Between his father's bloody garment and his grizzled breast lay the fragment of Haggadah from which Gozán had read at the seder. Shiloh removed it and laid it aside. Then he rent his own shirt in half.

That morning, with two female cousins, he cleansed and wrapped his father and laid him on a bench in their workroom. They would bury him on the morrow. After they had shrouded and composed his father's body, he said a brief Kaddish, swaying with reverence, grief, and exhaustion. Then he went out again into the city and walked its rough circle, from the well-kept road of the Calle de los Reyes Católicos to the crumbling stones of the Calle de los Alferitos.

He descended from the keyhole arch of the Puerta del Sol in
the Plaza de Zocodover, and walked over the old Roman bridge to
look in the reeds on the banks of the River Tagus, though he knew
it was hopeless. The gates had been closed in the night, and how
could Leah have climbed the city wall to hide by the river? When
by noonday he had not found his wife in the city's winding pas-
sages, or at the house of the family Selomó, or at home in her
kitchen, he made his way to the dark building by the Church of San
Vicente and hammered on the front door. "Take me," he said to the
priest who answered. "Put your knives in my flesh. Benito Gozán
for Elizabeta de la Cerda. My life for hers!"

"You disturb a Holy Office that must take its course," said the
priest. "If your wife be true Christian she has nothing to fear. Look
to your own conduct, man."

"Let me see Father Bartolomeo," Shiloh begged. But the priest
closed the door in his face.

Shiloh hammered again on the door, then ran to the side of the
building and yelled "Elizabeta! Elizabeta!" A member of the Holy
Brotherhood came out from the place and bade him begone.
Shiloh thought wildly that if he hit the man he would then be arrested, taken into the place, brought to his wife, but he knew it
would not be so; they would take him and lock him in a cell and he
could do her no good.

He ran downhill to the cathedral. Traversing its huge stone
floor from transept to nave to saints' chapels, he asked every priest
and layman he encountered for Father Bartolomeo or Father Lope.
None knew the whereabouts of either.

By a side wall Shiloh saw an old woman exiting a confessional.
He walked quickly toward the wooden structure, entered, and
closed the door behind him. He saw the dim profile of the priest
behind the screen. "Is it Father Lope?" he said. There was a pause,

and then Hiyam's cautious voice whispered, "Shiloh?" Shiloh leaned his face against the screen. "Gozán my father is dead."

Hiyam moaned faintly.

"And I cannot find Leah!"

"I fear she is taken," whispered Hiyam. "Rumor runs that the bishop wants another auto-da-fé. He is collecting Jews. Shiloh, I cannot help you. Were I to speak out, it would only pull his gaze toward me, and then he would see others, like you, coming into the confessional and asking for Father Lope. . . ."

He began to sob, and Shiloh could get nothing more from him but tears. He came out of the confessional, leaving Hiyam slumped behind his screen crying silently and whispering a vow to say the prayer of Kol Nidre at Yom Kippur, that he might be forgiven all of his sins.

Shiloh ran from the cathedral. The sun was hanging low in the west now. A bloody disk, it cast slanted rays over the Tagus and the pinkish tan stone of the square houses of Toledo. Hemmed in by the close-leaning buildings, he could not see the sun. He walked fast back to the building by the Church of San Vicente and pounded again on the door. No one answered. He circled the edifice and came upon a woman scrubbing cookware in a tub near one of the outbuildings. "Señora, have you seen any-one going in or out today?" he asked, gesturing toward the main building.

"They brought Jews in there last night, I have heard. From different parts of the city. All they could catch at their devil's feast. An hour ago they brought three of them out, shackled. Then they led them through another door, down there." She pointed to the far end of the building.

Shiloh grabbed her arm. "Was a woman among them?"

She eyed him suspiciously. "At least one she-Jew was taken. So my husband told me, and he is a guard of the place. But no women were among the group I saw."

"But the men? How did they look?"

"Bad!" the woman said. "They had horns and tails!"

Shiloh dropped her arm in disgust and ran back to the front of the building, where he knocked hard again, then put his ear against the door. He could hear loud shouts from deep in the labyrinth, but none were the cries of a woman. He pounded the door for ten minutes. No one came.

At last, in desperation, Shiloh limped up the high hill of the Alcázar and asked the first hidalgo who came out through the high wooden front door to direct him to the house of Sebastian de la Cerda.

THE HIDALGO SEBASTIAN De la Cerda stood with his legs planted wide, as if to steady himself. His ruff was loose and hanging, and he was clad below in unlaced silk breeches and a peacock blue doublet stained with wine. Shiloh, though as disheveled, was sober. Only his outside was unkempt, his wool shirt and breeches sweat-stained and muddy, his hair in a tangle. He had not bathed or changed his garments since just before the seder the night before. He looked like a madman or a zealot.

He fell to his knees before de la Cerda in the luxuriant room. "Your daughter," he said. "They have taken her. Save her, I beg of you!"

The don spat on him. "For you she was taken," he said. "For a dog such as you. I was told of it this morning. She has made her choice, and is dead to me already."

Wiping spittle from his face, Shiloh looked up in rage. "She carries your grandchild!"

De la Cerda laughed harshly. "A good argument for the mercy of the Inquisitors, but her child will avail her nothing if she does not forswear Judaizing. E'en if I would, I could not help her did she not repent. And she will not." He suddenly picked up a carved chair and threw it at Shiloh, who raised his hands and caught it just before it struck his face. *"Elizabeta Santa Leocadia de la Cerda will not!"* the hidalgo bellowed.

IN THE DEPTHS of the Inquisitional building, Father Bartolomeo anxiously conferred with Bishop Quiroga. "I don't care what the boy told you of them," Bartolomeo pleaded. "You paid him silver. He was bound to say something against them! This woman is of an Old Christian family, and furthermore she is carrying a child!"

"Her mother was Jewish, her husband is a New Christian who was already under suspicion of Judaizing, and she attended a seder. Her father has forsworn her, as is well known. Though Don Sebastian de la Cerda gives no reason for his coldness, his very silence damns her."

"But the child!"

"If she conducts herself well neither she nor her child will come to harm."

"ARE YOU A Jew?" asked a tall priest.

"Yes," Leah said.

The seated clergy looked at each other in surprise. They had not expected this. Two of the priests shared an uncomfortable glance. The prisoner was young and female and her belly swelled.

It would not be easy to punish such a one, or to justify her correction in the eyes of Toledo.

A red-capped canon who sat at a table tapped his quill against a parchment roll. Leah had been allowed to sit on a stool, and her eyes were at the level of the canon's. He gazed at her sharply, cleared his throat, and said, "Do you wish to amend what you have just said?"

"No."

The tall priest put his face inches from hers and said, "Do you confess that you attended a seder?"

"I say nothing to that." Turning her head, she looked at his eyes rather than in them, for they were flat and hard and admitted no access. It seemed there was nothing behind them. It came to her that she knew him. He was the hooded penitent with whom she had collided in the Plaza de Zocodover, on Ash Wednesday the year before. Few could have such eyes.

The priest withdrew and conferred with the canon, who sat flanked by several lesser clergy and the ecclesiastical lawyer. In a moment, the canon said in a reasonable tone, "This is perhaps a madness under which you suffer. You are the daughter of an Old Christian hidalgo of this city. You were baptized in the cathedral and catechized. You are young and have been misled by men whose eyes are closed to the light and who misunderstand holy scripture. Perhaps you yourself, as a child, were not well enough instructed by the Sisters of Santa Catalina. This happens sometimes—the nuns are often ignorant, country women—and can be corrected. For the sake of yourself, your child, and the eternal soul of each of you—for your child, should you perish, will perish with you, and languish in the nothingness of Limbo—I invite you to forswear what you have said to us here. Embrace the love of Christ, who has not forsaken you, for all that you have turned your back on Him."

"No, I thank you," said Leah.

All in the room stiffened visibly, and a look of anger came over the canon's face. Without looking at Leah, he gestured to one of the guards who stood at the door. "Take her back to the cell."

As Leah left the room, guided by a guard, she heard the lawyer beside the canon say, "As you know, rank denial of Our Lord gives the Church ecclesiastical license to enforce stricter instruction."

ABASHED BY HIS duty, the guard mumbled an apology as he guided Leah down an ill-lit hallway toward the small, windowless chamber where she had spent the previous night. Her feet had been bleeding then, and a man had brought cloths to bind them, but this morning they still pained her, and she walked slowly. Desperately, she considered her plight. She had recognized another of her Inquisitors, besides the shark-eyed priest. One of the men in the questioning room had so closely matched Shiloh's description of the monkey-faced fellow who had tormented him at knifepoint that she thought it must be he. That one had been bribable. She wondered briefly if she might gain his help by offering him silver. Shiloh had bought freedom that way. But Shiloh had been alone with the knavish fellow, away from the eyes of the officials of the holy Church. She was surrounded by priestly eyes.

She began to perspire, and her head felt light. The guard gripped her arm tightly as they rounded a corner. He led her gently to her cell, but did not hesitate to lock her in. She was given bread and a small stoup of wine. She ignored both. It was Passover. She sat on the hard bench that jutted from the wall, turned her face to the cold stone, and prayed.

Hours passed.

———

SHE KNEW THE time of day only from the dimming of the faint light in the hall outside the cell. Her bladder ached, and in shame she relieved herself in a pot she found under the bench, in full view of any guard who might pass. Afterward she stretched on the hard bench and tried to sleep. After an eternity a key turned in the lock and she opened her eyes to see Father Bartolomeo at her side. At this sight, for the first time since her capture, she began to weep. She sat up. "Where is my husband?" she said. "Our family?"

"Safe, but frantic for your release."

He did not tell her of Gozán. She collapsed against him and continued to cry, burying her face in the soft wool of his soutane.

He patted her shoulder. "Ah, Leah," he murmured, quietly enough that no listening guard could hear him use her Jewish name. "You have denied them their desire."

"How so?" she sniffed.

"All the questions they would have asked you. Did you poison a well? Do you change your linen on Saturdays? Does your husband sway when he prays?"

"Would you eat a pork sausage?" she said, smiling slightly and wiping her nose with her fingers.

"Yes, all that. Where is the sport, when you come right out with it at the beginning?"

"Thou shalt not bear false witness," she said. "It is the Law."

"Yes," he said, patting her hand. "Yes. That is our Law as well as yours. But Leah, I must advise you to do it. Lie. You must think not only of your husband, but of your child."

Leah put her hand on her belly. "The child is kicking," she said. "Wants to come out of prison, as I do."

"And you must give the answers they want in order that the child may. You know what the answers are."

"I cannot," Leah said.

Father Bartolomeo was quiet for a moment. Then he said, "Your husband has been to your father. Nay, do not flash fire at me with your eyes. He has gone to him, as have I. Your father is not inclined to help you, and says even if he would, he could do nothing without your own recantation. Though a fool in many things, Sebastian de la Cerda is right in this."

"Then he will not help me," said Leah. The child suddenly kicked hard against her belly, and she smiled through tears. "Do you know, this babe in my womb makes me less afraid. Boy or girl, it is of the seed of the chosen. How can I stand before Hashem having denied it its birthright?"

"They will torture you." The priest's voice was blunt. "Bishop Quiroga himself is going to question you. The canon that spoke to you today is from Madrid. He thought to make short work of the interchange, and to bring you back to Madrid for an auto-da-fé. Your punishment would have been lighter than that of some of the others."

"To wear the sanbenito," she said scornfully. "Ugly yellow, and a silly hat."

"So you do not like the fashion?" the priest said, smiling sadly.

"I do not like the fashion of men choosing things for me. Such as the things I may believe or say." She clung to his soutane. "Father Bartolomeo, I love my life. I love Hashem, the Most High I cannot see or name. I love my husband!"

"Who begs you to lie."

Leah flinched as though she had been struck.

"Yes," Bartolomeo said. "He found me as I was coming from

the bishop's palace to this place. He begged me to beg you to save yourself."

Leah blew breath out in a long sigh. "Shiloh," she said softly, caressing the syllables of his name, as he so often had done with hers. She looked at the priest with wide, sad eyes. "When you see my beloved, please tell him this. I am eighteen years old. There is nothing I desire more than to see him, to live my life with him, to give birth to our child." She rested her hand on her stomach. "And so I will do anything to make them relent." She leaned forward. "Anything *except* lie about what I think. I have seen what lying does to *him*. I gave my love a ring, and with that ring I gave him myself. He will not ask me to be less than myself."

"Leah, tell me this." The priest gripped her arm. "Do you imagine I can help you?"

"I hoped you would try."

"I *have* tried. But I tell you, a process has begun that I cannot stop. There was an age in Spain when priests were human, and charity mattered. Now we enter the age of the machine. The Inquisition is such a machine. It will crush you, Leah."

"What would you have me do?"

His eyes were deeply sorrowful. "I? I would have you believe, as I do, that Jesus of Nazareth was the messiah some of you await. I would have you confess Him honestly. Oh, Leah, our hearts are curved inward by sin. No law can save us. Only love!"

"Then human hearts made this Inquisition. You cannot blame a machine."

"You have me, Leah. It is so," he said sadly. "But the warped heart and the new machine make a diabolical combination."

"And you speak to me of Christ's love," she said bitterly. "May I find love in this place?"

"In all places. But you will not receive it from these men. I do not think you know what awaits you in there."

"It would not matter," she said. "I am who I am."

His face twisted with the effort not to weep. Then he said, "In the worst of the ordeal, do not confuse Him with His ministers. They are in error. For He was gentle, and knew that hearts choose as they choose. That we know Him, and show Him, through our free choosing."

She was silent. Then she said, "I choose truth."

"Do you believe Christ was the Son of God?"

"No."

The shark-eyed priest who stood by Bishop Quiroga ripped the cloth from her breast, half-baring her, and two other men stretched her on a table. She tried to cover her belly with her hands, but they pulled her arms wide. One of the two men moved behind her, pinning her at the elbows to the table. "Approach," said the dead-eyed priest to the monkey-faced man. Grinning, that man walked forward, bearing a wooden dipper.

When the first drop of hot oil hit her chest she screamed. It was as though a thousand red ants were biting her underneath the skin, spreading and multiplying as they fed on her flesh. She felt her child contract in her womb. Another drop, and then another. Her flesh sizzled.

"Stop!" she yelled.

The priest and the man with the dipper stepped calmly back. The bishop approached her where she lay. "Do you think we will stop at your command, infidel? Do you imagine that the Church Militant will desist from the conversion of heretics, from the unification of her scattered parts? *Every knee* shall bow to the Christ. The remnant shall rejoin the whole. I would save your very soul, and that of your child."

She sobbed. Her chest felt as though it were aflame.

"Elizabeta de la Cerda, do you want your child to be doomed to Limbo?"

"I am called Leah," she said. "And it will not!"

"Will not?"

"There is no such cruel place."

The bishop slapped her with the flat of his hand. She almost welcomed the pain, which distracted her for a moment from the throbbing of her chest.

"What year do you say it is?"

"Five thousand three hundred and twenty-eight."

The bishop slapped her again. "Do you believe that Christ was born of a Virgin?"

"No," she moaned.

The hot oil fell again. Her screams resounded through the mazelike passageways of the prison, and several of the guards shifted uneasily.

"Haul her up," said the bishop.

They sat Leah up on the table, then tied her arms with ropes that were hooked through rings in the wall. With a crank the men raised her halfway to the ceiling.

"How can you," said Bishop Quiroga, "a woman who bears within herself a child who is yet no heretic, deny the sanctity of Christ in the womb?"

"I—got—my—child—from a—man!" Leah gasped.

The bishop reached to slap her again, but he could not reach her; she was too high on the wall. He bade one of his servants turn the crank. As the machine raised her it tightened the ropes around her arms and she yelled again.

"You have joined yourself to a black flock that spreads plague, that poisons wells, that kills Christian children, that castrates men!" the bishop cried. "Will you repent?"

"It is not true," Leah sobbed. "Do not ask me to lie. None of it is true! Have pity on me!"

"You have joined yourself to an evil tribe that killed the Christ, that crucifies boys, that kills children and eats their flesh!"

Leah felt her child kick hard within her, and shouted, "*You* kill children!"

The bishop, aiming for her face, struck her hard in her upper stomach.

"Ah, Father, Father!" Leah wept.

"Bitch, do you call on your father? Sebastian de la Cerda has rejected you."

"My Father in Heaven will never reject me!"

"Then you believe in Him?" asked the bishop, holding a finger up to the priest and the Holy Brother who manned the crank.

Leah panted. Her eyes began to lose focus, and she saw the bishop doubled, tripled, and quadrupled before her, like a flock of crows. She heard the other priest's urgent whisper, "Only the civil arm can order death, divine señor!"

"Death?" the bishop said angrily. "I am trying to save her *soul!* She is in grievous error. Only discipline can return her to her right path!"

Leah fought to keep her eyelids from closing.

Bishop Quiroga came closer to her and looked in her pain-stretched face. "Do you want water?" he asked.

"Yes," she whispered.

He took a glass from the table and dashed it in her face. "Do you believe," he said, "in the God who is three in one and who reigns in Heaven? Do you believe in Christ, the bridegroom of His Church, who died on the Cross and was raised on the third day?"

Her face dripping with sweat and water, Leah let her chin rest on her bare collarbone and sobbed for a minute, while the bishop and his servants stood suspended, awaiting her reply.

Then, slowly, she raised her head. Taking careful aim, she spat in the bishop's face. Then she yelled every curse she had ever heard spill from the lips of men tumbling from taverns in the twisted streets of Toledo, from beggar boys in the dusty lanes who vied with dogs for crusts of bread. She yelled that she shat on the bishop's gold cross and on his gold and silver monstrance and on his hell-bound Church.

Trembling with fury, the bishop raised his finger. As the crank turned again, Leah felt a huge tearing in her womb and then blood flowing in a sea down her legs, soaking her skirt, pooling on the floor. Before she fainted she saw the bishop's face turn white, not with rage, but with fear of the red tide that issued from her. She heard a whirling rush in her ears, and only dimly did she hear him say, "Bring her down. Bring her *down!*"

NINE

Shiloh stood hidden in the shadows by the building, facing the wall, whispering and swaying softly. He heard a tumult of voices at the back of the place, and he jumped and ran toward the sound. By the light of the torches affixed to the wall he saw Leah, drenched in blood, being carried out by two guards.

"Leah!" he cried, forgetting to hide her secret name. The guards looked at the wild-haired madman, but kept walking. "She is my wife," he sobbed, running to them and clasping her in his arms, knocking one of the guards to the side. Leah's eyes were closed, but she moaned softly.

In pity, the guard said, "We take her to the Sisters of Santa Catalina, close by. In his mercy and consideration of the child, the bishop—"

"Give her to me!" said Shiloh.

The guards looked at each other nervously, but their faces showed their agreement. The situation was dire; the woman yet bled and was sobbing in agony. Dead or alive, the child forced its passage. They were glad to wash their hands of this pregnant Jew.

Shiloh laid her to earth. A nun came running, robes flying, from out of the Church of San Vicente, and knelt by Shiloh's side. "Mother of God," she said, and crossed herself. She raised Leah's skirts and placed her hands on the child's bloody crown. "Push!"

Shiloh pulled off his shirt and handed it to the nun, that she might stanch the blood. He cradled Leah's head in his arms, pinching and slapping her whitening cheek with his fingers, saying her name. But her eyes remained closed and her breaths came sparser and sparser. He put both his hands to Leah's face and kissed her brow. A cry came forth on the air.

Shiloh was kneeling in the starlight, his face against Leah's hair, when the nun pulled him away from her. In his hands she placed the baby, hale and hollering, wrapped in his shirt. "A daughter," she said. Shiloh's fingers were slippery with Leah's blood, and so he found it easy, holding the baby against his chest, to slip off his ring and wipe it on the stained shirt. He held it out to the nun. "Take it," he said.

She gazed at him with pity. Then, pushing the turquoise back at him, she reached for the squalling bundle. "A young woman serves in our priory," she said. "A new mother. I will take the child to her. Seek her later. Now, stay with your dead."

THEY BURIED LEAH and Gozán in the ground behind the old Sinagoga del Tránsito, once a place for Toledan Jews, built in Moorish design and carved with Hebrew and Arabic runes that hardly anyone could now read, but that the Christians had not yet scraped from the walls. Afterward Shiloh stood with Daniel the elder and the priests Hiyam and Bartolomeo and Astruga and Reuben and young Yehuda and Aaron in the front rooms of the family Selomó, by the hearth, and said Kaddish.

Don Sebastian de la Cerda sat stupid with wine in the upper room of his great house and bellowed with rage at a servant who tried to draw a window curtain. He did not appear at Astruga's dwelling, but others did, bringing the mourners food, roast chicken and fish from the Tagus, and Manchegan wine. Among the neighbors who left their offerings were some Old Christians, not only Father Bartolomeo, but shoemakers of the Calle de la Chapinería and their wives, who knew of Leah and pitied her wifeless husband and motherless child. They hated the Inquisition, and they feared it, and they trembled at the risk they ran in giving even such small succor to Jews. These men and women looked kindly at Shiloh in the weeks that followed as he passed them in the winding streets, bearing his hanks of wool, but he looked down at the dust or ahead at nothing, and did not see them.

THE SUN WARMED the city and the sky turned as blue as the stone of the ring he now kept in the genizah, in a box beneath the floorboards of his room. The lemon tree in Astruga's courtyard flowered and bore fruit. Like a candelabrum its branches reached out and up toward a flawless turquoise heaven. Astruga sat beneath the tree with her housemaid, tickling Leah's child.

Shiloh carried bales of merino wool to his shop and worked the loom and made his trades. At dusk he walked the twisted streets of Toledo, his shoulder bent under his merchandise. Remembering

Leah, he passed by the churches and under the cobertizos, and he hated all places because she was not in them.

In early September, just before Yom Kippur, he sold his shop to Daniel, the elder who had blocked the door to Leah at her first Shabbat. He told Astruga and Reuben he was leaving Toledo; he would no longer live in the shadow of the cathedral.

"*Zakhor*," said Astruga, kissing him and the child. "Do not forget to remember."

"Farewell," said Daniel the elder. "To each his road."

With his babbling child peeping from a pack on his back, Shiloh crossed the old Roman bridge that stretched over the Tagus. He bore a sack of remnants and oddments and bread and cheese, and a purse of silver. A skin of goat's milk for the child and another of water hung by straps from his shoulder.

Rain had come that August, and the green hills surrounding the city were only starting to brown on their heights. Today a storm was coming; the clouds were a blue-black mass crowding a white sky that peeped through in patches. Toledo looked gray underneath, its bulky Alcázar brooding on its highest hill. Below and north of the Alcázar, the cathedral's Gothic spire pointed upward, like a dead man's finger. On three sides, the silver-gray Tagus hugged the town like a ring. The broken maze of the holy city lay spread on its dark green hills like a painting in oils by a great master. But Shiloh walked with his eyes turned away, and did not look back.

He traveled east, across the dry, rocky plains of La Mancha, sleeping in fields with his child, waking and saying, by rote, his morning prayers, keeping clear of the main roads, which he knew were traveled by the Holy Brotherhood. For weeks he walked, coming out of the mountains and into the thickening air. At length he reached the low wooded hills above Barcelona. A day later he stood on the shores of the Mediterranean.

In Barcelona he found a sea captain he'd heard would bring Jews to Turkey in exchange for their jewels, and they set sail by a long sea path, first docking at Marseilles, then winging southeast. The captain's route lay past Sardinia and Sicily and Greece, but Shiloh did not go so far. With his daughter he disembarked at Genoa. At the wharf, which was loud with the cries of sailors and the creaking ropes and flapping sheets of docked vessels, he followed a line of other travelers toward an agent of the port who sat at a high desk. That man glanced briefly and curiously at the child strapped to Shiloh's back, and then, in Italian, asked him his name.

"Shiloh ben Gozán," he said, as his daughter woke and began to cry.

"Shilocci?" said the man, cupping his ear.

"Shiloh."

"Shiloch." The man wrote the name on a list. "From whence come you? Marseilles?"

"From Spain." Shiloh's tongue struggled with the unfamiliar language. He added, "I am a Jew."

"You'll not get special treatment for that," said the man.

"Good," Shiloh said.

"Do you plan to stay in Genoa, Shyloch ben Gozán?"

"I am bound for Venice."

"What will you do there?"

"Live." Shiloh shifted the crying infant to his other shoulder. In a low voice, as if to himself, he said, "Learn to be a Jew."

The man stamped a piece of paper and handed it to him. "For the port of Venice," he said. "The way is by river. *Buen camino,* Spaniard." He turned to the woman behind Shiloh, who herself bore a baby, as well as three full baskets of clothes and oddments. "From Marseilles?"

Shiloh moved down the docks. Behind him his daughter whimpered, but he had no food for her now. He walked slowly, smelling salt, hearing the gabble of tongues and the cry of seabirds. He listened for Spanish, as he passed women selling mussels and a sailor with a parrot and a lost-looking pilgrim with a shell-shaped brooch on his hat, who sought passage to Galicia and the shrine of Santiago Matamoros, patron of Spain, killer of Moors.

JESSICA

Venice, 1590

"Who chooseth me shall get as much
as he deserves."

TEN

Jᴇssɪᴄᴀ ᴘᴇᴇʀᴇᴅ ᴏᴜᴛ the window, holding fast to the casement shutter, balancing herself on the sill. Her room stood on the fourth floor of their tall, narrow house, but the tenement next door reached to six stories, and she had to crane her neck and hold her head in a painful position to see around its corner and catch a glimpse of the street beyond. Like her the sun was up, peeking around the dark angles of the crazy ghetto buildings. Its rays shone on a bobbing mass of red disks in the street. These were the tops of hats. Massed together, the scarlet circles were a red sea that widened as more men locked their doors and descended their stairs to join the throng flowing toward the gates to Venice proper.

Jessica shaded her eyes. A few yellow turbans, worn by the more distinguished of the Sephardim, the Spanish and Portuguese exiles, stood out among the red hats. She leaned farther to the left, squinting, then cried *"Maria!"* and grabbed the shutter to steady herself. She had almost fallen into the hard cobbled street. *Sixty-three feet straight down!* Her father's angry rebuke of the week before hung in her mind, and her heart pumped quickly. *Sixty-three feet straight down!* She might have died. It happened twice a year or so, folk falling to their deaths or grave injury from the high floors of the tall, thin ghetto buildings. Her father had barred most of their upper casements to prevent such accidents in his house, but when he'd brought the bars and the carpenter to her room she had resisted, complaining that she lived in a birdcage already, begging to be vouchsafed a clear space of sky. For a rarity, Shiloh ben Gozán had granted her wish.

She stared not, however, at the sky, but down toward the street.

"He left before dawn."

She looked behind her as she hauled herself back into her chamber and dropped heavily onto the Turkish rug. Launcelot Giobbo, her father's servant, was standing in her doorway, smiling mockingly.

"How do you know what I was looking for, sirrah?" she said crossly, dusting her hands on her skirt.

"For a kiss I won't tell him your hair was hanging down the wall like the German Rapunzel, beckoning a man to climb up it and fetch you away."

"For a kiss? For a *kick* you will learn to keep your fool mouth shut, or I'll tell him the meat you brought home yesterday was not pure."

"He knew it already. One sniff and he had thrown it to the dogs, and cuffed me himself." The man affected a Spanish accent and shrugged. "Such a nose!"

Really angry, Jessica balled her fists threateningly, and Giobbo held up his hands in mock terror. At that she smiled in spite of herself, but said sternly, "Do not mock my father, sirrah! He is your master. He pays *you* well enough, though you do half the work our last servant did. Honor him!"

"*You* do not." Giobbo disappeared from the doorway.

Fuming, she bound up her hair with a lace veil, and covered that with the hated yellow headdress bordered with red. She would go out today, if only to the Jewish market. Perhaps, though her father forbade it, she might slip out the gate to visit the Piazza San Marco. . . .

Grimacing, she wrapped herself in her olive green cloak and thrust her arms through its slits. On the cloak's left sleeve above the arm slit was stitched a red badge. It was the size of a ducat and the shape of a heart, and the council of Venice had decreed it must be worn by all Jews.

As she closed the front door of her father's house she heard from afar the bell of San Marco's, the signal that prompted the city guards to open the locked gate between the Jewish quarter and the Fondamenta della Pescaria. The Jews paid them to do it. She wondered what her father had hoped to gain by leaving so early for the Rialto Bridge, where he conducted his business. Rich though he was, he would still have been penned in with the rest of them until the ghetto was unlocked. Perhaps he had gone to the synagogue to make one of a minyan, and say his early prayers with his mystical friend Rabbi Amos Madena. Or perhaps he had met a Jewish associate in the heart of the ghetto itself, to strike some secret deal concerning silk or cloves or silver. Many were the rituals that busied her father, and most were murky to her. The fact was, she did not care where he was as long as she was elsewhere, her free flight unmarked by his stern hawk's gaze.

To the devil with the Jewish market! she decided. Today, no detestable testing of vegetables and fish for freshness, no eyeing the shohet to see that he cut the beef correctly, according to the rule of kashrut. Eyes cast down to her shoes to evade the looks of her father's friends, she merged determinedly with the mass of red-hatted and yellow-turbaned walkers who moved toward the gate at the rim of the ghetto.

With the throng, she passed over the wooden drawbridge that spanned the thin, green-gray canal dividing the Jews' island from the city. In Venice proper, she stood in the shadow of three lopsided buildings all in various states of slow collapse. She pulled off her green cloak and yellow headdress, rolled them into a tight bundle, and tucked that under her arm. Then, like an unhooded falcon, she flew straight toward the heart of the city, braving the cold, wrinkling her nose at the smell of the offal that floated in the water of the canals.

It was a long way to the Piazza San Marco, and despite the December chill she was sweating when she stopped just short of the huge square, in the shade of the tall tower of the Campanile. She smoothed her hair, then walked more slowly into the open piazza. The sun was still low, and no silk-clad gallants were yet strolling. Not slackening her pace, she ascended the steps of the great Church of San Marco. She passed through the narthex into the deep, shadowy womb of the basilica, to the chapel of the Madonna dei Mascoli. There she gazed rapturously at a high spot on the wall, where hung a huge framed canvas in whose center Mary sat between two apostles, holding the Christ child. Over Mary's shoulder hovered a small, fat, smiling angel.

"An angel were you, that did preserve me," her father had told her again and again, when as a child she had begged to hear the story of how they had come from Toledo to Barcelona, then set sail in a rot-planked ship for Italy. "I carried you in a pack on my back, and you bounced. You guzzled goat's milk, and you laughed at the cows and their bells and the fish jumping out of the sea south of France. And when we came on the boat into Venice you pointed up at the towers and turrets and the giant gold lions and said, *Sì! Sì!*"

She curled her lip at the memory of his storytelling. How had that laughing child and kindly father become the pair they were now? Once she had spent hours at her father's knee, joying in the old parchments and the crooked Hebrew letters he had taught her, laughing at how the lines ran from right to left in no Christian fashion, memorizing laws and tales of the old Israelites. Of their journey from slavery in Egypt across desert sands into Canaan! Of bold Deborah and Queen Esther, who succored their people! But as Jessica had grown tall, hemmed in by the tenements, built higher each year, she had seen no place in the ghetto where she might play a part in such colorful stories as were found in the Torah or Prophets. Her colors were the yellow turban and red badge that marked her narrow place in the city. Real life lay outside the Jews' gate, where the ladies of Venice strolled wearing heavy jewelry and splendid ruffs, the godruns made by the fine clothiers of the town. Jewish maidens were denied the godruns, and when she complained for one her mood was not lightened by her father's dry voice saying only, "I have heard that they scratch."

One day when she was fifteen, after the hundredth instance of her begging, her father had taken her with him outside the Jews' gate, to the Fondaco dei Tedeschi, the street where Jews and Gentiles did business before the building of the Rialto. She had meant to sit quietly, to watch and listen as he worked, to calculate interest on loans and check her figures against his. But her eyes had gone wide with distraction at the shapely legs and trimmed beards of the merchants who strolled and laughed and talked. He had seen the track her eyes took, and for a rarity had cut business short and pulled her home by her arm as she cried with rage.

In their house he had forced her up the stairs, saying, "What an unholy spectacle you make!" He had thrown her into her chamber and, his eyes raking her face and body as she lay sobbing on the rug, said to her cuttingly, "You are your mother's image. But you lack her heart. You are like *her* mother, who wasted herself on a silk-clad baboon." Then he closed the door, locking it from the outside. Late at night, not speaking, he opened it, so she might come down the stairs for her supper. But such was her rage that she would not come out until he had left the next morning for the Fondaco dei Tedeschi.

Then she sat in the kitchen at the cutting block, plotting slow revenge.

In the years since, the rift between her and her father had grown. Rarely did he take her now to help with his daily business, and when he did, she hated it. She loathed sitting among the free, fine people, marked by her red heart, her badge of shame, and the yellow turban that hid her rich, long hair. When he was absent from home she stole out when she could, illegally doffing her Jewish garb, haunting the Merceria where the Christians bought goods, gazing at the shopkeepers' jewelry and fine cloth. Often she went accompanied by a Christian guide. For she had found solace in befriending the Gentile maidservants and manservants of her house. Much wealth could be found in the ghetto, and many Christians sought work there. Her father hired them because they could do work on the Sabbath and holidays, could perform labors forbidden to Jews by holy law. But his daughter's easy friendships with the hirelings angered him. She would not consort with young women of her kind, but more than once his associates on the Rialto had seen his daughter in his Gentile servants' company, laughing, browsing among the forbidden wares of the Merceria. He was always dismissing the men and women he'd hired, only to have her befriend the new ones.

Six months past, he had pushed out the door a young woman to whom Jessica had become close. Jessica had stood by impotently in the upper hall as he had cursed the maid in Ladino, calling her a zoná, accusing her of lying with a Christian man in her chamber near the kitchen. A Christian pig, a rich fool who gave her gifts of sheer scarves and bracelets for her body, gifts she then shared with Jessica, though he had forbidden his daughter to wear such things! And what other things had she shared with his daughter? What whores' wisdom, unfit for righteous ears?

Jessica had known nothing of these charges of whoredom until she'd heard them hurled behind the serving girl as she tumbled down the stairs to the street, then jumped to her feet before gawking neighbors and shook her hand at Jessica's father, giving him the figo, the fig of Spain. Her father had slammed the door and, when he'd seen Jessica in the hallway, her eyes a brown and white blaze of hatred, he'd only raised his hand as though to slap her, then dropped it to his side and said quietly, "Sit in your room."

Few were his stories of Toledo now, and of their long journey eastward during her infancy. His remarks about his Spanish past were vague, barbed comments about the shame she would be to her mother if she were alive, and how like Jessica was to her grandmother, who had changed her name from Sarah to Serafina and married a worthless drunken son-of-something. In her room Jessica would cry with frustration, wishing she could talk to either lost woman, and wondering how she could so desperately miss a mother and a grandmother she had never seen.

She knew her mother had been baptized a Christian but had married a Jew. Yet whatever her mother had sought, it could not have been this forced imprisonment in the ghetto, this jail of dietary laws and womanly duties and dress restrictions. And whatever her grandmother Sarah—no, *Serafina*—had wanted in the house of her rich hidalgo, it must have been more than frivolity. Might she not have wanted true kinship with the people, her countrymen, among whom she lived? Might she not have wished for the folk of her city not to eye her askance and mutter *Jewess* as she passed?

Or that a finely dressed fellow, of a family much esteemed in the high circles of her society, be not forbidden her for the mere shape of his manhood? Although perhaps in Spain, she reflected, Christian and Jewish manhoods had the same shape. Jews would not dare to circumcise there; there *all* the men quite likely were as Lorenzo must be. . . .

In the dark of the church Jessica blushed and crossed herself. *Think not of Lorenzo's manhood before the image of the blessed Virgin,* she thought, then put her hand to her mouth to cover her smile.

There were many in the church, kneeling before saints' images, murmuring prayers in hushed voices. Turning from the painting, Jessica walked past workers repairing columns and a priest lighting candles by the altar. She stopped at another chapel at the far end of the left arm of the transept. There in an alcove stood a statue of Mary, her palms joined before her breast and pointing heavenward in prayer. She was clad in a blue cloak sewn with cloth-of-gold stars. Her face was gentle and loving beyond thought.

Jessica knelt before her, placing her bundled cloak and Jewish headdress below her knees to cushion her bones against the hard stone floor. "Holy Mother," she prayed softly. "Heal me! Teach me freedom."

She stayed kneeling for a time, hands clasped but head unbowed, gazing upward at the Madonna. After a time she rose, feeling calmer. She retraced her steps past the row of saints' effigies that lined the transept and led back to the center of the church.

Once she paused before the painted Magdalen, to whose carven hair some supplicant had affixed a real silver comb. She smiled at the statue, which smiled back at her in a fixed wooden way.

"Sister!" Jessica whispered. "Friend."

Behind her a candle flickered. The Magdalen's painted blue eye seemed to wink.

ELEVEN

OUTSIDE THE CHURCH Jessica bunched her folded cloak and headdress tighter and again tucked them under her arm. She straightened the lace veil she had loosely pinned to the back of her hair, and emerged from the shadow at the corner of the church stairs.

She strolled the streets near the plaza, moving toward the Canale Grande, gazing covertly at the well-dressed young Christian men and women, most of whom strolled in pairs or groups of three or more, engaged in ringing, bell-like chatter. Both sexes wore sparkling jewels on their fingers and dangling from their ear-lobes, and fox skins over their silk robes, and lovely wide ruffs above. She avoided the eyes of the red-hatted Jews, averting her face from a few of them. She felt her loneliness, and was briefly sorry not to have asked the servant Launcelot to come with her. But she did not fully trust him as she'd trusted the maid who'd been his predecessor. And she hated being in his constant debt, owing him ducats to seal his mouth, enduring his teasing requests for more than coins, for a caress or a kiss. She feared that, given enough license, those requests might become demands, and he might try to press them home.

Besides, in the church, as she'd gazed at the Magdalen, it had occurred to her that if she stood at the juncture of the Canale Grande and the Canale di Cannaregio at just the right hour she might find her friend today, might hear what news she had of Lorenzo. And Jessica wanted no witnesses to *that* colloquy.

The air trembled with the blows and rasps of hammer, saw, and chisel. It seemed on every corner buildings of marble and granite were being raised, as fast as, on other corners, they were sinking. Two workers passed her, pulling blocks of stone and wooden beams on carts. She heard them chattering about the Rialto, their destination, still under its final construction, though crowded daily with investors, merchants, and moneylenders. She walked quickly in the opposite direction.

When the bell of the Campanile tolled eleven she was standing nervously at the opening to the Canale Grande, scanning the flat-bottomed boats that came and went bearing passengers or merchandise. At length the great, carved prow of a very fine gondola came into view, and she gave a birdlike hop of excitement. This boat had two oarsmen, both dressed in red and green livery, who skillfully guided their slim craft among the crowd of lesser vessels, bringing it to rest at the quay. One of the men reached out and grasped a ring that jutted from the canal wall, while the other put his hand back to raise the beautiful woman who had half-lain, recumbent under a cloth-of-gold canopy, fanning her powdered nose against the stink of the water.

"I thank you," the woman said warmly, offering each boatman a gold cruzado. Jessica stood by a pillar, admiring the towering headgear of silver and silk the woman wore above her loose, red-dish brown tresses, and the low cut of her bodice. Thinking envi-ously, *She evades no eyes,* Jessica stepped from the pillar's shadow and said, "Nerissa!"

The woman turned with delight and hugged her. "Ah, Jessica! You are most clever at slipping out, dearest! Not like me, who prefers to be cursed at and thrown down a hard flight of stairs."

"Both methods serve the purpose," Jessica laughed, returning her friend's tight embrace. "Now, tell me at last who fits you with this boat and this fine wear. From whence do you come, wicked Jezebel?"

"From the palace of Cardinal Grimani!" Jessica looked shocked, and Nerissa laughed. "A man is a man, little Jessie. I can tell you that under his red robes is a thing that—"

"*Stop,*" Jessica said, though she laughed. "This only makes good what my father thinks of all Christians. *And* of you."

"Oh, not all Christians are bad," Nerissa said, suddenly serious. "Your father thinks things are all one way, always. As for what he thinks of *me*—"

"I do not think what *he* thinks," Jessica said, squeezing Nerissa's gloved hand and pulling her along the canal. The greenish water was high, and it licked at their slippers. "Let us come out of the wet. Let us walk in the Merceria. You must tell me whether you gave my message to Lorenzo di Scimmia."

"Are you sure you want *that* one?" Nerissa said. "I will tell you frankly, I have seen him with other women, and not only in the houses of Malipiero, among the courtesans. All the gallants go there. But I saw him in the Piazza, with the daughter of a noble-man. One of the Ten, from the signiory."

Jessica was silent for a moment. Then she said, low and angrily, "He wants her wealth."

"No doubt of it. But you think he wants something else from you."

"Yes," Jessica said fiercely. "I have seen his eyes on my—"

"Body," Nerissa said boredly. "Well, perhaps you know what you are about. I will say, the maid's father walked with the two, down the steps of San Marco's, and your Lorenzo seemed more entranced with the signior's jeweled chain than with his darling daughter."

"And she?" Jessica asked nervously.

"She seemed to care nothing for Lorenzo's chatter, though her father had her so swathed in veils that it was hard to know the direction of her ears and eyes. But even did she desire your chosen fellow, still, Lord Brabantio di Paolo of the Signioria is not like to grant his daughter to the youngest son of a man who has lost his fortunes. I think you are safe there." She smiled. "But come, Jessica. You cannot be seen with me in the street. I have new apartments by the Canale Grande—no, fear not, not near the Rialto! And not in the plain brothel where I started, where we were forbidden to wear jewels and rings." She flourished a diamond on her hand. "What think you of this?"

"The cardinal?" said Jessica, at once admiring and disapproving.

"And this?" Nerissa cocked her head so Jessica could see the silver comb affixed to her headdress. "Yes, yes, the cardinal! Come, walk!"

JESSICA LAUGHED OUT loud at Nerissa's new fortune when she came into the house near the Ca'd'Oro and saw the black and white marble floor of the entryway, and the oil painting by Titian that hung on the wall.

"A portrait of the cardinal himself!" Nerissa said proudly, gesturing toward it.

In a room hung with velvet drapes, she called for refreshment and bade Jessica put her feet on the settle. Jessica did, and tried to relax, though she worried that her father would somehow learn of her escapade today, and though her blood boiled as she imagined Lorenzo di Scimmia strolling and laughing by the side of a noble-woman. That Christian maiden, though veiled, no doubt wore a gorgeous godrun on her neck.

"I gave Lorenzo your message when he came here with his nitwit friends," Nerissa said.

"And?" Jessica leaned forward.

"He kissed the paper."

"Ah!"

"And said he would steal a red cap and slip past the ghetto guards on Thursday next."

Jessica clapped her hands.

Nerissa stared at her pityingly. "You believe this?"

"Not altogether, but it could come to pass." Jessica joined her hands prayerfully like the statued Virgin in the cathedral. "He is something of a liar, but he did come once before, and climbed halfway up the wall, two stories, before my father threw open the shutters and poured—"

"Shit on him." Nerissa laughed. "There is something about your father that I like, for all that he threw me downstairs. With him, you know where you are."

"Well, I hate him," said Jessica, pouting. "And I do not like where I am with him, and I will not stay, I will fly and never come back, I will—"

"Live in paradise with golden Lorenzo," Nerissa said, yawning.

"*Freckled* Lorenzo," said Jessica. "I tried angling for one or two golden ones, but even my father's money was paltry bait for the nobles who have enough money already." Her voice was grim and resigned. "Not sufficient for them to risk sullying their fine lineage with the blood of a Jewish wife. Though they do look!"

Nerissa gazed at her with sympathy and understanding. "They do, do they not? Well, play this game for yourself. Perhaps you have chosen the best one, after all, if you would enter their silver society. It's best not to be in love with the man who marries you for your money."

"So I think."

"Mmm," Nerissa said, swallowing some wine. "For all his family's ill luck, he has wealthy friends and a name that will open doors to you. If you can get enough from your father, some nobleman may give him a post or a title. As long as he can drink every night and is not asked to dirty his fingers, he'll do well enough, and then you and I"—Nerissa grasped her friend's hands—"can cavort the day long, in the Merceria, or frolic among the grand estates of the provinces, the Terra Firma—"

"But what are you saying?" Jessica asked, glancing at the glass of wine a servant had brought her. The wine was not kosher, and she silenced the voice inside her that told her so. Defiantly, she picked up the glass and took a swallow. The liquid was fine and sweet. She smiled at Nerissa's notions. "You are mad, girl," she said. "We may walk the Merceria, but you will never be a country lady in the Terra Firma."

"Ah, will I not?" said Nerissa. "Little bird, you do not know everything." She had taken off her heavy jeweled headgear, and her red-gold mane lay in loose curls over her shoulders. She sipped her wine, then raised her hands and tousled her hair. "That thing scratches me! Well, Jessica, I will do my best with Lorenzo. He may swear to an assignation, but that will mean nothing unless he knows he will get something from it, and so I will promise he shall."

"Shall what?" said Jessica nervously.

"Get a first payment on what he will one day receive in full, but only if he marries you. You may have to give him a little more than a kiss."

"Not much more," said Jessica cautiously. "That might ruin the gambit. And I am not a whore."

"Oh," said Nerissa. Her voice was faintly chilly.

"Pardon me," said Jessica quickly, touching her hand.

Nerissa smiled with her usual warmth. "No matter. Anyway, you are right. Only a taste of bait. Your trout's on the hook. Play him." Nerissa sat quietly for a moment, rolling the stem of her glass between her palms. "*His lovely infidel,* he calls you. Do you like that?"

"He will call me something else when I am Christian."

Nerissa put down her glass abruptly. "Well, God bring him wisdom and charity. Right now he's a fool, like the rest of them."

"Of whom?"

"The men of this city."

Something made Jessica say defensively, "My father's not a fool."

Nerissa looked at her shrewdly and nodded. "No," she said. "He is not. So have a care."

WHEN THE KEY turned in the lock of the door to their upstairs rooms, she was seated placidly on the settle, reading a verse of the Torah, which promised that the Lord would refine the children of Levi like gold and silver. She rose and gave grudging greeting to her father, suppressing a grimace at his long beard.

Unwinding his turban to free his thick brown hair, he doffed his black gabardine, and laid on a table the prayer book he habitually carried. Even stripped of the marks Venice made him show, he looked different from the other citizens with whom he did business. He looked, indeed, different from many of the Jews, most of whom, apart from their legislated dress, strove to resemble their Christian townsmen as much as they could.

But apart from his business, her father shunned the company of Gentiles, and welcomed his difference.

The table was set. Arriving at home past two, Jessica had busied herself to do chores she'd neglected that morning, laying the table for supper, a meal of meat untainted by cheese, livened with a bowl of onions and asparagus. Launcelot Giobbo had done his work middling well that morning, and she was glad she had not sought his guardianship outside the ghetto. There would only be more late afternoon scurrying for them both if she had.

Her father nodded at her, washing his hands in a bowl. There were voices behind him on the stair, and she sighed, recognizing that of Rabbi Amos Madena, who would go on at length about the Torah. The other voice was not familiar. "Three of us," her father said, cracking his dark-bearded face in a smile. "A trinity."

DESPITE HERSELF JESSICA was drawn to the speech of her father's guest, a man named Benjamin Ha-Levi from Amsterdam. He was a seller of silks, come to Venice to see to a trade. As tall as Shiloh, he was a great deal fairer, and, for a novelty, blue-eyed. He was a Tudesco, a Jew of Polish ancestry, larger and fairer than any of the other northern Jews who dwelled in the ghetto. Speaking good Italian, the man spun prices and numbers with her father, while the rabbi, listening, laughed and said that Shiloh ben Gozán should have studied kabbalah with him, because all their dizzying figures sounded more mystical than his own numerology.

"Not a kabbalist," said Ha-Levi, pointing at Shiloh. "This one should have been a tradesman. A seller of goods."

"I was one," said Shiloh dryly, tasting the soup Jessica had placed on the table. "I wove wool and sold it in Toledo. I was good at it."

"Ah, there is naught here for Jews but trading in nothing. Used, threadbare clothing or money to lend at interest."

"I'm good at that too."

"Citizenship denied you even though you were born here, and no honest work allowed," the man teased.

"I was not born here, and my work is honest," Shiloh said briefly.

"But do you not tire of these ghetto walls?"

"*I* do not," said Rabbi Madena. "The wall is like the fence we put around the Torah in our lives. It is easier not to transgress the Law when we do not mix with the others"—he smiled at Shiloh—"too much."

"I tire of the walls," Shiloh said.

The rabbi frowned slightly. "I fear Shiloh may someday move eastward, to Turkey or Constantinople or even Jerusalem. Our people would suffer to lose him. He has been a pillar of the Temple of Scuola Levantina, and a help to the fatherless."

"Children need fathers," said Shiloh, flashing a stern look at Jessica.

I am no longer a child, Jessica thought. She looked at her plate and said nothing.

"Signior Shylock should go north and west," said Ha-Levi. "Come to Amsterdam. There the religion is money, and the only heresy is bankruptcy."

Shiloh laughed at that, as did Jessica. Resentment faded for a moment, and the eyes of father and daughter met in a camaraderie as brief as it was rare. Shiloh looked back at his foreign guest. "I came to Venice to learn to be a Jew," he said, smiling wryly. "Would you have me convert to a new faith?"

"I tell you this, Signior Shylock—is that not your name?"

"No." Shiloh shrugged. "It is what the apes of the Serene Republic of Venice call me. I am Shiloh."

"I will call you what you call yourself, Shiloh ben Gozán. Now, let me say this. In this year of Our Lord fifteen hundred and ninety—pardon," he said, noting his host stiffen, "year of *their* Lord—in this time of schisms, I say, there are different ways of being a Christian. Why not different ways of being a Jew?"

Jessica looked at the man with new interest. But her father's eyes were hard and skeptical. *"Por su camino,"* he said. "To each his road. I say there is one way to be a Jew. I have spent twenty-two years learning it."

"Well, you may at least allow that there are different places to be one!"

"That, we allow," said Rabbi Madena.

"But not Amsterdam," Shiloh said. "Spain still has its finger on Holland's pulse. I'll not live again under a Spanish flag. I'd sooner pay taxes to the Ottomites."

"It won't come to that, after Lepanto," Ha-Levi said. "And the Spanish won't last in the north after the sea drubbing the English gave them two years ago."

Jessica heard herself saying, "Here, it has been said that a storm gave Spain that drubbing, and that the English were just lucky in the chance." As she'd expected, her father frowned at this slight to his precious English. But Ha-Levi gave her a broad smile. He seemed both pleased and surprised that this ghetto-sheltered girl should know something of world events. Yet why should she not? She had ears. She heard things on the streets of Venice.

Ha-Levi shook his spoon. "Young mistress, you may be right about that, but be assured, on land the Protestant armies also triumph. England will drive Spain from the Lowlands before another year is out."

"They may," said Shiloh thoughtfully. "They may."

"And meanwhile, the Dutch are nothing like the Spanish. Jews practice openly there. They live side by side with Moors and Catholics and Calvinists."

"Calvinistas!" Shiloh said, smiling at an old memory. "Like the Luteranos, but to the pope, even worse!"

"What do you know of Luteranos?" Ha-Levi asked in surprise, as he wiped a spot of flan from his beard. Jessica found herself staring at his northern habit—dark clothes, but exceptionally well made ones. She recalled the fine leather hat with the white feather that she'd hung for him on a wall. The man's collar was lace, and his thick woolen cloak, which she'd put below his hat, was unmarked with the red badge. An alien in Venice, he was allowed to dress like the Gentiles for the time of his visit. The city relaxed its laws for him, for both the Lowlands and Venice profited thereby. On any street, she would never have known this man for a Jew.

The man wore a wedding band. She closed her eyes in envy, imagining his wife at home, clad in Dresden lace and a pretty Holland cap.

"I know little of Luteranos," Shiloh said. "I met some once in Spain, in Valladolid. I sold them wool, and they trusted me for a partner in secrecy. I attended their meeting for my curiosity. An odd thing! A bare upper room without a crucifix or a chalice. They prayed and sang and recited the sayings of the Nazarene. Then they spit on Rome." He laughed. "I did that part with them. It was they who taught me of our Maccabee, who purified the Temple in the year three thousand five hundred and ninety-five, when the Greeks put their statue of Zeus inside it. They loved Judas Maccabee. Tossed Zeus out, and the Greeks after!"

"*They* taught you?" said the rabbi, tugging his unruly hair.

Shiloh clapped him on the shoulder. "My knowledge was partial back then, you see, my wild-eyed Amos Madena."

"Man's knowledge is always partial," said the rabbi.

Shiloh nodded. "Still, in Spain it was especially so. Nothing but fragments. Our 'rabbi' learned *his* Hebrew from an Old Christian priest!" He chuckled. "So I myself learned some things from the Luteranos. Renegade fellows, they were. I liked them that day." He took another bite of lentil soup. "But I never went back to Valladolid."

"Toledo was your place," said Ha-Levi. "A wondrous city, is it not?"

Shiloh spooned his soup and said nothing. The rabbi stopped eating, watching him.

"But you still speak the language of Spain!" the guest persisted, tearing a chunk of bread with his teeth. "Signior Shiloh, do you never cast your mind's eye back on the city of your birth?"

"Do I look like I'm made of salt?" Shiloh said, pushing his bowl from him.

The guest looked perplexed, and the rabbi laughed gently. "Benjamin Ha-Levi, tell us more of *your* city."

"Ah, Amsterdam!" The big man's face lit up. He loved the very name of his town. "We've Protestants in Amsterdam, but very respectable now, not like the rebels you saw. Ours have church buildings of their own and are grown haughty enough. You'd see them, and see the rest of the world, and the rest of the world's silver. *You* have enough of *that* commodity. Why not pour it into our money-sea? You'll get it back a hundredfold." He looked around admiringly at the room's heavy wooden shelves, and the damask curtains that shaded the windows. "I can see you know how to breed your coin."

"Shiloh ben Gozán spent nearly all his money coming from Toledo to Venice, and now he rents this whole house, a place as tall and thin as he is," said Rabbi Madena proudly.

"And with as many hidden compartments," said Shiloh.

The rabbi laughed delightedly. "The first floor is sublet to others. Still, the house is too big for this pair"—he gestured at Shiloh and Jessica—"without a son-in-law and one or two grandchildren." He smiled at Jessica, and she ducked her head, partly to avoid his eerie eyes, one of which was milky and blind, while the other seemed always to harbor a mad glint. But she also ducked so the rabbi could not see her frown. She feared he would now speak of his son, Isaac, a passionate fellow who spent hours reading the Talmud with his father and hers, arguing in Hebrew or a Spanish Jessica could ill understand, speaking of words and dates and arcane points of law in the Mishnah. *If to light a fire on Shabbat saves one the labor of sweeping up shards of the glass one would otherwise drop while stumbling in the darkness, is the lighting of the fire then lawful? Since the Law was given for life and not death, if honoring it brings death, is its violation not lawful? What said Rabbi Akiva?* They found their paradoxes endlessly entertaining. When Jessica had trouble sleeping she would creep down the stair and listen to the three of them, and that would shut her eyes.

Eyes. It was true that those of Isaac, Madena's son, were lovely, long-lashed and green. But they were so like a puppy's when they gazed at her that his ardor only made her want to pat his head and pull his ears, which were large. And besides, those same eyes were weakening from excessive study. He wanted to be a rabbi like his father, but he'd be blind before he was fifty, and then his poor wife would spend all her free hours reading aloud to him. He was a kind youth. He and she had played together as children, and she well knew he was her father's choice for her. But she would never, never, never be that bookworm's wife.

She dreamily prodded the fish bones on her plate with her knife. *Lady Jessica di Scimmia . . . Good morrow, Lady Jessica! Lady Jessica, do you know the doge's son, Lord—*

"Jessica! My son Isaac said yesterday—"

Jessica jumped to her feet, murmuring an excuse, and collected the plates. Her father frowned deeply at her. She could feel the heat of his glare, but she did not look up as she hurried to the kitchen. At her back, her father's dry voice began listing figures. *Eight million pounds of New World silver, coined into cash by Holy Catholic Spain every year! Four hundred thirty-five pounds of raw silk catalogued in the port of Venice!* Jessica rolled her eyes.

Tending the kitchen fire, Launcelot Giobbo winked as she passed. She made a face at him, and went to the side of the kitchen closest to the doorway. As she scraped table scraps into a bucket, she heard Ha-Levi's confident voice. "You can trade in *all* of those goods, just as you like, in Amsterdam."

"I suppose Amsterdam is the new Jerusalem," said her father. "Streets paved with gold? Or silver, I should say."

"Laugh if you wish, Signior Shylock, but I think our love of silver—the love of *all* of us for silver, be we Moors, Jews, Old Christians, or any Eastern infidels—is the only thing that can conquer our hatreds. Why kill each other, when we can profit from trading our skills and our wealth?"

The rabbi laughed softly. "I would hope something more than skills and wealth might bind us in the end."

"Of the peace of God we may dream, Rabbi. But what I speak of now is a thing we may lay present hands on. Money and the skill to make it are respected in my city. Jews can thrive in Amsterdam.

And we don't have to live in a ghetto there. I have two friends who *own* large houses, mansions—"

"And no Christians hate Jews in Amsterdam." Her father's voice was sour.

Jessica suppressed an impatient click of her tongue. Shiloh ben Gozán would not cease ridiculing anyone who tried to loosen his stiff thinking! She scraped the plates faster, hating him.

"Mock on, signior my host," Ha-Levi said. She heard him smack his lips over the flan. "It is better up there than down here."

TWELVE

TWO MORNINGS LATER Launcelot Giobbo, leering, handed Jessica a folded paper. She snatched it from his hand and dismissed him, but he dawdled, making kissing noises with his lips. So high was her mood at seeing Lorenzo's script on the paper that she could only laugh at him.

At the fownten in the Piazza San Marco at three on first Monday Advent, he had written in his childish hand. *Meet me that I may kiss your wrist, my bootiful Jewiss, and speak of days too come.* She folded the letter and tucked it into her sleeve, wondering whether Nerissa was right about the caliber of Lorenzo's intelligence. "But it matters not," she told herself. "What harm if he cannot spell his *name,* as long as that name is di Scimmia?"

When the Campanile struck three on the appointed day, Lorenzo was nowhere in sight. Jessica stood in the piazza, nervous but warm in a fur-lined cloak Nerissa had lent her, and scanned the busy crowd of dark-clad businessmen in furs, and jeweled ladies and laughing gallants in silks of purple and green. She did not see him. She shifted from foot to foot, avoiding the gaze of some lone men, one of whom, she was sure, would have approached her had she not walked quickly to the other side of the fountain just when he began to move in her direction. *Dear God,* she thought, *perhaps he thought me a* bona roba, *a courtesan, like Nerissa!*

It was twelve minutes to four by the tower clock, and she was blinking away tears, when she felt a light tap on her shoulder. She turned and almost threw herself into Lorenzo's long arms, but then, thinking better, deferred their embrace. "What became of you?" she asked. "I have so little time; my father dines abroad, but will be home at eight—"

"Ah, I am sure he will be late. Business was brisk on the Rialto today. I passed by there on my way and saw him twisting his knife in a poor farmer who was late on his debt." Lorenzo gestured with his wrist. "Only he uses his tongue. Sharp talking! That's what they all fear."

"It could not have been a farmer," Jessica said. "He lends only to the richer merchants. The ones he is sure can still pay in a year of bad harvest."

"Come, let's walk. We have hours, I tell you! When the cat's away . . ."

She frowned. "When he says he will come home at eight, he comes home at eight." But she allowed herself to be led across the piazza to the Rio di Palazzo, past a group of worried-looking councilmen examining the water-rotted pilings of a bridge, to the streets behind.

"I heard magnificent music on the way here, dear Jessica!" Lorenzo said. "Spilling from the windows of a house near the Palace of the Doge. Lutes and oboes, like larks and nightingales!

So I stopped to listen." He hummed, plucking an invisible lute with his fingers. "Who knows how long I was there?"

"Me," Jessica grumbled, though she was no longer really angry. He had come. He was on the hook. "It was forty-eight minutes, less the time you spent wandering the Rialto Bridge spying on my father. Shall I buy you a timepiece?"

"A very fine one. Gold, with tiny diamonds about the face. You have ducats enough, or your father does. But do not. I'd only lose it, fair infidel!" They had reached a narrow street, and he pulled her into the shade of a house wall. She returned his kiss, but when his hand began to lift her skirt she stayed it. "Enough, my love!" she whispered.

"*Not* enough," he said, pressing her thigh hard. But he released her. "Enough, then, beauty, just now."

A maidservant came out of the house and scowled at them. They walked toward the Canale Grande. Lorenzo hailed a gondola, and Jessica opened her purse to pay the oarsman.

They lay together in the bottom of the boat, nearly hidden from view, as the gondolier rowed them through a series of widening waterways. They passed petty craft and some fine gondolas, and once a magnificent craft where, through half-drawn curtains, Jessica saw one of the city's Signioria, the Council of Ten, being ferried from some important place to some other. He was frowning in a businesslike way under his red cap, which thrust heavenward from the back of his head as though to increase his height and grandeur. She sighed, imagining that he had several sons, all affianced to Christian maidens.

Their random journey brought them at length to the city's eastern port, from which tall merchant ships sailed into the gulf, then south, and finally east for Turkey or the Indies, or west for Marseilles, Amsterdam, Hamburg, and Antwerp. At the port the oarsman rounded the bay as she and Lorenzo busied their eyes and huddled together against the wind. Jessica watched the horizon, entranced, as the sailborne ships gained speed, flying out to the open sea on woven wings. Then she looked closer at hand, at the sweating black slaves on the docks who loaded bales and boxes into the bellies of the great wooden vessels. She thought of her father's cutting remarks about slave-owning Christians, and frowned, tapping her forehead as though she could shake his voice from her mind.

Lorenzo pointed to a pretty, trim ship that had *Andrew* written on its prow and said, "That belongs to a great friend of mine. A trader in Indian spices. I've not seen him for weeks; I owe him two hundred ducats." He sank slightly lower in the gondola, and peered over the edge.

"I could pay that with ease," Jessica scoffed.

"Good," came Lorenzo's voice from under a blanket. "I believe I saw him on the quay, with his brother." He reached out and tugged at her ankle. "Come down here."

"No. Here, before all the world, you would shame me?"

"I would shame you under a blanket."

She pointed to the sun, though she knew he could not see her finger. "It is past six, Lorenzo! We run hazard." She leaned down, pulled the woolen mantle from his laughing face, and kissed him. "And you know you are not to shame me *at all*."

The oarsman steered them back toward the web of canals. As he rowed he kept his face expressionless, but hummed a song. Lorenzo pulled himself up and began to sing it. He had a fine tenor voice, and she listened with pleasure until he grew too loud, his sound echoing off the close walls of San Giacomo dell'Orio. Then she bade him hush.

"Ah, Jessica," he said sweetly. "Only marry me and my fortunes will improve. I knew it the day I caught your eyes on the Rialto, sitting behind your father, under your yellow cap, counting his coin with your little brows knit together and your lips moving quietly. Lovely lips!" He kissed his fingers to heaven and embraced her.

"It is almost seven by the sun," she said, pulling away from him. "It lacks less than a quarter of an hour til the Campanile's bell."

"I know, fair pagan, I know!"

"*Fair pagan.* I will be one of the two."

Lorenzo poured wine from a skin into his mouth, then offered it to her. "What two?"

"It says in the Talmud that two out of six hundred thousand Jews will cease being Jews."

"Such a scholar!" Lorenzo said, in a mock Spanish accent that reminded her briefly of the servant Launcelot's raillery. "And *such* a teller! With your counting skills, why do you not help your father now, on the Rialto?"

"You know why! He does not want men like you looking at my lips."

"Then he hoards you. But I will marry you and make you yield interest."

She was tired of this jest, but she half-smiled at it. "When, Lorenzo? When?"

Like her father, she was no fool. She knew as well as her friend Nerissa did that Lorenzo wanted her wealth as well as her heart. The family di Scimmia was an old and noble one; Lorenzo's father had once served in the Council of Ten. But the old man had spent money lavishly, and had finally degraded his fortune entirely. Though loath to dirty his hands by trafficking in merchandise, he had in the end tried to rebuild his substance by a speculation on the

Bourse in Madrid. He had lost money, and afterward had been forced to sell his country estate in the Terra Firma, the Venetian provinces on the mainland. Lorenzo had two brothers, and would gain only a small share of his father's house in the Piazza Patriarcato after the sire's death. There was always the Church, but the Church was not for Lorenzo. He had friends among the other impoverished gentry, but more and more he sought the company of merchants. These new friends were worth less in rank, but more in cash—more than Lorenzo himself was worth—and their habit was to lend money in exchange for the company of lords and introductions to their titled sisters. Lorenzo thought the exchange a fair one.

In truth, he admired the merchants. They were like Christ, whose first miracle was one of conversion. Jesus turned water into wine, and the traders turned spices and silks into silver coin. More often than not Lorenzo turned that silver into wine again, and thence back into water. This to him was not blasphemy, but magic.

Though it occasioned debt on his part.

Jessica knew of Lorenzo's debts, but believed that with the help of her father's money his fortunes could revive. With five thousand ducats Lorenzo could himself launch a trading venture into both the Indias, East and West, the lands of spices and mines, and re-store his own fortunes for life. She had not met any of Lorenzo's family yet, but Lorenzo had told her that they were beginning to welcome the plan.

"Choosing me, you will at last get as much as you deserve," Lorenzo told her, kissing her once more as she hurriedly debarked at the Canale di Cannaregio. "Ducats for spices, and spices for ducats, and ducats for a house on the Canale Grande. A string of happy conversions!"

"Including my own."

Lorenzo looked blank.

"Conversion."

He waved his hand in a disparaging gesture. "Nothing. Some water sprinkled on your head, and mass on Sunday."

She did not speculate on the cost of changing faiths. Her father had left Spain and never looked back. She would not look back at the ghetto.

"Will you not see me to the gates?" she asked.

"I cannot." For the first time that afternoon, Lorenzo glanced at the sun. "Late, by the cross. I have an appointment to dine with Bassanio back in San Giacomo dell'Orio. But I will send to you!" The boatman pushed off. "By Nerissa!" Lorenzo winked.

SHE CLOSED THE door only ten minutes ahead of her father's entry. But when he came in, Shiloh seemed tired and distracted, and after they prayed and lit the menorah's third candle, honoring Hannukah, he only bade her go to bed. "'*Ora*," he said. "Now I, too, want only to sleep."

She felt guilt assail her. He had dined with other members of the Sephardim, the exiles, who always spoke of Spain. For an instant she thought of going to him and smoothing his creased brow. But then he loosened his coat and took out a leather bag, and her thoughts were converted to considerations of its likely contents.

Late that night, when she heard his restless steps below her, she shifted on the floor where she had lain for an hour, and peeked through a knothole in the floorboard of her chamber, into her father's private room below. By the slight flame of the candle he carried she saw him loosen and remove a piece of the wall and place the leather bag behind it. *So,* she thought. *The same place as always.*

As he rummaged inside the wall, she moved quietly back to her bed and closed her eyes, hoping Lorenzo's twin passions, for her body and for his wealth, would be enough to impel him to marry her.

What did her dry father know of passion?

IT WAS HIS genizah, where he kept his most precious goods. He reached his hands inside it to unwrap the linen that held the turquoise ring. In his palms he cupped the ring, as he stood by the wall with his head bowed, swaying slightly with weariness. He whispered something that might have been a prayer.

THIRTEEN

Nerissa was gone from Venice.

Jessica had waited a week for a message from Lorenzo. On the seventh morning that Launcelot returned empty-handed, she grabbed her cloak and ran down the stairs and out into the streets of the ghetto, binding her hair with yellow cloth as she went. She walked briskly through the gates and south into the city without bothering to shed her shameful red-hearted robe or her headgear. Within the hour she was knocking at the door of the fine house near the Ca'd'Oro where, less than three weeks before, Nerissa had poured her wine and bade her rest her tired feet on a velvet settle.

The servant who opened the door grinned widely at her headdress and said, "Happy Christmastide, Jewess!"

She frowned. "I seek Nerissa," she said. "Nerissa d'Orocuore, of the—"

"You will not find her in the city, but if you are that same fine lady to whom I brought wine in the week before Advent, I have her message for you." He peered at her curiously. "Certain, you are much changed, all covered up!" He left her standing in the doorway and pushing her turban back impatiently to show a bit of her hair. She wondered where Nerissa could have fled to, and how she would ever find Lorenzo now, without a friend among the prostitutes. She envied those ladies who walked freely among the gallants, in their brothels and other places where men threw dice and played cards at hazard.

When the servant returned with a sealed paper she tore it open without moving from the stoop, though the youth bade her good morrow and closed the door.

Beloved Jessica,

I have been gifted with a most unmerited fortune that is too strange to explain in brief. It concerns a wondrous person I have met in a most unexpected way, who has convinced me that a binding love is possible between two hearts destined to belong together. I have removed to dwell with the author of my bliss at a fine estate in the Terra Firma, though from its description it should not be earth but a very paradise. Should you determine to fly from your cage in the Ghetto Nuovo, you will find a welcome here with us. Lorenzo di Scimmia would be passable means for such a flight. He knows of my leaving, and bids you send your servant to his dwelling with news of your present fortunes. I think he means news of your father's fortunes, and how you might best lay your hands on them.

A thousand kisses
Nerissa

Below her signature were inscribed two sets of instructions. One directed the reader to Lorenzo's dwelling in Venice, the other, to an estate across the Gulf of Venice in the Terra Firma, north toward Treviso.

Jessica folded the paper, tucked it behind her belt, and raced home, her heart and mind running before her steps.

When she reached her father's house, she climbed three flights of stairs and quietly opened the door to his study. She tapped the wall, creeping along the floorboards and listening intently, until she heard a resonance that bespoke hollowness. She fumbled with the masonry until the wall piece came loose in her hand. The piece was heavy, but she held it without placing it on the ground. She gazed into blackness behind it. It took her eyes a moment to discern the outlines of the box.

It bore a lock, of course. When the time came, she would need an iron to break it.

Carefully she replaced the masonry. She had no broom, so she licked her hands, then knelt and used her palms to lift up the dust that had fallen to the floor. When the boards looked clean, she rubbed them with her skirt and rose, dusting her hands against her apron.

She closed the door to the study carefully.

As she turned to go down the stairs, she felt herself suddenly grabbed hard around the waist. She shrieked, and Launcelot's voice whispered, "Stop thy mouth, my falcon, my dove, else I will stop it myself!" She felt the hardness in his groin as he held her from behind, and she stiffened, repelled. "Do not worry," he said. "I'm not such a dolt that I'd ravage *his* daughter. But I'll have some of that silver you took."

She kicked him backwards against the wall, and turned for the stairway.

"I'll tell him you were in there!" he said warningly.

"The box is locked!" she said furiously, turning to glare at him. He was even-featured and sandy-haired and might have been handsome were it not for the sly grin he wore always, even now, as he clutched his kicked shin. "I took nothing! I have nothing for you!" Her tone softened. "Have you a crow? Could you teach me to use it?"

"I could get one," he said, still rubbing his leg. "But I trust you not. I am the first your father would accuse."

"I wouldn't be sure of that," she said.

"Besides, I want something else from you."

She looked at him, scorn returning to her brow. "That will never happen."

"Not that; I told you. I will leave you to your Lorenzo, your Romeo, that you may lean out your casement to him, like Juliet."

"Who are they?"

"A story."

"You read trash."

"Never mind! I will tell you what I want. I want you to get me a place with one of your fine friends in a house with marble floors. A place with Flemish pictures on the walls. I tire of the ghetto."

"*My* fine friends?" Jessica said, and laughed. "*My* fine friends have lost their palaces, and that's why they have aught to do with me. Their tiled floors have been sold to merchants and courtesans."

"Ah, but they have richer fine friends, do they not? I can leapfrog upward, from a poor gentleman to a less poor one and thence—"

"To the doge. Next, to the pope."

"And why not?"

Jessica sat on the stair straightening her skirts and shaking her head. "You are a crafty villain. I have no doubt you will *be* pope one day."

"When I am he, I will see that you are made a saint. Get me a place, my fine mistress. With your Lorenzo, if you would have me play Mercury the messenger between you. Or get me hired by his fellow gamester Bassanio di Piombo. Then I'll plague you no more."

She nodded, thinking. "I will try, clown," she said. "I will try."

But in the end she did not have to try.

She had dispatched Launcelot with a message for Lorenzo. After supper that evening she was peering from her window, awaiting his return, when she saw Bassanio di Piombo himself approaching the house. She was amazed to see him among the scarlet-capped Jews of the ghetto. His feathered hat and blue silks drew other eyes than hers; she saw children gawking and pointing as he climbed the outer stair to her father's door.

Bassanio? She had never seen him away from the Piazza, where he went strolling with this or that noblewoman near the central fountain; or the Rialto Bridge, where the gallants went sometimes to listen and stare at the merchants and moneylenders (though, as her father said mockingly, they knew little of the game). What was he here for?

She raced down the stairs, fearing something had happened to Lorenzo. Part of her heart hoped he was as agonized as she over the drought of messages, the absence of letters once faithfully delivered to him by Nerissa, and that he had sent Bassanio to seek some word of her and give her an inkling of his own doings. But that thought terrified her, too. Surely even Lorenzo could guess how her father would storm at such a visit! Lorenzo would not have sent him. Bassanio could only be here for the other reason, the only other cause that brought Christians to the Ghetto Nuovo.

He needed money.

She sat on the bottom step of the back stairway, her head against the closed door of the spare room in which her father received guests who had come only for business, who were not welcomed to the upper floor for meals and conversation. The room in which he dealt with Gentiles. Jessica listened hard, hoping to hear Lorenzo's name.

"The state frowns on large loans," she heard her father say sardonically. "That is, when Jews make them."

Bassanio muttered something she could not hear.

"Three thousand ducats," her father replied. "Well." She heard the clack of the beads on the Chinese abacus he kept on a table.

"Ay, sir, for three months." Bassanio spoke a little louder. She could hear the sheepishness in his youthful voice as he hastened to reassure her father. "But you will have the money back in no time, no time! In the twinkling of an eye. By next week, I am sure."

Three thousand ducats! Had he lost it at hazard? For like Lorenzo's father, Bassanio di Piombo had spent his dead sire's once mighty resources at the gaming tables of the city. For what folly could he need this present sum?

"For three months," her father said wryly. "Well!"

"For the which, as I told you, Antonio shall become bound."

She could almost feel her father stiffen, though she could not see him. *Antonio di Argento.* She had never met the man, had only seen him at a great distance on the Rialto, and listened more times than she could count to her father's bitter complaints against him. *A monkey-faced clown! A merchant investor who knows nothing of the trade!*

According to Shiloh, Signior Antonio had mistaken his early luck for skill, had amassed wealth he was now busy wasting on reckless sea ventures, though that mattered little to her father. What plagued Shiloh was that Antonio haunted him in the Rialto. Antonio hated Jews, and though in this he was not alone among the Venetians, his insults were constant, and cast a pall on Shiloh's business. He was a shameful man, said her father, a fellow of fifty or more whose chosen companions were youths in their twenties, men like Bassanio and Lorenzo and the young merchants those lordlings had chosen as friends, the twins Salerio and Solanio della Fattoria. Antonio's monkeyish face, her father had said, was wrinkled but painted with rouge, his brown hair a wig. His neck was shrunken and sinewy, and his teeth were dyed. Only from a distance could anyone mistake him for one of the young men, who only stood him because of his sudden wealth and willingness to squander it on them. He played the grand benefactor to get their attentions. Even they saw through him, all but Bassanio, who was as taken in by Antonio as the older man was besotted with him. Bassanio thought him a wizard of commerce, and hung on his words, despite the canary disaster of three years before.

That event had brought Bassanio and one of his friends close to ruin.

It had happened because Bassanio, though he thought it generally loathsome to sully his hands with the sale of material goods, found the high-stakes gamble of mercantile commerce a happier prospect than actual work. A place in the Church, or a high secretarial post in the doge's court, were dull, demanding, and devoid of the thrill of hazard. So, having brought his substance dangerously low at the gaming tables, he launched a more ambitious gambit, joining Antonio, Lorenzo di Scimmia, and a Florentine named Graziano di Pesaro in a wine venture. Defying the embargo laid by the Christian League on trade with the Ottomites, the partners shipped eight hundred barrels of Spanish canary to the port of Constantinople. Their ship miraculously survived all sea hazards, including swift chase by one of Venice's own gunboats, and sailed into the Turkish port with its cargo intact. Great was the feasting of the four men when they heard the news of their bark's triumph over so many odds. It had cruelly surprised them later to learn that since the Moslems of Constantinople were forbidden to drink alcohol, their canary wine must be poured into the sea or stored, unsold, at their continuing expense in a Turkish warehouse.

Shiloh and his friend Tubal-cain had howled over the story at supper. Even Jessica had laughed.

But that merry meal had occurred before she cared a fig for those Christians' fortunes; she and Lorenzo had then not exchanged looks on the Rialto Bridge. Now, all was changed. Now, when her father spoke cuttingly of Antonio, her covert alliance with the merchant through Lorenzo made her smolder. "Why not leave them to themselves?" she had lately snapped in the middle of one of Shiloh's tirades. It irked her that he saw the Christian Venetians as an undifferentiated mass of fools. He could not see that Lorenzo, for all his folly, knew and loved music; that Antonio tried to help his friends; that Bassanio, though not clever, had . . . had . . . a good eye for clothing! She could not abide her father's bitterness. "Why cannot Signior Antonio be as he is?" she said. "I have heard he has an open hand."

"I know he does. I've felt it. He pretends to slap me with good humor on the back when I'm eating my cheese, with the hope that I'll choke," her father had replied with some heat. "A fine jest for those with a heavy wit. And all is made good because he finds Jews abhorrent to his taste. Well enough! I have known such hatreds since birth. But this one's a *bufón*, a clown for children. He mocks us for sport in front of his pretty friends, hoping only to make them laugh. I see him daily, come so smug upon the mart. He is one of those *bravucones* who delight in tormenting those he believes to be weaker. Pretending to a holy charity when what he cares for is what everyone else on the Rialto cares for. Silver! He puts me in mind of a cruel ape I encountered once in Toledo; indeed, he could be his brother. Both the sort to kick those they think won't kick back."

Jessica knew her father could kick anyone back, and hard, when it was worth his trouble. In Antonio's case, it was not. Did a Jew strike a Christian in the Rialto, he would not see the outside of a prison for years, if he even lived to be dragged into one. And things would not be well for such a Jew's daughter, either. Her father's hatred of Antonio would have frightened her if she had not known Shiloh as she did. She saw daily how tightly he reined in his fury against the Christians of Venice. At home, he mocked Antonio, as did his trading friends of the Sephardim, all except Rabbi Madena, who listened, sad to hear of such ill will outside the ghetto, where he rarely traveled. But even the gentle rabbi knew that Shiloh's ability to mask his anger was the means by which he had thrived.

Now Jessica pressed her ear harder against the door. Bassanio was arguing on behalf of Antonio, who had agreed to be his surety. "*He* lends out money gratis!" Bassanio said. "No interest, and open terms!"

"What a fine fellow," said her father. The abacus clacked again. "Why don't you borrow money from him?"

"He has none just now."

"Ah, I see! That must be because he lent it out gratis, with open terms. He gave none a reason to pay him back before your Christian Judgment Day. Now he can lend no more, no matter how badly his neighbor needs it." In the silence that followed, Jessica imagined her father's sharp glance at Bassanio's silks. "But you do not look as though you need it."

"I tell you, Signior Jew, Antonio gave me the money to buy these clothes."

"A very poor investment, it seems."

"He did not do it so I'd give him money back!"

"What, then? What did he want back, Signior Bassanio?"

Jessica cringed at her father's mocking tone. She heard Bassanio rise from his chair and stand, speechless with confusion. Then a knock came on the door. "That is him," Bassanio said. "That is Antonio."

"Jessica!" her father called.

She jumped to her feet. She had forgotten that Launcelot was not in the house, and she ran down the stairs to open the front door. There, standing on the stoop, was the man her father hated. Shiloh had described him well, marvelously picturing the pasty powder he wore on his cheeks, and the rouge and dyed moustaches. She curtsied, trying not to stare at the merchant, and brought him to the room where the others were. Her father had doubtless heard her jump from her perch on the stair-bottom, but she could not forbear returning to the step and listening hard.

She heard her father ask Bassanio if he needed his three thousand ducats in order to make some holy pilgrimage. A fire iron scraped the hearth as he added, "This I will lend you for a palmer's staff, good Christians!" Bassanio said nothing—Jessica envisioned his handsome, vapid face frowning, as he searched for a witty reply—but Antonio said harshly, "What know you of pilgrimages, Jew?"

Her father said he was in the habit of conducting backward pilgrimages, walking miles out of his way to avoid cathedrals.

Bassanio began to laugh at this, then abruptly stopped. *Shamed,* thought Jessica, *by Antonio's glare.*

The men now moved to the far side of the room and their conversation became a mumble. Various numbers were mentioned, and then the word *interest* was said in an angry tone by Antonio, and she heard her father explaining something about Jacob and Laban and Abraham and sheep. She blushed in the darkness, imag-

ining Antonio and Bassanio sharing a mocking glance, sneering at
the Jew, the Jew, the Jew, who cited his scripture instead of signing
over the money.

And money was indeed what they had come for. It was clear
they bore no word of or message from Lorenzo.

She rose and went to her room. There she knelt by her bed and
crossed herself. From under the mattress she removed a rosary, and
began to tell the beads with her fingers, whispering words she had
heard mumbled in the Church of San Marco. *"Ave Maria, gratia
plena, Dominus tecum. Ave Maria . . ."*

But twenty minutes later, when she heard the house's main
door open two floors below, she threw the beads on the bed. She
tiptoed quickly into the upper hall to hear the visitors' last words.

"A bloody bargain in a season of Christmas!" Bassanio was saying. "You shall not swear to such a bond for me! I would cut off my
own head first!"

"Why, fear not, man, I will not—"

"Enough, you have persuaded me," Bassanio said quickly. "To
the notary tomorrow. Now, to the gates before the guards lock us
in with them."

Antonio moved ahead of Bassanio through the door, and she
could not hear what he said next, but then she heard Launcelot's
name. "And the first three ducats for the wage of that Giobbo fellow, to take him out of this house!" Bassanio was laughing. "Do
you think the Jew does not trust him in the upper rooms with
pretty Jessica?"

SHILOH TOLD HER the rest at supper the next day. She let her
knife fall to the cloth and stared.

"What could you mean by it, Father?"

He shrugged. "A jest. Those two mock my usury as though the Christians of Europe did not practice it as well."

Their guest shook his head. He was Tubal-cain, who also worked on the Rialto, and who studied the Talmud on Tuesday evenings with her father and the rabbi. "Venice is losing her place among the nations by not following England and Germany and the Netherlands in this," he said. "If their great merchants might lend at usance, and not only we—"

"We would have less money."

Tubal-cain pointed his knife at Shiloh. "And be less hated!"

"I do not think it. And pray, put your knife to its proper use! No, I do not think it, Tubal-cain. The hate of such as those two who were here today is deeper than their empty pockets. It is themselves they hate, for having to borrow from me. Never will you hear one of those pork-eaters admit the truth."

"And what is that, Father?" Jessica could not help asking, with false sweetness.

He frowned at her tone. "The truth is that I have more to lend not because of the rates I charge, but because I am a better judge of a surety, and know what investments will show a return. No, you will hear that *they* lack funds because they are generous, and *I* surfeit because I am a bloodthirsty dog, a greedy wretch, a ravening wolf, what have you!" He shrugged again and poured himself a glass of water. "So I play the part. No interest I charge those two, but a bond of blood. Repayment by our Passover feast or Antonio di Argento gives me a pound of his flesh. Why not? Let them laugh at the story on the Rialto."

Tubal-cain frowned. "Your sense of humor will get you in trouble. What would our fathers say?"

"I don't know. I don't consult ghosts."

"Of course not! Who believes in those? But why did you sign

any bond that threatens to take you from the Jewish court into the courts of the city? Rotten fish!"

Shiloh spread his hands, as though to say, *Is this not obvious?* "This will never reach the Municipio. Antonio di Argento has an argosy bound to Tripoli, another to the Indies, a third to Mexico, a fourth for England—there's no end to the silver he's cast on the waters. He will squander the money when it sails back into port, but some of it *will* sail back. Enough will. And I'll have my payment before he spends the rest on his dear Bassanio di Piombo."

Shiloh swallowed half his glass of water. "Besides, even if Antonio's ventures *did* all fail, I'd have my chance to shame him. I'd not press the bond. What would I do with a pound of flesh? 'Tis not mutton. If I were the cannibal they think me, I'd find meat less stringy than his to dine on. I'd eat that little fat parrot Graziano di Pesaro, who dogs di Piombo's steps and never stops talking. Venice would reward me for that."

Tubal-cain chuckled, and the corners of Jessica's lips twitched. She put her hand to her mouth.

"I do not need di Argento's money," said Shiloh. "I would show him the mercy that is supposed to be only Christian, and forgive his bankruptcy before all Venice. Pour hot oil on his head, is that not how the Nazarene said it? Or was it burning coals he recommended?"

"How would I know?" said Tubal-cain. "You learned much in one visit with the Luteranos in Valladolid, Shiloh. And *you* never stop talking about *that*."

"Di Piombo asked me to dine with them," Shiloh said. "I wish you had seen Signior Antonio's face when he said it! What do you think the Ma'mad would make of it, had I accepted?"

"You know what the council of elders would make of it. No need to ask. They would put you under the cherem, as they did poor Mordecai, for drinking the wrong wine with the Christian flax trader from Hamburg. They would bar you from prayers."

"How rude the signiors must think me, not to go," said Shiloh. "Only for a few prayers."

"Three thousand ducats!" said Tubal-cain. "What did they want with such a sum?"

"No honest trade, I am sure. Some monkey business. Signior Bassanio has debts. He owes everyone, including those foul-mouthed twins who delight in poking the Jews on their badges, Solanio and Salerio della Fattoria. Were those two born in a cage?" Shiloh pushed back his chair as though to give his rage room. "To say nothing of that chimpanzee who hangs chattering about the Exchange with the rest of them, though he has no business there. The ginger-haired gallant di Scimmia!"

Jessica stiffened, though she had known the name would be spoken.

"No doubt they all want new clothes to impress the doge's daughters," Shiloh said, looking straight at Jessica. "Would you not call them a worthless tribe, daughter?"

She rose from the table, her face set. She bowed to their guest and mounted the stair. After a minute her door shut.

Shiloh's frown loosened, and he looked at his friend and sighed.

FOURTEEN

Launcelot returned with no word from Lorenzo.

He had waited, he said, for two hours at the door of Lorenzo's lodgings by the Rio di Greci, while water seeped into his boots. Lorenzo's manservant had finally raised a window and grudgingly seized Jessica's missive, saying he'd add it to the store of letters and tradesmen's bills that awaited his master, but he'd not venture in search of him; he was paid ill enough only to mind the house. "And I think that fellow just in his complaint," said Giobbo grouchily. "These missions I do for thee are what make thy father scant my wages." He held out his hand. "You'll make good the difference, my dove."

"Here's gold for you," she said sourly, crossing his palm with a cruzado. "But you will find you have your profit of his dissatisfaction with you. He has preferred you to Bassanio di Piombo."

"Is't so?" asked Launcelot, grinning widely. "Di Piombo! I'll fit him well. That man has a streak of poetry in him."

"And you think *you* do, as well?"

"I *know* I do. Ah, freedom!" Launcelot jumped and clicked his damp heels. "No more haunting the ghetto market for the sukkot's bloodless beef, and for fish prepared cashew!"

"Kosher," said Jessica. "And our butcher is a *shohet,* not a *sukkot.* But you'll not need those words now. Practice French, not Hebrew. Now you'll patrol the haberdashers for capes cut in the Gallic style. And my father's ducats will pay for those, too!"

"How so?"

"He's taken a loan, your Bassanio. Do you know where he lives?"

"I do."

"My father bids you be gone tonight, before he returns from prayers. I'll do your drudgery here, I doubt not." She looked at him in disappointment and exasperation. "Who will ferry my messages now?"

Launcelot pinched her cheek with a boldness rare even for him. "Ah, fair damosel, thou knowest Signior Bassanio is fast friends with your love. I will yet play the post between you. We will make of your plight a romance, like the French *lais* of the knights and their ladies, and I will fly with wingéd feet bearing pledges of love—"

"For cruzados and ducats."

"Thy father's." He winked.

"YOUR DAUGHTER SCANTS evening prayers," said Rabbi Madena.

The minyan was disbanding, the other eight men rising to walk from the triple-arched synagogue of Scuola Levantina. Some moved

THE TURQUOISE RING   149

toward the baths, others homeward. Shiloh walked forward and seated himself on the benches normally reserved for the old, under the raised platform of the bimah. Rabbi Madena stood on the bimah, majestic under his wild cloud of hair, replacing the scrolls of the Law in the ark.

"I know," Shiloh said, "but how do you know?"

"My wife tells me. They talk of Jessica at the mikvah." The rabbi adjusted his robes and came down from the platform to sit beside Shiloh. "Your daughter has not sat with the women for two months."

Shiloh was silent.

"Where does she go?" asked the rabbi.

"*Qué me sepa!* How should I know!" Shiloh said with irritation. After a moment he added, "One day a Christian I know said he saw her in the Church of San Marco." He looked at the rabbi, his dark eyes wells of pain. "Staring at one of the painter Titian's graven images. And she had unwound her headgear."

"Ah, well, we all hate the colored hats."

"'Tis not that!"

"I know," said Madena quietly.

They sat in companionable sorrow for a moment, looking at the closed ark. "She will break my Isaac's heart," said the rabbi after a time.

"And mine!" Shiloh turned suddenly to Madena and said in an anguished voice, "The Church took her mother, yet she runs to it with open arms! She—"

"She does not know the Church took her mother," Madena calmly interrupted.

Shiloh fell silent. After a moment he said, "You and no other man in Venice know what became of my Leah. I spoke of it once, and will never do so again. I will not defile my daughter's ears with the story."

"Well, then," Madena said enigmatically.

Shiloh brooded for a moment, not responding. Then he reverted to his earlier theme. "I know not what to do with her. I have defied all custom to teach her, a woman, the Law. And she spurns my instruction! My Leah would pant for the Law like a thirsty deer. She drank learning like sweet water; swallowed it like manna, but Jessica! And the girl says little to me; she is a closed box."

"Yes."

"It hurts!"

"Yes."

"She is the image of her mother, and I love her more than I love my life. But she angers me beyond thought. She worships . . . surfaces! And she knows not how to value herself. She tempts danger from those young Christian apes who know not how to prize *her*. I have seen them stare at her, even when her hair is covered. Their very gaze dishonors her!"

"Perhaps she knows it, Shiloh. Jessica is not stupid."

"Then *why* . . . ?"

Madena sighed, and was quiet for a moment. Then he said, "I have five sons. I know not the way of daughters. But I think your rigor—"

"You call our Law rigor?"

"I call our Law freedom. I call hatred rigor."

Shiloh looked as though he'd been pricked by a sword point.

"I am saying," said Madena, "that you seem to hate the Christians you traffic with on the Rialto, and to share your disdain with Jessica as though you wish to make it her own."

"I tell her their worth, in order to protect her from them. What does she think of them?"

"She thinks them young folk, like herself! She would like to dress as their sisters do." Madena raised his hands against Shiloh's outcry. "I do not doubt your judgment, Shiloh ben Gozán. And I grant you, Jessica is unruly. It is your sacred obligation to guard her against men who would harm her. But Leviticus tells us to love our neighbors as ourselves, and—"

"Do I not? I give food to the hungry of this ghetto. Even to the shiftless who eat impure food and never make one of a minyan. But the men out there"—he gestured eastward, toward the Rialto— "who call us dogs and spit on us from the corners of their mouths— these are our neighbors?"

"There are some who would say so," said Rabbi Madena, raising his bushy brows.

Shiloh grunted. "You talk like a Christian. But they only talk."

The rabbi frowned. His one good eye glowed like a coal. "I talk like who?"

"Ah, Rabbi, forgive me," said Shiloh, his face contrite.

"It is rare for a refugee, a converso who once chewed the sacrament, to liken a ghetto-born Jew, who has never set foot in a church, to a son of Ishmael!"

"You are right. Forgive me."

Madena's frown relaxed and his face resumed its genial mildness. "I forgive you, my neighbor!" he said, laughing a little. "In Spain they do the best they can. But touching this question of love, I will remind you that Deuteronomy says we must love aliens *as well* as our neighbors."

"Well. That's me," said Shiloh. "I am the alien."

Shiloh left the prayer room in a sour temper. At its entrance he paused, tucking the new leather case that held his prayer book inside his topcoat. Though he was not superstitious by nature, something made him button the coat's right side over its left to ward off the evil that might come from that sinister direction.

Rigor, the rabbi had said. Was the word just?

Shiloh did not think all Christians evil. Good Gentiles lived. He himself had known four, in Valladolid. And two in Toledo. One of those was even a priest! And he knew, further, that not all Jews were the stuff good husbands were made of. He knew a married man in the Ghetto Nuovo who kept two mistresses and had the boldness to justify his acts with the claim that, since the mistresses were widows, he was no adulterer. *"These are not my neighbor's wives!"* Shiloh had once heard him tell the rabbi. The rabbi, no less! Yes, a Jew could monkey with the Law. Even good Tubal-cain, who loved the Talmud, had once paid a Gentile broker to start a rumor on the Rialto, to drive the silk price up by making whimsical suggestions that two ships from the Indies had met with ill luck on the high seas. His defense? He claimed that while the law of Moses forbade *him* to give false witness, neither Moses nor the Mishnah said a word against paying Christians to lie!

Yet Tubal-cain and even that rascally Ben the Lecher were men of substance. They paid their debts and fed their families. In the main, they were good for their promises. Antonio, and Bassanio, and Lorenzo di Scimmia . . . these, on the other hand, were hardly even men! Shiloh's fist closed against the mass of them. He hated their weak, many-jointed Italian names. Too many syllables!

Still standing in the doorway of the synagogue, he rubbed his head, battling the rising tide of his anger and his fear for Jessica, reciting scripture to calm his beating mind. *The Lord is gracious, merciful, and righteous. It is well with the man who deals generously and lends, who conducts his affairs with justice. For the righteous will never be moved; he will be remembered forever.*

Sighing, he forced his hand to relax. He began to walk slowly through the small, well-kept courts of the Scuola Levantina.

Perhaps in Jerusalem, he thought. *The Christians of Europe have abandoned the East to the Ottomites. There the muezzin calls the Moslem to prayer alongside the Christian and the Jew. There the chosen walk on holy ground! There none dresses in the Paris fashions, the little purple parrot feather, what an imbecile di Piombo looked with it waving from his velvet cap like plumage . . . To the East . . .*

But he dreamed, did he not? "Israel is within," the rabbi had told him once. "That is the best lesson I took from the kabbalah. There is no sacred place but the human heart. No Compostela, Mecca, or Jerusalem. Your Luteranos are right in this. Only the heart."

"Ah, but they think the heart desperately wicked," Shiloh had replied. "A heavenly sky shot through with black streaks of sin."

"It is desperately good as well," Rabbi Madena had answered, looking for a moment like Father Bartolomeo of Toledo. "Good will always be stronger."

Once Jessica had angered Shiloh by telling him that the heart could not choose what it loved. Could not *choose?* What good was a heart, then? *His* heart had chosen! Out of a thousand, it had picked a woman whose price was above rubies.

Shiloh stopped again before the temple gates, to pin the red badge on his sleeve before he entered the outer world of the ghetto. He glanced inside the women's courtyard, where seated wives and daughters were laughing. He heard one of them speaking rapidly in Ladino, and felt an old pain.

For twenty-two years he had lived like a Capuchin monk in Venice, though many fathers had offered their daughters in marriage, especially as his worth grew. And there were widows enough in the ghetto. At times he regretted not having taken a *mujer*, a woman, who might have made sense of Jessica.

A few times, when he was younger, he had allowed the lusts of his body to drive him to the *zonas* of the houses of Malipiero, in the Gentiles' Venice. But he did this no longer. It was no way to live, and it dulled the edges of his memories of Leah. So he kept alone. He would not forget Leah. Dead, she still owned his heart.

He felt keenly his solitude and the emptiness of his bed when he heard, as he sometimes did in the ghetto, a woman's voice speaking Ladino or Spanish in the accents of central Spain, of Castille or La Mancha, or saw one whose special gestures and phrases marked her as a Toledana. For it was not true what he'd implied weeks before, to Ha-Levi of Amsterdam, that he never thought on that city. He hated the *neschech,* the biting usury he practiced in Venice. He pined for the sheep-shearing and carding and weaving he had done in Toledo with his hands—hands that now spent hours each day counting coin, scribbling figures, and telling the beads of the abacus. He missed the trees and dry hills of La Mancha with an ache he felt deep in his ribs. Here wet was everywhere, in the air, on his skin, in his throat, and still, nothing grew but mold and moss. Venice was a city of water and stone. In Toledo, orange and lemon trees flowered, even in the very heart of the city.

He stopped at the side of the ghetto street and leaned his head against the wall.

Jessica was all he had left of Leah, and Jessica had never known her. No man he now knew had known Leah. No woman had, either, and if he took a wife who knew nothing of what Leah had been to him, Leah's image would blur and then vanish. He alone bore her face in his heart.

Zakhor, Astruga had said. *Do not forget to remember.*

"Signior?"

Shiloh opened his eyes. A boy was gazing at him questioningly. "Your head?"

"It is filled with weighty thoughts," Shiloh said, straightening and patting him on the shoulder. "Home, now, to your supper. The law prevents ghetto-wandering at night."

DESPITE LAUNCELOT GIOBBO'S fanciful visions of busy message-carrying between Jessica and Lorenzo, it was February before he returned to their house. Jessica had lost flesh because of her anxiety, and from the double burden of chores laid on her shoulders by his departure.

"Fair Jewess!" Launcelot said when she opened the latch. She stared at him goggle-eyed. He was dressed in peach-colored hose and powder blue livery, and sported a feathered cap. "So *this* is where my father's shrewdly earned ducats have gone!" she said, pulling him inside.

He preened and shook his leg before her. "And I have three pair!"

"You clown, what is the message? I am ready to strangle Lorenzo—"

"He has been visiting friends in the Terra Firma; he regrets his silence—"

"He has been gambling with Bassanio!"

"Yes, and 'tis a great gamble Lord Bassanio now has afoot!"

"*Lord* Bassanio?"

"Soon to be, or as rich as one, if he succeeds in this. A lady of the mainland, richly left—"

Jessica's heart climbed to her throat, and she seized Launcelot's neck. Was Lorenzo at issue in this? Had he abandoned her? She had passed him one day in the Piazza San Marco, walking with his father, and though the youth had winked, his father had stared at her as though she were some horror from the lagoons. Yet she had been exiting the Church of San Marco and wore Christian woman's gear given her by Nerissa. Her heart had beat fast; she had thought Lorenzo might introduce her to the senior di Scimmia, but her lover had only made a furtive signal to her as they passed. In a low voice he had said something to his father, to which the sire had loudly replied that a sow's ear was not convertible to a silk purse. Her face burned at the memory.

"Is Lorenzo making plans to marry a lady?" she said, shaking Launcelot. "What says he?"

Launcelot freed himself from her fingers and handed her a note. Quickly she unfolded it and scanned its contents.

"Too long a pause for that which you find there," said Launcelot, smirking as he straightened his embroidered collar.

She threw her arms around him. "Clown, I know you have read it already. You may tell Lorenzo yes, I will be here on the appointed night; yes, my father will be hours studying the Talmud with his friend; yes, I will be a Christian's wife, yes!"

FIFTEEN

Five weeks later a hard knock sounded on Shiloh ben Gozán's front door. Jessica opened it to find the severed ear of a sow on the stoop.

Her lip curved in shock and disgust, and on the heels of those feelings came understanding. She closed the door and sank against it, fighting tears. So. Some brother or cousin of the grand di Scimmia family had thought it a merry sport to slip into the ghetto and leave her this coarse message. Marriage with Lorenzo would not raise her status from that of a barnyard animal.

She rose and opened the door. The thing was impure and disgusting, but she picked it up anyway and took it inside. Then she wrapped it in paper and threw it far into the alley behind the kitchens.

She thanked all her saints that her father had not been home to see it.

Still, by afternoon she had convinced herself that the foul gift was a good sign, a proof that Lorenzo intended faithfulness to his promise. It was clear that he had told his family, or some of them, of his and Jessica's plans.

"Do not worry, beloved," he said to her the next day, as they kissed in the shadow of the Church of the Madonna dell'Orto. Her father had watched her doings more nearly of late, and now when she and Lorenzo met it was here, closer to the gates of the ghetto. "Fear not," he said, stroking her hand. "When you are baptized and I have placed a ring on this fair finger, they will be well pleased." He frowned thoughtfully. "Though my cash runs low. We may have to wait for a ring."

HE WOULD COME for her on Shrove Tuesday, when the city was at its peak of carnival. The canals and rivers and ports would be crowded with musical boats; the citizens would run drunk and disguised; so dense would be the street crowds that, for all Jessica's father's timeliness, he would surely be more than an hour coming home from the house of Tubal-cain. The Jews, of course, did not observe the Christian holiday, but it was the custom of masked Christian boys of Venice to climb the gates of the Ghetto Nuovo and share their good will with its residents, throwing wine in folk's faces and pulling men's beards and throwing flaming paper-wrapped bricks into the synagogues, all the while singing loudly and merrily.

To help Lorenzo, Bassanio di Piombo had visited the Rialto today and once more asked Shiloh ben Gozán to sup with him, intending to keep the moneylender late or even overnight in some discussion of their business. Shiloh recounted the story of Bassanio's absurd invitation to Jessica, at home. "Those fools think it a mere whim that we will not eat shellfish or pork!" he said, shaking his head. "As though we could do it with ease if we would!"

Jessica had herself often thought so, but she knew better than to risk her father's ire by sharing the notion. Not tonight.

"Tubal-cain and I will study our Law while the Venetians are busy breaking theirs," Shiloh said. His eyes were alight with the love of Talmud and Torah.

"What will you study tonight?" she found herself asking.

"This and that. After the Talmud, we will continue an argument about the punishments inflicted on our captors in Egypt. Were they plagued with many small frogs, or just one big one? The Hebrew is ambiguous."

They shared a smile. She felt a small kindling of warmth toward him, and with it a stab of guilt.

He took her by the shoulders and straightened the veil with which she had wrapped her hair. "What is this costume?"

"'Tis the day of disguises, is't not?"

"What, are there masques?" He frowned. "Yes, the drunken crew will be here with their torches! Lock up my doors, Jessica." He shook his finger gently. "And clamber not up to the casements to look, nor thrust your head into the public street to gaze on Christian fools with varnished faces."

She rolled her eyes.

"Ah, well you might look to the Most High to save you from me. But I would save you from *them!* Daughter, Christian youths mean no good to Jewish maidens. They are—"

"A tribe of monkeys!" She finished the sentence with him, and for a rarity, they laughed together.

She looked after his straight back as he descended the stairs, clad in his dark cloak and his turban. Her leaden heart would break if she thought of the hard road he had traveled to come to Venice, or recalled the times she had read with him from the Pentateuch, and he had helped her trace the Hebrew letters with her fingers. So she did not think of those things. Instead she ascended the stairs and pushed her hands under her mattress, seeking her rosary. Her fingers touched the beads, and then, next to them, something harder.

It was the fire iron she had brought up from her father's study that morning.

Shiloh descended two floors, then paused on the far side of the door above the last flight of his house's stairs. He pondered for a moment, and the look on his face was agony. Slowly he took a key from his pocket and locked the door from the outside. *"Para estar seguro,"* he said under his breath. "Only to be sure."

By a quarter past five the ghetto was alive with the sounds of shattering glass and singing. From her high window Jessica could see dots of flame in the streets below, and some buildings burning. A group of laughing youths ran below her window dragging a cursing youth whose red cap had slipped from his hair. She watched as they deposited him at the corner and circled and kicked him.

She closed the window.

She was dressed in the service breeches Launcelot had left behind in his rooms, and an old shirt of her father's. She had pinned her hair to her head in a tight coil and covered it with a Spanish cap she had found buried deep in his trunk. Now she took the fire iron and a candle and went downstairs to his private room. Her heart beat so hard she could feel its hammering. She crossed the room, placed the candle on the floor, and removed the piece of the wall that hid the genizah.

It was dark inside the hole, but after groping for a few seconds she found the locked casket. It was so heavy that she strained her arms lifting it from its place, and then dropped it, jumping back as it fell loudly to the floor. *Is it lead-lined?* she wondered, as she hit the lock hard with the iron. After several blows the latch flew open, and she knelt with her candle to peer inside.

Oddments lay within. A fragment of an old scroll, inscribed in Hebrew and decorated with geometrical patterns and images of flowers and plants. It was discolored with rust, or blood. She pushed it impatiently to the side. Underneath it were the bags of silver and gold her father had brought from the Rialto. Their contents she poured into a large leather bag she had bought in the Merceria. Three diamonds sparkled in the light of the candle, and she scooped those into the bag as well.

She took as much as she could carry, then rummaged among her father's papers for other small and precious things; emeralds, or rubies. A faded cloth unrolled itself at her hand's brusque gesture and a ring fell from its folds.

She held it up to the light of the candle. It was a turquoise, its stone stained with something and shot through with dark, veiny lines. Its band was black with grime, but she could see it was fine silver, and well crafted.

She heard a yell in the street outside, and pushed the ring quickly into her pocket. Then she jumped to her feet and crossed to the window. It was not Lorenzo; only some sailors from the port pleasing themselves with the local mayhem, drinking and singing and calling out loudly for women. Jessica blew out the candle. She dragged the sack of coin outside her father's door and bumped it down the stairs behind her to the lower landing. Her heart felt as heavy as the bag, and she walked more slowly at each step. She thought of her father's warm brown eyes.

The ground-floor tenants were at the synagogue. She would wait for Lorenzo outside their apartments, by the front door.

But perhaps she would tell Lorenzo that she could not leave her house this way.

Above the first floor she turned the knob and pushed.

The door stayed fast.

She stopped, aghast.

And then her heart fired with the rage of her confinement. The flames of resentment bore it heavenward and made it light. "I will jump, then!" she said aloud, and ran into her father's study. But of course, the windows there were barred. She sat on the floor and wept with anger, but only for a minute. Afterward she rose and ran through the house, ransacking bedrooms and closets and buck baskets and taking every sheet, clean or soiled, that she could find.

Then she sat in her room by her relit candle and tied the linens as tightly as she could.

At seven, the appointed hour, Lorenzo was not there. In the darkness she bent over her rosary, mumbling her prayer to Maria. *Keep me angry, Holy Mother,* she begged. *Keep me angry!* She pulled her rope of sheets, tightening the knot that tied it to her bed frame. Fifteen minutes went by, and then twenty.

Her father had said he would return at eight.

At last, as the Church of the Madonna dell'Orto struck the half hour, she heard Lorenzo in the street below, and let her breath out in a gasp. She jumped to her feet and looked out the window. "Here!" she called down. "Lorenzo, up here!"

She saw him swaying on the cobblestones, dressed in wild colors and covered with holiday confetti. Next to him stood his grinning friend Salerio, the merchant. This was the man on the wharf to whom Lorenzo had confessed owing money, that day in the gondola, and she wondered briefly if Signior Salerio had come for the sport of this carnival masque or for his payment. But it did not matter which.

A short man bearing a torch stepped from behind Salerio, into the middle of the street. He wore the mask of a wolf, and he pushed it up to his brow. "Fair Jessica!" he said, opening his arms.

"God be with you, Graziano!"

"Come down, fair one!" said Lorenzo, slurring his words. "My falcon will slip her jesses!" He stumbled, then caught himself, and raised a bottle to toast her. Her heart sank as she saw his unsteady gait, and she abandoned all thought that he might climb halfway up the house to help her down.

"I cannot," she called. "The door is locked."

"Then send out the money!" yelled Graziano and Salerio as one. They screamed with laughter.

"I must send it first, perforce," she called, thanking the Blessed Mother that the singing and yelling from all parts of the ghetto gave some cover to her voice. "Stand back!" She heaved the tightly bound leather sack to the sill of the casement and shoved it over. The bag hit the street with a clank, and the three men whooped and rushed to open it. None of them watched as she pushed the rope of sheets through the window and pulled herself onto the sill. She yanked the highest sheet as a test. It was tied fast. "Sixty-three feet straight down," she whispered. Then she turned and swung her legs into the night air.

The silvery sound of pouring coin greeted her ears as she approached the ground. "I'm here!" she called excitedly. "Here, my love!" Only then did the men look up.

"See her climb!" laughed Graziano. "Like a monkey!"

I *WILL GIVE thanks to the Lord with my whole heart, in the company of the upright, in the congregation.* Shiloh spoke to himself as he picked his way through broken glass and shards of brick in the street.

Great are the works of the Lord, studied by all who have pleasure in them. Full of honor and majesty is his work, and his righteousness endures forever.

As the bell of Madonna dell'Orto chimed the first stroke of eight, he rounded the corner, then stopped. Hanging from the top floor of his house, a white rope blew sideways in the hard March wind.

IN THE CHAPEL of Madonna dell'Orto the revelers giggled as the hired priest sprinkled Jessica's head with water. He asked her something about the Christ, who languished on his wooden cross above the altar, his eyes rolled skyward as had Leah's in response to her father's sour gibes. Her hand in Lorenzo's, she said what the priest told her to say. But while her lips moved her eyes swept past the crucifix and rested below the cross, on the blue-clad Madonna in a painting that hung on the wall, on the face of Mary the mother.

SIXTEEN

THE STORY SPREAD everywhere in Venice, though it began on the Rialto, where business was done even on the first day of Lent. The Jew's horns had grown an inch and the devil had carried him over the wall of the ghetto, then abandoned him in the Piazza San Marco, where he stood howling his rage at the loss of his Frankfurt diamond and his ducats and, only incidentally, his daughter. Solanio della Fattoria, the merchant Salerio's twin, could barely speak for laughter as he pantomimed the gestures he thought should be those of a robbed Jew. "My daughter!" he spluttered, spraying his mouthful of wine on the sleeves of the rapt merchants on the bridge. "O my ducats! O my daughter! Fled with a Christian! Justice! The law! And—and—two stones!" He grabbed his crotch and raised his voice to a falsetto, as his listeners roared. "Two rich and precious stones, stol'n by my daughter!"

What had actually happened was that Shiloh had vaulted the ghetto wall where it was lowest, by the Fondamenta degli Ormesini, and then hired a boat to cross the small canal that divided the Jews' neighborhood from Venice proper. Twenty minutes later he had appeared below Bassanio's balcony, where that young man sat coatless and merry, singing a catch with Solanio. From the street Shiloh yelled a rich litany of insults sprinkled with Spanish curses, and demanded to know the whereabouts of Lorenzo di Scimmia. Bassanio and Solanio cupped their ears and affected not to understand his alien tongue. Outraged, Shiloh reached for a stone to throw at the pair, but just then someone came careening from the left and gave him, with his fist, a blow to the head. Shiloh fell to the cobbles and looked up, his left ear ringing, to see Antonio standing grinning, the pasty skin that peeped through his unlaced shirt a stark contrast to his salmon pink face, which was dusted with powder.

"For once in the year you are dressed for the season, *bufón*," Shiloh sneered, as Antonio raised a foot to kick him. Shiloh grabbed the foot and pulled it, and Antonio fell to the street with a yell, while Bassanio and Solanio yelped with laughter above. Shiloh raised his fist to smash the Christian's cheek, but when Antonio cowered and held his hands up before his face, Shiloh lowered the fist in disbelief. "*Marijosé,*" he whispered contemptuously.

A stream of liquid splattered his head, and he jumped up, looking above. Solanio had unbuttoned his breeches and was making water on the street. "You are baptized, Jew!" he said. "Like your daughter!"

Bassanio rose unsteadily on the balcony, looking pained by the merchant's crass behavior. "Go home, Signior Shylock," he called down. "Jessica will be fast married by now. Joined to Lorenzo, as close as a ring and a finger. At the Church of Madonna dell'Orto—"

Solanio covered Bassanio's mouth, laughing. "*Now* what have you done?"

Shiloh ripped from his head the turban Solanio had soiled and threw it at Antonio, who was struggling drunkenly to rise to his feet. "*Cochino*," Shiloh spat, and left the street, racing back through a mass of carnival revelers toward the Ghetto Nuovo, slipping on the wet, mossy stones of the streets, then righting himself and running still faster. But when he reached the church by its northeast wall, the building was dark.

In the lane outside, Shiloh seized a torch from a masked, singing man too stupefied by drink to note its theft. The man stood gazing in surprise at his empty hand as Shiloh rounded the church, seeking an unlocked door. In the end he climbed through a window. Though he knew the place was empty, still, he searched everywhere, in the sacristy and behind the altar, until finally, in tears, he turned to quit the sanctuary. But at the door he turned, holding his torch high, and pointed to the painted Christ who hung suffering on his cross in the chancel. "*You!*" he yelled in fury. "*You* are a *piece of wood!*"

It was nearly midnight when he reached the city's eastern port, but the place was still crowded with masquerading citizens. Shiloh fought his way through a crowd of face-painted, bare-breasted women; gawking Dutch travelers, dressed in black despite the holiday; brightly clad Venetian revelers; Turkish seamen and merchants in fezzes; and a lone, balding Englishman who sat on a wall, scribbling furiously on cheap paper and muttering, his eyes awash in a dream. Of the costumed celebrants and foreign visitors, few noticed the tall, hatless man with the heart-shaped patch on his sleeve who solicited the porters and agents of the wharf, asking for news of his daughter.

At length a ferryman counting coin at the westernmost dock gave Shiloh the answer he'd feared. The man had been approached

by a couple who matched the description Shiloh gave. He showed
Shiloh the small diamond they'd given him in exchange for his
promise to deliver a message to Signior Antonio di Argento, whom
in their rush to embark they'd had no time to seek. At Shiloh's insis-
tence the man held up the paper, and in the flickering light of many
torches Shiloh read the hastily scrawled words. In misspelled Italian,
Lorenzo thanked Antonio for the loan of his one remaining sloop,
that would give him and his new wife passage to Genoa. They assured Antonio that, as the payment agreed on in advance, they had
met on the wharf the vintner who had supplied wine for Antonio's
carnival feast. For the clearing of Antonio's debt to the vintner and
the bonus of the man's pet monkey, they had given him an old
silver ring.

The next day Shiloh sat in his private room, next to the open,
lead-lined casket Jessica had abandoned on the floor. He rocked
back and forth, wearing his tallit. Then he rent his garments and
murmured Kaddish, the prayer for the dead. Outside, the Jews of
the ghetto swept glass and bricks and trash from the street. Rabbi
Madena stood in the street and called his name. But Shiloh closed
his ears.

That evening he knocked on Tubal-cain's door.

His friend embraced him. "You were missed on the Rialto," he
said. "Will you return?"

"Yes." Shiloh's eyes were deeply shadowed. Tubal-cain looked
at him anxiously. "You know they are in Genoa," he said. "Will you
pursue them?"

"No."

"I know not what to say to you, my friend. I stood by today
when one of Antonio's creditors approached him and shook his
hand. He showed him a ring that he had of your daughter for a
monkey."

THE TURQUOISE RING   169

Shiloh stared down at his long-bare finger. "It was my turquoise," he said after a moment. "I had it of Leah when I was a bachelor."

"Ah," said Tubal-cain. "Ah."

Shiloh's mouth twisted, in pain or contempt. "I would not have sold it for a wilderness of monkeys."

"What can I do, Shiloh?"

"Give me your help."

"My purse lies all unlocked to your occasions!" Tubal-cain grasped Shiloh's hand. "How much did she—"

"Not that," said Shiloh. "Not money. This. You have heard that Signior di Argento's spice shipments are delayed?"

"Of course. But fear not. Only a sea calm. The wind will blow. One crashed on a barrier reef, repairs already effected; and some sailors fled ship in Africa, but those will be replaced."

"Even so," said Shiloh. "Even so. I wish to start a rumor on the Rialto."

By THE NEXT afternoon the brokers' tongues were clacking, from the eastern port to the traders' bridge. Against all odds, all Antonio di Argento's ships appeared to be lost. One had run aground on the Goodwin Sands; a second, coming from Tripoli, had been attacked by pirates. The third, bound back from Mexico, had simply vanished in the western Atlantic, near the Bermudas, as though swallowed by sea or by air.

Shiloh quietly did his business in his booth on the Rialto, as conjectures and surmises sailed past his ears. Antonio did not appear, although his creditors did.

After the close of business, Salerio and Solanio della Fattoria dogged his steps in the street, on his walk north to the Ghetto

Nuovo. "Jew." They spat at him. "Dog Jew! Will you not look at us?"

"If I am a dog, best beware my fangs," he said, not slowing. "And tell thy friend Antonio that Passover nears. Let him look to his bond!" He stopped and took his knife from his robe, then from a pocket fetched a rind of kosher cheese bought in the ghetto. As they watched, he carved a slice and threw it at the pair. "Have you dined, pigs?"

"Your daughter married a Christian!" cried Salerio, dodging the cheese.

"That is true, and she is damned for it," said Shiloh, resuming his walk. "And so may you be damned, in your Christian Hell. You knew, none so well as you, of my daughter's flight."

"That's certain!"

Shiloh stopped again, and the twins stopped too. Shiloh looked at them in irritation. "Will you stop following me? Have you only one brain between you? And no homes to go to?"

"What will you do with Antonio's bond, devil?" asked Solanio.

Shiloh laughed. "Enforce it. Take his flesh."

The men looked horrified. "What's *that* good for?" asked Salerio.

"To bait fish withal. If it will feed nothing else, it will feed my revenge." He shook his head in exasperation. "Look you now, mannikins! Shall I explain what would be clear to a half-wit? Antonio has laughed at my losses, mocked at my gains, cooled my friends, heated my enemies—and what's his reason? I am a Jew. Hath not a Jew eyes? Hath not a Jew hands, organs, dimensions, senses, affections, passions? Fed with the same food—" He looked at the remains of the cheese in his hand, and tossed it at the pair in disgust. Solanio reached for it but it slipped through his hands. Immediately two curs appeared and fought for it at the twins' feet. "In a manner of speaking, I mean!" Shiloh went on. "Is a Jew not hurt with the same weapons, subject to the same diseases, healed by the same means, warmed and cooled by the same winter and summer as a Christian is? If you prick us, do we not bleed? If you tickle us, do we not laugh? If you poison us, do we not die?" The men were staring at him, whether baffled or stunned by his words, he could not tell. He spoke more slowly. "And—if—you—wrong—us, will—we—not—*revenge?*"

Salerio opened his mouth to respond, but Shiloh stopped him with a gesture. *"Bufones,"* he said, almost kindly, "the questions were rhetorical."

NAKED, JESSICA LOLLED on fine linen sheets in a Genoan inn. Her hair, thick, dark, and long, lay loose on her shoulders. The pet monkey was perched on the bedpost, and she fed it scraps of the sweetmeats they had bought on the docks.

Her husband sat sprawled on the carpeted floor, arranging piles of ducats between his bare legs. "But this is not all," he said.

"Greedy!" Jessica smiled at the monkey. "It is enough for a trading venture, if a small, shrewd one. No canary wine to Constantinople." Her laugh was brittle. "At any rate, this money will give us a start." Lorenzo was silent, and she wondered whether he was listening to her. She glanced over at him, and saw him staring at her, as pale as a death's-head. "What is the matter?" she asked.

"Jessica," he said slowly, "this is not even enough to cover my debts."

She sat up. "You have *more* debts? How great are they?"

"Great enough to swallow this sum and still bellow for more hard food."

"And you did not *tell me?*" Jessica's shriek set the monkey chattering. She jumped to her feet. She and Lorenzo stared at one another in horror, like Adam and Eve after their fatal meal.

"Where is the rest, Jessica?"

"What do you *mean,* you—you—*liar?*"

Lorenzo batted the air as though to wave away her insult. "Your father has more money than this!"

For a moment she thought she would strike him. "You stupid fool, did you mean me to ruin him? His money is in the bank of the Exchange, of course! Had I known we needed more, I would have planned things another way! This"—she stamped, and the coins on the floor jumped and toppled from their piles—"is only his week's profits. I got nothing but that and the spare jewels in his genizah!"

"His what?" Lorenzo blinked at her.

"Oh, you . . . *you!*" She sank back on the bed and placed her forehead in her hands.

"Jessica, we cannot live on this. You must go back and get his blessing!"

"I must *what?*"

"You could do it, i'faith! I have not stolen your virtue as he feared, I have properly married you! I may even give him a grandson who will be called a Venetian citizen. And as a Christian—as a *rich* Christian—that boy may one day sit as my father did on the Council of Ten! Think how the old Jew would like that! The di Scimmia name is four centuries old; he will be proud. . . ."

She sat staring at Lorenzo as he talked on, gesturing in his excitement. She felt the blood slowly drain from her face. At her shoulder, the beast she had bought with her mother's ring grinned, bounced, and chattered in her ear.

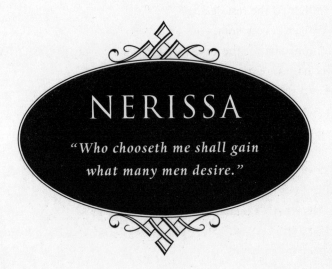

NERISSA

*"Who chooseth me shall gain
what many men desire."*

SEVENTEEN

WHEN NERISSA'S POSTERIOR bumped down the steep stairs of Shiloh ben Gozán's tall house in the Ghetto Nuovo, she minded the pain less than the thought of the bruises likely to follow. Purple and green would mar the fine surface of what Signior Pietro Delfin had the night before called a masterpiece of God's creation. "Perfect," he had marveled, appraising her from behind, then kissing his fingers and raising them heavenward. "Of a roundness rarely encountered on this earth, and the *rosiness!* I have seen the cheeks of Titian's Maddalena—"

"You have?" said Nerissa, thrilled. "'Tis no wonder the Protestants rage against our holy images!"

"I meant her face, of course! And too, I have noted the pink and white of the tender Christ child's visage as painted by that very same master in Rome, before he sold it to the cardinal Aldobrandini. The softness, the lushness, of the infant's tender skin, shadowed by the plumed feather held by Saint Jerome at his side—ah! It moved me to tears. But dear Nerissa, even *these* holy sights did not impart the ecstasies, or the gratitude, I now feel in regarding a work created not by the hand of man, but that of God! I should like to return here with my canvas and oils—"

A firm step on the floor above interrupted Signior Delfin's rhapsody. Quickly Nerissa turned, lowering her nightgown, and said, "Off you *go!* Did I not warn you? The master's private room is above, and he walks there at night sometimes. He told me if all was not quiet in this room after ten, he would throw me from the top step to the street, and now I fear he has heard you. . . ." She bundled the signior's cloak into his arms and pushed him quickly through the door that opened into the alley, whispering thanks for the gold brooch and the silver coin, and abiding his final kiss and his vow that he would come the next time with his paints. But Signior ben Gozán heard him running down the alley toward the ghetto wall, and threw open his casement, intending to pour slops on the fellow's head. Nerissa blew out her candle and watched her adorer disappear around the corner. Delfin escaped the slops but not the harsh voice calling *"Vaya, lujurioso!"* from above.

She had guessed that Signior ben Gozán would wait until morning to expel her so that he could show his daughter that he did it, and let her hear why. So instead of lying sleeplessly in the bed she and Signior Delfin had planned to rumple, she'd risen and packed her belongings—a modest store, but amplified during her six-month stay in the house by a satisfactory number of jeweled trinkets and a well-filled pouch of silver—and waited until the sun rose. She almost stole from the house before dawn, since she was not inclined to cook breakfast for a man who, before he ate it, would fire her from the open door like a ball from a Spanish musket. But then she remembered that if she did not ready the meal, the labor would fall to his daughter. This, along with the lack of farewell, would seem a betrayal to Jessica.

Besides, she harbored the small hope that a passionate plea for forgiveness would regain her Signior ben Gozán's goodwill.

That hope proved vain. *"Zoná!"* the signior said fiercely the next morning, pulling her by the elbow down the stairs to the open front door. Under his left arm he carried her trunk, which he tossed into the street first. Jessica had run from her room at the noise, and stood openmouthed at the second-stair landing, too angry or frightened to make a sound. Nerissa did her best to flash her an apologetic wink, though she then was sorry, since when ben Gozán saw it his face grew darker. He hissed something in Spanish about the putas of Venice corrupting his daughter. *"Your city floats in sin!"* he said, pushing Nerissa down the stairs after her trunk. "You all live by the doctrine of Epicurus; you defy the Law; you worship the body!"

Nerissa did not know who Epicurus was, and was unsure which law she had defied by enjoying herself with Signior Pietro Delfin, though as she flew through the air she resolved to find out. The third part of the master's accusation tugged at her heart, however. *You worship the body!* Could it be true? She delighted in adornment, and in the compliments men showered on her face, her form, her hair. She joyed in the appearances of others: the well-dressed donnas on the street, their ruffs wide and their hairnets dusted with silver; the men in their furs. And at times she came close to forsaking her prayers at night because her mind was busy with memories of intimate encounters with men's bodies. Even Signior Delfin, who was duck-footed and slightly pockmarked, had some fleshly features that had caused her to smile tenderly after his hasty departure the night before, as she lay in her sleepless bed. No doubt she should have directed her thoughts to more spiritual matters, or at least to planning where she might go from the ghetto.

"Float into your city and wash away!" Signior ben Gozán cried from the stair-top.

She was angry at the master for tossing her streetward. She had done her work well, and found it unfair that she should be cast from his house, where the wages were good and paid always on time. To shame him before the neighbors who had come out to their stoops to gawk, she raised her hand and curled her fingers into an insult she had learned there, among them, in the ghetto with the Sephardim. "Venice is not my city, signior!" she yelled. "I was born in Padua!"

Or near it, I should say, she thought, dropping her hand to smooth her red-gold curls. She bent and picked up her trunk, then began to limp toward the ghetto gates and the Fondamenta della Pescaria on the far side of them. *Shall I go back to the country?* But she could not, of course. Her parents had sent her forth to find good employment in a decent house. To creep back to their dwelling would be shameful, and they would not welcome her no matter what the cause. On her father's tenant farm lived nine other children, all younger than she. Busy with their brood, her mother and father would not keep her, a woman grown.

And as for Padua, her reputation was not good there.

At the age of sixteen she had walked barefoot on grape-stained feet from her father's vineyards to the home of a Paduan shop-keeper whose wife had died shortly before. The affable man had agreed to provide her with shoes, clothes, room, and board in ex-change for her weekly scrubbing of the floors of his house and cooking and laundering for him and his two daughters, aged twelve and fourteen. Nerissa had performed her work well enough, but her friendship with the elder daughter had pained the master, or at least the results of that friendship had sent him to tear his hair. Such was the affinity between Nerissa and young Katherina that the girl would slight her studies in music to help Nerissa make meals in the kitchen, just to hasten the labor and allow the pair time to rove the town. That Nerissa hooked eyes with shopkeepers' lads on those jaunts seemed not the worst thing to her master, though the town chattered that Signior Baptista Minola's hired girl was kissing Padua's favorite sons under moonlight by the boxwood trees. This talk was not good, but what Signior Minola disliked most was the other talk: the quick, bold, combative speech which emerged from his daughter Katherina's mouth at the supper board on the evenings after her walks with Nerissa, as though the servant girl had put the spirit of the war goddess Bellona into his daughter's mind.

"Why should a woman wear a veil to church?" Katherina would ask, tossing her head and eyeing her father with a challenging stare.

"Because of ancient custom, and—and—because the men—"

"Custom so ancient may be foul and rotten!"

"Ah, clever is your tongue, my dear. But the good maidens of this town—"

"Are simp'ring fools who do what they are told."

"And so should you, Katherina! 'Tis a child's office, as well as a woman's."

"A woman is full grown, no more a child."

"And you think *you* are full grown, and ready to bandy words with your betters?"

"Perhaps not with my betters, but with you."

In his confusion Signior Minola could only splutter, "*Who* presented you with these ideas?"

Turning the spit in the kitchen, Nerissa would hold her breath, praying, *Let her not say "the cook"!* Katherina, clever enough to guard her friend without God's intervention, would answer, "Think you I can't concoct them by myself?" or "They are extempore, from my mother wit!" Still, Nerissa was suspected.

In the end Minola, stammering his apologies, had sent Nerissa home to her parents, saying that though she was a fine house-servant, he could not harbor in his home one so intent on toppling its modest hierarchy. The charge was not fair, since Nerissa had never meant to sow dissent in the Minola household. In her walks with Katherina she had only voiced certain memories that seemed to strike a chord in the younger girl's mind; to pluck a string that awaited a touch. She had spoken of her country home, a place far too chaotic and needful of many hands' labor to be ruled by the law that boys mattered more than girls, or mothers than fathers. Nerissa had brothers, but had herself manned a winepress from the time she was ten until the next eldest, Giacomo, was big enough to take her place. Evenings on the farm had seen merry or sometimes violent argument around the supper board, in which the females took part as happily as the males. Her own mother had once poured a jug of spoiled olive oil on her father's head when he'd accused her of buying maggot-eaten cheese to save money, and he had known better than to punish her for it. Nerissa had done no more than share these and other such recollections with Katherina, but the stories had blown angry life into the young girl's imaginings, as though she were a dragon-painted sail and Nerissa's speech the magical west wind.

So Nerissa had been dismissed, and left Padua. She would not miss the lads of the town. Handsome some had been, but not one of them had made her heart tip into love. She walked not home-ward, but farther east, toward the coast. Behind her she left a town-ful of youths who spoke rapturously of her kisses by the boxwood trees, and a flying boot, thrown with enthusiastic displeasure from the signior's upper window by Katherina Minola.

———

AND NOW SIGNIOR ben Gozán had dismissed her as well.

The moon-eyed fellow whom Nerissa had allowed to carry her trunk to the Piazza San Marco was reciting lines of the poet Petrarch in praise of her skin. He invited her to lodge with him in his quarters by the western docks, but the fact that he had time at midmorning to trundle her belongings about and follow her, doglike, through the town gave her pause. Whatever employment he had was likely night-work, dishonest, and liable to bring her into trouble with the law.

So she gave him a coin and sat on her trunk near the doge's palace, gazing up at the fig-leaved Adam and Eve carved in pink marble and white limestone on the wall.

She had served three wealthy families in Venice, and while with each of them she'd paid close attention to genteel fashions of dress and habits of speech. She had learned much in these houses, but had been dismissed from them all for similar reasons. The first donna had disliked Nerissa's habit of sharing her eldest son's bed-chamber in exchange for lessons in reading. The second had caught her kissing a family cousin in the kitchen. So anxious had that lady been to remove Nerissa from her own husband's gaze that she had sent her, demurely dressed in some of her own mod-est clothing and with the best of recommendations, to a signior in the Rialto, where her husband did business. That signior had been Shiloh ben Gozán, who would now know better than to trust a Gentile's word on anything—or so, among other things, he had said as she flew from his front door that morning.

She herself had known better than to ask him for a reference.

The Campanile struck ten. She felt the dampness of the stones soaking through her thin shoes. A guard of the palace approached her and asked what she was doing. She said she was sitting on her trunk. He asked her what she would *like* to be doing, and whether, if it was what he would like to be doing, she might do it with him, when his duty was done for the day. She thanked him prettily, but said she hoped by that time to have found some more gainful employment.

He seemed friendly enough, and she was lonely, so she told him her morning's history. "Pray tell me," she asked him, "what law in this town does a woman break by performing the act of Venus with a man?"

"That will depend," said the guard. "Perhaps your Jew master referred to the law against adultery."

"Ah, but that concerns the breaking of marriage bonds. I am not married, and neither was Signior Delfin." She looked regretful. "There was once a married man who came to my rooms in the ghetto. A guest of my master's. He crept in after the evening meal when Signior ben Gozán thought him bound for home. Benjamin was his name, and he spoke so sweetly to me and I was, I must tell you, so curious to see a circumcised—well—i'faith, I will confess, *that* was adultery, and I asked Christ to forgive me for it! His poor wife, at home!"

The guard laughed. "Venetian wives are accustomed to it. And they do it too."

"Less in the Ghetto Nuovo," she said, frowning. "So I think."

"I see no harm in your amorous pursuits!" The guard winked at Nerissa. "Though Christ forbids them."

"No, he doesn't," said Nerissa. "I read a Bible through and through, studying my letters. Christ says nothing about my amorous pursuits."

"Well, the priest forbids them."

"The priest is like the fox who cannot reach the chickens and so thinks no one else should."

"I don't know that fox, but I know some priests who eat chickens. Which is to say, women."

"Then why should I not eat men? As I might say. Where's the harm? I do my work in the house. Why should the master call me *zoná?*"

The guard frowned. "What is that?"

"I am sure it meant *prostitute.*"

"Ah, here we have a law to contend with! If you take money for your work—"

"The act of Venus is not work."

"Still, if you are paid for it, then the law stipulates that you must be licensed, and live in the houses of Malipiero, allocated for the purpose. You say you read?"

"I do."

"Then I will help you. Go to the street behind the inn whose sign says 'Ox,' near the islands of Rialto. The castellans will ask you for six ducats, and the madam may examine you, but if under your garb you are as good as you outwardly seem"—he winked again—"they will give you a license and a room."

Nerissa frowned. "This is the law?"

"The law of the Serene Republic!"

"Well, I will try to follow the law." Nerissa rose and lifted her trunk. "I will try."

"I cannot leave my post, or I would carry that for you," said the guard.

"Another will come along, I am sure, signior."

"Speak to the castellan. The shorter one. Tell him Giuseppe spoke for you."

"You seem to know much of this place," Nerissa called back over her shoulder.

"'Tis a place of business, like any other." Cupping his hands, the guard spoke to the receding red-gold curls. "I may see you there tonight!"

EIGHTEEN

So NERISSA BECAME a meretrix in the houses of Malipiero, where she lived for five months. These were clean houses and the women were kept from injury by guards paid by the city. Men with knives were forbidden entry. She found herself able to choose among customers, though since she chose only men she liked, she called them friends, not customers. She did her best to avoid the married ones, although of course the men often lied. None of the men she met tempted her heart to fall. She was glad of that. She was freer that way, after all.

The women of Malipiero were a mixed lot, containing those of both good and ill temper and many in between. But they all liked Nerissa, who bought their good will not only with her wit and warmth but with the lore she'd learned in the country about preventing the conception of a child. These tricks of boiled herbs and moon-watching were helpful, she said, though it was well known they did not always work.

In the main Nerissa enjoyed the loose sisterhood of the prostitutes, and especially joyed in her freedom not to sweep floors or seek kosher food in the market or remember to avoid putting beef on a milk plate or serve both meat and milk at one meal. Yes, to Signior ben Gozán's frustration, she had mixed up the crockery. But how could anyone do all of that right? In the houses of Malipiero, she did not have to try. Here her job was to strut through the Merceria, and later to lie on a bed.

Still, it irked her that the silks and jewels that winked at her from shelves in the Merceria were forbidden her now by Venetian law. The guard at the doge's palace had not thought to warn her that necklaces and pearls and all manner of jewelry were denied the courtesans of Malipiero, and that they were made to wear gowns of a special color (a drab one at that!), as though women who lived by the law of Venus should walk in the habits of the Sisters of Santa Maria. Nerissa especially scoffed at the rule that forbade her to wear rings not only on her fingers, but *in any other imaginable place.* Now her trinkets from Pietro Delfin remained mostly hidden in her locked trunk, although now and then she gave in to her heart's promptings and slipped a bracelet on her ankle, where none could see it when she strolled the piazzas.

In any other imaginable place, she thought as she walked, and rolled her eyes heavenward.

The dress restrictions wore on her the more when she regarded the velvet caps and the furs of the gallants who bided their time in the Malipiero residences, drinking and jesting and disappearing into rooms with the women. Upstairs, they all stripped naked. But why, in other places, should she not look as splendid as they?

She put the question to a raucous wit named Graziano di Pesaro, who lay with her one night in her room. His ostrich-plumed hat hung from the bedpost, and his velvet sleeves, cut with fine eyeholes to let the red silk of his shirt peep through, now lay discarded on the floor. "I see you admire my gear," he said loudly, to vie with the laughter that flowed up the stairs, and the squawk of a pet parrot in Giovanna's chamber, next door. "*Do* you admire my gear?" He winked at her, but gave her no time to answer. "My man's gear, I mean, and my clothing as well! The doublet comes from France; the ruff"—he gestured toward a yellow-dyed collar that hung from a doorknob—"from Madrid. Not that they flew by themselves over the Mediterranean, no, no!" He laughed. "They were brought with much labor."

"Whose?" asked Nerissa. "I doubt it was yours."

"The weavers push their shuttles, and the ships that carry this merchandise strain against the winds, as much as I myself might strain to throw—"

"Dice?" quipped Nerissa, but Graziano babbled on as though he did not hear her, speaking of his new silk breeches and the detestable number of foreign workers in Venice and the speed with which a lucky hand of cards had repaired a portion of the losses he had suffered in an unfortunate shipping venture that had ended in Constantinople. She turned to the side, thinking his chatter might lull her to sleep, but just before she reached slumber her ear was suddenly caught by a gold-glowing gem in the silver nothingness of Graziano's talk.

". . . my good friend Lorenzo di Scimmia," Graziano was saying. "The cardinal was irked when he refused the seminary, after his father had labored for his admission, and after the cardinal himself had promised Lorenzo an eventual bishopric. Cardinal Grimani even assured Lorenzo, privately, that priestly orders were no bar to dalliance with women, as long as the ladies were hosted covertly, as was his own rule—"

Nerissa sat up and said, "What is this you say?" startling Signior di Pesaro, who was unused to people listening to him. "Lorenzo di Scimmia a bishop!" She laughed. "What folly!"

"Do you know him?"

"He is the same long-armed lover who climbed halfway up a wall last year to visit my mistress in the ghetto, and was sent back down again by a bucket of foul matter on his head!"

"What?! Jessica baptized Lorenzo with—"

"Not Jessica. Her father!"

"Shylock the Jew!"

"His friends call him Shiloh, but he is the man. And Lorenzo gives up a bishopric to pine for his daughter!"

"Why, Lorenzo is in the lower rooms now!"

"*Is* he!"

"Or in one of the uppers."

"More likely. But let's not speak of him, signior. Tell me more of this amorous cardinal!"

AN INTRODUCTION BETWEEN Cardinal Grimani and Nerissa d'Orocuore was arranged by Lorenzo, to repay the great man in some measure for his wasted efforts on behalf of the youngest male di Scimmia. For her part of the bargain, Nerissa happily agreed to ferry messages between Lorenzo di Scimmia and Jessica ben Gozán. Nerissa met Lorenzo in the houses of Malipiero or, once the cardinal had installed her in state, in her new apartments near the Ca'd'Oro. She met Jessica in the piazza, or at the fondamento near the Canale Grande and the Canale di Cannaregio, or in the Church of San Marco by the statue of the Magdalen.

Now she dressed in fur robes and wide godrun collars and towering jeweled headdresses, unlike the prostitutes who walked the city modestly, dressed in their simple gowns, without jewels on their fingers or ears or *in any other imaginable place.* Now, with her eyes lined with kohl and her hair held with silver combs, with her plunging bodice and her silver slippers, Nerissa looked like a lady of Venice.

She felt no deep passion, no slip-slide of the heart, for the cardinal. But she liked him well enough. He was kind, though unable, it seemed, to follow the law of the Church regarding priests and women. His own rule for Nerissa was a simple one. He was a busy man, a great favorite of Pope Gregory, and he traveled often to Rome. He would require her company at his palace only infrequently. At other times she might enjoy the luxurious apartments provided for her near the Ca'd'Oro, with their five rooms, their hired servant, their plush settles and damask curtains, and their oil paintings by Titian and Caravaggio on the wall. All was hers, and in return only one thing was asked. Nerissa must not use the place for any other merry meetings.

She tried. For two full weeks she carefully avoided the enticing gazes of men in the piazzas, in the Church of San Marco, in the Merceria. But in the third week she was felled by the limpid eyes of a workman who carted stone and boards toward the Rialto Bridge, and by his muscular legs, which brought to mind a sketch of David's statue, done by a Florentine sculptor, that she had seen in the cardinal's palace. After that first evening of the broken promise, it had seemed a small matter to open her apartments to other friends, if only, at times, to make merry with wine and conversation. She knew one day soon the cardinal would know of her lapse. But perhaps, if she begged his forgiveness, he would let her stay on.

Yet within the month a thing happened that prevented her caring what the cardinal said.

She had been descending the stairs of the Church of San Marco after vespers, considering what a bungle she had made of her confession. "I have borne false witness," she had said to the priest through his screen.

"To whom?"

"To a man to whom I am obliged."

"Is he your husband?"

"No."

"Is he your lover?"

"Yes."

"Why does he not marry you?"

"Ah, signior priest, I believe this question should be left for *his* confession."

"Do you presume to tell me my spiritual duty, young woman?"

"Look you, Father, I want only to confess that I have betrayed a trust."

"You are fornicating with a man who is not your husband. I find that a greater sin than a—wait, young woman!" The priest's whisper grew angry as Nerissa rose, sighing, and left the confessional.

"Christ, forgive me for whatever it is you think worst in my behavior," she murmured, as she glanced at the carved figure on the crucifix above the high altar. If the rules of the Church really did forbid her delight in the pleasures of Eros, perhaps there was something wrong with the rules.

Though perhaps not.

"Hssst," said a voice at her elbow as she descended the church stairs.

She looked to her side, and saw a slim young man dressed in the robes and cap of an acolyte. His voice was standing water, between youth and maturity, and his blue eyes shone. "I heard your confession," he said.

"You *what?*"

"I was lurking in the transept."

"That is against the rules!"

"No, it is not. It is within the rules. Can you cite me any portion of canon law that forbids me to lurk in the transept and hear whatever it is I hear?"

Nerissa gazed at him in perplexity, and said nothing.

"I thought so. You cannot. I have made a little study of it."

"Why?"

"I am interested in law."

"Why are you talking to me?"

"Because I liked your reply to the priest. I am interested in further debating the matter." The youth fell into step with her as she walked the piazza.

"Have you no duties?" asked Nerissa. "What kind of acolyte are you?"

"I will speak truth. I am no kind of acolyte."

"Then what in the devil might you be?"

"I might be a lawyer if I could grow a . . . No. None of this here. Take me someplace where we may be alone, and I will speak freely to you."

She stopped and regarded the fellow suspiciously. She was used to such gambits from men, but this lad looked unusually young to have mastered the way of eloquence, and there was something in his face that suggested he sought more than love's embraces—if indeed, he sought those at all.

"How old are you?" she asked.

"Twenty-six."

"Twenty-six! But your voice . . ." Nerissa peered at the youth's face. "*You* are no—"

"Not here!" The youth grabbed Nerissa's elbow and guided her to the edge of the piazza. Pedestrians looked askance at the odd pair they made: a well-dressed beauty, being briskly marched down the flagstones by an altar boy who gripped her arm. "He'll bring her to Mother and a whipping," a woman remarked to her companion, nodding knowingly. "Brother and sister."

"More like sister and sister!" the false acolyte laughed, pushing Nerissa into the street.

In her apartments near the Ca'd'Oro the clerical robe and cap were removed, and straight golden hair fell to the youth's shoulders. She was, sure enough, a woman, and the oddest one Nerissa had ever met. Apart from her hair, she lacked beauty. Her jaw was square, her voice was hoarse—"from smoking tobacco, shipped from the New World," she explained—and her form was spare and muscular, not ample and soft like Nerissa's own. Legs spread apart, as though she gloried in the freedom of the breeches she wore under the acolyte's robe, she sprawled on the settle where, two days later, young Jessica, fleeing her father's house for the morn, would sip nonkosher wine and fret about the whereabouts of Lorenzo.

"My name is Portia," she said. "Lady Portia Bel Mente. Have you any ale?"

Nerissa had not, but she poured the young woman some canary, asking, "*Where* did you find the cap and the robe?"

"I borrowed them from a church in Treviso."

"Borrowed?"

"Indeed, yes. The rules of that city make it quite clear that the ceremonial habits of the clergy are the property of the nobility who pay taxes in the region, and my father was a nobleman. So if it came to a debate I could make a good case that these clothes belonged to me. Not that I want them." Portia sipped the wine and smacked her lips. "I'll put them back straightaway on my return. But truly, I am interested in the point of ecclesiastical law you raised in your colloquy with that idiot priest."

"In my what?"

"Dispute. Debate."

"I had not meant to debate him, and I know nothing of Church law. I spoke only from common sense."

"'Tis sure, you have a great deal of it."

"I thank you, lady. And again, you were in the Church of San Marco to . . . ?"

"Spy. Had you not heard of the council of bishops that met here this week?"

Nerissa shook her head. The cardinal did not speak to her of Church matters.

Portia leaned forward in her enthusiasm. "A busy discussion of many points of ecclesiastical law, and of the pope's position regarding the Inquisition of Spain and whether such a venture should be maintained by the Church in Venice, whose Inquisition is exceedingly lax. And great argument concerning Venice's resistance to the Church's general policies concerning Jews and Moors in Christendom."

"You attended this meeting?"

"In disguise. I took vast notes; here, look!" From the folds of her discarded gown Portia removed a thick sheaf of paper covered with spidery writing. She hesitated, looking at Nerissa. "Can you read?"

"I can," said Nerissa. "Though not as well as you, I am sure, and I would not begin to look at *that* before I had downed at least three glasses of wine."

Portia laughed so that she spilled drops of her own wine on her manuscript. She hastily dried the pages on her gown. "There. Well, I cannot blame you, my lady—"

"Nerissa d'Orocuore. And I am not a lady."

Portia shrugged. "The word has an imprecise definition. You speak well."

"I have taught myself that."

"You have a strange name. *Goldheart*. But you are right—despite your strange name—much of what passed at this meeting was dull stuff, and a thousand times I wanted to intervene because I saw the answer to a question right away when the half of them would spend hours debating the tangles of it. But at length I could see that those bishops only wanted to hear themselves talk."

"Quite right you must be, I think."

"I am always right."

"And you have come here from Treviso by yourself? All alone from the Terra Firma?"

"Indeed, yes. I hired a boat. It was not difficult. Why should I not travel?" Portia rose and assumed a debater's stance, and Nerissa laughed. "I did not notice that *you* were accompanied by an army of servants, for all your fine wear," Portia added, seating herself once more. "You, too, are unafraid to walk alone."

"I once walked alone from Padua to Venice."

Portia frowned thoughtfully. "That cannot precisely be true," she said. "There is a watery gulf between Padua and Venice."

"Well, to be sure, I came part of the way in a boat."

"You should say what you mean."

"You can be most annoying, Lady Portia."

"So my father would tell me, before he lost his mind completely."

"Oh, I am sorry."

"There is reason to be." Portia sighed and looked pensive, then, after a moment, more cheerful. "Still, I will find a way out." After this cryptic utterance, she raised the wine bottle in a toast, and winked. "I will drink to you, then, Nerissa."

The wink and the confident voice touched something deep in Nerissa. To her own surprise, she felt her heart begin to tilt and slide. "No, Lady Portia Bel Mente," she said, holding her glass high. "To the pair of us!"

NINETEEN

NERISSA HAD NEVER before been drawn to another by the force of mind rather than flesh. She had felt a faint foreshadowing of the current that now swept her when she'd walked by the waters of the Brenta, in Padua, sharing lively banter with young Katherina Minola. But Katherina had been a child, and Portia was . . . a *woman*, although she baffled gender. She seemed neither male nor female, but both things at once.

The least of the confusion was the matter of her favoring masculine garb, like the robe and hat of the clerical acolyte and, the day after she appeared in that holy disguise, the jacket and breeches of a Venetian sailor (where *could* she have gotten the gear?). Her real androgyny ran deeper.

It was notable in her forceful gestures—her fist pounding a tabletop for emphasis, her manner of tossing her lovely blonde hair at the same time she was shaking her head in aggressive disagreement with a thing Nerissa had said, which she did many times during the hours they sat and drank wine in the cardinal's apartments.

A woman given to argument was not a strange thing. Nerissa herself had shouted at Signor ben Gozán and given him the figo the day he'd tossed her from his house. The women in the houses of Malipiero wrangled and pulled one another's hair, and Nerissa's own dear mother had been quick-tempered, prone to screech her dissatisfactions, and handy with pails of water or jugs of olive oil to throw on her children and husband when she saw the need. But Portia's manner of arguing was otherwise. She seemed to have studied debate as an art form, and now pursued it in her speech with cold passion. Never did she show anger; never did she raise her voice, except in a studied, rhetorical way. Yet she pounced on illogic like a cat on a mouse, in a manner that often confused Nerissa, but enthralled her, too. Portia had read much: Greek and Latin sages in their original texts, Biblical commentaries, canon law. Nerissa had read little beyond the Bible, in the house of her first employer in Venice.

But the two women spoke of everything that night, or what seemed like everything: of the wars between the Catholic states and the Ottomites, of the peculiarities of Englishmen in Venice, of the proper harvesting of grapes (about which Nerissa had much to say, though Portia still proved her in error on several points). Listening to Portia, Nerissa felt herself pleasurably floundering in a sea of eloquent discourse. She felt like Herod had when preached to by John the Baptist. Portia vexed and baffled her, but she loved to hear her talk.

And talk Portia did, nearly all the night. She continued to analyze the debate she'd just witnessed among the bishops of the Church, as she'd scribbled in the shadows like a secretary and nearly bitten off her tongue, she told Nerissa, to keep herself from lecturing those learned men.

"They are all shaking with wrath about Venice's recalcitrance to admit papal rule!" she said gleefully, pouring herself more wine.

"Venice's what?" said Nerissa.

"Resistance! Unwillingness! Venice is a merchant state, as well it should be. It thrives on its commerce. The clerics cannot see that its independence from Rome gives it its freedom, *and* its wealth. Oh, I wanted to tell them that the rule the Church would impose on nations would tax its own coffers in the end! Why not let the states profit and then take in the tithes?"

"But how would the Church constrain Venice?"

"Do you have any food?" said Portia. "So please you," she added, as Nerissa rose to ring the bell for her servant. "I have manners, you know, when I need them. But here we are sisters, are we not?"

"And sisters can belch at one another, is that the way?" asked Nerissa, moving toward the door.

Portia laughed behind her. "Well argued! I shall take care not to belch."

Nerissa spoke to her servant through a crack in the door. She paid him extra coin not to tell the cardinal of her visitors, but Portia was an apparition so bizarre that she preferred her manservant only to hear her guest's voice. A woman in breeches under a clerical gown would, perhaps, be too great a story for a young man to keep to himself, even for a ducat.

"But to my question!" said Nerissa, returning to the settle.

"I had not forgot it," said Portia. "The Church sits uneasy with the *estado mezclo* of Venice. How can there be a mixed state, it says? A state is Christian or it is pagan. At issue is Venice's harboring of Moors and of Jews in especial, without requiring their conversion."

Portia deepened her already low voice and raised her fist in the air. "'*No Christian state can thus survive!*' said Bishop Dembo. '*The Ottomites will destroy us!*'"

"Ah, marvelous! Had you thought to swipe the cope of a bishop rather than the gown of a humble acolyte, perhaps you might have said your piece after all!"

"And told them all, if discovered, that the signiors of the state and not the Church owned the gear? That would have been a merry disputation! A thing thought of too late, dear Nerissa. Though I wanted to speak my piece even as an acolyte. I wanted to tell Bishop Dembo that in their own lands the Ottomites tolerate Christians, Jews, and Moors to live side by side."

"Perhaps he knew it already?"

"If he did, he did not make good use of the information. And I would have reminded him that Pope Gregory himself frowns on forced conversion."

"That is not what I heard in the ghetto."

Portia put down her goblet and looked interested. "Nerissa," she said, "you will not tell me that you are a Jewess! Why, you look just like . . . like . . ." In a rare moment, she searched for words. "A Christian woman," she said at length.

"I am not a Jew," Nerissa said, laughing. "I worked for one in the Ghetto Nuovo. But none of the women I saw there had horns or tails."

"Only the men, then?"

Nerissa looked hard at Portia, sure she must jest. But beneath her blonde brows her guest's eyes were rapt and serious. "Lady," Nerissa said, "in all your study, have you come across no descriptions of Jews?"

"Yes, many!" said Portia. "There is Mandeville's *Travels,* which tells of the Jews' secret language and conspiracy to enslave Christians. There are John Foxe and Martin Luther, who prove most conclusively that the Jews are the brood of Cain. And there are of course the writings of Archbishop Alonso de Fonseca concerning the peculiar stench of Jews, the *foetor judaicus*, as well as the Jews' crucifixion of a child in La Guardia. De Fonseca was most specific about the horns."

"Your reading is wide," Nerissa said admiringly. She rose to answer her servant's knock, and returned with a capon, which she carved for herself and Nerissa. "Did Christ have these horns, as well? And Saint Paul? Did he stink?"

Portia laughed. "Admittedly, I have never known a Jew."

"I have," said Nerissa a little distantly, thinking of the man Signior ben Gozán called Ben the Lecher, and his visit to her room. She sensed Portia looking at her sharply, and sat up straight, clearing her throat. "If ever you had, you would see that the Ten only make them wear badges and hats for fear that Christian women will fall in love with them and bear their children."

Portia frowned. "But I have never read this!"

"Nor have I." Nerissa tapped her head. "It is extempore, from my mother wit."

"Common sense again," said Portia. "Well, here is what I think. Horns or no horns, I think the Jews' existence should be suffered in Venice for the good of the state. Our Church frowns on usury. The Jews' faith does not. Someone must practice it, or loan-giving will not be profitable, and Venetian trade will totter and then sink into the sea. We will be like the lost city of Atlantis in Plato's myth."

"I know not the myth, but I know that this very house has sunk an inch deeper into the Canale Grande since I came to it a month ago."

"Perhaps this is due to the weighty conversations you hold herein."

"Oh-ho-ho!" said Nerissa. "I would say that this is the first weighty chat these walls have ever heard."

"Or *floors* have ever *borne,* you should say," said Portia, delicately raising a chicken leg with her fingers. "To sustain the metaphor. Of sinking, and so on."

"What is a metaphor? For that matter, what is usury?"

"A poetic figure of speech, and lending money at interest."

"Ah, what my Jewish master did."

"Which?"

"The moneylending. Not the poetry."

"Then your Jewish moneylender is a pillar of Venice, upholding the city. Whatever the bishops say, why should he not continue his happy life here?"

Nerissa began to speak, but Portia held up her hand. "It was a rhetorical question, Nerissa! The Venetians are well disposed to embrace their flock of Jews."

Nerissa was quiet, thinking of the time Jessica had run home weeping because a woman had spat on her and torn her turban in the Merceria.

"Now you may speak," Portia said lightly. "What is your thought?"

Nerissa told her.

"But that unhappy event is regrettable and was avoidable. The woman who spat objected to the girl's false faith, and not to her person."

"That may be so, but she spat on my friend's back, not on her false faith."

Portia again raised a hand high, palm to heaven. "Yet! While it was wrong of the woman to do it, our mixed state is organized to prevent such unpleasant acts. The maiden may do one of two things." Flourishing both hands now, Portia told Jessica's options on her fingers. "She may stay in the Ghetto Nuovo, in peace among her own. Or she may become a Christian and discard the offending garments of the Jewess."

Nerissa felt herself half-persuaded. "In fact I think she is disposed to do the latter," she said.

"On the other hand, however, if her father wishes to be Jewish—"

"He *is* Jewish."

"If he wishes to remain so, and be a moneylender, let him also stay in the sphere the city accords him. Then all will be well for him."

"Yes, perhaps you are right."

"And how have you gone from serving a Jew to serving a cardinal?" Portia said.

Nerissa's eyes popped wide in surprise.

"Oh, do not think I can see Titian's portrait of Cardinal Grimani on the wall and fail to guess who commissioned it! How is it that you left that Jew's service?"

Nerissa smiled widely. "Ah, milady, that is a new story entirely."

PORTIA SEEMED SOMETHING less or more than a woman even when she slept, clad in a fine and frilly nightdress Nerissa had bought with the cardinal's allowance. She was tall, and the gown only came to her knobby knees. Her calves, which poked from under the hem, were finely shaped, but bony. She snored raucously, like a big man or an old woman, and scratched her stomach in a way that reminded Nerissa of her peasant father. And she lay with her legs splayed, just, Nerissa guessed, like the sailor whose clothes she had borrowed for her journey. Perhaps she was already dreaming of playing his part in a gondola on the morrow. Nerissa found her un-gainly appearance in sleep amusing, although Portia's sprawl and her snore forced her onto the floor and, at length, onto the plush settle in the next room.

The next morning Nerissa helped Portia wrap and pin her glorious blonde hair under the sailor's cap, and straightened her seaman's cloak. Portia bowed and kissed her farewell, and without meaning to the two fell into lively laughter.

THE LETTER CAME one week later, from an estate called Belmont, near Treviso, in the Terra Firma. *I am disposed to save all whom I find languishing in fearsome plights, and lift them to better lives,* it an-nounced in a bold scrawl. *Thus you must go with the trusted servant who bears this missive, as he leads you to Belmont, where you will be my companion. I believe the offer will find you grateful. Here is a draft. The banking firm it names will honor it, and supply you with ample means for passage. Do not bring the cardinal; I fear his company would be too dis-putatious even for me. He and I would agree on nothing except for the delightfulness of Nerissa d'Orocuore. Yours in warm friendship, Lady Portia Bel Mente.*

Nerissa unfolded the draft, and stared. Portia had sent her a note for five thousand ducats.

She had never seen a draft for money in her life, and had never dreamed of possessing one tenth of the amount this note named. Her first impulse was to cash it and flee from Venice, west and south to her own father's farm, and present him with the swag—well, a piece of it—to show her family that her failures had, in the end, proved lined with gold. But her common sense won out. Across the Gulf of Venice, she was likely to be hit on the head and robbed, and left worse off than ever before.

And besides, she had thought of nothing but Portia for a week. Ducats or no ducats, she was drunk with joy.

She would see Portia again, and hear her talk.

What was more, she thought, folding the letter and note and tucking both in her bosom, if Lady Portia could dispense such sums so readily, there were doubtless even more ducats to be had at Belmont. Nerissa could keep these, and send her parents some of those.

"Do you think my plight fearsome?" she asked the young servant in scarlet livery, who was dividing his appreciative glances between Nerissa's sumptuous apartments and Nerissa herself. "Your mistress doth," she added.

"If to live here with gold cushions is fearsome, then your bedchamber must hide some demon whom I cannot see," said the servant, looking as though he would like license to investigate the matter. "If I may say so. Yet my mistress is always right."

"Does her eternal rightness ever grow tiresome?" Nerissa took the delighted servant's arm.

"I . . . *should* not say so," said the young man.

"Fear not," said Nerissa. "I will give her a healthy dose of olive oil."

"What mean you, olive oil?" asked the servant.

She winked at him. "Common sense."

TWENTY

A GONDOLA FERRIED them to a vessel at the eastern wharf. Nerissa breathed the sea salt and heard the cries of the gulls and the laborers. She watched the black slaves rolling barrels into the bowels of the ships, and only briefly wondered whether those men would be moved by Portia's arguments regarding the justice of the mixed state in the Serene Republic of Venice.

Nerissa had written to Jessica and to the cardinal, who would be pleased that she, unlike his last mistress (long absconded to Florence, and now dead of the plague) had not carted off his silver plate. She had left the two letters with the servant of the place, thinking to let him and her friends amuse themselves guessing to what fairy-tale land she had fled.

Now, wrapped in a warm cloak, she stood on the deck of the ship. A sluggish breeze blew the sloop east around the point of the city, past the isles of the dead. Then the vessel tacked westward, and a stronger wind tightened the sails. The boat sailed along the coast of the mainland, north toward Treviso and the river Fiume Sile. On the widening river they passed farm buildings with red-tiled roofs, and brown stubbled asparagus fields. Far ahead of them, like strong, broken teeth, the white Alps bit the cold blue sky.

If NERISSA HAD read myths or romances, she would have thought Belmont sprung from the pages of Virgil or Ovid or Ariosto. As it was, she was able only to compare the place with the description of Eden in her old employer's Bible. Here were the streams from the river, watering the ample garden; there was the bellium and onyx stone sparkling in the mansion's white walls; there were the bright flowers that throve in the hothouse, even in the cold of January. This Eden was fantastic, but worldly too, for here she and Portia strolled clothed in satin and silver and cloth-of-gold, and musicians played lute, flute, and viol during supper, and afterwards, too. She and Portia dined on pheasant and berries and cream and drank the wines of a half dozen nations.

Portia seemed the end point of mystical journeys Nerissa had heard spoken of, by the merchants who came to the houses of Malipiero; by Signior ben Gozán and his Rialto friends at their suppers. For Portia's sake the silkworm performed its yellow labors, spinning itself into thread. For her, Incan laborers dug gold from their mountain mines; bent-backed East Indian women culled pods from their plants and pounded them into saffron; men picked oranges in sunny Seville and packed them on ships in December. Their conversions complete, these goods poured through the portals of Belmont.

With awe Nerissa watched barrels of grain roll into kitchens and storerooms, and counted the casks of new wine—fruit of the work of peasants like her father, who stretched their arms and bruised their feet to pick and crush their landlords' grapes. She marveled at Portia's serene acceptance, as her due and tithe, of things for which thousands labored unto death. Lady Bel Mente thought herself the arbiter of some natural order, unlike Nerissa, who in the Merceria had always felt like what she was, a courtesan buying jewels with a lover's money.

But Belmont was not the Merceria. Here Nerissa felt gifted, not purchased, by Portia's bounty, even by the unimaginable thousands of ducats she had sent Nerissa in Venice, in order, Nerissa was sure, that she might not be humbled by a constant need to ask for money. In Portia's presence she felt a guest and a friend, and though she set herself to help manage the vast household, she sensed that friendship was her real obligation. For Nerissa, that was no labor. She loved the duty, which was spiced with laughter. In addition, as anyone might, she loved the hothouse blooms and the fine fare and the constant music of Belmont.

And the place was awash with men.

Portia explained the visitors to her, and what was at stake in their presence—no less than the mansion itself, and the lands surrounding it, past the poplars, out of view of the wide windows that looked over the garden. There were the sheep farm and the vineyards and the fields of grain and poppy. There were the holdings that yielded over fifty thousand ducats a year, to none of which Portia could lay claim without claiming something else, or someone else, or rather, letting someone else claim both her and her money. That someone, she told Nerissa with a look of ill-hid distaste, should be a husband.

So said her father Bel Mente's will.

"Absurd!" said Nerissa, holding a half sausage out to Portia's silky spaniel. The dog snapped at it and gobbled.

"Agreed," Portia said. "Until I marry, I have been given a mansion, but not possessed it. And I hate the thought of a husband! But I'll have the money somehow, won't I?"

"Will you?"

"I *will*," Portia said, her eyes like steel. "I'll puzzle out a way."

"A way to have money? But Lady Portia . . ." said Nerissa hesitantly. They were strolling in the hothouse, near the January roses, while snow fell outside. "You sent me—"

"Five thousand ducats, yes. Not from Belmont. From an investment I made by proxy on the Rialto. An English lord who visited here advised me to buy shares in something called the Levant Company. A group of Londoners who do business with the Turks. I profited a hundredfold."

"But—"

"Even Venice frowns upon trade with the Protestants—not to mention the Moslems—but it is not precisely illegal, and commerce should know no borders. I understand what you ask. You want to know why, if I can profit so mightily on the Rialto, I should care a fig about my father's estate."

"I would not go so far," Nerissa demurred. "But more of this profit from investments might lessen your need to—"

"Marry, and be more than a guest in my dead father's home. Yes. But such an outcome would not satisfy me, Nerissa, though I grew as rich as Reyna Nasi."

"I have heard of Midas, but who is Reyna Nasi?"

"A very wise Jewess."

"Horned?" Nerissa teased.

"For aught I know! She traded in spice and started a bank, and now she has more gold than the sultan!" Envy and admiration fired Portia's eyes. "She was arrested and fled Venice before I could do more than read stories about her, and now she dwells in Constantinople."

"Well, why not be like her?"

"And get arrested?" Portia said, laughing.

"You know that is not what I mean!"

Portia shook her head vigorously. Her gold hair was sparked with flecks of light, caught from the torches and braziers that warmed the hothouse. "I will be no Reyna Nasi. I will be Portia Bel Mente. I will have my own money and my father's, too." She punched a fist in the air. "I will solve his riddle!"

Fascinated, Nerissa studied her flushed face. Though Portia spoke of money, what burned in her eyes was not greed, or not the usual kind. After only a short time in Belmont, Nerissa knew Portia's passion was the knot of a logical problem. She wanted silver and land, but most of all she wanted to win a game against high odds. Her mind craved puzzle and challenge like a man craved a woman's kiss. Portia would torture her mind and rack her brain to bend the world to her desire, and find pleasure in the struggle. The road to her father's estate lay through a husband, and she hated the thought of one. "Do you think I would be ruled by a male master?" she asked Nerissa, who guessed the question was *rhetorical*. Yet Portia would turn her back neither on Belmont nor on her own desire to rule it. She would win her father's game, and when all was done her triumph would be total.

Her eyes glowed with an inner assurance of victory. Meeting those eyes, Nerissa could not believe she would fail.

Until Portia told her the second condition of her father's will.

———

"How can she win it?" Nerissa asked Graziano di Pesaro. Her old customer from the houses of Malipiero was gawking at the tiled floor of Belmont's lobby.

"How can they know how many slabs of marble will fill a room?" Graziano asked. "How is it that just the right number are ordered?"

Nerissa looked at him in silence for a moment, then answered, "I believe that when there are tiles in excess they are sold back to the supplier, or used somewhere else in the place."

"Ah!" said Graziano, clapping his hands. "Most ingenious. And what was it you asked me, my little lecherous nymph?" He raised a brow lasciviously.

"Nothing important," said Nerissa, wishing the suitors gone so that she and Portia might catalogue the fellows' faults. She sighed. "Something *rhetorical.*"

She had not been especially pleased to see Graziano among the group of Venetian gallants who had arrived by swift ship the evening before, since she found his chatter tiresome. But he'd attached himself to her like a burr, winking and nudging her in not-very-covert congratulations for her shrewd self-elevation in fortunes since they had known one another in the houses of Malipiero. She let him know quickly that Portia was well acquainted with her history, fearing more than anything else the tedium of heavy-handed jests with double meanings, and suggestive private glances in the lady's presence. "She will know what you mean, and knows it already," she told Graziano. "And do not think Belmont a bawdy house just because I am in it."

Graziano's face fell, and Nerissa, repentant, took his arm and offered to show him the grounds. He had time enough to wander. He was not himself a suitor of Portia's, but had come as a hanger-on to Bassanio, whose ears had pricked up in Venice at the news of the death of the old grandee who'd been Portia's father, and the rumor that the signior's wealth was available to the man who won his daughter. Bassanio was not the only one to try to profit from the news, which had circulated rapidly at a Twelfth Night masque. He had thought himself clever and quick in obtaining a loan from Shiloh ben Gozán, with Antonio as bondsman, and in ransacking the Merceria for shoes with silk roses on the tips and dyed Spanish ruffs for his neck and velvet capes and sleeves cut with eyelet holes. "I am a Jason," he had exulted to Graziano. "I go in quest of a golden fleece!" "To fleece *her*, you mean," had replied Graziano, who sometimes showed sparks of wit.

But when Bassanio had appeared in the office of the agent of the wharf, fresh in his courting clothes, to hire a boat for Belmont, the tired functionary had directed him toward a list on the wall and told him to add his name. "A ship has been chartered," the agent said. "There is room for one more."

Bassanio had wished to appear to Lady Portia in solitary splendor, descending the ramp of a hired sloop (rentable for five hundred of Signior ben Gozán's loaned ducats), trailed by a servant in peacock blue livery. Yet no such boat was to be had, so great was the mob bound for Treviso, so he reluctantly joined the throng of hopeful Venetian Argonauts on a leaky vessel that pulled out onto the westward river several weeks after Nerissa arrived at Belmont. He did manage to squeeze his new servant on board, though Giobbo slept below with the rats. At the last moment Graziano, not wanting to be left out of anything sportful, jumped onto the deck. This precipitated a pileup of crushed-velvet doublets and snagged earrings, as well as a hubbub of curses issuing from perfumed mouths, and a flurry of manicured hands smoothing beards on delicately barbered chins.

At the least, travel was less costly this way, though Bassanio lost the extra ducats in a game of primero played under the mainsail.

Once in Belmont the suitors had more idle time to play bowls and turn cartwheels in the snow, all of them hoping Lady Portia would glance through the window of the room where she spent hours sequestered each morning and notice a shapely leg in orange-tawny. Nerissa knew that Portia would converse with only one man a day, and that the rest of the time she spent writing and reading. If she looked out her library window at all, it was to take notes on ridiculous sights about which she and Nerissa might laugh in the evening, when they sat by the fire, their stays unlaced (though Portia hardly needed stays), and tippled ale and wine.

In the days, Nerissa performed the duties of household management, ordering an army of cooks and grooms and footmen to prepare meals and clean stables and ride hither and yon to the dwellings of local learned men, bearing messages from Portia requesting the loan of still more books. Nerissa's labor was easy. She found much time to walk in the hothouse and flirt with the men, many of whom tried to pinch her bottom, which was still bruised from her flight down the ben Gozán stairs.

"All to the good," Portia said of the suitors' lechery. "You are to separate the sheep from the goats. Let them pinch you if they will, and then send those ones packing."

"That is fine for *you,* who spend your days reading in a cushioned chair!" said Nerissa. But she did not truly mind the duty, which came naturally to her.

Indeed, she found one young man's discourse so sweet that she barely wanted to yield him to her mistress. Though as it turned out, he decided for himself that the lady Portia was not, alas, for him.

Nerissa had been twelve weeks in Belmont when she heard a loud voice announce, "I am Petruccio Bella Lingua!" Clad in pink muslim sewn with silver diamonds, she was humming and listing names in a ledger. At first she ignored the man's announcement, but she looked up at the slap of his hat on the table beside her. There he stood, a giant of a fellow with a barrel chest and arms that could have wrestled a stag. His face was plain but his eyes pleasant, wide-spaced, and snapping with wit.

"And what might you be?" she asked him politely.

"I might be a bear from the Scottish highlands. But I'm not! I am a gentleman of Verona, that, hearing of your beauty and your wit—"

"Waste not your *own* wit. I am not the lady Portia."

"Ah, but perhaps I speak of *you!*" he said, not balked in the slightest.

"What can you have heard of me?" Nerissa asked, a little nervously.

Signior Bella Lingua dropped to one knee and began to sing in a Paduan dialect a song about the white of her skin and the gold of her hair, only he reversed the words so as to praise the gold of her skin and the white of her hair. "I find you foolish," she said, though she laughed. "How do you know I come from Padua?"

He jumped to his feet. "Any man could tell that, from your speech. Now. You have guessed me aright; I do come to woo the lady Portia, though the agent of her port is most beautiful as well as quick-witted, and if I fail with the lady, which is impossible, I will take you away with me to Verona."

"No, you will not," said Nerissa. "Here is my place, with her, whatever befalls your suit. And be not so sure of yourself!"

"Why should I not? I am the man who, single-handed, defeated the Ottomites at Lepanto some nineteen years gone."

"When you would have been, as I guess, six years of age."

"Five! Four years afterward, I went on a seafaring venture to Mexico. My ship was struck by lightning in the middle of the Atlantic, and sunk, leaving me, the sole survivor, treading water and conversing with a dolphin. He carried me a mile or two, like Arion's water steed, before he tired. I swam the rest of the way myself. Once in the New World, I defeated a tribe of Indians by snapping their heads off with my teeth, and returned to Italy with a thousand pounds of gold."

"Swimming?"

"With one arm. Once home, I celebrated the fourteenth anniversary of my birth with a hundred ladies from Padua—the town where women are loveliest"—he winked at Nerissa—"and as to how we disported ourselves, modesty and thy blush forbid my recounting the tale."

Nerissa, of course, was not blushing, but laughing. Behind Petruccio a line of men was forming, and voices were starting to grumble. Nerissa tucked her pencil behind her ear, and folded her list into her waistband, to prevent suitors from altering the order of names. As she stood she brushed from her lap a tiny hoptoad, one of the many that throve in the nooks and crannies of the well-appointed house. "I must supervise the gardeners' work in the hothouse," she told the waiting men, who began to groan loudly. She held up her hand. "Complainers shall not be entered in the log." The groaning dissolved into whispers of dissatisfaction.

"Come, Signior Petruccio," she said. "I will advise you of the challenge, which will be as nothing to one who has traveled the globe at sixteen to pluck a hair from the beard of the great Cham."

"Did I tell you of that?" said Petruccio, happily taking her arm.

"You were on the brink of it, I know."

But to her surprise, once she had told Petruccio of Portia's father's conditions, he would have none of them. "A fool's enterprise," he said bluntly.

"But why?"

"This is no test of wit, or even discernment. Only blind luck! Look you, lady, I would hazard my life for a thing I knew was worth the risk. And I would undertake to turn a sow's ear to a silken purse, and do it, too. But I'll know something of the goods before I buy. I'll take their measure. What do I know of the lady, besides that she's rich? Not that that's nothing."

"It's something to you, I think. It's why you came here."

"True enough."

"I think you would like her. And she you." But Nerissa's heart quailed as she said it. The truth of her words struck her. This man *did* seem a match for Portia. Portia had said she was disposed to love no man; that she wanted to find a way—short of postmarital murder—to reject all her suitors, and still win her father's wealth for herself. But Signior Petruccio's wit could change her mind.

And then, what place at Belmont for Nerissa?

Still, she could not bring herself to betray Portia by discouraging a man who might bring her friend happiness—who might change Portia's game entirely, and for the better. If he wanted no part of Belmont, let the decision be his. She looked at him, raising her eyebrows questioningly.

"No," Petruccio said. "Were it a contest of wit, I'd undertake it. Something to *do*. Not mere guesswork, as in a fairy tale. I'll be off. You come with me."

"No!" Nerissa said, laughing. "I am not what you wish. I have little money, despite my gown."

He looked disappointed. "Well, perhaps I will marry you anyway," he said. "You've a ready wit. And I could sell the Veronese lechers glimpses of your loveliness."

"My golden skin and white hair?"

"Think how pleased they will be to see that those colors are in fact reversed!"

"No, signior," Nerissa said, touching the petal of a flower.

"What!" he scoffed. "Reject me for roses in March?"

"'Tis not for roses," she said. "Another thing keeps me here, good signior."

"Another *thing* will keep you there, in Verona."

"And so you will win me with your bawdy speech?"

"Parrots will speak. Petruccio will *do!*"

"You will do well enough, I think, for any witty maiden."

"Not *well enough*. A husband past all hoping!" Petruccio slapped Nerissa so hard on the back that her pencil flew from behind her ear and bounced on the hothouse floor. He bent to retrieve it for her, but looked up as he knelt. "No kicking when I am down here."

She shook her head, laughing helplessly. "Signior Petruccio, I am pleased by your attentions. But I've made my choice, here at Belmont."

"For money?"

"For love."

"Show me my rival!" the big man bellowed.

She covered her ears. "Good signior, I think you would exhaust me in a day."

"Yet I need a wife! One witty and beautiful! And rich!"

Nerissa took back the pencil and pulled folded paper from her waistband. "I think I can prefer someone. In Padua."

"I have a friend who would host me in Padua," said Petruccio thoughtfully. "She is wealthy?"

"Very comfortable. Her father's a dealer in dry goods, but he owns five shops in the city. Ask your friend if he knows of the family Minola. Here is the direction."

"How does she look?"

"Her looks are no hedge," said Nerissa, writing.

"How long has it been since you saw her?"

"Some six years, I think."

"Six years!" said Petruccio. "Then she may already have found a husband."

"No," said Nerissa, tearing a corner of the paper. She pushed it into Petruccio's paw. "I would wager she has not."

THAT NIGHT SHE and Portia were both in ill humor.

In the afternoon, after Signior Petruccio's departure, the lady had cruelly mocked a suitor who had come very far to woo her. His face had displeased her, and she had therefore done what she could to dissuade his suit before he even assayed the test he must pass to win her hand. The man had persisted, gracefully bearing her sharp insults, which had continued after he'd lost the challenge. At length she had slammed the door on the disappointed fellow, dusting her hands and pronouncing herself well rid of him. Nerissa, who until today had enjoyed mocking the foolish fortune-hunters behind their backs, was for the first time angry with Portia for her behavior, though she had tried to contain her distress before the other servants.

"You might have waited until he was out of the house before attacking his appearance," she said now, as they toasted their feet a foot from the fire.

Portia yawned. "My jests were for you. He was so vain he had no inkling of what I meant; he thought all a compliment."

"I am not so sure of that. He was doing his best to be gallant. And I saw your maidservant wince when you laughed at his face."

"The Moor? She does not matter."

"How not?"

Portia made a clicking sound with her tongue. "Well, from now on I'll be kind to all of them, to please you, Nerissa," she said crossly, rising to take the book she had left open on a table that afternoon. "All the peacocks and monkeys and parrots and popinjays who want my money, not me. Now I will read what Cicero the orator says. I am sure he will not chide me, like you do. I'faith, I thought I had left off being scolded when my father died. I'm not your child!"

"No. You are my friend," said Nerissa, with some heat, wishing for a moment that she'd gone off with Signior Petruccio. "And as your friend I must tell you that though your mind is a thing of beauty, you have no heart!"

TWENTY-ONE

I<small>T WAS PARTLY</small> because of that quarrel, their first, that Nerissa did what she did the next day.

By late morning the Venetian suitors were gone. They had enjoyed themselves mightily playing primero and hazard at Belmont, but in recent weeks they'd decided to think still another while on whether to assay the wooing challenge. This had been their second visit, en masse. United in gamesmanship these three months, they all now thought themselves friends, and spoke of returning from Venice replenished with more borrowed money, perhaps in a flotilla of four ships, rather than a single galleon; racing one another, in fact! They were all Argonauts, they claimed. Between them Portia and Nerissa called them the Ship of Fools, though not today, because today the women did not speak to each other.

Graziano and Bassanio kissed Nerissa's hand before they embarked. "We will return in a fortnight," Bassanio pledged. "Borne hither on the wings of our eagle-like sailing vessel!"

"I take this to mean you will drag into port on some leaky and overpriced scow," Nerissa said, holding her pencil and calendar. "What day?"

Bassanio calculated. "Good Friday, of a certainty."

"With so many visits, and a new suit of clothes each time, you wear out Signior ben Gozán's endowment," said Nerissa.

"Whose?"

"Signior Shylock."

"Ah," said Bassanio. "Well, perhaps next time Lady Portia will let me face the wooing challenge, which I am certain to win. And in the meanwhile, Graziano and I will put what is left of our money into a new trading venture that Signior Antonio has thought on."

A faint look of worry crossed Graziano's face. "There are rumors, Bassanio, that Antonio's present ventures—"

"I shall not believe them!" Smiling, Bassanio held up his hand. "Surely his argosies will return in triumph from the Indies and the New World. And then he thinks to send a shipment of rosaries and kneelers to England."

"That Protestant nation to our north?" said Nerissa.

"Is it?"

"The wind is in our direction," Graziano interrupted, holding a finger in the air. He dropped it and kissed Nerissa's wrist. "We must be off, fair courtesan!"

Nerissa snatched her hand from his grasp. "By all means, go. I find your company less sweet when you call me whore."

"I said courtesan, beauty!"

Bassanio put a hand on his friend's arm. "He has not the graces," he apologized. "But he is . . ."

"Short?"

Graziano winked at Nerissa. "But to speak of endowments, you know what is said of men of small stature and theirs."

Nerissa wanted to remark that she had more than once seen the saying disproved, but thought it wiser to say naught. She feigned not to understand the jest.

Bassanio's absurd servant, Launcelot, scurried from house to wharf, bent by the weight of two trunks he held under his arms. "I was thirty minutes finding the peascod-padded doublet!" he complained.

"Begone, Argonauts." Nerissa waved as she walked toward the mansion.

In the lobby she sat in a damask-covered chair, her heels tapping the fine Carrera marble of the floor. She knew that behind the closed doors of the main lower chamber Portia was entertaining the wealthiest suitor yet to throw in his lot with the rest. He was a noble of Aragon, in Spain, and he spoke Italian vilely, although Portia, with a pointed glance at Nerissa, had counseled her servants not to mock the poor man but to remain as grave as English Puritans from now on.

Nerissa kicked the leg of her chair, frowning. She had chosen not to view the wooing test today. She wanted to show Portia she had not yet forgiven her for her behavior the evening before. After Nerissa had called her heartless, Portia had risen from the settle with her book and gone out of the room and slammed the door. And her frostiness this morning was proof that she herself had not forgiven Nerissa.

The nobleman was almost as wealthy as the Spanish king, made so from his family's sponsorship of Cortés the explorer, who had come back from the New World with Indian gold. Were he to wed Portia, the two of them would be fantastically rich. Of course, he would have to meet Portia's father's conditions first. But Portia claimed to be smart enough to steer her own choice toward success.

She had wanted Nerissa's collaboration in that choice. Was she now angry enough to choose on her own, and thrust Nerissa from her life?

From behind the presence room's locked doors she heard Portia's silvery laugh. Her stomach clenched. *Enough listening and brooding,* she thought. *I will see to the kitchens.* Abruptly she stood.

It was then that she noticed the handsome soldier lounging against the far wall of the lobby. He was tapping his belted sword with his finger as he silently appraised her. When she caught his eye, he put his hand to his breast and bowed, a quick duck of a dark head. Then he smiled. He had excellent teeth, of a whiteness rarely seen in Italy, although common among the Spaniards Nerissa had met in the Ghetto Nuovo. His eyes were quiet and dark, and his bearing was graceful: a straight, soldier's back, though he stood not at attention now, but at ease, with one leg bent, his knee jutting forward and his foot on the wall behind him. The hilt of his fine silver weapon caught the sunlight that slanted through the high windows of the portico.

"You are not a suitor," she said, returning his gaze evenly.

"I serve in the guard of Aragon, lady," he said, gesturing toward the closed chamber doors. He spoke with a Spanish accent that recalled to her the voice of Signior ben Gozán, though her Jewish master's Toledan inflection had weakened with time. This man spoke as though he had left Spain only a month before, though his Italian was smooth enough.

"I am not a lady," she said.

"I am not a gentleman, though I hope to rise in rank."

"In the army?"

"Where else?" He took his foot off the wall and walked toward Nerissa. "If you are not a lady, perhaps you would not begrudge an hour of your time to a common soldier."

She looked at his trim form and the arm that rested on his sword hilt. Even relaxed, the arm's muscles swelled the broadcloth of his military coat. She looked up, and saw, again, his eyes appraising her. He slowly smiled. "I am not called again into service until this evening."

"I may not be called again into service at all," said Nerissa. "So I think I may spare you something more than an hour."

GRAZIANO TOOK MY *measure, for all he's a fool,* thought Nerissa, as she lay beside the soldier later. She ran her hand along his arm. *Still,* she thought, *this was pleasant.* She met the man's eyes. They were very dark, and, on close examination, very strange. They seemed to absorb and swallow the light. She looked away from them at his hand as he raised it and caught her fingers. For the first time, she noticed his ring.

It was polished silver. Five clean, twisted strands of metal comprised the band, which was set with a black-streaked turquoise stone. "Who gave you that?" she asked. "Have you a wife?"

"I have."

Nerissa felt sick shame descend on her. Why had she not thought to ask him? Why had she not thought at all?

"She did not give me the ring. And as we speak she is doubtless fucking a servant in the house where she works, so talk not of her." He threw off the sheet and sat up. She saw scars on his broad back, and touched them lightly. "What are these?"

"What are they not?" He turned his head, and pointed. "These mark the beatings of my father. This, a knife fight in Córdoba. And this came from a shattered musket ball. I felt its fire in the seige of Lepanto."

She stared at him. He could not be less like the fantastical Signior Petruccio, but here was the same lie. "You could not have been at Lepanto. You would have been only—"

"Nine years of age. I was a ship's boy in the Spanish arm of the Christian League. I will not even begin to tell the things done to me there, by our own side's soldiers. Now I am twenty-eight, and glad to turn mercenary. My ship was sunk by a storm west of England in fifteen eighty-eight, when the Spanish Armada was blown to hell. Not me, though. I clung to a spar and the current took me to Calais. I almost drowned. But I washed onto shore and then limped back to Aragon to get my pay from my noble master. I came on this fool's errand with him, but when it's over I'm done with him and the armies of Spain." He untied a skin of red wine from his sword belt, squeezed a swallow into his mouth, and offered some to Nerissa.

She declined, saying, "But you spoke of rising in rank."

"And I will, but not in Spain," he said, capping his wineskin and wiping his mouth. "In Venice. I hope to be a lieutenant, and perhaps an *arráez*."

"A what?"

"*Un capitán.* Manhood is proved by the sword. A slave driver for whom I once swept floors told me this, and I find it to be true. *La pura verdad.*"

"I cannot speak your language," said Nerissa.

"We do not need to talk," he said, reaching for her again.

BUT AFTERWARD HE seemed to want to. He told her he had taken the turquoise ring he wore from a box in a vintner's shop, where it had lain with some other pieces of jewelry and coin. The wine merchant had carelessly left the box open on a table when he went in the back rooms to bring out a cask of canary for him. "I took it because I had seen it before, and it pleased me. Only the devil could know how a Venetian vintner came upon it, but it could be no other than one that had sat on my old master's shelf. I watched him piece the silver strands while I swept the floor of his workplace. He said it was for his daughter, that one day she would make a gift of it to her husband. But he thought better of that, I suppose; the stone was flawed, and he gave it or sold it to another woman. I saw it later on that second one's husband's finger." His face went dead and blank as he said this.

"Where?" Nerissa asked.

"At a Shab—at a secret meal."

"What kind of a meal?" she asked. *A Shabbat meal?*

"'Tis not thine affair," he said coldly. "It was a kind of secret meal held in Spain. I'll not put myself at such an event again. I quit the practice when I left Toledo."

"What brought you to go from there?"

"I hated the place. Half its Christians were Jews or Moors. And some—" he stopped himself. "Why do I speak to you of things dead and buried?"

"*I* know not. Say nothing if you wish."

But he went on. "It is that I did the Church's business in my own city, and the result was, a woman died. It came to light who had racked and burned her. The officers and the priests were known, even by the woman's own family, and shunned by some. Even by some Old Christians. Her father was a hidalgo of some note. He was dead of drink a month after his daughter's death. Some thought he killed himself." The soldier half-smiled. "At any rate, I did not wish my part in the thing known."

Nerissa moved as far away on the couch from the man as she could, and pulled the linen sheet up to her chin. "Do you say that you were—"

"An Inquisitional torturer? Of course not. I was an innocent child. They paid me in silver and sweets. I only did my duty; only told an officer where the Jews might meet."

"And you feel no guilt," Nerissa said, horrified.

He looked again at her with his dead stare, then smiled in a friendly way. "Why should I tell you of my guilt? Are you a priest? What's it to you if I hate Jews?"

She drew her breath in suddenly, without knowing why she did so. He looked at her sharply. "You are not one."

"No. But I have known some."

"So have I." He laughed harshly. "The first was my own father." He pointed to his back. "He who gave me these stripes, though he'd some help with that from my mother, before I was big enough to kick her in the teeth. And that was after he'd left us both, and she'd put me out to beg. Gave me some bruises to help me look needy." He looked at her quickly. "Had I any plan to live more in Spain, I would not have told you my father was a Jew."

"In Venice Jews declare their faith openly. They have no secret meals. They are free."

He laughed hard at that. "Free? I have seen the Jews in Venice. Wearing their heart-shaped badges on their sleeves, and their red caps. Denied any post in the civil affairs of state, or in the army. I despise them."

"Why? Because your father was one and beat you, you despise all of them? Your mother, I guess, was a Christian, and thrust you out to beg." Three months of banter with Portia had sharpened Nerissa's speech. "Thus it follows you should hate all Christians."

"I do."

Nerissa gave a brittle laugh. "And Moors?"

"Them worst of all."

"Why?"

"Because they wear their difference on their skins. Their black-ness is even clearer to the eye than a heart on a sleeve. By Janus, I should pity them. Moors cannot hide their evil."

"Evil?" Tears came to her eyes, as she recalled the cause of her quarrel with Portia: her friend's mean-spirited mockery of a suitor's face. "Perhaps all men are evil. But what can be evil in *skin?*"

"Why should I tell my thought to a woman?" the soldier said. "Whores and thieves and tigers, all of you. I say I do not care for Moors. But I will serve one in Venice. A fine jest, is it not? I have a letter from my old master in Spain, whose floors I swept. A general reference. He wrote it for me some two decades ago, before I left him, though perhaps it was only to get me to go. I did my work well enough, but he hated my singing."

"Ah, you sing?"

"No. He once made a fine sword for a Moor turned Christian, a great hero who is now a general of the armies of Venice. The Moor's command is the place for paid soldiers; they come from all over Europe to fight the Turks. And I served with him at Lepanto, though I was but a child. I'll tell him of that and show him my scar, and I'll show him my letter of preferment. And I'll send for my whore of a wife. In Venice I'll find my fortune."

"I hope you will speak more courteously to your hero Moor than you have to me since I satisfied your desire."

"Of course I will," said the Spaniard. "I know the trick of it. I am not what I am. Now let me sleep."

Within five minutes he was breathing deeply, enjoying the quick rest of a soldier. Nerissa looked at his handsome face and his beautiful form, and felt disgust at both, and at herself. Her heart was suddenly touched with longing for her friend, for laughter by the fire with Portia. She missed Portia's beautiful mind.

This one was a devil. She'd tell it to Portia, who had doubtless made short work of the lord of Aragon, and was looking for Nerissa at this moment to tell her how. Portia would agree that though the soldier's parents were monsters—if he spoke of them truly—that fact in no wise excused his own villainy. Why, in the houses of Malipiero Nerissa had met women who'd been served worse; who'd been raped by uncles and beaten by a dozen men; and who yet showed cheer and hope and kindness. This fellow, on the other hand—well, he deserved what ill luck befell him!

Was it not, in fact, a Christian duty to rob him? So Nerissa thought as she wrapped a sheet around her and then lightly plucked his purse from his sword belt. She tiptoed toward the door of the small closet where they'd lain. She put her hand on the latch, and then turned to regard him once more. He lay still save for the gentle rise and fall of his chest.

So she crept back to the bed, knelt, and carefully slipped his ring from his finger.

TWENTY-TWO

SHE HAD NOT expected Portia's tears.

"You said I had no heart," she wept. "Well, now you see that I have, for you have broken it."

She looked almost beautiful, with her face flushed the color of a rose, and her fine yellow hair spread on her shoulders, like spun gold against the white silk of her nightgown. But after two hours of sobbing, her eyes were puffy and red.

"How could you have done it?" she asked Nerissa again. "How *could* you have? I thought you were good, but you are cruel. You wanted to hurt me and punish me. Did you not?"

And Nerissa, herself weeping at her friend's distress, could only tell her that yes, perhaps a little, but nothing like this, nothing like so much as this. It was only a man, and she herself was common coin, Portia had known it when she brought her to Belmont. What was the matter?

"You have—"

The Moorish servant woman opened the door of the chamber, bearing new linens for Portia's bed. Seeing Portia's state, she stopped in the doorway. "Leave us!" Portia cried. Nerissa looked at the woman sympathetically, but nodded. The woman bowed quickly and left, closing the door.

Portia looked at Nerissa. "You have been mocking me, with the suitors—you, with your beauty and your graces. *Odd Lady Portia; she walks like a man and talks like one, too.* Have I not heard it? *She is disputatious and far too clever. No man would take her if not for the money!* As though I *wanted* a man! Did you think I had not heard it?"

Nerissa looked at her in amazement, and shook her head. "Lady, you may have heard those words at some time—"

"More than once, from those simpering damsels of the neighbor estates, who have pretended so long to be brainless that the fiction has become the fact!"

"But Portia!" Nerissa knelt by her side on the carpeted floor of her chamber. "You have never heard me say those things. I am your friend!"

"And well I pay you to be my friend!" Portia said hotly, sitting up straight in her oaken chair. "Are you not grateful?"

The women's eyes locked in silence. Portia's cheeks paled, as though she knew she had said an unforgivable thing, and awaited the slap of courteous, cold rejection.

But Nerissa only said softly, "Did you think you had to pay me for that?" She put her head in Portia's lap and smiled up at her. She made an antic face, and Portia began again to cry, but to laugh at the same time.

Nerissa slid back on the carpet. "Portia, I think you the most wondrous person I have ever seen! A thing of wild beauty! You stole an acolyte's gown!"

"As a point of law, the Bel Mente family were entitled to the thing," Portia sniffed, raising a finger.

"You spied on the bishops! You—you—i'faith, your talk is a draft of Ponce de León's Fountain of Youth. 'Tis like music, though I don't always know what you mean. I hazarded the loss of a good life in Venice to come to you, not knowing what you meant with me. Do you know I prayed and read the cardinal's Italian Bible beforehand? Paul wrote to the Hebrews that faith was the surety of things hoped for. I shut the Bible and sailed here on hope that your friendship was real and lasting. I would pay *you* silver to be near you," she added, laughing. "And so here is some!" She threw the Spanish soldier's purse in Portia's lap. "I took it from him as he lay, naked and sleeping—"

"Ah, don't!" said Portia. The look of pain had returned to her face. "That you *touched* him! Did you not know how I loved you?"

Nerissa looked at her solemnly. "Perhaps I did not."

"Well," Portia said miserably, after a moment. "I suppose you will leave me now? You have the money I gave you; you may share it with your family; I will not demand its return."

"No," said Nerissa. "No. Many think they want fleshly embraces, but a deeper longing fires them. I think I have learned this. Bodies have their beauty. But I want something else more."

"What, Nerissa?" sniffed Portia, drying her eyes gracelessly with the sleeve of her gown.

Nerissa rose and kissed her. "Someone to talk to."

"WE MUST FIT you with a husband," Portia said the next day, as they strolled in the springtime sun. At their heels bounced her brown and white spaniel, hoping for a game of fetch.

Nerissa laughed. "How can that suit our plans to be merry companions?" She reached down to pat the dog.

"I will think hard on the matter, but 'tis plain you cannot do without some sort of man."

"'Tis better to marry than to burn, saith the Apostle."

"An interesting claim," said Portia pensively. "Did he mean it was better to marry than to burn in hell, or better to marry than to burn in the flames of thwarted fleshly desire?"

"Which do you think?" Nerissa knelt for a stick and threw it toward the trees. The spaniel raced for it, but then veered, distracted by a mud puddle.

"Or did he mean it was better to marry than to run about with a torch in one's hand, burning fields, buildings, spare useless papers—"

"Such as thy father's will?"

"There you have hit it!"

"Walk slower!" Nerissa said, puffing. "Better to marry than any of that, I suppose. But I will have no husband who would separate us. And that may be much to ask of a man."

"I'll construct a bargain that will make him grateful," said Portia, stopping beneath a tree. "I'll tell him that we are to remain joined, like two cherries on a stem."

"Hmmm," said Nerissa. "Well enough. But I claim the right of refusal, if your arguments fail to persuade me." She put her hands in her pockets, and cried, "Ah, this! I had forgot it!"

"What?"

Nerissa pulled the turquoise ring from the folds of her apron. "I also stole this from that Spaniard."

"Nerissa!"

"My defense is that he also stole it, from its proper owner," Nerissa said, handing it to Portia. "And that he was the devil."

"A plausible defense," Portia said, squinting at the ring. "A turquoise!" A strange look crossed her face. "I saw a ring like it somewhere, long ago. . . ." She thought a moment, then shook her head. "Perhaps it was only a dream." She tossed the ring in the air with one hand and caught it with the other. "So you stole this from the devil. I saw your devil walking graciously behind his lord to their Spanish ship today. The lord looked glum, but the fiend's look was serene enough. He seemed not to have noted his losses."

"Well," said Nerissa, "you know how the devil behaves. Always putting a fine face on things. And to whom could the fellow complain? You are a great lady, and I hold the keys of your house. He is only a common soldier."

"Common sense, as always." Portia put the turquoise ring on her finger, where it dangled loosely. "The devil's ring is too big for me. But we'll think of a use for it. We will give it some great meaning, to make the suitors tremble."

"It was made for a man, he said. The stone is flawed, but the silver is heavy enough. And the work is fine. I think you might use it as a gift to make someone *grateful*."

Portia colored. "Ah, Nerissa, you think me a proud fool, do you not?" She dropped the ring into the pocket of her man's breeches.

"I have told you what I think of you."

"Heartless?"

"Perhaps not."

"Heart outweighed by brain?"

"Perhaps," Nerissa conceded. "But for all that, I love thee."

New tears came to Portia's eyes. She reached for Nerissa's hands and held them tightly. "Then teach me, Nerissa."

"Me? How could I teach *you*?"

"I have more life before than behind me, and small training in kindness. I may fail many times before I succeed. But I have watched you."

"Watched me how?"

"With my suitors. With the servants, who love you. With the stray cur I kicked near the Ca' d'Oro, the day we met. You called him back and fed him a bun. Be my heart, Nerissa. And teach me how you do it."

Nerissa was red as a poppy. "Portia, I am not as good as you think me."

"This depends on our sense of the word *good*. It has two—"

"Stop!" Nerissa laughed. "We will debate meanings later. I will stay! Now let us go and watch the new barks fly in at the dock."

"Ah, the suitors. Borne by hope?" Portia asked.

Nerissa looked at the stately mansion, at her friend's laughing face, and at the gold-set diamonds that hung from Portia's ears, in odd contrast to the rough woolen shirt and breeches the lady always favored for walking. She thanked God for her ridiculous fortune, while, at Portia's question, she shook her head. "Few men even know what they hope for. Yet to Belmont they sail, on the wings of desire."

PORTIA

*"I may neither choose who I would nor refuse
who I dislike; so is the will of a living daughter
curbed by the will of a dead father."*

TWENTY-THREE

"WHAT WE NEED," said Portia, "is two very stupid men."

"Lorenzo di Scimmia is already married," said Nerissa, wrinkling her brow in thought. "Unfortunate. Yet not so, neither. He shows a streak of willfulness that would vex your purposes."

Portia turned a page in the ledger where she logged her investments. "Do I know this Lorenzo?"

"You shall." Nerissa's new, heeled slippers clicked on the marble floor as she crossed to hand Portia a letter. It had come that morning, and was signed *Jessica di Scimmia*. It told all her friend's news: that she was fast married; that the family di Scimmia had disowned Lorenzo, denying him his meager patrimony and shutting their door in the Piazza Patriarcato to the pair of them; that their welcome was growing overripe at the Milanese estate of Lorenzo's third cousin, from whom Lorenzo had borrowed a thousand ducats, since lost in a bet on hounds.

"His new wife, my dear friend Jessica, begs our indulgence and requests that she and her husband might visit for a time," said Nerissa.

"Jessica?" Portia peered at the paper.

"The daughter of my former master, the usurer."

"Ah, the little Jewess."

"Do not call her that, my dear. She writes that she has been sprinkled with magic water and is a Christian now. And especially blessed, because especially poor."

"Then why should she not come to Belmont? Every other fortune-hunting fool does. Write. Tell her she may come as soon as she likes."

"Thank you, Lady Portia."

"I think it wise that she chose a Christian, but how did she end up with a penniless one?"

"He lied to her about his debts, and she misjudged the sum he needed. He led her to think what she could bring from her father's house would pay for all. She knew he was no sage Solomon, but she never guessed he thought she had access to *all* her father's money. Look, she writes it here." Nerissa tapped the page. "He thought Jews kept all their wealth in bags of gold in their walls!"

"And they do not?"

"Portia! You asked me to school you in heartfulness. Let me begin by instructing you that Jews are human, with their own hearts, *and* brains. They are not fairy-tale ogres!"

"I have never read fairy tales, my dear."

"No, I suppose you have not." Nerissa removed a cat from a chair and took its cushioned seat. The cat yowled in protest, but quieted when Nerissa placed it in her lap and scratched its ears. Then it stiffened, quivered, and pounced on the fringe at the edge of the Turkish carpet. A small frog jumped from the fringe, escaping the clawed paws by inches, and disappeared between the wall and the back of a settle.

"Anyway, I jest," Portia said, returning the letter. "This Lorenzo sounds like a prize fish. 'Tis a pity that I did not hook him before your Jessica did. I could have afforded his losses. Paid his debts and put him on a halter, as per prior contract before admission to the game. And I would have made him agree to live in Venice, and not annoy us here."

"No, 'tis as I said, dear Portia. A di Scimmia is not for you. If you and I are to live as we wish, unhaltered ourselves, we need men who are not only idiots, but who can be led like oxen with rings in their noses. Men who will believe anything, and do as they're told."

"Yeesss," said Portia pensively. "Well. Bassanio and Graziano return this Friday."

Nerissa rose, dumping the cat from her lap, and looking stricken. *"Graziano?"*

PORTIA WOULD HONOR Nerissa's right of refusal, but was confident that with her golden tongue she could persuade her of the rightness of her choice of Nerissa's husband, or of any other plan that came to her mind. Had she not, at the age of four, defeated her father at chess? At seven, had she not proven her uncle wrong in a debate over the bounds of his property, by locating a provision in her grandfather's deed of ownership concerning an easement? Her father had not noted the clause until she brought it to his view, and had been grateful to her then—the profit was his own—until she suggested that his knowledge of contracts would improve if he learned to read Latin as well as she.

That, it seemed to her now, was the moment their bond had begun to crumble.

He had loved her when she was three. But as she grew taller, strolling his parks and reading books as big as herself, Signoir Bel Mente grew more hunched and sour. Before she was eight he'd exhausted three wives in vain pursuit of a son. When the third woman died, his desire shifted course. Then he thought only to raise a daughter discreet, demure, and gracious enough to win the heart of a nobleman's heir. A former soldier, perhaps; one who had proved himself with a sword, fighting pagans, and was now disposed to embrace the fruits of peace, now that the Christians had battered the Turkish fleet to near-ruin in the Gulf of Lepanto. The fruits of Christian peace in Signior Del Mente's view were rich holdings of land, a marble-floored mansion, and the fruitful bed of a docile young lady.

The son of a nearby Trevisan landowner seemed promising quarry. But the signior's plans for the youth were modestly threatened when Portia, in her fifteenth year, stole the boy's father's horse and rode it halfway to Verona to buy a case of books with her birthday money. Signior Bel Mente had given her the silver to spend on slippers and gowns with the guidance of an old female servant, and combs to amplify the singular beauty of her hair. But the coin went for Tycho Brahe's *De Novê Stellâ,* Galileo's treatises on the undulation of the pendulum, and three books on Roman law so thick she'd had to pull them back in a cart. She'd justified the theft of the horse by pointing to a century-old Trevisan statute that set limits for free-ranging livestock. In a rage, her father returned the beast to its owner, who accepted the horse, but made it plain his family would not accept the girl.

Portia could not see why she was not the heir her father wanted. She lacked interest in swording, her father's passion, but what good was soldiery to the acquisition of wealth? Prosperity, she learned early, was a matter of shrewd investment, careful land management, and exploitation of law. So she pored over the statutes and rode to the courts, taking notes and sitting with the students in the galleries. She spoke to the men of Treviso regarding doings on the Rialto and the Bourse and the Dutch Exchange. Her father should have thanked her for her counsel, in her view. But he didn't. He railed at her for roving, and he hated her disputatious manner. Never did she shriek or wail or weep or pout to win arguments, as a regular female would. She only coolly stated her points and refuted contending logic. She studied oratory and practiced rhetorical gestures: the open hand for *munero,* the offering of a money concession; the closed fist for *pugno,* the refusal to yield; the empty palm for *demonstro non-habere,* the showing that what is requested cannot possibly be supplied. She would stand in her father's library, her hair pulled back with a rough piece of string, and theatrically punch the air while her even voice proved, in eloquent terms, that he was a fool, a buffoon, a waster of incomes that had been better poured into the sea than invested where he had put them (why not in Asian pepper before the price rose, as she'd warned it would?). He lacked the brain of a kicked cur, and should not presume to argue with one who had taught herself seven languages, including Latin and ancient Greek.

She should have been beaten, of course, but he was loath to raise his hand against his only child. So he threw her books into the Fiume Sile, which was the first thing he ever saw put her into a rage that was real and not a rhetorical display. Her anger frightened him so much that he locked himself in his chamber rather than her in hers. He stayed there for a day, listening through the door as his eighteen-year-old daughter gave commands to local fishermen for dredging and drying. He never asked whether she recovered her books that way. The question would have been logical, but by the time he unlatched his bedroom door the next morning, wearing his late third wife's yellow farthingale and a pair of her pearl ear-rings, he had abandoned logical discourse forever. He would fight his daughter in a new way, becoming the fool that, in her rhetorical flights, she had so often claimed he was.

For all her shrewdness, Portia was never able to tell whether her father's madness was fact or strategy. What was clear was that it served his desire to flee her conversation. He would seem sane enough when requesting partridge eggs for breakfast, but would crow like a rooster and crack one of the eggs on his head when she came with her account books and proposed a land purchase that called for his signature. He could or would not allow her to act as the heir he was convinced should be male, and whom he seemed to have despaired of acquiring.

Seemed to have, that was, until his last revenge was revealed.

It happened after his funeral, at the reading of his will. As Portia heard the testament's terms declared, her tears ceased to fall and her face became first pallid, then red with rage. Her real grief for her father's loss—a loss that, she was sure, had befallen her years before he'd actually died, or begun to be mad—was swal-lowed in her anger at how he now reached out of the grave, a god on paper, to convert her back into a smiling poppet of three.

"By these present let it be affirmed," the lawyer droned, *"that the lands, moveables, house, incomes, rents, and additional possessions of Francesco Bel Mente be held in trust for the future husband of Portia Bel Mente, and that this man shall be he who without prior instruction and fully by chance and hazard correctly chooses the special magic lovely splendid and well-tooled box containing my daughter's picture, which box shall be one of three caskets of gold, silver, and lead which I bought in the shop of Maestro Julian del Rei, swordmaker of Toledo, in 1567, because my daughter craved them when she was small and far more charming than she grew afterward."*

More was written in the will, of course. The servants were to run naked thrice about the barns on the Feast of the Epiphany, and the signior's spaniel was to be dressed in a cloth-of-gold vest and toasted with mulled wine on alternate Easters. But Portia shut her ears to the colorful provisions that enthralled the other hearers of the will. She rose and walked stiffly from the room to her own chamber. She did not throw herself on her silken sheets to weep. Instead, she knelt by the wall, next to the silver box the will had named, now filled to the brim with sharpened quills for her writing. Beside that box lay the gold one, which held paper. She removed the stack of parchment, along with the box's false bottom, made by a carpenter whom she had paid to do the task five years before. From the box's real base she drew out her bound copy of commentaries on the laws of inheritance in the Serene Republic of Christian Venice.

TWENTY-FOUR

Although Bassanio had told Nerissa he would return on Friday fortnight, he seemed to have meant the pledge figuratively, with Friday signifying Monday. He arrived at midmorning three days beyond the promised time, and one day after Easter, a holiday whose most notable event had not been the mass, but the spaniel's investiture in gold raiment and mulled-wine toasting, a ritual whose date had fallen on this year. Bassanio descended from a rag-sailed passenger boat wearing tight plum-colored hose, a Spanish cape of purple silk, and a green velvet cap set with a red brooch. Behind him skipped Graziano in a blue satin jacket and pantaloons and a splendid velvet cap of his own. (He later confided to Nerissa that his hatter was owed eight ducats for the thing.) The crown of Graziano's hat was stitched with parrot feathers.

Trailing the two gallants' steps came Bassanio's servant Launcelot Giobbo, puffing under the weight of a clothing trunk.

Portia watched from her study through her opened window of leaded glass, as Nerissa, flanked by the Moorish servant Xanthe, curtsied to the men at the dock. Looking displeased or perhaps a little ill, Xanthe lent Launcelot assistance with the trunk. He spared her the leer he generally cast over the maidservants' bodies, which surprised Portia. Perhaps Launcelot had no interest in Moorish women.

Nerissa led the two gentlemen, gesturing toward the beauties of the new-blossoming gardens as though inviting them to stroll there. Portia saw that Nerissa was trying her best to show greater than usual warmth to the guests, and was sorry for her, since she was sure the parrot feathers on Graziano's head had increased what misgivings Nerissa already had for Portia's fine plan.

"HE IS A popinjay among popinjays!" Nerissa had shrieked earlier that week, when Portia had proposed Graziano for Nerissa's future spouse. "A pretty piece of flesh, I'll grant you, but how could you match me with him until death did us part?"

Portia had looked at her coolly. "I thought you liked pretty pieces of flesh."

Nerissa sat abruptly back in her chair. Her skirts billowed about her, then settled like a shaken sheet. "Ah, this is the game. You have not forgiven me for my Spanish soldier, so you wish to punish me for life by saddling me with a mean-spirited fool."

"A chatterbox, I'll grant you, but mean-spirited?"

"I have heard him rant in the foulest terms about the aliens in Venice, those whom you praise for giving life to our markets. The Jews, the Moors, the French, the Germans, the horrid Dutch Protestants—he would strike them with axes, he would whip them with ropes, he would dump them in brine! Each group has a flaw.

Hollanders are drunkards who would eat the world's profits—as though he's not, nor would not! The French sell inferior wine and talk through their noses—as if he knew anything of grapes, or I found *his* squawk musical. The Moors work for less than a Turkish soltani and so keep the good men of Venice begging instead of earning their bread carting crates on the docks. He, of course, would not lift a hand to carry a basket of peaches from the garden. And as for the Jews—ah, there's no end to it! The Jews make gunpowder and sell it to the Turks, to be used to blast Christian soldiers into three parts, and all upwards into heaven! Jews spread the plague, they—"

Portia held up her hand, chuckling. "I begin to think better of thy Graziano already. He is a man of thought."

Nerissa laughed scornfully. "No thought is behind his ranting. He only repeats what he has heard his father and his friends' fathers say."

"Well, his father may not be altogether a fool. I would deny that the men of all nations should be shipped from Venice. Let them show their colors on our Rialto! Yet there is something to these complaints. Have I not seen the bad behaviors of all nations on display here in my own house, where the Spaniards and English and everyone else flock in, bleating and baahing like goats and sheep?"

"*Lady* Portia, you have met one of each sort, at most. Would you tar whole nations with the sins of particular men?"

"A good answer! You begin to learn logic."

"More than logic. 'Let he who is without sin—'"

"Enough!" Portia raised her hand. "Bible later, at our prayers."

"You rarely have time for those, with this getting and spending and plotting to get more and spend more, my dear lady," Nerissa chided.

"I promise you, I will find time for confession this evening, and will tell the priest all my horrid wrongs. Meanwhile, I have you as my scourge for the daylight hours. Now, attend!" She clapped her hands, sitting straight at her table. "Let us address things in the proper order." She ticked off her list on her long fingers. "One. I cannot evade my father's will; it is ratified and well applauded by the nitwits of Venice, and might as well be set in stone. Two. Nevertheless, I will find a way to make its restrictions answer to my desire. Three. That desire is a sheeplike husband foolish enough to follow my direction in all things fiscal once he has acquired those things according to the terms of the blessed will. Four. Such a sheep, name of Bassanio, is expected this week. He will descend down the ramp of his hired vessel full ready for the slaughter. Five. With him will come Graziano, a *pretty piece of flesh* with strong views on the bad habits of foreigners, and were Bassanio to win our marriage game, said Graziano *would* serve as a passable match for Nerissa, to satisfy the lusts of her flesh—"

"And to give me a child as foolish as the sire?"

"Or as wise as thee! And we'd make Graziano follow Bassanio's lead in sheepish obedience. We'd have him sell us his desirable absence in exchange for a gambling allowance. Oh, Nerissa, he would do it!" She leaned forward in excitement. "He mimics everything Bassanio does, down to the discharge of a sally of leaden wit that falls from his mouth like a ball from an ill-fired cannon."

"This fantasy has gone too far."

"Not far enough! I *will* persuade you."

The dispute was not settled by the time of the Venetians' arrival. The women spent ten days bickering like a married pair, as Bassanio played cards with Graziano or sat in the lobby and kicked the rungs of a chair, as Nerissa had on that unhappy day of the lord of Aragon's visit two weeks before. Within those ten days three more suitors arrived and departed in discouragement or horror after being informed of the full terms of Portia's father's will, as so many men had done before them. Among other absurdities—such as to dine on raw plovers' eggs seasoned with garlic on the morn of the wooing challenge, and to dance a morisco while clad in yellow garters—the will required each gamesome man to sign a contract forswearing further wooing anywhere. The rule would apply even if the man guessed wrong, and failed to win Belmont and Portia. In that event the clause would have been nearly impossible to enforce, and both Portia and Nerissa guessed that the men who had thus far failed at the game had no intention of staying celibate. Indeed, two weeks past, the lord of Aragon had exited the house muttering something about the sail-route to the house of a rich heiress in Barcelona. But the language of Bel Mente's contract was fearsome for some, as were the one-in-three odds of passing the marriage test, and the veil Portia wore over her face while the men made their choices.

Bassanio of Venice already knew what Portia looked like. He had visited the house when her father was still alive, having heard that a mad Trevisan was trading priceless silver for tiny swamp frogs. That rumor had inspired Bassanio to boat from Venice to the isles of the dead, across the lagoon, and to hunt for small hopping beasts in the low, wet foliage that grew among the stones of the crowded cemeteries. Though he had stained his velvet breeches with kneeling, he had managed in three hours to collect ten tiny frogs in a wire-lidded box. He had boarded a sloop to Belmont and had nearly completed a transaction with Signior Bel Mente when Lady Portia had burst into the room wearing a man's riding breeches and brandishing one of her father's Spanish blades.

"Look, daughter!" her father had crowed, holding out his hand. "Three exquisite hop-toads in exchange for this old, dusty head of Christ done by Cellini, good for no purpose I can see—what, daughter!" He'd jumped to the side, upsetting his chair. The toads had escaped severing, jumping to safety on the floor, while both Signior Bel Mente and Bassanio had rushed from the room to evade Portia's sword of justice. Signior Bel Mente had retired, shaking, to his chamber, and Bassanio, crestfallen, to the dock to await the sloop's return. The frogs had made their way to the damp parts of the kitchens, where, months later, Nerissa scooped eight of them into her apron and deposited them in the garden. The remaining two had multiplied, so that every so often at Belmont, frogs appeared on mantels or mirrors or on the delicate ivory keys of the virginals in the grand presence chamber.

Portia's sword had been daunting, yet Portia herself had been wonderful. She'd looked a very Athena to Bassanio, her plain, severe features exalted by her righteous wrath at the spectacle of an unjust bargain in the making. Such a woman would suit his need, he thought. He could wear her on his arm like a buckler, and she would quell the tongue of rumor with her fire-flashing eyes. She would be a goddess of the household, seeing well to the hiring of servants and the pricing and buying of goods for their table, which would be amply stocked not only with fine fish, flesh, and fowl but with witty guests brought from Venice. She, of course, would be grateful to have a husband to watch over her more public fortunes, especially one with so capable an advisor as that master of commerce, Antonio di Argento.

Nor did Bassanio forget Belmont itself, with its damask curtains, velvet settles, and Turkish rugs; its farmlands extending miles downriver toward Venice, and its Cellini silver. Assisted by the sage investment advice of Antonio—who would be often a guest in residence—how nobly the estate would prosper!

And so, the word of Signior Bel Mente's death had found Bassanio full ripe to woo the man's daughter.

Why not, thought he? He was a well-favored fellow, and though his fortunes had ebbed of late, his clothes would not show it.

And no doubt she'd forgotten about the frogs.

"A LAMB TO the slaughter," Portia said to Nerissa with satisfaction. She let the curtain drop on the view of the rainy garden where Bassanio and Graziano were walking and shielding their feathered caps with their gloved hands. "It is April, and time for weddings. The other Argonauts have fallen by the wayside. This is the third visit of this pair. Now is the time."

"Why?" asked Nerissa. "Because three is a lucky number?"

"*Imprimis,* because Bassanio thinks it is; and second, because he has worn the plum-colored hose twice. He's almost out of money."

"Ah."

"And now, let us think which casket to put my portrait in this time. We must consider quite carefully. Which one will be the most hint-worthy?"

"I think you had best choose." Nerissa smiled. "Let me take charge of finding the new horrors for the other two caskets."

"Can you catch one of the frogs?"

"Ah, they could not breathe in there."

"You and your warm heart for cold-blooded things. Would you take the same care with a leech?"

Nerissa shuddered. "I would not. A leech would be apt for Bassanio, but I won't touch one. Better a pound of dirt in one of the caskets, and in the other, what of a deck of false cards, so if he fails in his choice he can still make his living?"

Portia clapped her hands. "Excellent! Now, the lead casket this time, I think. As for the placement of the three boxes, I think we must bring them out from the walls into a semicircle, on altars, in the middle of the room, with me also on the rug and you at the far wall—"

"Portia." Nerissa sat with her hands folded in her lap.

Portia stopped in midgesture. "What is it?" She dropped her hands, looking suddenly anxious. "You'll not abandon me in this venture?"

"Of course I will not. But if you want Bassanio, why do you not simply tell him the answer?"

Portia shook her head. "It would ruin the game."

"Game! My dear, we speak of a husband. It is your life you put at the hazard."

Portia again raised both hands, palms upward. "I cannot help that. All is spoiled if I do not play by the rules."

"I cannot understand you! To hint and hint til Bassanio guesses aright is hardly keeping thy father's law."

"Ah, but it is! He says nothing against hint in the will."

"If we go by the will, we must allow that it also says the man must choose *fully by chance and hazard.*"

Portia raised one palm higher, and with the other hand pointed theatrically at Nerissa. "You need not quote the will to me; I know it by heart. I say he does choose by chance and hazard even if I hint, because who is to say he will understand the hint?"

"Portia, I care nothing for thy father's law, but if you wish to abide by its spirit—"

Portia stamped her foot in a rare display of genuine anger. "*My father was insane when he contrived this plot!*" she cried. "What should I care about the *spirit* of his mad rules?"

Nerissa spread her hands in bafflement. "Then rip the will and do as you please! Or are you as mad as your father? Write your own marriage contract for Bassanio—"

"Oh, I will," said Portia determinedly.

"And let the other one go!"

"But then where's the sport?"

"*Sport!* Now we are back where we started! I am ringed by your crazed logic, and I start to doubt your wits. To you, the sport is to win while staying inside the bare letter of your father's law, and the devil with the spirit. You will not simply denounce the game as madness, though the choice of a husband depends on it. And my fortunes depend on it too, Portia, because whether or not you persuade me to marry Graziano, I have thrown in my lot with you. Think, Portia! A husband is . . . a grave matter. If Bassanio loses, then a stronger-minded man may win. You won't have chosen him, he might not love you, and he could defy all your schemes. He could cast me out, and make you miserable."

"I know it!" Portia sat in her chair and put her forehead in her hands. "I fear it!"

Nerissa went and knelt by her side. "Then stop the game!"

Portia turned her face to the side and looked at Nerissa steadily. "Why did you not counsel this before, when the lord of Aragon was here, or the Moroccan one you liked so well? Or the Dutch drunkard? Or the Russian noble? The danger was then as great."

"No, it wasn't," said Nerissa. "Before any of them chose, I stole your portrait from the casket without telling you."

"*What?*"

"Yes, I did. The risk was too frightening. For the Dutchman, I put bottles of ale in all of them."

Portia stared in mock outrage at her friend, and then laughed. "Ah, but they all chose the ones I wanted them to, anyway."

"You were lucky. They might not have."

"And I knew nothing of your trifling. So I am still not forsworn—"

"Yes, you were faithful to your odd rules. But now the game is different. You want this man, and he may choose awry. Well? Why not end the game now?"

Portia dropped her hands into her lap and said quietly, "I can't."

"Portia, if you cannot share your heart with me any better than this, I will leave you. I cannot stay."

Nerissa began to rise, but Portia tugged at her sleeve. "No! I will tell you why I cannot. Have you noted the old man who sits in the far corner, by the purple drape, whenever a man is present in the room with me?"

Nerissa nodded. "The man with the black cap and cape? I thought him some old retainer, kept here for charity's sake."

"Ha! He is an old retainer, but I'd throw him out on his bony buttocks if I could, right down those stairs—"

Nerissa winced.

"Forgive me. A sore subject for you. Nerissa, he was my father's lawyer. If I am found compromising the least article of the will, in *his* interpretation, not mine own, then I get nothing. I lose all, even the very roof over my head. The estate will go to a Milanese cousin I've never even met. And Nerissa, he watches *you,* too, to make sure you don't alter the dice. I am amazed he did not see you take my picture from the caskets."

"I did it at night. I crept down, with pillows under my blankets in case *you* peeped in on me," Nerissa said. "Why did you not tell me this part?"

"Forgive me!" said Portia, folding her hands prayerfully. "I should have, I know. And I would have, before Bassanio took the test. But I feared you would not approve the risk I was taking, in giving my chosen suitor such hints as I had to, to win the game for us. Eluding Signior Nemo Fontecchio's eye will be the hardest part of the game." Her eyes glowed as she said it, as though she meant, the *best* part of the game.

"But Portia," said Nerissa, "I am not like you; I know little of laws. But could not the law work for you in this instance? From all you have told me of your father, it should have been a small matter to prove him—"

"*Non compos mentis.*" Portia spoke matter-of-factly. "If you knew how I tried! And if I was anyone else, the thing would have been done, and I a merry heiress. But I needed three witnesses to his madness besides myself, since I stood most to gain from the judgment. I could not find *one*. The priest *saw* him out rowing in the yellow petticoat, and still pronounced him sane as San Giovanni. All the lawyers and lords of Treviso applaud my father's plan, though they laugh behind their porticos." Her voice turned sour. "You see how it is? They all think proud Portia needs a man to bring her to heel. I tell you, a woman of wit is not liked in north Italy!" Suddenly rueful, she darted a glance at Nerissa. "Or perhaps it is only I who am not liked."

"Oh my dear. You are liked by *me*."

"Then help me!" Portia slipped from her chair and knelt next to her. "Old long-faced Fontecchio can't watch us both at once. He'll not be a match for our paired wits!"

That evening Portia sat late at her desk as the sun set, inscribing her own contract for Bassanio. So intent was she on her labors that she did not stop to light a candle, even as the room darkened.

The young man would sign two documents. The first would be her father's mad contract, which specified not only the terms of the game but the punishment of eternal celibacy for losers. The second contract, better crafted than her father's, was the one she even now copied onto fine parchment. She would show Bassanio this second paper after the game was played. It made her bed, together with any hope of heir, contingent on Bassanio's agreement to invest her as titleholder of Belmont and its monies, lands, buildings, and moveables. The second contract would come as a surprise to her father's lawyer, but she was by now better versed in marriage law than he, and he could not contest it, nor could Bassanio, even had he the brains to do so. *Ergo,* if Bassanio chose not to sign, then short of rape—not likely to be done by the sheepish fop—his marriage must stay unconsummated.

And no man would want that.

Portia dotted the last *i* on the document and wiped her ink-stained hands with a handkerchief. She smiled. It was well. She would win her father's game if Bassanio did.

And he would.

She opened the top drawer of her desk to push the document inside it. There, among the pencil stubs and sharpened quills, lay the turquoise ring Nerissa had taken from the Spaniard and passed to her. She picked it up. This time she did not slip it on her finger, but only held it in her palm, gazing at the bright blue of its flawed stone, at the black streaks that marred its beauty. As when she'd first regarded the ring, she had the thought that she'd held it before.

The door between the hallway and the adjacent room suddenly opened, and she started like a guilty thing surprised. She heart Nerissa's voice as her friend entered the other room talking to Xanthe, the Moorish house servant. Portia dropped the ring back into the desk drawer and half-rose to greet them. But when she heard her own name mentioned, she sat slowly down again and listened.

"You may be sure of her kindness," Nerissa was saying.

"I am . . . not sure of it, lady," said the Moorish woman's soft voice, in slightly halting Italian.

A chair creaked as Nerissa sat. "Come, rest," she said to Xanthe. Hearing this, Portia frowned slightly. The maid was to be laundering sheets at this hour.

"Remember that we will help you to a fine husband," said Nerissa. "Do not forget my counsel."

"If I do, believe that I will never forget your kindness," came the soft, accented voice.

"Do you know, I may marry myself, soon," Nerissa chuckled. "Lady Portia has urged me to take Graziano, and assured me that he can be brought to ask for my hand."

"That one?" Xanthe sounded doubtful. "He is almost as bad as—"

"I am not at all sure that I want him! But she has half-persuaded me. She thinks I may make Graziano into a mate tolerable at long distances. She has great faith in my power to reform others' morals. And she has contrived an additional plan, to save me if faith leads us astray. If I cannot abide him, I may use my influence with an old friend. A cardinal, who has the ear of the pope. My union shall be annulled, the lady says! Ah, but you shake your head."

"Forgive me," said Xanthe. "But is it wise to wed at such . . ." She sought the word. "Such risk?"

In the other room Portia gripped her pen so hard that her knuckles whitened. Who was this servant, to give them advice?

Nerissa's voice betrayed only thoughtfulness and a little melancholy. "Perhaps not, Xanthe. But no men are perfect. Nor women neither. There is something wrong with all of us."

"With some more than others, lady," came the reply.

Nerissa laughed gently. "Even Launcelot may improve."

Portia heard the servant sigh. "Let me not speak of him," she said. "I thank you, lady, but the linens await me." Portia heard her rise and curtsy with a rustle of skirts, then walk to the door. Upon reaching it, she stopped. "Lady Nerissa . . ."

"What, Xanthe?" Nerissa's footsteps went toward her. Portia strained to hear their speech.

"The soldier who came with the lord of Aragon. I saw you speaking with him."

"And?" Nerissa's voice turned a little sharp.

"Nothing. Only I thought I knew his face. And when he passed the door to the kitchens, I saw a picture in the . . ." She paused. "The top of his sword."

"The haft."

"That. It was a woman on a bed, clothed as a duenna, white, bleeding. . . . I thought he might do you hurt."

A hint of merriment entered Nerissa's voice. "Do not be so frightened by those devil's pictures you see in your mind. He did not hurt me. And I was not . . ." Portia heard Nerissa brush her hands against her gown, as though to rid them of dirt. "Xanthe, fear not for me. He stood in *my* danger, not the other way around." She made her voice a stage whisper. "I robbed the fellow! Of some silver, and a ring. Never fear for me, dear. He may do other women harm, but I think his part in our story is done. God sent him to show me something."

"What, lady?"

"That a beautiful body may harbor death."

Nerissa explained no further, but Xanthe made a sound of assent, as though she understood.

"Here is a riddle, Xanthe," Nerissa said. "Theft is wrong, but I am glad I robbed that handsome soldier. God does not often tell us to steal, but somehow I think that I did it this time at His prompting. I think He can be larger than His laws."

Xanthe laughed. "I think Lady Portia would . . ."

"Chide?"

"Yes, chide you for saying something is bigger than *law*. She loves it so! But I know not. I speak small things to her. Her tongue is too quick and sharp for me. And it is as we spoke before. She says not my name. She looks not at me but . . ." Again she stopped, at a loss.

"Through?"

"Yes, through me. As though I am not there."

"Her heart is good, Xanthe," Nerissa said, as the two left the parlor and closed the door.

Portia sat straight in her chair, the darkness hiding the flush of her cheeks from any who might have seen it. But the room was empty. She was alone.

And it is as we spoke before. So. They spoke of her in private, Xanthe and Nerissa.

She half-rose once more, thinking to follow Nerissa and warn her she should not talk in familiar terms with a common drudge who folded linens and cleaned the scullery; that if Xanthe was with child, as Nerissa's first sentences had implied, she must straightaway be married not to a "fine husband" but to a peasant in the countryside; and that Nerissa should not jest about theft to those who worked in the house. But she sat down abruptly, as shame heated her skin.

Though your mind is a thing of beauty, you have no heart.

She mused for a time on Nerissa's works, and on Xanthe's.

After a few minutes she struck a flint in the darkness and lit a candle. From a bottom drawer in her desk she took a long-stemmed pipe and a paper of Virginia tobacco. She lit the pipe and began to smoke, drawing the harsh herb deep into her lungs and then breathing it out, stopping now and then to cough.

TWENTY-FIVE

"HERE. NO. JUST there."

Following Portia's instruction, Xanthe hauled the marble pedestal to the left edge of the soft Turkish carpet. Nerissa followed with the closed silver casket. In the corner of the presence chamber, Signior Fontecchio sat with his arms folded, squinting suspiciously at them from under his black cap. He did not offer to help them.

"'Tis more commodious, this arrangement, is it not, good signior?" Portia called to him, smiling graciously. Her hair was coiled and braided today, and interwoven with double loops of pearls. But the coils and pearls and the very gold of her tresses were barely visible under the dark gray veil that covered her head. Like Xanthe and Nerissa, she wore a leaden-hued gown and slippers dyed black. From her neck hung a pencil.

Signior Fontecchio gave the barest of nods, as he shifted in his chair and tapped his foot. His frown deepened.

"How could I not have known?" Nerissa whispered to Portia, after she'd returned to the center of the chamber. "He is quite disrespectful, and that gown—"

"The habiliments of a lawyer," Portia responded, low-voiced, and with something like envy. "He flaunts his office. Of course he knows what we want to do; he's no fool. But he can't stop us if all we do is hint."

"You are convinced of that?"

"Did he quibble when I stuck out my foot and tripped the Dutchman as he staggered toward what I *thought* was the winning casket?"

"Noooo," said Nerissa. "But I thought he attributed the stumble to the ale the man had used to wash down his garlic and plover-egg breakfast."

"He would not have been able to prove otherwise, whatever he thought. And so it will be today, as long as we are subtle." Portia tugged at her large dangling pencil. She saw Nerissa share a covert smile with Xanthe, who had joined them in the center of the rug. Their closeness pricked her heart. "Do not laugh at me," she whispered sharply. "I know what I am about!"

Nerissa curtsied elaborately, still wearing a teasing smile. Xanthe withdrew to stand against the wall.

Portia surveyed the room. "Now 'tis perfect."

The three box-bearing pedestals stood at equal distances from one another on the enormous red and brown rug. At one end stood the silver casket, at the other the gold. Xanthe had polished both boxes to a high sheen. The dull lead casket stood unpolished on a slightly raised pedestal in the exact center of both the rug and the room.

Portia clapped her hands, and a manservant clad in leaden-hued livery opened the door to let Bassanio enter. Graziano stood a foot behind Bassanio in the lobby, and began to follow him in as though connected to his friend by an invisible string. But Nerissa moved quickly and closed the door on his outraged squawk. Then she joined Xanthe by the wall.

Although Bassanio had thrice been to Belmont since the frog incident, this was the first time since then that he and Portia had stood in one room. It was, in fact, the same room in which, on that early occasion, he had tried to purchase a silver Cellini head of Christ for a wire-topped wooden box of hop-toads. Now he looked nervously about the floor, as though he expected one of the small beasts to leap, peeping, across his dancing slipper. In fact, he did think he saw one, just disappearing into the shadow of a music stand. He glanced covertly at Portia, who only smiled behind her veil and tugged at her pencil.

Now Portia drew herself up straight and tall. She took a small step from the rug's edge toward the leaden casket, and opened her mouth to speak, just as Signior Fontecchio rose and said in a reedy voice, "The lady must stand at an equal distance from all the caskets." He sat down again abruptly, with a flare of robes.

She was miffed. The rule had not come into play before, and indeed, she was quite sure it was *not* a rule. But she was not disposed to argue with the lawyer now, and compromise her case later, after Bassanio had won the choice. She took the lawyer's interjection as a warning that he was watching them closely.

Well, let him watch! She would transgress no stipulation that could be found in the contractual bond.

Bassanio stood watching the drama, looking awed at the spectacle of the boxes, and a little glassy-eyed. *Good,* thought Portia. *The less he thinks, the better.* She raised her arms and said loudly, theatrically, "I could teach you how to choose right, *but* then I am forsworn. *So will I never be.*" She turned her head and looked pointedly at Signior Fontecchio. "So may you miss me."

"Let me choose!" said Bassanio, in a voice as theatrical as hers. "For as it is, I live upon the rack."

Against the wall Xanthe stiffened slightly. Portia caught the movement and glanced at her curiously, then returned her gaze to Bassanio. "Upon the rack, Bassanio? Then confess what treason there is mingled with your love."

"Uh—" Bassanio pondered, then his face lit up. "None but that ugly treason of mistrust, which makes me fear the enjoying of my love!"

"Ay, but I fear you speak upon the rack, where men enforcéd will speak anything."

Xanthe was visibly trembling, and Portia again looked at her, this time with alarm. *Was she ill? Pregnant indeed?* This morning, busy arranging the chamber and herself for Bassanio's choice, Portia had had no time to question Nerissa on the matter. She had been, in fact, reluctant to do so. She did not know what was right to say, how to define her own feelings with regard to Xanthe's friendship with Nerissa, and her presence in the house. But perhaps she should have forced the question. The servant had a part to play in Bassanio's ordeal; if she collapsed, their plans could go awry.

Bassanio was now raising his hands to heaven as he stood before the closed chamber door, glibly pursuing the witty conceit Portia had introduced. "O happy torment, when my torturer—"

"It is time for the lover to make his choice!" said Nerissa. Portia looked at her in surprise. She had taken Xanthe's hand in both of hers, and Xanthe, though still trembling, seemed calmer. Nerissa looked urgently at Portia as she said, "Lady Portia, lead him on!"

"Yes," said Bassanio, seeming happy to abandon the labors of poetry. "Let me to my fortune and the caskets."

Portia gave a slight nod to Nerissa. "Away then!" she said. "I am locked in one of them. If you do love me, you will find me out." With a sweep of her hand she indicated the caskets, at which Bassanio had been darting glances since he came in the door. "Let music sound while he doth make his choice," she added.

Signior Fontecchio opened his mouth and jumped up to protest, but was drowned out by the loud sounds of flute, lute, viol, and drum that commenced immediately in an adjacent chamber. From the folds of her gown Portia produced a small bell with a leaden clapper. As Bassanio walked forward to survey the caskets, his hands folded behind his back, Nerissa and Xanthe—who had stopped trembling—stepped forward and began to sing.

> *Tell me where is fa-a-ancy BRED,*
> *In the heart, or in the HEAD?*
> > *Reply, reply.*
> *It is engendered in the eyes,*
> *With gazing FED, and fancy dies*
> *In the cradle where it lies.*
> *Let us all ring fancy's knell.*
> *I'll begin it—Ding, dong, BELL.*

Bassanio was approaching the gold casket. Portia rang the bell loudly and suddenly, and he started and covered his ears. He stared at her. She pulled on her pencil, and said, "What are bells made of, Signior Bassanio di Piombo? Do you know?"

Signior Fontecchio was staring at her furiously. He started to speak, but at his first word Xanthe and Nerissa renewed their song.

"Signior Fontecchio!" Portia called to him over their voices. "Were you about to offer your thought on how bells were made?"

"A silvery sound have they!" said Bassanio, grinning widely. He turned toward the silver casket, and bent to read the card Portia had placed before it. *"Who chooseth me shall get as much as he deserves."*

"Bread, Bassanio?" Nerissa said, breaking off her song. She gestured to a table by her, on which Xanthe had put forth a loaf of barley bread and a pat of butter. *"Bread?"* She pounded the tabletop. *"BREAD?"*

Bassanio shook his head at her in puzzlement. "I am not hungry just now, so please you." But her question had diverted him from his purpose, and he turned again. "Now what was I . . . ," he murmured. He passed his eyes briefly over the lead casket in the middle of the floor, and read the inscription on its card. *"Who chooseth me must give and gizzard all he hath."*

"Hazard!" said Portia. "Hazard!"

"Ah, pardon. Hazard. Hmm!" He turned away from the lead casket and looked again at the gold box.

Nerissa rolled her eyes at Portia. Portia rang her bell, but this time Bassanio did not look up. He was engrossed by the gold casket, although he did not seem to be reading its inscription, only appraising its workmanship, or perhaps its color. He seemed mentally to be weighing the box.

"What does it say?" called Nerissa.

"What? Ah! The inscription!" Bassanio bent. *"Who chooseth me shall gain what many men desire."* He straightened, smiling. "And all desire Portia!" he said. "She is gold among women." He reached his hand forward. "Here I make my—"

Nerissa pushed Xanthe, and she stumbled forward with a loud and fake-sounding sneeze. She crashed into Bassanio, whose elbow hit the gold box, which tumbled and hit the floor with a thud. He bent to retrieve it, but Signior Fontecchio, spry for his years, sprang forward before he could touch it. "Do not handle the boxes!" he hissed. "Stand back there!" He gestured Bassanio off the rug while he replaced the box and its placard on the pedestal.

"Ohh," Xanthe said dramatically, clutching her forehead. She walked with Bassanio to the edge of the rug and nudged him. "My *head*. My *head*. It feels . . . feels . . ."

"Heavy, does it not?" called Portia. "Your head feels *heavy*, I think."

"That cold in your *head*," said Nerissa, who had joined Portia at the middle wall. "You should be in *bed*—"

"Cold?" said Bassanio, his expression lightening. "Cold? Gold!" He moved again toward the gold casket.

"What did you put in that gold box, a lodestone?" Portia whispered frantically to Nerissa. "All he sees is gold!"

"I put in a pretty little mirror and passage money back to Venice!" Nerissa hissed. "The marked playing cards are in the silver box."

"Well, stop him before he opens the wrong one!" Portia retorted, ringing her bell violently. Bassanio stayed his hand at the very lid of the gold box, and looked at her.

As she gave back his gaze, all Portia's well-laid plans fled her mind, and she felt herself suddenly blank and witless. She opened her mouth, but no words came. She saw Bassanio's questioning look and, behind him, Signior Fontecchio's frown, and knew at last that she could not make either of them do or not do anything. So she closed her eyes and prayed.

"You have not always fared well at the game of *hazard*, Signior Bassanio," she heard Nerissa say calmly at her side. Her friend's voice was low, but it rang loud in the quiet room. "Perhaps you will do better today."

There was silence. Then Portia heard Bassanio take two steps to the side and raise the lid of a box. She held her breath, and slowly opened her eyes.

Bassanio was standing before the open lead box, holding up a tiny portrait of a velvet-clad woman whose head was piled with intricate coils of golden hair. The pictured woman wore a soft and pleasant expression, and her eyes were painted a gentle turquoise blue.

"This is not you, is it?" he said.

OF COURSE, ONCE it was made plain to him that he had won the game, he had no end of praise for the portrait and its likeness to fair Portia. Her veil removed, Portia withstood the comparison for a full minute. "What demigod hath come so near creation?" Bassanio cried, one hand holding the portrait, the other cupping her chin. "Here in her hairs the painter plays the spider, and hath woven a golden mesh to entrap the hearts of men. But her *eyes!* Having made one, methinks it should have power to steal both his, and leave itself unfinished! Yet look how far—"

"That is enough, Signior Bassanio," Portia said briskly. "You'll be pleased to know the portrait was done by the famed artist Giulio Romano, and is worth a pleasing sum. Now, you have papers to sign." She looked across the room at Signior Fontecchio, who was speaking rapidly and angrily to Nerissa, while on his left flank Xanthe tried vainly to interest him in butter and barley bread. In the anteroom the musicians played on.

"Will you offer my Hercules his congratulations, Signior Fontecchio?" Portia called across the rug. "He has met the challenge."

Portia could hear Graziano pounding on the oaken portals. "What has happened?" came his muffled cry. "Did we win?"

"Oh, let the fool come in," she told Nerissa, who rolled her eyes once more, but went to the door.

"Lady Portia, I am not entirely sure that this challenge was *fairly* met," said the lawyer, breaking from Xanthe and striding toward her, his robes flapping. "In the spirit of your father's will—"

"Is there a spirit in this will?" asked Portia, pulling the document from her sash and unfolding it. "I must say, I found no spirit in this will, only some words setting forth conditions. Those conditions were met."

"*Fully by chance and hazard,*" said the lawyer, tapping the sentence in the document hard with his pointed finger. "*Fully by chance and hazard* the suitor was to pass this test!"

"*Signior* Fontecchio." Portia crumpled the will in one fist as she placed her hands on her hips. "Many a time and oft you have found pleasure in reminding me how this will constrains my spending. I beg to remind *you* that by now I know its wording at least as well as you. Fully by chance and hazard? Today you have stood witness to the performance of Signior Bassanio di Piombo as he made his deliberations over *my* caskets."

"They are not yours, Lady—"

"They were once, and soon will be again! Now, whatever you think you saw and heard, can you deny that this young man's very unsupported walking—even his choice to come inside out of the rain today—has occurred by *anything* but chance and hazard? Is it not a very miracle that he remembers to breathe?"

Signior Fontecchio opened his mouth, but found no reply. At length he said brusquely, "I will bring the marriage contract," and withdrew.

TWENTY-SIX

Bassanio signed the contract left by Portia's father. But he would not sign Portia's addendum.

Portia stared at him, openmouthed, as he explained. True, he had promised in letters to her that, did he win the wooing game, she might be his gracious mistress and command him in all things, yea, even that he would swim to the Antipodes to gather her wild strawberries from the untrodden woods of Virginia ("He'll learn I'd prefer tobacco," Portia had told Nerissa, crumpling that letter). Still, he said, as Graziano nodded and smirked, as master of Belmont, he must be assumed to be the arbiter of his wife's fortunes. Let Portia hold sway in all things domestic. Let her send to Seville for oranges, to India for spices for their feasts! Let her engage and discharge servants at will!

"I'll begin with him," Portia said, interrupting and pointing at Launcelot Giobbo. Launcelot jumped guiltily and took his hand out of a bowl of candied figs that stood on a cedarwood table. "Let him pack up his ridiculous plum-colored tights and be gone by morning. He'll take no more sport with my serving maids. And you, sir." She turned her sharp gaze back to Bassanio, who, fishlike, was opening and closing his mouth. "We have more to discuss before the marriage is consummate."

Launcelot sucked his finger and looked beseechingly at Nerissa, as Portia grasped Bassanio's elbow and pointed at her study. She heard Nerissa whisper a few words to Giobbo about speaking to the mistress on his behalf if only to prevent his darkening his old employer's door again. Xanthe, standing behind them, scowled furiously at something, and Portia looked hard at Nerissa and said, "My dear, 'tis best you speak to *Graziano* now. I believe he has some suit to you. As for my groom, leave me closeted with him for a time." She marched Bassanio into her small study with its large wooden desk, and slammed the door behind them. "Now," she said. "Sit."

Obediently, Bassanio began to lower himself into the comfortable armchair behind the desk.

"Not there!" she said. She gestured toward a stool on the desk's other side. He moved, and sat himself upon it.

"Signior Bassanio," she said, seating herself in the desk chair. She softened her voice. "That is to say, my love." She folded her hands before her. "You may think me an unlessoned girl, unschooled and unpracticed, but I assure you that the full sum of me is something quite other than you imagine."

Bassanio looked confused. He raised a finger and began to speak, then subsided into baffled silence.

Portia sighed. "What would you hear?"

"Ah!" Bassanio leaned forward. "Some sweet words befitting the fancy of a new bride, I think."

"Ah, words! So it is the gilt of poetry you crave, as seal to our marriage contract. Very well, then. Let me see." She rose and stood back from her desk, spread her arms wide, and curtsied deeply. "My gentle spirit commits itself to yours to be directed, as from her lord, her governor, and her king!"

Someone rapped at the door. Impatiently, Portia opened it. Nerissa stood outside with her hands clasped before her. "Shall I still send a man for the priest?" she whispered anxiously. "What has happened?"

"I am advising Bassanio regarding his rights and interests."

Nerissa looked both worried and exasperated, though she held her tongue. Portia knew her thought. Things were fully evading their control, they had gone wrong since the very start of the day, and Portia should confess it and do her best to extricate them both from this mad arrangement. But she set her face grimly and closed the door on Nerissa's distress, though not before her spaniel, still clad in his Easter cloth-of-gold jacket, had raced in, yapping. She sat again in her armchair, and ignored the dog as it gamboled at her feet. "So!" she said. "To pick up the thread—"

"Like Theseus in the maze, with Ariadne!"

"If you will." She spread her arms again. "Myself, and what is mine, to you and yours is now converted. Before, I was the lord of this fair mansion, master of my servants, queen o'er myself! Yet now, this house, these servants, and this same myself are yours, my *lord's*."

"I accept these gifts!" cried Bassanio, bounding from his seat.

Portia dropped her hands and pointed at the stool. *"Sit!"*

The spaniel sat, and Bassanio sat, too.

"We have had enough poetry. The fact, *Lord* Bassanio, is that you would waste my wealth in a year, had you the mastery of its spending. And that is why *this* contract guarantees that you will have no such mastery. Yes, the money is yours now! But consider this. I have three years been its steward, and I will tell you plainly in your ear, under *my* stewardship since my fool father died, Belmont's incomes have increased fivefold. I acquired a pretty sum by proxy in Amsterdam, dealing in East Indian pepper, and I presently stand to gain even more from the profits of the Levant Company—"

"My sweet, I am so glad that your lovely head harbors thoughts of commerce," said Bassanio. "For I have come to think it of the highest importance to our commonwealth. Our merchants are the new Jasons, sending their ships to all points of the world for golden fleeces. They are the Galahads, in quest of new grails! I myself am noble, and do not dabble personally in the trade other than to use such men as my agents. Yet together we shall profit not fivefold but tenfold, twentyfold, nay, a hundredfold! For I have as my advisor a dear friend, the best of all possible friends, a Merlin of merchantry, a Solomon of the silk and spice trade, a . . . a . . . by Christ's blood, a very wise man, and his name is—"

"Antonio di Argento," said Portia in a voice of controlled wrath.

"Then you know him?"

"*Of* him."

"And you know of his—"

"Scheme to sell wine to the abstaining pagans of Constantinople, yes. And of the newer one, to sell rosaries and items of Catholic prayer to the English."

"Ah, well, as far as that goes, I have received new information about England's position with regard to the pope—"

"*New?*" Portia half-rose, then sank back in her chair. She smiled politely. "Bassanio, I will waste no more time in idle chat with you." She pointed. "There lies my addendum to your marriage contract. Sign it, or this marriage—which I cannot now prevent—shall remain unconsummated. For your access to my chamber is something I *can* prevent. And I warn you, an unconsummated marriage is not hard to annul, especially when one's dearest friend has the ear of the pope."

A pounding came on the door, along with Signior Fontecchio's angry voice. "What is the meaning of this, Lady Portia?"

"Are you still here, signior?"

"What does he sign? Have you any witnesses? I warn you, you shall not evade the provisions of your father's will—"

"I do not intend to evade them!" Portia called to him. "All will be done by the book! Though I amended the book," she said in a lower voice. She stood. "Bassanio, I leave you again to read, and to consider."

She strode briskly from the room and went to the garden in search of Nerissa. She found her in the arbor, kissing Graziano, and grabbed her friend's arm in anger. "Come with me!"

"KINDLY LET ME propel myself along these walks!" Nerissa said, shaking her arm loose. "*What,* lady? You begin to confuse me. You gave me license to tempt Graziano, he has proposed, and I have agreed to consider his offer, to indulge you, though I have grave doubts. I begin to think you concocted this whole scheme while chewing the seed of the Turkish poppy. Graziano for husband? He has a fine leg, and a soft lip—"

"Ugh! Nerissa, leave your thoughts of clawing and pawing long enough to discuss our condition. Bassanio says he will not sign my addendum! It seems I have a rival for his trust, and it is no other than that *idiot* Antonio di Argento! I've never met him, but I hate him. I *hate* him!"

"Calm thyself," said Nerissa, stopping along the garden path. "This rage and hate do not become you. Now, lean against this peach tree. Breathe!"

"I know how to breathe! What am I to do? How am I to convince him? If he can still think Antonio a wise counselor after the losses he has sustained through taking his advice, what can I possibly do to cut their tie? Yet Bassanio has won the game, and is determined to marry me! Oh, Nerissa, Nerissa!" Portia sank to the base of the tree and put her head in her hands. "I had reconciled myself to the marriage night. Even to children! I knew in time he would turn to others in Venice, and leave me *alone.* These things I could endure, but the *money!* To put it in the hands of a fool!"

"Oh, heavens." Nerissa knelt by her side. "Perhaps we should pray."

Portia laughed shortly. "The last time I prayed, Bassanio won the wooing test. Now I am starting to wish he hadn't! How can we pray for sinful things?"

"What sinful things?"

"I have read that Bible you are so fond of quoting, though you think I have not. *Wives, be subject to your husbands.* How can I pray for mastery of my own possessions, when I'm supposed to give them to him?"

"Well," said Nerissa after a moment of thought, "I do not know. But I am going to pray that things turn out as they should."

The two sat, holding hands in silence. Both closed their eyes. After a minute, Nerissa said "Amen" just as Portia said "I have an idea."

They opened their eyes and looked at one another. "I may have to play at hazard," Portia said. "Once more."

A drop smacked her brow, and she looked up. It was raining again.

"LORD BASSANIO," PORTIA said. It was late afternoon, and the sun had finally slipped from behind the clouds that had reigned all day over Belmont. Its slanted rays fell through the wide windows and lit her hair, which Nerissa had redressed with the pearls. Portia had changed her gown. Now she looked regal in crimson and cloth-of-gold, her train of silk coiled about her feet on the marble tiles of the lobby. She could read the admiration in Bassanio's eyes as he looked at the garment.

"I am persuaded that in God's judgment you, my husband, are to me a very Christ. Lord of myself and my fortunes!"

"Oh, but you shall be the dear mistress of my heart—"

"Shush!" Portia caught herself, and smiled tenderly. She curtsied low. "I mean to say, I gratefully accept your compliment. And to honor your penchant for hyperbole and the symbols of hearts' commitment, I have brought you a gift."

"Lady, any gift of yours will be received as a blessing from heaven, as manna in the desert, and I will guard it as the thousand-eyed watchdog guards the gates of hell," said Bassanio.

"I am as sure of these pledges as I am of your vow to fetch me strawberries from the New World. Therefore, receive this gift, and its provisions, which I have inscribed in that"—she pointed to a sheet of parchment on a small table—"amended contract. Nerissa?"

Nerissa opened a box and extracted the turquoise ring she had stolen from the Spanish soldier. Portia held it aloft. "My worldly possessions and myself, I give you with this ring. When you part from it, lose it, or give it away, your title to *all* those things shall revert to me. So says the contract. But this is a ritual, dear Bassanio. Signing the paper, I mean. Surely you will never lose the ring."

"Of course not!" said Bassanio, his face alight with the poetry of the moment. He took the ring and placed it on his long, slender finger, where it hung almost as loosely as it had on Portia's. He frowned slightly. "The stone is—"

"Lovely, is it not? A turquoise as blue as my eyes, shot with streaks of black, to remind us that only God, and not ourselves, is perfect."

"Ah. An excellent conceit. And the band—"

"Made to signify the knitting together of our two souls in marriage." Portia noted his discomfort with the bumpy feel of the entwined strands of silver. She smiled with satisfaction.

Twisting the ring, Bassanio said, "But there seem to be four strands—"

"Five, in fact," said Portia.

"They stand for the five festal garments given Benjamin by Joseph," suggested Nerissa. "In the Book of Genesis."

"Ah, the festal garments! Excellent." Bassanio nodded sagely. "Well, I can only say that when this ring parts from this finger"—he held his hand up; the ring slid so the turquoise hung against his palm, and he corrected its position, pushing it back as far as he could on the digit—"when this ring parts from this finger, then parts life from thence!"

"It would not be necessary for you to die in such an instance," said Portia. "The consequences would be merely fiscal." She tapped her newly drafted document with the quill pen handed her by Xanthe, who stood at her other side. "Signior Fontecchio has agreed to witness your signature."

As Bassanio approached the paper, Nerissa nudged Portia and whispered, "More *sweetness* in thy discourse!"

"I have indeed agreed to serve as witness," Signior Fontecchio said sourly. "But Signior di Piombo, I must advise against—"

"Ah, what traffic hath dry advice with the thrilling risks of love?" said Portia, throwing her arms wide. "Sign to the sacred rules of the mystical ring, my Bassanio, and be lord of this mansion! This body! My heart!"

"Give me the pen!" cried Bassanio.

TWENTY-SEVEN

It was lorenzo di Scimmia who brought the news of Antonio's wreck.

They came at the supper hour, with their empty purses and their mournful letter from di Argento. Nerissa, Graziano, and the newlyweds Portia and Bassanio sat at table. Portia was trying to evade the hand of Bassanio, who was holding cherries dipped in cream to her lips. She was calculating how she might prolong his wine-bibbing unto the hour of sleep, and so escape her marital duties until the next night. She glanced at Bassanio's gloved hand, so clothed not only for elegance, but to prevent the loose turquoise ring from dropping into the salad. "Until the band is smoothed and tightened, my love!" he had said. She'd smiled noncommittally.

Xanthe was presenting sliced Sevillan oranges to Graziano, keeping the table between herself and Launcelot, who stood behind his master. The manservant had been retained for the nonce due to Nerissa's intercession. Nerissa sat at the table end, laughing at Graziano's fool jests in spite of herself. Portia noticed she had downed more than her usual share of Spanish canary. But when the servant ushered in a tired-looking young man and woman wearing threadbare silks, and announced them as the di Scimmias, Nerissa jumped to her feet without swaying a bit, and ran to embrace the woman with the Spanish eyes who stood shaking the dew from her hood. Portia narrowed her own eyes briefly, assessing the visitor's dark, full hair and olive skin. The girl returned Nerissa's embrace, but then stood a little apart from the others. In her face shyness and defiance were mixed. Portia saw her eyes spark with brief envy as they wandered about the gold, wood, and marble of the room. *Married to a fool who spent her money,* Portia thought, feeling a stab of sympathy for her. She rose and extended her hand. "You are Mistress di Scimmia."

The girl curtsied deeply. Clearly, she had learned the arts of Christian civility from someone, Portia thought, perhaps from the gentry of the houses they had lately frequented. It seemed unlikely she knew it from her husband, who was even now clapping backs with Graziano and Bassanio and loudly boasting of the distance he and his wife had traveled from Milan. It surprised Portia to note that Jessica looked like any other young woman, though prettier than most—certainly prettier than Portia herself. Her skin made her Spanish heritage evident, and Portia recalled what Nerissa had told her: that Jessica's grandfather had been a Toledan hidalgo. So. She was at least one-quarter Christian.

Though fully Christian now, of course.

"My dearest Lorenzo, you have missed my wedding!" Bassanio said as he hugged his friend. "A short ritual for a long . . ." He sought a word. Portia suppressed the ones that sprang to her mind. *Penance? Sentence?*

Lorenzo supplied him. "Holiday! I congratulate you, Bassanio, and your fair bride, Lady Portia Bel Mente, in the name of the noble family di Scimmia of Venice, and of myself, Lorenzo di Scimmia—"

"Recently disowned," murmured Nerissa in Portia's ear, as she left Jessica's side to relieve Xanthe of her tray of oranges. She feared Xanthe would drop it; the woman seemed spellbound in another of her mystical fits, and was standing immobile while the tray teetered on her fingertips. Nerissa seized it, and raised her voice. "A slice of Sevillan sunshine, dear guests?"

"And my wife, Jessica!" said Lorenzo, accepting an orange crescent. "My dear pagan! My fair infidel, gentle Jessica!"

"*Gentile* Jessica!" Graziano hooted.

Portia saw the girl wince. "Sit, Jessica," she said, as kindly as she could. "So you have fled to us from the house of your father, in the Ghetto Nuovo."

Jessica's face turned pale. She remained standing and, not looking at her husband, said, "Lorenzo, you had best share our news."

"By the cross, I had forgot me." From his cloak Lorenzo brought a folded paper. "I had this from Salerio della Fattoria, whom we met on the boat coming up the river, though his business has taken him back to Venice." He handed the note to Bassanio. "This thing concerns you, friend."

"What is it?"

"A piece of paper with writing on it."

Nerissa glanced humorously at Jessica, but Jessica only looked at her in white desperation, as though she were trapped in the bottom of a well. Silence settled on the group as Bassanio unsealed the letter. In a moment he looked up at Portia, wearing a face as pale as Jessica's.

"Antonio di Argento has lost his money," he said in a whisper. "All of it. The rumors look true. His ships . . . not *one* of them has yet come to port."

"Ah," said Portia, sampling one of the long-stemmed cherries. "How fortunate that I had sunk no money in *his* enterprises."

Bassanio looked at her, still ashy-faced. "But I have."

She stopped midchew and stared at him. Jessica, Lorenzo, and Graziano exchanged stricken glances. Portia said slowly, "Dear Bassanio, you told me this very afternoon that you had no money at all. The admission did not surprise me, though I did think you discourteous to confess it *after* you won the game, rather than before. But no matter. What fresh tale is this?"

Bassanio sank into a chair, looking miserable. "Portia, when I told you my fortunes were nothing, I should have told you they were worse than nothing. I had . . . impawned myself to the fortunes of Antonio di Argento. I am sorry. I *should* have told you."

Portia began again to munch cherries, looking at him fixedly. "Yes, you should have told me. It is much safer to tell me now that you have my fortune, is it not?" She glanced at the new guests and Xanthe and Nerissa, who stood bunched at the rim of the table, their hands folded before them and their mouths downturned as though they suddenly found themselves at a funeral instead of a wedding celebration. "Well, sit you down, all of you!" she said. "There is still wine, and half a haunch of a whole roast boar."

Jessica sat, looking a little ill at the remains of the boar's head on the platter in the center of the table. Xanthe went to the kitchens and returned with a plate of fruit and bread, which she set before Jessica. Jessica glanced at her curiously, smiling a brief thanks.

"Let me see that letter," Portia said, taking it from Bassanio's shaking hand. She read aloud. *"Sweet Bassanio—sweet Bassanio? — My ships have all miscarried, my creditors grow cruel, my estate is very low, my bond to the Jew is forfeit. And since in paying it, it is impossible I should live, all debts are cleared between you and me if I might but see you at my death. Notwithstanding, use your pleasure. If your love do not per-suade you to come, let not my letter.*" Portia folded the document. "Peevish. Well, that is that, then. I know not the full sum of this case, and can see it is a sad matter, but at any rate, my husband, your debt is cleared. He says so, here." She tapped the paper. The group stared at her speechlessly. She spread her hands. "What? What is it?"

Nerissa spoke quickly. "What Lady Portia meant to say is that Bassanio's debt to Signior Antonio is cleared because *she* will clear it, of course, and redeem Antonio from whatever hellish pending death he refers to in that letter. Is that not what you meant, Lady Portia?"

"Why, yes, of course!" Portia said quickly, altering her face to show grave concern. To herself she wondered how she would ever survive this life of festive dinners without Nerissa, and vowed for the twentieth time she would never let her friend leave her side. Nerissa was a peasant, but she was at home among these gentle Venetians. Portia herself was a noblewoman born, but among their urbane chatter she felt as foreign as a stranger from a strange land, as though her life and faith were something alien to theirs.

She looked up and, to her surprise, saw Jessica di Scimmia gazing at her with a look of compassion.

Portia half-smiled at her, then watched the girl's eyes grow somber as Nerissa asked, "But death for a debt, in Venice? I have never heard such strangeness. Who is this Jew who threatens to kill Antonio?"

Jessica looked mournfully at her friend. "I grieve to say it is my father."

A SOFT KNOCK sounded on the door of Portia's study, where she had secluded herself after supper. "Come in, Nerissa," she said.

"Not Nerissa." The voice was another woman's. The door opened several inches, and a dark-eyed face looked anxiously in. "It is Jessica di Scimmia. May I speak to you, lady?"

Portia gave Jessica a more comfortable seat than the stool she'd allocated to Bassanio that afternoon. Half anxious and half relieved, she had watched after supper as Bassanio rushed to his rooms to pack garments for a short return to Venice. He would attend Antonio's trial in the civil court. He would bear in his hand the scrip for the money—Belmont money—that would pay Antonio's debt. He would return at once when the trial was ended. "I shall not sleep until I am once more at your side," he had told Portia.

Portia had resisted her impulse to ask him why, in that case, he was bringing three changes of clothes with him. She did not care about that. How long he stayed in the city was not her chief concern.

His friendship with Antonio di Argento was her worry.

As though she could read her thought, Jessica said, "Lady, pardon my boldness. But I think it meet for you to know that Antonio di Argento has your husband in absolute thrall."

Portia put her hands together and rested them against her lips. She nodded slowly. "So it doth seem."

"If I may say so—Nerissa has written to me of your wisdom and wit. I myself know what it is like to marry a fool who knows nothing of money, and who lets your silver slip through his fingers like water. So I know—lady, I will speak plain—that whatever your feelings for your husband, you cannot wish him to manage the wealth of your estate, and still less can you wish that he do so upon the advice of a harebrained Venetian merchant."

Portia raised her eyebrows.

"Forgive me, lady. Perhaps you find me blunt. I was raised in the Ghetto Nuovo, and have much to learn of the courteous discourse of the Christian gentry."

Portia laughed her rough chuckle. "Well, you will not learn it from me. I am an odd duck among the gentry. Say on, Jessica. I find you most eloquent."

"I think you must find a way to discredit Antonio. Lorenzo has told me of ten more schemes Antonio has, to lose *all* our money."

"Are you saying I should not send my money to redeem this Antonio from his paltry three-thousand-ducat debt? That I should let your strange, bloodthirsty father plunge a knife into his breast and cut out a pound of flesh, so as to rid myself of Antonio's meddling advice?"

Jessica looked pale. She said, "I do not think it would come to that, unless my father has . . . gone mad."

"Fathers have been known to go mad."

"But if he did hurt Antonio unto death—if the law let him go so far—it would not solve your problem. Bassanio would revere Antonio all the more for his sacrifice. Like Lorenzo's, his head has been filled for years with Antonio's plans. Antonio has rarely made money on any of them, but Bassanio would put them all into practice, whether Antonio were still living or not. He would drain your coffers. And Antonio would seem—"

"A martyr," said Portia. "A saint, to be worshiped."

Jessica nodded.

"But would your father really kill Antonio?"

"He is angry," she said, looking deeply pained. "It is I who have hurt him, but Antonio who will suffer. I do not think your money will make a difference. My father has money enough. That bond of the pound of flesh was drawn up as a jest. He wants to humiliate Antonio."

"So do I," said Portia.

"But though my father may mock Antonio in court, Antonio will still seem heroic to Bassanio, for baring his breast to the knife of the *evil Jew*." Jessica's voice turned bitter. "Whether the *evil Jew* uses his knife or not, Antonio will have offered himself as a—"

"Lamb to the slaughter."

Jessica smiled at her. "Sheep for the shohet, I was going to say."

"The what?"

"No matter." She leaned forward. "Lady Portia, you must prevent Antonio's sacrifice, and win control of your wealth some other way. You must interrupt this thing, or all you own is at hazard."

"And all you might yet own, since your husband came here to borrow my money."

Jessica blushed deeply.

Portia reached across her desk and patted the girl's hand. "Now it is I who have been blunt. Fear not, Jessica. I pity your state." She leaned back in her chair. "Look you, I care not to whom I give money, as long as it is *me* who gives it! You and your Lorenzo will have enough, if I can gain title to what is mine *own*. I find you wise in your counsel. I share your conclusion. Bassanio must be brought to respect me. But how to *interrupt this thing* of Antonio and your father, as you say? How am I to do it?"

"I know not!" said Jessica. "But from what Nerissa tells me, you can, with your brain."

"Ah, she thinks well of me."

"She loves you," Jessica said simply.

Portia smiled softly. "And I her."

Jessica rose, curtsied, and then hesitated. "There is another thing," she said. "This news of Antonio's ships. Six ventures failed; six vessels sunk, coming from Tripoli, England, Mexico, Lisbon, Barbary, and—"

"India, yes. Most unlucky."

"Un*likely*, is what I think. Lady Portia, there are men who spread rumors on the Rialto, to drive up the prices of their own stock."

"So I have heard."

"I only suggest that you employ whatever agents are at your disposal to investigate the mystery of Antonio's total bankruptcy. If it is done in time, perhaps the case will never come to court. There is a man called Tubal-cain, who works on the Rialto. After the close of business he often visits the eastern docks. He should be sounded."

Portia wrote down the name. "I thank you, Jessica." A thought struck her, and she looked up at the visitor. "The men think your father a bloodthirsty dog. Your view of him seems . . . more complicated."

Jessica was silent.

"Why did you leave his house?"

Jessica looked down and said in a small voice, "He wished me to be—other than I was. He tried to make me learn the Law. . . ."

"To *make* you . . . ?" Portia stared at her. For a rarity, she had no words.

The girl raised her head, and her face showed again the strange mix of shyness and defiance Portia had first noted there. She no longer shrank, but returned Portia's gaze without blinking. The brief intimacy they'd shared had fled, but still Jessica stood, as though awaiting a silver coin for the intelligence she'd given. Was she as anxious for profit as Portia herself? Yet no. Portia saw a hunger for something more than money in her eyes, and knew what it was. The girl craved friendship, and inclusion in a magical world she thought Portia ruled. It was those things she'd hoped to buy.

Portia pitied her, not least because Nerissa was starting to show her that such things could not be purchased.

But other things could. Always there was money, and that, Portia could give. So she said stiffly to Jessica, "My dear, all will come right. And I will reward you for helping me."

NERISSA HAD FORCEFULLY bade good night to Graziano, and was saying her prayers, when her door opened and a man entered her chamber. She gasped and sprang to her feet. "Who are you?" she cried.

The man laid a gloved finger to his lips. He was slender and tall and wore wispy moustaches. His chin showed a faint dusting of brown beard. His boots were black with silver buckles, and his cap was soft leather, as were his breeches, which looked made for riding. They looked, in fact, like a pair Nerissa had seen the day before, on the legs of Portia.

"*Who are you?*" she whispered, sitting down on her bed and assessing the man's graceful movements. Inwardly she said the Paternoster, laying stress on the request that God not lead her into temptation.

The man sat in a chair by the door, outside the circle of light cast by Nerissa's candle. "What is your guess?" he said in a rough whisper.

Nerissa squinted at him. "Say something else."

"Bassanio is a nincompoop, and so is Lorenzo, and so is Graziano, and I have a plan to put all of them in their proper places forever."

"*Portia!*" Nerissa put her hands to her cheeks. "This is no time for a masque! What can you mean by this?"

Portia took off her leather cap and scratched her head. Nerissa cried out again. "Your *hair!*"

"Yes, I cut it!" hissed Portia. "Now be quiet!" She brushed her head again. The golden hair stuck up in spiny tufts. "I feel quite light-headed."

"Then lie down. You are drunk, drunk, drunk."

"Not so. I have a plan. Bassanio explained to us the ridiculous contract Antonio signed with the Jew. Any fool could win this case for Antonio. I know the lawyer they've engaged; he used to lend me books in Padua. He is greedy; with silver I can persuade him of anything. We'll visit him tonight and pull him from his bed. He'll write a letter for me. I *know* the law. I will redeem Antonio myself!"

Nerissa looked at her sadly. "Your father was mad, too," she said. "A shame that it should strike so young."

"Nerissa, this *can* be done. My voice is oft mistaken for a man's. Many's the time I've seen folk look twice at me when I talk. And you, who know me better than anyone I will encounter in this court—including Bassanio—did not recognize me at first just now, even when I spoke."

"You sit half in the dark!"

"This disguise was hastily contrived. I will work on it further, and on the voice. Now, get up! We have said our farewells to our husbands—"

"*Your* husband. I have not agreed to marry—"

"Do not quibble over words. I need your help in this. Get up! Dress!"

Nerissa fell back on her bed, groaning "No, no, no!" A bodice, a kirtle, a cloak, and boots bounced on her stomach as Portia, rummaging in her friend's wardrobe, threw the articles at the bed. "The trial is set for Friday," Portia said enthusiastically, her head in the wardrobe. "We will leave a note for Jessica and her fopling Lorenzo. They may play the lord and lady here, awash in cream and strawberries. Let her wear our clothes. Let's off; my ship is fast; it will make no stops. We'll return before Bassanio doth. Come *on*!"

THE GRAY LIGHT of dawn entered the westernmost room of Portia's house, where Signior Nemo Fontecchio had spent the last night of his paid service at the Bel Mente estate. He rose in his nightgown and walked creakily to the jordan. Having relieved himself, he pulled on a cotton shirt and breeches, and reached for the nailed board on the wall where he kept his lawyer's cap and gown. "What the devil?" he muttered as his hand touched the empty hook.

TWENTY-EIGHT

THEY PASSED GREEN asparagus fields, and wild iris and honey-suckle on the banks, and poppies that glowed like rubies in the river grass. But when they crossed the gulf, the colors faded. The city of Venice loomed before them like an island of gray stone.

Nerissa sat sulkily on the deck of Portia's sloop, dressed in a clerk's gown Portia had borrowed from the Paduan lawyer. That man's practice was thriving; he was glad to let his Venetian client Antonio hang if Portia would pay him for the duty. She had paid as well for Nerissa's clerkly garb, which they took from the room of his assistant. Nerissa thought it little of a bargain. "This gear does not suit me," she complained to Portia now. "Why do I do these things for you?"

"Because I thrill you with my boldness."

"My life contained spice enough before I met you," Nerissa responded crossly.

"But not enough witty conversation, nor swans floating on ponds," said Portia. "Now you have those things. Are you not grateful?"

"If I am so blessed, then why do I shiver on the wet boards of this boat, in a pair of woolen breeches that squeeze my tail so I cannot walk without pinching?"

"Can you never stop talking about the injuries done to your tail?"

"No! And speaking of those injuries, I have something to say about Signior ben Gozán."

"Shylock, you mean."

"Portia, he *cannot* press the terms of his bond. He will drop the suit before we come to the court. A pound of flesh! It would kill Antonio, and my heart tells me ben Gozán is no murderer."

"It is manifest on the court docket that he intends to become one. So it is written."

"Whatever is written, I *know* him. I do not call him friend, I assure you. I have a dent on my left buttock from my fall down the stairs—"

"Again the buttock! And a dent! Is't possible?"

"Incredible though it seems, it is so. But Portia—" Nerissa lowered her voice, though only sailors crossed the deck, glancing curiously at them from time to time. "I have known killers. I have seen them in the houses of Malipiero, with their eyes blank and dead. Why, in your *own* house, that soldier of Aragon—"

"Yes?" Portia said in a brittle voice. "More of him?"

Nerissa fell silent. Then she said quietly, "I only say I do not think Signior ben Gozán can mean it. Antonio will be spared this ordeal, and so will we."

"Well, my dear, I have listened to his daughter both at last night's supper and afterward, and I have a different idea. Ben Gozán blames Antonio because he lent the ship that made Jessica's flight

possible. Had he caught them he'd have brought her home before
Lorenzo bedded her and made her irredeemably a Christian's wife.
Now he craves revenge. The Jews always crave revenge! I have read
that they love to wield knives. And what of those Psalms you are
always telling me to read? I read them. I found them full of King
David's pleas that God shoot arrows at his enemies and burn them
up and throw them in pits and cut off their lips—"

"Portia, the Catholic bishops preach the same verses against
the Ottomites!"

"But who *wrote* them, I ask you? I am only being logical." Portia
assumed a wounded look. Throwing her cape dramatically across
her breast and shoulders, she sailed with her long stride to the
stern of the vessel.

Nerissa put her head on her knees and groaned softly. She felt
seasick.

WHEN SHE WALKED up the marble steps of the Municipio and
entered its cool, columned lobby, Portia was struck with a passion
that was two parts awe and three parts envious rage. Around her
strode gowned, black-hatted men, speaking confidently of suits
and appeals and judgments of the Forty, spicing their talk with
Latin terms like *caveat emptor, magistratibus urbis,* and *quid pro quo.*

This! she thought with wild satisfaction, flourishing her own
borrowed robe. *This!*

Behind her, Nerissa whispered frantically. "*Portia!* Your left
moustache hangs loose!"

Portia rubbed her face thoughtfully, frowning as though she
were deliberating how best to defend an agent of the port against a
bribe-taking charge. "There," she said out of the side of her mouth.
"Better?"

"Yes."

"And call me Balthazar. Walk quickly, now. Our case's hour is three, and whether it begins on time or not, our earliness argues in our favor. We appear before the fourth bench, and a venerable magistrate. One of the oldest of the Forty."

"*You* appear! Not I. Portia—"

"Balthazar."

"Put method in your madness. You are a passable young lawyer, I will confess. But *none* would mistake *me* for a boy."

Portia halted midstride. "Your common sense speaks wisely in this instance, young Buonaventuro. Roll not those eyes at me! I find myself well persuaded by you, not least because your Graziano, who clings to Bassanio like a burr, and who may be said to know your person well—"

"To say nothing of Signior ben Gozán, in whose very house I lived!"

"—is bound to be a witness in the court. *Ergo,* you may stand outside the door, hat pulled low."

Nerissa sighed with relief.

Portia thought her heart brazen, but it raced like a human organ as she opened the door to the fourth bench of the courts of the Forty.

She blinked in the April light that poured through the window. She wished it were less. The first thing she saw was Bassanio's back, splendid in watered silk, and his yellow-gloved hands gesturing, as he stood by the rail that divided the judge's high stand from the area where witnesses stood. He was talking with someone. Fearing he would sense her gaze upon him and turn, she averted her eyes and walked forward to the far side of that rail, arranging her book and papers. These were a volume of Venetian civil statutes and a second copy of Antonio di Argento's bond with the

Jew Shylock, witnessed by Bassanio, and hastily unearthed by her the night before, from under a pile of gauzy garments in her new husband's wardrobe. She could hear her heart in her ears, and feared the babbling men in the chamber heard it, too. But none did more than glance at her as she inserted herself among them, calmly looking over her documents. They were businessmen, from their talk: merchants and a handful of lawyers come to witness the case for its oddity, speaking of their own ships, commenting fearfully on the wreck of Antonio's, remarking with relish the famous savagery of Jews. Her eye was caught by the scarlet cap of a young man with large ears and melancholy green eyes. He stood near the wall by a tall, dark-haired gentleman who patted his shoulder in a fatherly way. The young man clutched a leather case. On the sleeve of his coat was stitched a red heart.

A chill gripped her as she heard Bassanio's voice almost at her elbow.

". . . had to!" he was saying. She turned her face and hunched her shoulders. Another man's voice, low and bitter, replied, "And so you are well pleased in your marriage."

"Dear Antonio," Bassanio said. "For me and my fortunes, it is best."

"Then I do not care what becomes of me."

Graziano's shrill laugh sounded suddenly from above and behind her head, and Portia jumped. She stole a glance upward, and saw the popinjay in the raised gallery at the room's rear, some fifty feet back. Then, once more, she saw Bassanio's watered-silk back, as her husband moved quickly toward the small stair that led toward Graziano in the gallery. She looked to the front of the court again, though not before her mind registered the singular sight of two identical twins, dressed like fine gentlemen, who stood next to Graziano, hissing and muttering.

A door behind the high judicial desk opened. Through it walked a white bearded judge, splendid in his high black cap. The dim peal of the Campanile sounded thrice, and the hubbub subsided as watchers moved toward the galleries. All had reached the court in a good hour.

Portia stayed put. She looked neither left nor right, thus avoiding the eyes of the men who remained on the floor. Calling on all her memories of civil disputes she'd witnessed from the galleries in Padua, in Vicenza, in Verona, she waited until the judge was comfortably seated, then left her book and bond on the rail and walked confidently forward. She handed the old man a paper. She felt all eyes on her back, but kept hers fixed on the judge as he read the message, which recused the Paduan lawyer, Signior Bellario, from the case on the grounds of illness, and recommended in his place Signior Balthazar, a young doctor of laws, expert in civil disputes, newly admitted to the bar.

She was happy to see that the judge squinted.

"Well enough," he said at last, shifting in his high chair. "Take your place, Signior Balthazar. Are you acquainted with the difference that holds this present question in the court?"

She had smoked three pipes of tobacco on the deck of her sloop the night before, hoping to roughen her voice, though the smell had given Nerissa the quease. Now she spoke as mannishly as she could. "I am informed thoroughly of the cause."

"Antonio di Argento and Shylock, both stand forth," said the judge.

Portia turned and faced the room, as two men stepped forward from behind the wooden barrier. A low murmur arose from the galleries, then died at the judge's stern look. Portia drew herself up to her full height and surveyed the disputants.

Apart from young Jessica, who was partly Christian, she had

never met a Jew in her life. At supper at Belmont, Bassanio, Lorenzo, and Graziano had derided the old, monstrous Shylock. Now she regarded the merchant's strangely simian face, with its powdered, hanging skin, the cheeks' unnatural pink exposed by the bright afternoon sun. She saw his sunken, kohl-lined eyes and his dark scowl. "Signior Shylock," she began, addressing Antonio. She was halted by laughter from the merchants in the gallery. Genuinely uncertain, hating the blush growing on her cheeks, she looked back at the judge and asked, "Which is the merchant here? And which the Jew?"

The judge pointed to the painted man. "Signior Antonio stands there. The Jew is the other."

Now she looked at that other, who stood by Antonio's side with his arms folded. She felt disoriented, as though she'd been misinformed regarding the particulars of this case, and of many other things throughout her life.

Antonio's antagonist was the tall, fatherly gentleman she had just seen patting the shoulder of the young red-capped man by the wall. He was a dark-haired, fine-eyed man of middle years, dressed in well-cut clothes of the sort worn by the wealthiest merchants on the Rialto. He looked younger than Antonio by at least a decade.

In fact, though Portia did not know it, Shiloh ben Gozán had clipped his beard the day before, and cut his hair to a length standard for a Venetian citizen. He had put aside his Jewish turban and badge upon entering the courtroom that morning, shutting the clerk of record's mouth with a dry, withering gaze. Now his head bore only a dark velvet cap he had bought in the Merceria.

"Is your name Shylock?" she asked him.

"*Shiloh* is my name."

Portia could hear little difference between the pronunciations, but she nodded as though she understood. She could see nothing in this man's face or on his body to mark his difference from the Christians. Yet in expression, he could not have been less like Antonio. While the Christian merchant wore a melancholy glower, Shiloh ben Gozán looked almost amused. He raised his brows as she continued to stare at him.

Collecting herself, Portia addressed him again. "Your suit is strange."

"His is stranger." Shiloh pointed to Antonio's green silk doublet and trunks.

The citizens in the galleries laughed, although, casting a sideways glance upward, she saw indignation on the faces of Antonio's knot of friends. She heard Graziano's yell: "Hold your tongue, Jew clown!"

Fool Graziano! Her anger at the interruptions restored Portia's confidence. She held up her hand. "Silence!" The noise subsided, and she looked at Antonio, who had roused himself from sluggish melancholy enough to realize—just now, it seemed—that the slim youth before him was not a mere clerk of the court, but his legal defender. "Where is Signior Bellario?" he asked.

"Sick." Portia stared boldly back at the merchant. His eyes showed a flicker of fear, then slack resignation. She pointed at the moneylender. "You stand within his danger, do you not?"

Antonio shrugged indifferently. "Ay, so *he* says."

"Do you confess the bond?"

"I do."

What was wrong with the fellow? *I do not care what becomes of me.* His complaint to Bassanio had been sad and strange. Could it be true?

Portia deepened her voice. "If you confess the bond—" She stopped to cough. A clerk of the court brought her water, and she thanked him. She swallowed, and said, "Then must the Jew be merciful."

"On what compulsion must I?" the moneylender said politely. "Tell me that."

Portia had been prepared for loud resistance, not for this man's quiet tone. She had meant to match the Jew's fierce outbursts with a passionate plea for mercy that would move the judge to tears. How vexing was this Shylock's calm!

But she'd match it.

In an infinitely reasoning tone, she began. "The quality of mercy is not strained. It droppeth as the gentle rain from heaven upon the place beneath. It is"—she held two fingers up to the judge—"twice blessed! It blesseth him that gives and him that takes. 'Tis mightiest in the mightiest; it becomes the throned monarch better than his crown."

She heard a rasping sound, and jerked her eyes leftward. Shiloh ben Gozán had taken a small knife and a whetstone from his pocket and was now sharpening the blade. The audience murmured. Portia turned her eyes abruptly from the man and again faced the judge, raising her arms and her voice. "Mercy is an attribute to God himself, and earthly power doth then show likest God's when mercy seasons justice!" The rasp of blade against stone grew louder, and she grimaced. She turned back to ben Gozán and spoke louder still. "Therefore, *Jew*, though justice be thy plea, consider this: that in the course of justice, none of us should see salvation."

Signior ben Gozán gave a short laugh. "That depends on a man's religion. But mercy and salvation have naught to do with this case." He placed his knife on the bar and took his contract from the breast of his coat. He shook the paper open. "I crave the law. The penalty and forfeit of my bond."

"You cannot enforce such a bond, Shylock!"

He raised his shoulders, and his hands, palms up, two fingers still pinching the paper. "It is a losing suit, but what can I do but try? I cannot help my wolfish and bloodthirsty nature."

Hearing guffaws from the gallery, she assumed a mocking smile to match his. "And so, beastly Jew, you would rend the flesh from a Christian. But flesh is not money. What could you possibly do with it?"

"I might convert it to money."

"How?"

"I might sell it to Christians to eat at their mass. You practice some kind of cannibalism there, do you not?"

The citizens in the gallery did not laugh at this, but hooted and hissed, and the judge shifted in his chair. Portia sensed her advantage, and pounced. "Your blasphemy is abominable anywhere. But in the Municipio of Venice we do not try heretics, but civil offenders. Is he"—she gestured at Bassanio—"not able to discharge the sum owed?"

"Yes, he can!" Bassanio sprang toward the gallery rail above, and Portia quickly turned her face from the audience back toward the judge. From the corner of her eye she saw Bassanio's gloved hand wave a note. "Here I tender it for him in the court. Yea, twice the sum!"

"Wha—?" Portia almost swiveled to glare at him, then quickly returned her eyes to the judge's platform.

"If that will not suffice, I will be bound to pay it ten times o'er, on forfeit of my hands, my head, my heart!"

Portia gritted her teeth in rage. *I'll have his hands, his head, his heart!* Still eyeing the judge, and not Bassanio, she forced her voice to stay quiet and reasoned, saying, "Even if Signior Bassanio truly *had* this money—which I doubt—this cannot be." Murmurs sounded in the gallery, and she raised her voice. "Venetian law upholds a contract freely signed, though its execution be deadly to a signatory. Only the Council of Ten can alter the law, and they have not done so."

"A Daniel come to judgment!" Shiloh ben Gozán said wryly. To her amazement, he winked at her. It came to her that he alone in the court had guessed she was not what she seemed. Quickly she averted her face from him, as her brain raced. Would the Jew call her office into question, and stop the proceedings? To continue was to gamble. Still, she thought he would not expose her. If he thought her a fraud, he more than anyone would expect her to botch Antonio's case. Perhaps his knowledge of her fraud was her safety.

In any case, she could not stop now.

The Jew leaned toward her and handed her his document. "Read," he said. "This contains my oath. I had sworn to take a pound of flesh from this merchant, did he not return my ducats on the day of payment. That day has arrived. Shall I break my oath and perjure myself? Not for *Venice*." His lip turned with scorn as he said the city's name.

Portia clutched the paper and extended her arms in a theatrical gesture of pleading. "Be merciful!" she said. "Bid me tear the bond!"

"No," said Shiloh.

Antonio coughed pitifully. "Most heartily I do beseech the court to give the judgment!"

Portia turned toward him, quelling her anger at this clown-faced man who strove to play the martyr before Bassanio. "Why, then, it is thus," she said coolly. "You must prepare your bosom for the Jew's knife."

The listeners gasped. Incredibly, Antonio unlaced his doublet, exposing a flesh so white it seemed never to have been touched by daylight.

"Do you know, there are more than one," ben Gozán said mildly.

Holy Mother of God! Portia flicked nervous eyes at him. "More than one what?" *More than one contract?*

"Jew."

She regarded him blankly.

"You persist in calling me 'the Jew.'"

The men in the gallery tittered. White-knuckled, Portia clutched the bond. This man would not let her orate! Yet he would *not* steal the stage from her, any more than would Antonio, who had now removed both his doublet and his shirt and stood with his arms spread like Christ, the pallidness of his flesh in startling contrast to the powdery pink of his doctored face.

So. A martyr here, an urbane wit there. Well, it would not serve. She had them both on the hip, and soon they would know it.

She looked at the judge, and saw to her surprise that he was dozing, listing sideways in his chair. His elbow hit the table and he sat suddenly upright, adjusted his high cap, and said, "Proceed."

"Antonio!" Bassanio called from behind the bar. "I am married to a wife as dear to me as life itself."

A look of jealousy flashed on the merchant's face.

And suddenly Portia understood what was between them.

Bassanio continued, rubbing an eye as though to wipe away tears. "But life itself, my wife, and all the world are not with me esteemed above thy life," he said theatrically. "I would die for you myself if I could!"

"Come down and do it then, *bufón!*" Shiloh ben Gozán, suddenly angry, gestured at Bassanio with his knife. "A pious Christian, liberal in offers! Were my knife at your breast you'd say anything to escape the pain." He pointed his blade at Antonio. "At least your friend's heart speaks through his mouth. It's more than I expected. He usually runs like a dog."

The judge roused himself to call for order. From the rear gallery Bassanio stared down at ben Gozán, openmouthed. As the cries from above subsided, Antonio turned and held up his arms to Bassanio. "Commend me to your honorable wife," he called. "Say how I loved you! Speak me fair in death. And when the tale is told, bid her judge whether Bassanio had not once *a love!*"

Shiloh ben Gozán stood by, nodding sagely at this passion play. "Very good, very good," he said. "Yet I have no time for this. Can we settle the business?"

"You are overhasty to shed a man's blood, Signior Shylock!" said Portia.

Shiloh shrugged. "It is Passover, a holy time, and my Sabbath approaches. I have three wells to poison before sundown."

Laughter swelled in the gallery, as the jest was repeated from man to man. Portia closed her eyes in frustration. *"Silence!"* When the place was quiet again, she stole a glance at the judge. His lids were half shut. No matter. It was not he but Antonio who needed to be shown who was master of the game.

She looked at the moneylender, who was now tapping his foot. "Jew Shylock, prepare your knife."

Smiling blandly, the tall man raised his knife and stood before Antonio. Antonio had dropped his arms and was standing head down, gazing at the floor, but now he lifted his arms again and stared defiantly at his antagonist. The citizen listeners watched in horrified silence. The judge slept.

Portia placed herself between the two men. To ben Gozán she said, "Therefore prepare thee to cut off the flesh. *Shed thou no blood.*"

Di Argento's eyes darted between her and ben Gozán, and the merchant looked confused. A hum of admiration rose from the listeners as Portia stared triumphantly at the moneylender.

Unperturbed, ben Gozán replied, "I will not *take* the blood. Isaac?"

The sad-eyed young man in the red cap rose from a bench and came forward, holding a pail and some rags. Shiloh leaned over the rail to grasp them, saying, "Of course I will catch or mop all that is spilled. The blood will remain the property of Signior di Argento."

Yells of outrage sounded from the gallery. Sweat trickled into Portia's collar. *Damn the Jew!* When she could make herself heard, she raised an arm to forestall ben Gozán, who had begun again to approach Antonio with his blade. She picked up her law book from the rail. "Wait!" she called. "If you take more or less than a pound, be it but so much as the division of the twentieth part of a grain—"

"Enough delay," ben Gozán interrupted. "The flesh will be weighed as precisely as this instrument allows." The young red-capped man was now handing a pair of butcher's scales over the rail. "I am no shohet," said ben Gozán, "but any man can cut meat in small slices and weigh as he goes. Isaac ben Amos is a rabbi's son—here today against his gentle father's counsel—but he is as skilled as you, my young Daniel, at the parsing of texts. Together you and he may avouch that I do not overstep one article of the signed bond."

Antonio moaned softly, but only Portia heard him. Again the court was a bedlam. Shiloh ben Gozán now raised his knife over the merchant's waiting breast. Portia met ben Gozán's eyes with a mix of horror and admiration.

She glanced back at the yelling citizens. In the very rear of the chamber, the door to the hall stood open a crack, and Nerissa's white face peered in.

That man is no murderer, Nerissa had said.

Portia tore her gaze from Nerissa's face, and looked at the lively eyes of the man whose knife was now poised a foot from Antonio's breastbone. In that instant she knew Nerissa had been right.

Shiloh ben Gozán would not cut. He was having a colossal jest at his foe's expense. At the last moment, he would throw his knife to the floor, bow courteously, forgive the debt, and walk from the court. He wanted only to drive up the price of his mercy; to trade his forgiveness not for money, but for his foe's humiliation. He had come here today only to show the Christians their folly, to body forth their nightmares, to play and overplay the monstrous Jew, and thus shrewdly to mock their superstitions and libels and lies.

But she understood something the Jew did not, which was that Antonio desired death.

He would not die. Perhaps he, too, knew that, now. But Bassanio did not know it, and Bassanio would never forget Antonio standing before the Jew with his arms spread, awaiting the fall of the knife. When the Jew spared his life, both he and Antonio would triumph.

And she would look the greatest fool in Christendom.

All this she saw in an instant, and knew things were as Jessica di Scimmia had said. She must halt both Shylock's mercy and Antonio's sacrifice. She must stop Shylock before he stopped himself. So as she watched his knife-holding hand slow, barely perceptibly, in its descent, she played her last card.

Quickly she looked down at the law book, then up in shock as though she had just seen the thing she had found the night before, poring over the thin pages at her desk in Belmont. "Tarry, Jew!" she said in a voice of command. "There is something else!"

Startled, ben Gozán halted and stared at her, his hands still firm on the knife hilt.

She raised the heavy book with both hands. "It is enacted in the laws of Venice! It is illegal for an alien to seek the life of any citizen, by direct *or* indirect attempts."

Ben Gozán's face paled. He regarded her in silence for a moment, as the watchers in the gallery took in their breaths.

Then he let his knife clatter on the floor. He nodded. "Ah, yes," he whispered. *"For an alien."* He seemed barely to hear as Portia lowered the book and read on, detailing the anti-alien laws of Venice. A foreign criminal's estate was forfeit to the state. A foreign criminal's life lay in the mercy of the state. When she finished, she met his eyes. Something in their dark depths shamed her, and she looked away.

"Is *that* the state?" said ben Gozán in a low, furious voice, gesturing toward the sleeping judge.

"He is the arbiter!" Portia growled back, ashamed of her shame. She met ben Gozán's eyes again, and this time glared. She pointed to the floor. "Down, and beg mercy of the judge!"

Ben Gozán glared back at her in dark contempt. He folded his arms, and did not move.

Antonio had sunk to the floor. The men in the gallery were now cheering and howling with laughter. The judge suddenly started and asked what had happened, and when Portia explained, he cried out for order. He declared Antonio's release and demanded that the Jew Shylock draw up a deed of gift of his monies, half for the state, and half for Antonio. Antonio first shook his head, baffled and dazed. Then he recovered himself enough to agree with his lawyer that the moneylender's confiscated wealth should be, as the young lawyer phrased it, "shared with Shylock's son-in-law, Lorenzo di Scimmia, during Antonio's life, and, should Antonio remain heirless, bequeathed to the same Lorenzo at his death." Shiloh looked at both Antonio and Portia in horror, then turned to the judge and, holding his hands up, said, "You may as well take my life, when you take the means whereby I live!"

"I pardon your life," the judge said, with sudden smug alertness. "*We* are merciful."

"Pardon it if he becomes a Christian!" said Antonio. For the first time, fight had entered his eyes and his voice. Graziano, now on the floor, took up the cry. "Make him a Christian! Make the dog a Christian! Drag him to the font at San Marco!"

"Be it so," said the judge. "The judgment shall be signed forthwith. The court is adjourned."

The merchants swarmed to the floor and past the barrier and began to haul Shiloh ben Gozán from the room. Young Isaac ran to help him, but was himself swallowed by the fray. The men of the Rialto pulled the youth's red cap from his head and the heart from his sleeve, yelling, "Baptize this one too!" The moneylender's eyes were closed and his lips were moving, and as they dragged him by both arms past Portia she heard him whisper a chanted, anguished sentence. *"He will be remembered forever,"* Shiloh was saying in Hebrew. But that was one language Portia did not know.

Bassanio fought through the pack to embrace Antonio.

Portia averted her face from her husband once more, and pulled down her cap. The door behind the judicial desk shut behind the black back of the judge. She walked as quickly as she could in the other direction, toward the portal that opened into the hall.

Made careless by horror, pale Nerissa still stood in that door's opening, not twenty feet from the hooting, kicking Graziano. She was staring at the riot. Portia grabbed her arm and hissed, *"Let's be gone!"*

They had just reached the wet street when she heard Bassanio's voice calling from the balcony above the Calle San Luca. "Young Balthazar! Your payment! Wait!"

"Don't wait!" said Nerissa, but Portia did. She turned slowly. Thirty feet above her, her smiling husband leaned into the air above the street. He seemed a bluebird, poised to fly. The Municipio, that hall of justice, so solid that morning, now looked to be tilting and sinking into the cloudy waters of the canal.

She cupped her hands around her mouth. "I'll have my payment," she called gruffly. "What of those yellow gloves?"

"These?" Bassanio said, eyeing his hands. Antonio appeared beside him on the balcony, reclothing himself in his gaudy green sleeves and doublet. Bassanio stripped off his gloves and threw them down to Portia. She stooped to retrieve them, and Nerissa, who had been hiding behind her, abruptly turned and strolled to the fondamento, as though she would hail a boat.

"But you'll have nothing else?" Bassanio called.

Portia slipped on the gloves. "The case is *pro bono. Gratis,* for the good of Venice. But I will take that fine silver ring, in return for saving your friend's life!"

"Ah, well, this," said Bassanio. "It's not a good ring. The stone is flawed, and the band is—"

"Are you not grateful to me?"

"We *are*. We are eternally in thy debt. Believe me, I would give you all the goods in the Merceria to show my thanks."

"Do you own all the goods in the Merceria?"

"No, no! A figure of speech. This ring, now. My wife gave it me—"

"Give it to the lawyer!" Antonio broke in, his voice harsh with anger. It was a strange tone from a man whose life had lately been spared, but Portia forbore to remark it.

"My love is worth more than your wife's," Antonio snapped.

Bassanio looked down at the ring that was already slipping from his finger. "It hurts anyway," he said. "I'll bring her a gift, and she'll forgive me."

In less time than it takes to say a credo, the ring was lying before Portia on the damp stones of the street.

THE SUN WAS low in the west as Portia hurried Nerissa toward the eastern docks. "Come! I need to question a man, and close to nightfall he will be gone."

Wrathful words washed back on her. "Is there *more* to your trickery? This was cruel, Portia, *cruel!* I heard most of it, and saw the last of it! And what of your husband and Antonio?"

"I think I need not fear my wedding bed as much as I'd imagined," Portia panted. "But I intend to claim what is mine even before I seek annulment." She twirled the turquoise on her finger. "This ring will do it."

"Do not *you* lose it then! But how could you *do* this to that poor fellow, Portia?"

"The world is the world, Nerissa. A stage where every man must play a part. I played Jesus amazing the elders with my wisdom, and he played the evil Jew. I did not write the pl—"

"Cruel!"

Portia stopped short and turned to Nerissa. "*I* cruel? Your man with the fine Spanish eyes was going to cut a man's heart out!" Grabbing Nerissa's elbow, she started them off again, not heeding her friend's look of outrage. "He was going to take his knife and—"

"You *knew* he was not! He was playing a *game.* And they took everything he had and kicked him into the street! Graziano was lead dog, yapping and biting. You may forget any thought that I'd knit my soul with that one; I'd be stretched on the rack before I'd do it! Do you know, not long ago a Veronese wanted to marry me, ugly of face, but the *wit* of him! Too late, I fear, for me; another will have him by now. So be it. I'll go back to my parents' farm, Portia! I will! I'll beg them to take me, rather than marry such a rogue as Graziano di Pesaro. Common sense pukes at such a pairing!"

Nerissa railed on as they reached the outer rim of the docks, where the slaves carried trunks and rolled barrels, the sweat on their dark backs shining in the last rays of the sun.

XANTHE

"If you do love me,
you will find me out."

TWENTY-NINE

In DECEMBER OF 1568, the year twenty-one-year-old Shiloh ben Gozán first passed through Venice's lion gates, bearing his baby in his boat, the Moors of southern Spain rose in revolt. The cause was the new Pragmática set forth by King Philip the Second. It banned the speaking of Arabic throughout Spain, and enforced the burning of the holy Koran. The day it was published, the Moriscos—New Christian Moors who had hidden their true faith for decades—ran from their homes shouting *Allá Akbar*, brandishing swords supplied by the Ottomites. They killed Catholic priests and those priests' defenders, and sold Christian women and children into slavery.

The whole region of Andalusia was bathed in blood.

It was more than a year before the uprising was quelled.

When the Christians had once more won Granada, its Moors who still lived were distributed among other regions of Spain. The king declared a new law: any male Morisco over sixteen years of age found within ten leagues of Granada was made subject to death; any female over nine and one-half to slavery.

The Pragmática was upheld.

In 1571, Spanish, Venetian, and Austrian forces killed thirty thousand Turks and destroyed the entire Ottoman fleet at Lepanto, near the Greek coast. All Christian Europe exulted (save for Protestant England, who, though it feared the Turks, hated the Spanish Armada just as much). Yet Spain mourned the thousands of its soldiers who had been killed, wounded, or captured during the great battle. A minor official of the Toledan Alcázar grew angry because of the wound his nephew had received at Lepanto. A Turkish cannon had almost destroyed the young man's arm. The nephew was a common sailor with the undistinguished name of Miguel de Cervantes Saavedra, and had never been aught but a soldier. With one useless hand it was unlikely he would contribute anything more to the world. Craving revenge, his uncle grew zealous in his pursuit of renegade Moors. Before long he uncovered proof that a Toledan Morisco had received a supply of money and weapons from the Turks in the summer of 1568, and had sent all on to his relatives in Andalusia. That Moor was seized and sent to the Inquisition at Valencia.

He was a cousin to the swordmaker Julian del Rei.

The old craftsman said nothing directly to his daughter of the matter. But at thirteen she was wise enough to guess why her father, who had always slighted the Christian holidays and not gone to mass above once a month, began to close his shop routinely during the Holy Weeks and to attend church every Sunday. Now he prayed in Arabic only in Ramadan, in the dark of his room. At other times he no longer knelt, facing east on his prayer rug, even behind shuttered windows, and he began to cross himself before the statues of the Virgin and Christ that were carried in the Easter processions. He never mentioned his cousin's name, but in the year that followed the town said it often, along with the names of the other New Christians who had disappeared into the prisons of Toledo, Zaragoza, Valencia, and Madrid.

Xanthe heard the talk.

One day, in her seventeenth year, Xanthe saw in the bottom of a copper kitchen pot the cousin's face and body, the man's mouth contorted and his frame stretched on a rack. She dropped the pot with a shriek and ran to her father, who was filing steel in his foundry.

"Your cousin Gaspar—"

His look silenced her. She saw that he had long guessed the man's fate, and saw further that he did not want their kinship mentioned, even in the privacy of his home.

That night he came to her as she lay in bed and placed his hand on her forehead. "Xanthe, you are crossed," he said. "Half Jew from your mother, half Moor from me. I do not ask you to be true to any faith. I ask only that you survive."

She said nothing, but he stayed by her bed as though he expected an answer. After a minute he said, "Hear me, Xanthe. Faith is not sacred. You saw where Gaspar's faith led him."

"Yes, I saw," she said in a small voice.

"Only life is sacred, and all life is sacred."

It was a strange utterance from a man who earned his bread making swords and knives. But though her father loved his art and was proud of his blades' keenness, he was a peaceful man, and she accepted his saying as heartfelt.

"The meaning of the Most High is life and love," he said. "Like the meaning of music. Promise me you will survive."

She reached out to touch the ropy veins of his arm. "I promise," she said.

———————

Her mother had died of the plague, and her father had never remarried. Instead he'd poured his pain and his love into his craft, and achieved a name that had spread to Portugal, Italy, and France, and even beyond the bounds of Catholic Europe, to Germany, Holland, and England. Xanthe knew he hoped his fame as a craftsman, if not his New Christian piety, would protect them both from the busy eyes of the Inquisition. But she also knew he feared it would not. All Toledo knew of the fate of Elizabeta de la Cerda, daughter of a rich hidalgo, who had scandalously married a marrano Jew. Her father's status in the Alcázar had not saved her from the Church's punishment, though de la Cerda was an Old Christian name.

"For such fears your mother forsook her parents' faith when she took me as husband, and I was glad she did it," her father told her the next night at supper. There was no wine at the table—there was never wine at the table—and he was not talkative by nature, so she could not guess what had prompted his recounting of this old story. As he had the night before, he seemed shaken from his usual taciturnity by some new, deep fear for her future.

"Your mother chose life, as I did," he said. "We shared it together as long as Allá permitted it."

"Do you think I would choose death?" she asked him.

He looked at her gravely. "I tell you not only not to choose it, but to run from it, as far as you can." He leaned over the table, brushing aside the flat bread and dates she had set before him. Though he played the Christian in most ways, he still would not eat pork, and scoffed at carrots and turnips when she brought them from the garden. They were the food of pigs.

"Run from death, and choose life and love when you can. Your mother fell in love with this"—he pointed to his chest—"but had she done so today, she could not have married me."

"Why not?"

"There is a new law. I was told of it yesterday, by a Madrileño who came for a rapier. New Christians may not intermarry."

"*What?*"

"*Limpieza de sangre.* King Philip is bent on purifying all the Spaniards, if it takes generations. Ah, poor Xanthe, you are tainted on two sides. All the more reason you must find an Old Christian to marry you, and give your child Christian blood. But I will help you there." He smiled a little. "I have forged swords for the best families in La Mancha. My silver and my name will persuade them that a dark little Morisca is not so bad. And one of their sons will cleanse your blood."

Her father's wry tone did not disguise the seriousness of his purpose. Xanthe felt chilled. Her heart constricted, as though her whole body was being squeezed into one of the boxes on her father's shelves, those oddments constructed from surplus silver or bronze or steel or gold.

But she was not a defiant child, so she only looked down and said softly, "I need not marry yet."

"You gave away the ring I gave you to give your husband," he said. "Gave it to that poor maiden, who suffered so in *her* choice. But that was only a metal ring. The ring that truly matters is—"

"My virginity; I know, Papi," she said, blushing.

Despite her obedience, or because of it, she could not bring herself to tell him that she had also parted with the ring that mattered. A mother might have taught her better to rule her passions and guard her body, but she'd had no mother since the age of four. The vague warnings of the nun who'd taught her to read had carried small weight next to the feelings kindled in her by a young Toledan Morisco. The boy had promised her marriage, and his honeyed tongue had seduced her, though she had been willing, she would have to confess. Three successive nights they had lain together by a crooked almond tree near the wall of her father's courtyard. On the fourth night he did not appear, although he had sworn to come. It was months before she'd seen him again. He was emerging from his house with friends, in the middle of a celebration of his wedding on the morrow to a Morisco maid of the countryside. He had called out a greeting to her and the news, as though there were nothing amiss and no need to ask pardon for anything. It was as though his habit of lying about his faith had bled into everything, invalidating all his promises, rendering him heartless and glib. Though her heart was broken, she pitied his new wife.

A few days later he had visited her again in her father's courtyard, as Julian del Rei slept in the heat of the afternoon. He had come to explain himself, he said. Yes, he had married another, but what else could he have done? He had discovered he loved someone else. You could not choose whom you loved.

She had given him her whole heart, and he had broken it. She had wept for a week, and then sworn that ever after she would choose whom she loved.

Now her father thought he would make that choice for her. Xanthe smiled at the old man as he beamed at her from across the table. He thought her a glorious untouched fruit whom any youth would be proud to pick.

Before the Pragmática, the Moriscos would borrow Christian garments to marry, then change afterward into Moorish dress and repeat the ceremony in their own way, behind their closed doors. On the morning after a wedding the groom would show the fathers of both marriage partners a cloth spotted with the hymenal blood of his no longer virginal wife.

If such a cloth could not be supplied, there was trouble between the families.

I have one thing to thank the new edict for, she thought.

XANTHE'S MIND HAD long been haunted by the fate of young Elizabeta de la Cerda, whom all Toledo knew had changed her name to Leah Gozán.

When the lady had come into her father's shop that cold February day when Xanthe was eight, she had seen only that the turquoise ring she herself had laid on the shelf had glowed as the maid walked toward it. She had been caught by the beauty of Elizabeta, but even more by the vision of the shining heart she'd seen beating on the young woman's breast. The maiden had looked like the Virgin Mother, her heart on the outside, raised like a scar burned into her skin, only radiant and pulsing with life. The ring too had pulsed as the woman held it in her hand.

That night, when Xanthe had stared into the ring's blue stone, seeking the heart of its mystery, she'd seen in its scarred depths the shadow of a tall man holding an infant. But the image had quickly faded, and for her the ring had not pulsed or glowed.

She was glad to cede the ring to Elizabeta. She had known the young lady would return for it. And in the year that followed, Xanthe had been happy to see the lovely woman and her tall, handsome groom walking the twisted streets of Toledo, laughing and talking, heads close together. Always they were so absorbed in one another's company that they did not mark her, a small girl, nearly as dark as her Moorish father, who smiled at them shyly, as though she herself had given them to each other.

When the boy who swept their floors told her of the young woman's death at the hands of the Inquisition, she ran to the far corner of her father's courtyard and vomited. She thought everything inside her would come out and leave her vacant, and that her loose, empty skin would shrivel and float up to the perfect blue sky of the Most High. She prayed to die, as she lay in the dirt. She felt sick and afraid.

But the sickness passed, and she rose to prepare the evening meal.

The next day she heard the same boy singing a Jewish wedding song, one her mother had taught her when she was three. Her father still sang or hummed it at times, when thinking of his late wife. But the boy twisted the melody into tunelessness, and put mocking, ugly words in place of the song's true ones. Her father spoke sharply to him and told him to stop, for if there ever was a soul with no music in it, it was the soul of that boy. A quarrel followed between them, and the next day the boy was gone.

JULIAN DEL REI did not live to choose an Old Christian husband for his daughter.

One evening in her twenty-first year Xanthe found him lying bent over his cold forge, his hand gripping the silver of a half-made sword handle, and a look on his face so peaceful that it belied the soldierly posture of his arm. In death as in life he was a cross and a paradox. To his funeral came not only his fellow Toledan Moriscos, but most of the Old Christian dons of the city and the Manchegan countryside. After they had given him the rites of Christian burial she came home and howled with grief. Without knowing why, she tore her clothes and sat for days in a darkened room, ignoring the door-knocks of neighbors, drinking water only, fasting and mourning.

On the tenth day she weakly arose and went to the kitchen to cook.

She reopened the shop and rehired her father's craftsmen. She did well enough.

As YEARS WENT by she had more than one suitor among the Old Christians, but she turned them all away. In their faces she saw frightening visions, of men and women hanging from ropes and racks, of children burning.

She had headaches. Leaving the great cathedral one day after mass, she saw workers hanging a painting of Christ in one of the chapels. In the oil the Messiah's robe shone blood red. He stood ringed by men: a soldier in Spanish armor, a dignitary waving a long, white-fingered, accusatory hand, a man who pulled Christ's hands cruelly with ropes. She halted and stared at the canvas in horror, barely noting the young painter who gestured toward the wall and babbled to the workmen in a mixture of Spanish and what might have been Greek. The workmen looked after her curiously as she ran from the place, haunted by the painted red of Christ's robe.

After that the visions came thick and fast.

Sometimes she saw pictures of human torment in the metals with which the artisans worked in the shop. So she retreated to the rear of the house, where she kept ledger-books and counted silver. She had always been good with tabulations, and liked the rhythmic stacking and telling of coin. Now she found comfort in the feel of hard money between her fingers. The faces on the coins stayed still. They did not move or cry out in pain.

The security her father's fame had bought her began to erode in the face of her evident strangeness.

Customers and craftsmen talked, and word spread of Xanthe's visions. She was a tool of the devil, folk said. One man had seen her muttering by candlelight and casting spells. It was true; he had seen this, though the wizardry she was practicing was only the forecasting of weekly profits and expenditures for the shop. Still, some women muttered and gestured against the evil eye when they passed her in the marketplace. That truly frightened her, for she knew from travelers who visited the shop that witches were being hunted in Scotland and parts of France. It was a Protestant madness thus far, but in this age of fear, who could say it would not spread to crazy Spain? And she was a Moor, and the daughter of a Jew.

One day in the Calle de los Capuchines she was beset by a trio of men who pulled at her hood and called her a pagan witch and told her the Holy Brotherhood had her name on a list. They pushed her into the middle of the street. One struck a flint and held it to a piece of wood, then touched the glowing wood to the back of her wrist. "Let's see if a black witch will burn," he said. She cried out and struggled, and finally they freed her, saying, "Run, sorceress!" She raced halfway home and then stopped, her heart knocking against her ribs. She thought of all the Old Christian friends of her father's to whom she might go for protection. But in front of their faces in her mind's eye rose a wall of flame and an image of Elizabeta de la Cerda—no, Leah Gozán—crying in pain.

She did not trust Old Christians.

She did not trust anyone.

She forced herself to walk calmly and slowly back to her father's shop. In her back room, in a trunk full of papers, she unearthed an old ledger with accounts and addresses of Julian del Rei's foreign clients from years past. She leafed through it, seeking the names of gentry in England, in the Netherlands, in Italy. At last she came upon a yellowed receipt for two hundred maravedís from a Signior Bel Mente, of Belmont, near Treviso, in the state of Venice.

She knew a little Italian. She had learned it to converse better with some of the foreign customers who came to the Plaza de Zocodover. She carefully placed the slip of paper in an envelope, and later went to sleep with it under her pillow.

That night she dreamed of Jerusalem, though she never had seen that city. She heard the muezzin's call to prayer as she walked among its pink-white buildings. But as the sun rose in her dream the pink of the buildings deepened to red and ran down the walls of the temples and mosques.

She awoke to orange torchlight and men's coarse laughter sounding from the street. "Here lives the Moorish witch!" said one voice. There was a hard pounding on the door to the shop, and then came the breaking of glass.

She jumped to her feet and grabbed a cloak and a leather bag containing maravedís, the profits of the month. She began to climb through the window of her chamber, but when she was halfway out she remembered the slip of paper beneath her pillow. She jumped back in to retrieve it, then vaulted through the casement just as the outer door to the shop broke. She heard the heavy tread of several men in the front room, and the scattering of ironware.

She had never been muscular, but some bold spirit gave her arms and legs the strength to climb the crooked tree in the courtyard and to scramble over the high wall into her neighbor's yard. From thence she slipped into the street. She ran to the Puerta del Sol where the beggars slept, and sat pretending to be one of them. In the morning when the city gates opened she crossed the bridge over the Tagus, and did not stop walking until she reached Madrid.

THIRTY

THERE WAS NO reason Portia Bel Mente should have remembered her.

Portia had been three years old and Xanthe only eight on the
day Portia's father had bought three metal caskets from Julian del
Rei in Toledo. Twenty-three years had passed when Xanthe came
to a side door of the great estate at Belmont, bedraggled and foot-
sore from walking and riding half of Spain, and gaunt from sea-
sickness on the sea trip east and the boat ride up river. She herself
remembered Portia only because her father had often spoken with
amusement of the Italian magnifico who was mad for swords, and
of his headstrong daughter. And also because Xanthe had never in
all her life seen another head of hair that really looked like spun
gold.

A servant brought her to Portia. Two of the lady's servants had
recently quit in disgust, "unhappy," she said, "with having the inef-

ficiency of their marketing habits amply demonstrated to them on paper!" Xanthe had looked sympathetically at the doña and shaken her head at the rank folly of those two servants. In the pocket of her cloak she clutched the receipt that showed her own identity and proved Signior Bel Mente's tie with her father. But when Portia asked her, in Spanish, whether she could make beds, she nodded, and left the paper in her cloak. If she had ever yearned to call special attention to herself, Spain had cured her of the desire.

In the months to come it surprised her that this strange golden lady, always talking or turning the pages of three books at once, so curious about all things in heaven and earth, should show no interest in her servants. Could they do their jobs? Would they steal? If the answers were "yes" and "no," she cared to know no more. Xanthe was one of three Moorish women at Belmont; the other two were North African slaves. Yet Portia confused them all. Xanthe was sent to pour wine for guests or to clean chamber pots, to look after a visiting neighbor's children or to scrape pots in the scullery. The Moors jested among themselves that the lady of the house thought them either all one woman or twenty. They knew better than to correct her. As their duties of the hour required, they freely exchanged service clothes that ranged from the silks of the maid-in-waiting to the faded aprons of the kitchen slut.

Yet Nerissa d'Orocuore knew who they were.

Xanthe had been at Belmont for nearly a year when Nerissa arrived. The young woman came dressed in silk and cloth-of-gold, and had Xanthe been new to the estate, she would have thought Nerissa the mistress. As it was, it took her a week to infer that Nerissa was not a guest but an exalted duenna, second only to Portia in authority. She was entrusted with the keys to the house and the management of servants and the entertainment of the bizarre flocks of suitors who played cards in the lobby. All this she guessed when

Nerissa took to walking with a bunch of keys dangling from her belt.

She was filling a vase with flowers in the hall where guests dined when she heard the merry voice behind her. "Xanthe."

She started so that she spilled water from the vase, and turned, her heart racing, to curtsy. She could not remember the last time she had heard her name said by any but the maidservants, but this voice was well spoken.

Nerissa stood smiling at her in the doorway. "That is your name, is it not?"

"Yes," she said, looking down.

"Lady Portia was not certain."

Without wanting to, Xanthe grimaced. She quickly straightened her expression, but not before Nerissa saw her mouth twitch. "Well, you Moorish women glide about like ghosts, doing your work so quietly and well! And your hair and eyes are all of a color!" Her own eyes danced. "You must forgive us Venetians for our mistakings."

Xanthe smiled a little.

"Also, my mistress's head is filled with weighty thoughts." Nerissa now smiled broadly. "She has little time for the crowd of us."

Xanthe knew well who her own father had been, and had never for an instant felt inferior to the great lady. So it surprised her that she was not irked but strangely pleased to have been included in Nerissa's "the crowd of us." She stole a look at Nerissa's eyes, and knew that it was this friendly, smiling woman herself with whom she was glad to be linked. And with that recognition came a great heart's pain. She felt the full thrust of her loneliness.

"What is wrong?" said Nerissa, looking distressed. "Please don't cry." She came to Xanthe and put her arm around her shoulder. "I am jesting. I know it is irksome to have one's name forgotten. Do you know, my own mother was always forgetting mine!"

Xanthe could not imagine such a thing. She smiled at the absurdity, and at the warm touch of Nerissa's hand.

Nerissa squeezed her shoulder, then dropped her arm. "I will remember yours. *Xanthe.* Is it from your own language?"

"My language is Spanish, duenna," Xanthe said guardedly. Open-faced, Nerissa smiled and nodded. Xanthe relaxed a little. "The name is Basque, I think. My father liked the 'X' because it was a cross at the start of me." She held up her hands to show two crossed fingers.

"Ah, was he very devout?"

Xanthe thought of Julian del Rei's careful mass attendance and genuflections in the last years of his life. "Some," she said carefully.

"How you must miss him!"

Xanthe felt tears start again, and blinked them back. "*Sí,* duenna. *Sí.*"

Her BURDENS AT Belmont were light. She did not mind cleaning plates in the scullery or bearing linens to the soft beds of Portia's guests, or picking flowers in the gardens, or even sweeping tiny frogs from the folds of the curtains. At times she still saw sudden pictures in windows and glasses and plates, of women burned by hot oil, of children stabbed, of men yelling in pain on ropes or racks. But such images, which had haunted her in Spain for years, came less often at Belmont. It took her months to get used to the heaviness of the moist north Italian air, and she was sick with coughing throughout her first winter at the estate. But in time she felt hale, and the headaches that had plagued her in Toledo all but disappeared. She grew accustomed to her new world. Her tongue grew more quick in Italian, and she learned to joy in the greenness of the fields around her.

Belmont was an Eden of sorts.

Though like Eden, it had its snake.

SHE SAW HIM first by the fire in the kitchen. He was a young man who gave his name as Launcelot Giobbo, and he was extraordinarily well dressed for a servant. His hair was fine and sand-blond, and his face would have been handsome but for the constant mockery in his eyes. Despite her reserve she found herself warmed by his attentions as he jested and rubbed his red hands, made raw by the January wind on the river that had borne him and his even better dressed master north.

"We come on a wooing quest!" he exulted. "We will slay the dragons of Belmont, and capture its lady and all her riches! We are Jason! Aeneas! Percival! Galahad!"

"And *your* name?" asked the cook, as he turned a whole pig on a spit.

"I am Launcelot, the perfect knight. Do you know the story?"

The cook spat in the fire. "I cannot read."

Launcelot looked at Xanthe, who was smiling as she shook pepper into a stew. "Ah, but *you* are a lady of distinction." He rose to his feet and offered a sweeping bow. "I see how daintily you turn your eyes from that dead animal." He pointed at the pig. "I see the curl of your lip. Lady, it is the trophy of a great boar hunt!"

"No, it is not," she laughed. "The dirty thing grew in a barn."

He had not, he told her later, been christened Launcelot. In the parish records he was Balbi, a name incommensurate to his poetic strain, and so he had changed it himself at an early age. He loved the stage plays and the ballads and the knightly romances of Ariosto and Malory that he had learned to scan in the library of his first employer, before he'd been sent to the austere house of an old

Jew who never read anything lively. "And now I am come to Arcadia, and I see you, a Moorish princess, speaking in the accents of thy far-off kingdom!"

"Arcadia?" she asked, huddling in her cape. They had come to the edge of the woods to pick up kindling sticks, and the wind was biting.

"A place of green pastures."

"We must wait a few months for green pastures. And I do not have shame at my birth, but am not a princess."

"I think you are an enchanted one, jailed in your dark skin."

She frowned. "I am no more jailed in my dark skin than you are in your freckles."

He laughed as though she had made a great jest, and pinched her. "Would you show me to the room where the knightly squires rest?"

She smiled, despite the pinch, which she resented. "Come, then." She led him back into the house and through a maze of back halls to a small, clean room that contained two low beds. "This be yours," she said. "Perhaps another in here before the week's out."

"I would be *charmed* by your company in this room, Moroccan princess!"

"Not me!" She stepped away from him.

"Ah, *you* wish only sweet discourse. You are a princess. I will be by the kitchen fire tonight, Princess Melisandra—"

"Princess *who?*"

"And I will fill your ears with story! Will you wait? At ten of the clock?"

She nodded, laughing.

She thought him a clown; a bufón and a peacock. So she was surprised that night when, not seeing him by the fire as he had promised, her heart fell a little. The jests of the cook and another servant suggested that Launcelot Giobbo was busy with another wench of the house, one who had proved more friendly to his eager hands.

Later, she lay in her bed and could not fall asleep. A sharp-toothed wind seemed to eat at her entrails. She gazed at the moonlit wall. Gradually, to her alarm, there took shape thereon the image of a woman bent over a table, brutalized from behind by a shadowy fiend. She cried out in fear and buried her head beneath her blanket. Her heart pounded.

In time a clock struck, and she peeped at the wall again. It was pale and bare. She closed her eyes, but her heart would not cease its knocking. She was still seized by terror.

For the first time in years, she began a prayer to the Most High. She could not see God's face in her mind or the color of God's skin. Her mind was blank with fear; even the words of the Paternoster and the Arabic prayers of her childhood fled her memory. She prayed almost wordlessly, *por favor, por favor, por favor.*

At last she slept.

THIRTY-ONE

Xanthe SPENT THE next day laundering linens. Late at night she came into the main kitchen, and started when she saw Launcelot sitting alone by the fire, his boots propped on the bricks. He smiled at her gaily. She frowned at him.

"What means that crossed brow, my princess?" he cried.

She felt foolish, and could not bring herself to say that she had sought him the night before, and been hurt that he had not been there. After all, his words of invitation had been light, a flirtation, not weighted with truth. Why should she have thought he meant them? She was a woman of thirty-one, settled in solitude. And he was a sly young dog with an eye for girls. What did she need, anyway, with a new broken heart?

But loneliness clawed her.

"Tonight I will tell you some stories," he said. She ladled soup for herself from a kettle, and said nothing. "What stories do you like, princess?" He leaned toward her.

"Stories where men do what they say," she could not help grumbling.

"Fanciful tales indeed."

She looked up, and saw his smiling face less than a foot from hers. His teeth were good—straight, and none missing—but suddenly his freckled face repelled her. She saw a hardness behind the light in his eyes.

He placed his fair hand on her dark one. "What kind of child would you and I make?"

She drew back, dropping the ladle into the kettle. "None, so please you. He would be piebald."

He grabbed her waist in sudden, startling anger. "Bitch, are you proud of your pedigree?" She began to cry out, but he quickly covered her mouth with his hand. He spun her and bent her forward over the cook's chopping board, which was littered with orange peels and a knife. She grabbed for the blade, but succeeded only in knocking it to the floor. He kicked it to the far side of the room. "Devil!" he said, pulling up her skirt. "You are no fair Lucrece, but I'll be your Tarquin. Remember that you are a slave."

AN HOUR LATER, as she lay, awash in tears, on her bed, there rose before her the same wall of flames that had marred the faces of Old Christian friends in Toledo on the day the ruffians had called her witch and burned her wrist. Now, over and over, she rubbed the shiny scar. In it she saw the fire, raging before the faces and forms who stretched their hands toward her. Nerissa stood beckoning behind the flames, and even hard-faced Portia held out her hand. But the fire blocked Xanthe's path, and would consume her utterly before she reached them.

When she closed her eyes against the vision it still flickered, orange and black, against her eyelids.

"*No más!*" she cried, muffling her own voice with her pillow. "*Stop!*"

In desperation, she pushed herself upright. She left her room in the far wing of the mansion. Taking a torch from the wall in the hall, she walked painfully toward the center of the house, where voices still sounded in laughter and talk which grew louder as she approached. At the half-open door to the large chamber where the ivory-keyed virginals stood, she stopped.

Portia was not there. By the rules of her father's will, she stayed secluded from the men who came to Belmont to seek her in marriage, sharing her company only an hour each day, and that hour strictly supervised by the old lawyer who had drafted her father's odd will. But Nerissa enjoyed company at all hours, and was in the room tonight, flushed and happy with wine, laughing in the company of the Venetian gallants Bassanio di Piombo and Graziano di Pesaro. The three sat at a table, playing a game of cards. Pouring wine, laughing with them, was Launcelot, looking smooth as an orange. As he filled Nerissa's glass she looked up and thanked him with a playful smile, and called him *good sir.*

All thought of approaching Nerissa fled from Xanthe's mind. With her torch she turned and walked back to the kitchens. Though it was late, she lit a fire, and by its light found and picked up something from the floor by the wall. Then she heated water. In her room she poured the water into a tin tub, stripped, and sat in it for an hour, soaking and washing.

She kept the cook's knife on the floor by the tub, well within reach of her hand.

———

Someone, probably Nerissa, must have told Launcelot that Xanthe was no slave, but a well-born Morisca of Spain, because after that night he treated her with straight-faced, unsmirking courtesy. He touched her no more, and when they passed in the kitchens or hallways he walked quickly, and his eyes flicked toward her in fear. It made her smile, his thought that she could harm him. It told her that she *could* harm him, with a well-placed word to Portia or Nerissa, or even perhaps to his master, Bassanio, who, though something heavy of wit and light of brain, did not seem unkind. But she gave no such word to any of them. Even her fellow serving women received from her no more than a warning to flee Launcelot in empty rooms or dark corners. A lock sealed her tongue on the subject of her rape. She wanted to forget it, so she never spoke of it.

But she could not forget it.

The weather warmed into spring. It was the season of Lent, and the servants and the guests ate fish and eel caught from the Fiume Sile, and vegetable pie, and no meat during the week. But meat was allowed on Sundays. When the first Sunday of the season arrived, the table creaked under a mighty pork dinner. Xanthe was queasy to begin with, and felt worse when she saw the roast pig, so she excused herself continually while setting the table, moving back and forth between kitchen and board like a shuttlecock, while Nerissa looked at her with concern. As Portia entered with her guest of the day, Xanthe was downing a cup of steadying water in the kitchen, and nerving herself to return and pour wine. Then she heard a loud voice say, "Ah, lady! Fair is your provision for this thy humble servant! Yet wine I would not drink, and I cannot eat of the habitation which our prophet the Nazarite conjured the devil into!"

"What is he saying?" she heard a servant whisper. Holding the wine, Xanthe came to the door and saw an enormously tall black man with rings in his earlobes and a shaven head. He had the handsomest face she had ever seen. He wore the bagged silk breeches and tunic of a Moroccan lord, and his hand gripped a curved sword, from which two platter-bearing servants were nervously backing away. Xanthe's eyes went wide, and for a moment she forgot her stomach's turmoil.

The African held the sword high. "By this scimitar that slew the enemies of Allá—"

"Enemies of Allá? Do you mean Christian soldiers?" Lady Portia's voice was barbed. She stood veiled, as she always did before her suitors, and wore a gown of shimmering gold weave.

The dazzling nobleman paused for a moment, then smiled brilliantly. "This sword has also won three fields from Sultan Suleiman!"

"Ah, very good," Portia said, clapping her hands. "Lay it aside now, please. We will be eating of the devil's habitation, and you may eat what you please. There are leeks."

From the other side of the table Nerissa shot her mistress an angry glance. But the African merely bowed and smiled, after giving his sword to a servant, who looked goggle-eyed at the jewels in its hilt as he bore it away. Xanthe saw that it cost the big man something to maintain a pleasant look before the platter of pork that sat on the table before him, as he loaded his plate with bread and leeks. She wished to stay and look at him more, but her own gorge rose again suddenly as she looked at the food. She handed the wine to the maidservant who was crowding behind her to peep at the visitor, and fled from the house into the cool spring air.

Hours later she stood in the lobby, sweeping the marble tiles, when the portals to the presence chamber opened to discharge the nobleman, his smile tarnished. His train of three dark-skinned servants or slaves followed him through the door. "Farewell heat, and welcome frost!" he said, his hands raised extravagantly to heaven. He turned and bowed deeply to Portia, who stood with her arms crossed, tapping her foot. "Portia, I have lost, and take my leave." He straightened and strode proudly toward the outer door. Xanthe leaned on her broom and smiled at him, but his eyes washed over her as though she were not there.

Behind him Portia dusted her hands and said to Nerissa, "Good riddance to his black devil's face."

The man stopped, one hand on his sword. He half-turned, and for the first time he seemed to see Xanthe, who stood near him clutching her broom, her lips tightly pressed together.

He bowed to her.

Then, followed by his servants, he walked from the house.

Xanthe followed him with her eyes. Past her ran Nerissa, saying, "Wait, milord!" Nerissa flew through the house's open portals to its porch and walked quickly down the wide marble stairs. On the walk she caught up with the Moroccan and said something to him, some word of apology for her mistress's ill humor, and curtsied and smiled prettily. The man bowed to her, then continued down the path toward the dock, followed by his servants, who, bearing his luggage, had elevated their noses so high in the air Xanthe thought it a wonder they did not tip backward. Nerissa stood clutching her skirts in the breeze, watching them go. Behind Xanthe, Portia banged shut the doors to the presence chamber, hiding herself behind them.

Nerissa turned and climbed the stairs back into the house. Xanthe met her gaze, and Nerissa said, "I am sorry, Xanthe."

———

"COME IN!"

Xanthe pushed open the door to Nerissa's chamber, just as the clock in the room struck eight. Fine clothes were strewn carelessly on the bed, chair, and floor, and even across the prie-dieu, meant for prayers, that stood below the gold crucifix on Nerissa's wall. To Xanthe's surprise, Nerissa was kneeling on the prie-dieu as Xanthe entered, right on top of the petticoat draped across its base.

"Pardon," Xanthe said, halting in the doorway.

But Nerissa had risen and crossed the room. "Xanthe, sit down. You looked ill today, even before our lady Portia made such short shrift of that Moroccan giant." She led Xanthe to the bed, and pushed aside a white handkerchief stitched with red cherries that lay across the sheets. Her voice was blunt, but not unkind. "Xanthe, are you carrying a child?"

Xanthe sat on her bed and buried her face in her hands. Her sobs told the answer.

Nerissa knelt before her. "Launcelot is the father, is he not?"

Xanthe looked up in amazement. "How you know this?"

Nerissa waved her hand, dismissing the question. "It is how he treats you. As though he has taken what he wanted from you, and now fears you might ask something from *him*."

Xanthe looked at her, her eyes still big with tears. For an instant she thought of telling Nerissa all that had happened, but the lock on her tongue sealed it tight. The rape did not matter. What was, was.

"We will get him to marry you," Nerissa said matter-of-factly.

"No!" Xanthe sat up straight, drying her face with her apron. "Not him!"

"But if he is its father—"

"He is . . . bad. Vile."

"A clown, perhaps, but vile?"

"I could not put faith on such a man."

"But we *must* use faith, Xanthe. Indeed, it is all we have. All life is a game of hazard."

"I do not know that game," Xanthe said. "In my house we had no cards."

Nerissa looked hard at her tear-stained face, and after a moment she nodded. "Well, then. Not Launcelot. Another husband will be found."

"To be father to other man's child?"

"Hush. With a gift of property, or a good position, why not?"

Xanthe shook her head. "I am ashamed to want such help."

"We are all in need of help, Xanthe."

"Ah, but whom could I trust for it? Friend Nerissa, are there men who will do what they vow?"

Nerissa laughed a little. "*I* do not think so. Few women will, either, all or even most of the time." She thought for a moment. "Yet I did work for a man once . . . a hard fellow in some things, but he paid me well, and always, always at the appointed time. And when he said a thing would happen, it did."

"But that man is not here to marry me. How will I do for this babe?" Xanthe said mournfully.

"Oh, hush. We'll find you someone. I will speak to Portia, and she will get you a man or a family to raise your child. It pleases her to give people things."

Xanthe felt her stomach roil. She bent forward, closing her eyes. Nerissa laid her hand on Xanthe's forehead. "Xanthe, how long has it been?"

"Near three months."

Nerissa furrowed her brow, looking as though she pondered not what Xanthe should do, but whether she herself should say what she thought. After a moment she said in a low voice, "I would that you knew this. In the houses of . . . in a place where I once was, I met a woman—more than one—who thought she could not sustain a growing child. She—they—had ways to rid themselves of the seed, in the early months. It is done by some, Xanthe, and none the wiser. There is rue in the kitchen gardens of Belmont. I know something of that herb's qualities when it is boiled into a simple. Dangerous, a little, but . . ."

The stitched cherries ran together on the handkerchief that lay by Nerissa's pillow. The berries turned liquid, like blood drops. Xanthe closed her eyes.

Nerissa said hastily, "No, then. We must not do that. Xanthe? What is it?"

Xanthe opened her eyes. "Pictures plague me," she said in a low voice. "Bad ones, of tortures and innocent suffering. I saw one now. But it's fled."

Nerissa looked shocked. "How long has this happened?"

"All my life. Less since I left Spain, but more since . . . since . . . the Venetians came. Signiors Bassanio and Graziano."

"And Launcelot."

"Yes." Xanthe gripped her forehead with her fingers. "The pictures come on me when I am not ready—though how could I ever be ready—when I hear talk of cruel things, or sometimes for no reason I know."

"Most strange! But those signiors from the city have gone now."

"They will return. And if the lady Portia marries Signior di Piombo, I cannot . . ." Xanthe had been whispering, but suddenly her voice burst strongly from her throat. "These pictures! I would do anything to be rid of them!"

Nerissa sat close to her and put her arm around her hunched shoulders. "They are the devil's faces," she said, her voice hushed. "But we are stronger than he. You must banish the devil, as I do."

"How?"

"By laughing."

Xanthe smiled faintly. "But his faces do not . . ."

"Amuse? Then think of a thing that does. And pray."

Xanthe let out her breath in a long sigh. "To whom shall I pray? My parents were a Jew and a Moslem who feigned to be Christians. Maybe they thought they were! For me, I do not even know God's name."

"He knows yours," said Nerissa.

Another servant called Xanthe from the hallway. She rose, straightening her apron. "I must see to the beds."

"Life is not so tragic, Xanthe!" Nerissa said. "We patch up the world as we can. It's good to laugh."

She looked at Nerissa's friendly smile, red lips curved like a bow in a fair-skinned face. She looked at her red-gold curls. Xanthe's forehead creased, not in anger, but as though she faced a difficult puzzle. She held up her right hand, its scar a pink slash in the brown skin. "How do I laugh, Nerissa," she said, "when the world thinks the devil's face be mine?"

Nerissa looked at her wordlessly for so long that Xanthe thought she had no answer. But just as Xanthe curtsied and turned toward the door, Nerissa said, "For your own sake, you must try."

THIRTY-TWO

In the hallway she closed Nerissa's door and sagged against it. It was not illness or visions that weakened her, but fear of what she had almost done. She'd come far too close to accepting Nerissa's last offer. She hated Launcelot Giobbo and wanted to root his sprouting seed from her womb. But in her mind her father's voice echoed. *Only life is sacred, and all life is sacred.*

In the following week she felt more peaceful, as though she had come safely through some ordeal. Her visions grew fewer and fleeting. Her stomach bothered her only early in the day, and Nerissa was careful to make her load light, keeping her out of the kitchens before evening, sending her to convey messages or to pick flowers, giving her time to rest on her bed.

But the men from Venice did come again, and with them returned her nameless fears. The night of Portia's marriage to Bassanio di Piombo was one of the darkest of her life.

Xanthe had begged Nerissa to say naught to anyone of her condition, and Nerissa had said that though Portia at least must know in time, she'd say nothing as yet. But Portia, who had rarely even looked at Xanthe, seemed still to have guessed it, and even to discern that Launcelot was the culprit. On the very day of her marriage she had been on the verge of dismissing Launcelot from Belmont, and Xanthe had exulted. But then Nerissa spoke on Launcelot's behalf, and so he was maintained. Perhaps, not knowing the fullness of Launcelot's knavery, Nerissa thought Xanthe despised him only for wounded pride, or some other patchable love injury. A part of Xanthe knew this. But fear argued loudly. It said that Nerissa was an Old Christian, and so was Launcelot; they were all Old Christians, all in league with one another, and she had been a fool to trust any of them.

That night she saw more visions.

She was waiting at table in the great dining room, keeping her distance from Launcelot, who stood behind Bassanio's chair wearing peacock blue livery stitched with the di Piombo crest, a wingless bird. It was Portia's wedding feast, and wine flowed freely as the new guests arrived. It was not unusual for finely clad folk to visit Belmont at all hours, interrupting breakfasts and dinners and suppers, and so she paid no special notice to these two young folk until the woman pulled back her hood to reveal the face of Leah Gozán.

Xanthe froze, not noticing when Nerissa took the tray she was carrying, not hearing the welcomes and felicitations that passed among the guests, until she finally understood that the young woman before her was no ghost, but flesh and blood, and that this face was real.

And then she stepped back and listened, and heard and understood all.

SHE SAT IN the darkness of an upper room, watching as Bassanio di Piombo and Graziano di Pesaro took ship for Venice, and then, an hour later, as Portia, clad in a man's garments, hurried someone—could it be Nerissa?—along to the wharf. Portia was chasing her new husband, perhaps, or embarked on some other mad plan. Dimly through the floor Xanthe heard continuing revelry; laughter, music, and snatches of singing. She sat, looking into the night, thinking of nothing.

When it was very dark she saw a cloaked woman bearing a torch come out of the house and walk in the direction of the chapel.

Xanthe rose and lit a taper.

Jessica di Scimmia was kneeling in prayer before Mary's image when Xanthe entered the small church. The torch was affixed to the wall, and the young woman's bare head was bowed between two high candles. Xanthe coughed quietly, and Jessica jumped to her feet in fright. "Who are you?"

Xanthe held up her hands. "Only a servant," she said. "Do not fear me."

Jessica clasped her hands before her. "Did you come to pray?"

"No, I . . . Well." Xanthe walked toward her and sat in a pew. "I come to talk. I once lived in Toledo."

Darkness passed over Jessica's face, like the shadow of a bird's wing. "I know nothing of your country, mistress," she said.

"You have the face of your mother. I knew her."

Jessica drew in her breath, but said nothing.

"*¿Hablas ustéd español?*"

The answer was abrupt. "No."

"Perhaps you do not believe me," Xanthe said, smiling gently. "What know you of your mother, lady?"

"Her father was a hidalgo," Jessica said, with a note of pride. "She had a Christian name. But my father called her Leah." She sighed. "I never knew her. She died when I was born."

"The Inquisition killed her."

Jessica drew her breath in sharply.

Xanthe leaned forward, her eyes shining. "She was brave. The town knew of her! She—" She stopped suddenly. Jessica was sitting absolutely motionless, as though in shock. *She does not know of this,* Xanthe thought. *She does not know.*

In a gentler tone, she began again. "Your mother feared nothing. She might marry the most rich hidalgo's son, but she loved your father and she chose him. Can I tell you what she was like?"

Xanthe saw a brief, hungry flash in Jessica's eyes, and then a veil seemed to drop before them. "I want to know nothing of her," she said. "Perhaps, if I had known you before . . ." She paused, then shook her head. "Her past is not mine now."

Xanthe felt sad and confused. It was damp and chilly in the stone chapel, and the girl seemed to be shivering. She picked up a crumpled green cloak that lay on the ground and held it out to her. "Perhaps you should wear this, lady." Jessica made no move to take it, so she took it back awkwardly. A stitched red heart was tearing loose from the cloak's fabric. "What is this . . . this brooch?" she asked. "I could mend it."

Jessica laughed at her ignorance. "I tried to pull it off, but I could not do it without tearing the weave," she said. "You may take it and burn it. God be with you, now."

Xanthe picked up her candle and walked with the cloak toward the rear of the church. When she turned she again saw Jessica kneeling, mouthing prayers to a marble statue of a mother.

Oᴜᴛsɪᴅᴇ sʜᴇ sᴀᴛ at the end of the wharf, far from the house and the chapel. She placed her candle next to her. The night was dank and still, and her stomach felt as heavy as though she'd swallowed lead.

Jessica's cloak was in her lap, and she looked down at the loose, ragged heart on its sleeve. As she did so, shadowy shapes began to move over the surface of the red badge. She saw a man at the hub of a mob, ringed by other men who dragged and kicked and beat him.

Dread gripped her, and she closed her eyes. But the vision was there, too, behind the lids.

Laugh, Nerissa had said. *Laugh!* But Xanthe could not. She felt the sorrows of the world on her back, her shoulders, her chest. In her mind she cried out that she could not bear it; she was only one woman. Fiercely she prayed, to Christ and María and San José and the Holy Spirit, to anyone, to the Most High. *My God, my God, visit me, help me, I am so alone, Adonai, por favor, por favor!* And suddenly she felt the creeping fingers of the fiend, climbing onto her body, making her skin crawl, and she screamed and jumped to her feet.

From the folds of Jessica's cape jumped a tiny frog, who sat blinking in the candlelight.

Xanthe stopped screaming and knelt to pick him up. He weighed nothing. He was less than half an inch long, and his small throat throbbed. He looked at her suavely, then jumped into the river grass.

She began to laugh.

As she did so, the black ghosts hovering in the air seemed to dry and break apart like ash or powder, then fall and dissolve in the muddy decay of the river. She watched them go, then looked up at the cloudy sky of the Most High.

She was halfway back to the house when a man on the highest balcony began to sing. His song was a love ballad of old France, and its notes sailed upward like the lark at dawn. She stopped, hugging to her breast the folded cloak Jessica had given her, transfixed by the beauty of the sound.

> Can vei la lauzeta mover
> De joi sas alas contral rai
> Que s'oblid es laissa chazer
> Per la doussor c'al cor li vai, Ai!

So pure and rich and sweet was the voice, she would never have guessed that it rose from the throat of Jessica's drunken and dissolute husband, Lorenzo di Scimmia.

PORTIA AND NERISSA returned from Venice a day later, tired and in ill humor. Nerissa went immediately to bed. Portia stayed below to tell her story to the di Scimmias, the careless stewards of her house for the past day.

"I won it," Portia said, her voice not jubilant, but grim and defiant. "I freed Antonio, and got you two money to live, and won what was my own. The price was your father's ruin."

Jessica stiffened and her face turned white. Not noticing, Lorenzo picked her up and whirled her in the air, crowing. He nearly stumbled over Xanthe, who was on her knees on the black and white tiles, gathering the dead leaves that had fallen from the box-trees.

Rising, Xanthe dropped the leaves into her apron and walked out on the porch.

She heard footsteps behind her. "Xanthe."

She looked back in surprise, and curtsied. Portia had followed her. "I . . . owe you something." Portia seemed embarrassed, and her words came with difficulty.

Xanthe looked at her in cold inquiry.

"I have not been kind to you, I think. Perhaps I have not been kind to . . . several." She swallowed. "I hope you will forgive me."

Xanthe said nothing.

Portia cleared her throat. "Nerissa has told me of your condition. I will help you, of course. You shall be married if you wish it."

"Thank you, Lady Portia," Xanthe said. "But I need no help."

"I think all of us require help. Myself included, though I triumphed over the Jew." She corrected herself. "Shylock the Jew."

"Shiloh ben Gozán."

"He. I beat him and I beat Antonio, and I won what should have been mine from the start. But Nerissa tells me that had I won the whole world, I would still have much to learn."

"Not *you*, Lady Portia!" said Xanthe.

Portia frowned at her tone, then relaxed her brow and laughed shortly. "Well you may mock at me, Xanthe. I am too weary to protest. I have heard a sermon preached me by our Saint Nerissa for five hours on a boat. I thank God she has gone to sleep! In any case, I hope you will stay with us." To Xanthe's surprise, Portia leaned forward and gripped her hand. "I wish I could give you something."

Xanthe felt a surge of unexpected pity for her. She looked a strange scarecrow or clown, with her tall, bony form and her hair cut shorter than a man's. What loneliness was hers?

She smiled a little. "I thank you, Lady Portia. I have been well treated at Belmont, by most. But I want nothing from here that I do not now own."

Portia nodded, and squeezed her palm. Looking down at their clasped hands, she seemed struck by a notion. She stripped off one pale yellow glove, then slipped a turquoise ring from her finger. Its veined stone looked almost black in the light of the dying torch.

Xanthe went completely still.

"I will give you this ring, Xanthe, when I have done with it," Portia said. "A remnant, left over from our escapade. The silver is fine, and worth some money."

Xanthe raised her hand slowly to touch the ring delicately with a forefinger. In a low voice she said, "Lady Portia, so please you, whence came it?"

Portia regarded the ring carefully. "It came to me from Nerissa, who had it from a Spanish soldier, who had it from a vintner in Venice, who . . . I lose the track there. I seem to remember a ring like it."

"I . . ."

"It will be yours tomorrow. Yet it first has a part to play. Wait and see!" Portia dropped the ring into a pocket of her cloak. Looking suddenly recovered in confidence and zeal, she turned and marched into the house. Her robe billowed behind her. Xanthe stood with her fingers outstretched, staring at her back.

XANTHE WAS ON the portico with a broom when Bassanio and Graziano disembarked from their ship the next day. With them was Antonio, splendid in fresh face powder and borrowed furs. The men found Portia waiting for them on the wide veranda, clad in a dress of silver weave; evening finery, though it was not yet noon. A gold scarf hid her butchered locks. Behind her was Nerissa, smiling in blue satin. To the side stood Lorenzo di Scimmia, with Jessica seated before him, wearing about her neck the widest pleated godrun Xanthe had ever seen. On her lap sat a ring-tailed monkey.

"You are welcome," said Portia to Antonio. "But not with any standing. Think not to stay long or to give orders to my servants while you are here. Indeed, depart today! I'll give you the money, though you now have much of your own. It is your good fortune that your bankruptcy was a fiction." She handed Antonio a letter. "This document is signed by an agent of the port of Venice. After your trial, one of ben Gozán's friends confessed to the practice. Your ships met with no more than some costly delays, caused by your faulty planning before they left Venice. Indeed, two of them docked yesterday in Genoa."

Antonio opened and shut his mouth like a fish. "You . . . I . . . My . . . I know you! You were—"

"Yes, I was the doctor of laws who won your case for you. Strange, is it not? Now I have other business." She reached into the folds of her gown. Her eyes met Nerissa's, and the two women shared the smile of the Mona Lisa.

Then Portia turned abruptly to Bassanio. "You, sir." She drew out her hand and thrust it forth. "Is this not your ring?"

Jessica jumped up, dislodging the monkey, who scrambled screeching up a column. The talk became a babble of accusations. Launcelot Giobbo, arriving with a corked bottle of canary, stood stock still in the doorway. From the corners of her eyes Xanthe watched the finely dressed group, all gathered together as in the last scene of some improbable play. She swept around them, making loops and circles like an artisan or a sorceress. She skirted Lorenzo di Scimmia's arm as he shook Jessica's shoulder. "Do *not* ask her how she got it from the vintner," he was hissing. "What is that to us? If you anger her, she may cast us out, and Antonio's not yet given us the money!" Xanthe swept past them, and past Nerissa, who was giving Graziano's roving hand a sound slap.

Hard by Graziano, Bassanio stood swaying like a clubbed sheep. He had dropped the ring Portia had placed in his hand to the stone floor of the portico. "My love!" he said. "I would cut off my *right hand* if it offended you. But—"

"But me no buts." Portia waved her finger an inch from his face. "It matters *not* how I got that ugly ring, or whether I wish to convert it to a pencil holder. It is a piece of trash that came from the hand of a common soldier. What of it? You promised to wear it *always,* or forfeit your winnings. Did you or did you not sign a paper?"

"You said that was a ritual!"

"And you thought a ritual a jest?"

"Not a jest, but—"

"Did you or did you *not* sign a paper?"

"She is a harpy!" Antonio called to Bassanio. He was smiling happily, seated on the top marble step. "We do not need her money." He waved the letter Portia had given him. "My ships are in! With this and the Jew's money I have infinite capital, and a scheme! I think to sponsor the conversion of cows' skin to leather, in India, where none have yet thought to launch such an industry. . . ."

The din faded in Xanthe's ears as she left the veranda and rounded the kitchens. In the servants' wing of the house she replaced the broom, then retrieved her small trunk from her room.

In the hubbub and confusion that reigned at the front of the house, none noted, or afterward cared, that the ring had disappeared.

THIRTY-THREE

SHE FOUND HIM. He was standing on his stoop with a pack strapped to his back. The door to his dwelling stood half open, and from the street she saw him cast a key through it. The key rang on the flagstone entryway where it dropped.

She would have known him anywhere, though twenty-three years had passed since he'd walked the streets of Toledo, grieving for his dead wife and looking at no one. His beard was partly silvered; and a few threads of gray streaked his hair, but that was still *moreno*, dark and thick, and his hawk's profile was unmistakable.

Her back hurt from the long walk through the Ghetto Nuovo. Her Italian was passable now, and anyway she'd found, as she'd guessed she would, that many spoke Spanish in the ghetto. But the first woman she approached looked away when she asked for his dwelling, as though to speak of the man might infect her with his bad luck. The second shook her head and said that his house had been taken from him and she knew not where he was. Xanthe at last asked for Tubal-cain, a man whose name Portia had mentioned early that morning when telling the tale of her triumphs. *Ah, Señor Tubal-cain! He lives by the northern wall.* She found that man's tenement, and when she told his wife her purpose, the woman's face clouded and she sent her back the way she'd come. Her directions brought Xanthe to two crossed streets, where she stood for a moment in puzzlement, then turned right, to find the high house that had lately been Shiloh ben Gozán's.

She was humming the old song her father had once hummed, to cheer her own spirits, when she saw him and paused in the street below. He half-turned and looked curiously down at her, as though he knew the melody, or, better, owned it, and was wondering what it did on the lips of a Moorish woman whom he did not know. She stopped humming abruptly. "Señor ben Gozán? *Puedo hablar consigo?* May I speak with you?"

He turned fully then, his back straight despite the pack he wore. She winced when she saw that his left eye was bruised and swollen, and that his cheek was gashed.

He descended the stair, eyeing her from the top of her veiled head to the tips of her dusty shoes. "You are Toledan," he said in Spanish. "If you want work, Toledana, you will be disappointed. Only those with houses need housekeepers."

"I do not want work from you." She fell into step beside him. In the street children threw a ragged ball, and at the housefronts men and women sat or stood, talking. Some of them bowed as Shiloh walked past. Some looked askance at the odd pair, a tall Jew and a short Moorish woman in traveling attire. Others seemed as though they would speak to Shiloh, but he walked quickly, and looked at no one.

On the sleeves of the folk they passed Xanthe saw red badges like the one on the green cloak Jessica had scorned; the cloak now stowed in Xanthe's trunk. Thinking back, she felt foolish. She might have guessed what the heart meant. She noted also the crimson or yellow head coverings worn by the ghetto residents, and looked again at Shiloh, appraising his tall form, fine face, and thick hair. He wore only a cloth cap on his head, and no badge.

Glancing sideways, he saw the question in her eyes. "Jews who are only passing through Venice are not required to wear the hat and badge," he said. "I have recently learned I am one such traveler. Today I have no house. But that is not all bad. It means I do not have to keep it clean for the Passover."

She smiled. "I heard your d—I heard someone say you were as long-bearded as a rabbi."

Touching his chin, he said, "I cut the beard, and I will keep it this way. I like it. And who are you?" He stopped in the street. "I can direct you to houses that will hire."

"Señor ben Gozán, I do not need to work for your friends. I think I have more money than you do."

"So does everybody. Why do you haunt my steps?" He asked this not with irritation, but with a brief, mirthless smile.

"I worked for a Christian who knew you. She had something that was yours, and I wish to return it."

"Very curious," he said dryly, without much interest. "But I do not need anything from Christians."

"Then let me walk with you, señor."

He raised an eyebrow.

"I am no courtesan, I assure you!" In his presence she felt unusually bold. "I want only to walk and talk with you."

"Then you will have to walk toward the port, Toledanita."

"Willingly," she said, warmed by the diminutive. "I, too, had thought to leave Venice."

"Let it sink into the Adriatic," said Shiloh, setting forth again with his brisk stride. "Let it be inherited by frogs."

"The frogs have come already," she said, scrambling to keep up with him.

"Good."

They reached the open gates of the Ghetto Nuovo and crossed into the city. She stopped on the low Fondamenta della Pescaria, where the fish smell was strong. She felt suddenly sick. "Wait, please," she said. "Wait, wait."

He stopped, concern in his eyes. He looked hard at her, and as her queasiness abated she felt her cheeks grow warm at his gaze. "You are ill?" he asked.

"I am not ill," she said. "I am with child."

"Ah." He took her arm. "Then you must walk more slowly. And give me your trunk."

She unfastened the crossed straps on her breast, and he put the trunk under his arm. "Come," he said in a kinder voice.

They started again. His fingers felt strong on her elbow, but though he seemed to think he had slowed, he was still rushing her along. She did her best to match his pace, though her legs were so much shorter than his that the effort kept her puffing. Still, she was blessedly relieved no longer to bear the weight of the trunk.

"Where is your husband?" he asked.

"I have none." She felt her shame rising. "I might have married the father," she quickly added. "But I did not want to."

"What was he?"

"A piece of shit. So please you."

He laughed.

"I do not often say such things. Yet with him, the word is called for."

"It is good to call things what they are," Shiloh said. "What of your child? Where are you bringing him? Is he Christian or Moslem?"

"I do not know. How could I choose for him?"

"You could not," he said fiercely. "Only the heart can choose." He walked in silence for a moment. "Still, you can give him a good start. You had better find a good husband. Not one of those Christians." He glanced at her. "But perhaps you are one."

"Well . . ." She hesitated. "It is what his father was, at least in name. So the child has Christian blood in him."

"Ah. Is that a different color than yours or mine?"

She laughed. "If it is, I have three bloods within me. My mother was Jewish, and my father was what my last mistress would have called a *blackamoor.*" She stole a glance at his face. He was squinting at the westering sun as though to assess the hour. "So I am a walking Trinity," she added.

From the twitch at the corner of his mouth she could see that the jest amused him, but he said only, "See that you do not blaspheme in this city. Its folk are far, far more pious than I thought when I first got here."

"Ah, yes." All morning she had been sick, half with the motion of the boat on the river, and half with nervous dread. She still felt queasy, but her heart was now light to find that it was easy to talk to him, to match the rhythm of his dry humor. "I heard of their piety yesterday in the Municipio, and at the font of San Marco's," she dared to say.

He kept his face expressionless. "Ah, yes. I am famous in Venice now. Stripped to nothing by a doddering judge and a pair of—what

can I call them? Signior Antonio di Argento, with his painted funeral face and his lime green suit, and his lawyer, so-called, with
the tobacco stink and the hand gestures from the tragic stage." He
squeezed her arm. "But you, whoever you are, do not know what
I am talking about."

"I know more than you think," said Xanthe.

They were nearing the Campanile, which chimed seven. Men,
red-hatted and otherwise, scurried by them, talking of prices and
trades. "Look at the world," said Shiloh, making a sweeping gesture. "The Rialto has not been open all day, and furthermore it is
Shabbat, but still they do business." He raised a hand at a passerby,
a red-badged Jew of middle years who looked at him bemusedly.
Shiloh gave a short bark of a laugh. "None of them know me in my
new beard. I have become a story. No matter. I will leave them to
it. Few in this city even knew my true name."

"Shiloh ben Gozán."

"Yes," Shiloh said, looking at her in mild surprise. "Son of
Gozán ben Eleazar, who worked with his hands." He peered at the
sky again. "I do not know when your boat leaves, or what boat it is,
but mine will pull up its ramp within two hours."

"Are you bound for the east?"

"No. Amsterdam. I know a man there. A strange-looking Jew,
but a Levite, as I am. He will help me begin. Their Exchange is bigger than the Rialto. I will have one of those fine houses he spoke of
by next year. Though I think I may also turn weaver." He spoke a
little proudly. "I was one once, in Spain."

"You have money?"

"Enough. They took all my accounts, but I had silver in my
genizah. And my page of Haggadah. It is here." He gestured back
toward his pack with a shake of his head. "One day I may go even

farther west than Amsterdam, if the Most High allows it. Though only one time in my life have I felt farther from Him."

"Do you go to seek Him?" she asked.

He stopped so she could rest. "A strange thing to ask. But you are a strange and mysterious Toledana who will tell me none of her story. No matter. I understand the need for secrets. Do I seek the Most High?" He considered the question, as she sat on a low, damp wall and waited for her stomach to settle. "I might."

"Perhaps we are like a ring," she said. "The point farthest from another on its circle is also the closest to it. Perhaps when we feel farthest from Him, He is closest to us."

He narrowed his eyes and peered at her. "You sound like a sort of kabbalist. I like numbers and geometry, but I have no use for mysticism."

She frowned in puzzlement. "What is a kabbalist? And a Levite? And a Haggadah?"

He shook his finger. "As though I had time to discuss these things! I told you, I must walk." He began to rise.

"Wait." She touched his arm. "I have a thing for you." She reached into the pocket of her wool cape. As she felt for the turquoise ring, she saw his eyes flick toward the livid burn scar on her wrist, and away again. When she drew out her hand, she turned the wrist to show the ring on her palm. It shone there, bright blue and silver against rose-tan skin.

His eyes went wide. "This!" He bent and raised the ring reverently. His voice was hushed. "Where did you get it?"

"That tale is long."

He looked at her in amazement. "I went to the vintner who bought it of my daughter, may she give birth to monkeys! I offered him anything for it, but he said it had been stolen from him. Then he tried to sell me some wine that was not kosher." Xanthe smiled as he slipped the ring onto his finger, where it rested, at home. A broad smile creased his bruised face. "My ring! My turquoise! I kept it in my genizah. I had it from my wife, so many years ago, in Spain!"

"From Leah. She chose it for you."

His eyes grew wider, and it seemed that a day dawned in them. "You knew my wife?"

She nodded vigorously. "Leah Gozán, as brave as she was beautiful! I will never forget her face."

He looked at her steadily and for so long she thought her cheeks would burst into flame. But she held his gaze, and at last it was she who said, "Your ship?"

He rose and helped her to stand. "Tell me," he said. "Tell me your story."

As they walked, she asked him first to tell her what a genizah was. "You ask many questions," he said. "You have much to learn. Your mother was Jewish?"

"A converso. My father said she wore a cross around her neck."

"But she was born Jewish."

"Yes!"

They passed, talking, through the city, stopping each quarter mile to rest. The sun had set by the time they reached the eastern port, but a hundred torches burned along the wharf, where men and women hurried. Against the starry sky the docked ships bobbed with their sails furled, their masts standing naked and high, like crosses. Men of the wharf called out the names of places. *Barcelona. Marseilles. Sicily. Antwerp. Constantinople. Amsterdam.*

"The *Drake* weighs anchor in an hour. It is bound for the Low Countries," said the shipman, perusing each of their sets of papers in turn. He handed them back. *"Buen camino."*

Shiloh said to her, "You will need help on the ramp." He reached out his hand.

Xanthe looked down at the ring on his finger, and saw her last vision. In the blue and black turquoise rode a ship, higher and wider than the one now docked before them with its sheets half rolled. The sails of the ship in the stone were fully unfurled, blown big-bellied by wind, and the vessel tacked due west, trailed by its shadow, along the path of the sun.

She blinked, and the image vanished.

She took Shiloh's hand and the two of them went down to the boat ramp. Night had fallen, but the moon was as round and bright as a new coin. Out in the gulf where the trade routes began, merchant ships crossed paths in its light, and the waves were washed with silver.

ACKNOWLEDGMENTS

Among the many scholars and friends whose writings or comments contributed to this book, a few deserve particular thanks. I'm grateful especially to James Shapiro, colleague and friend, who generously shared his time and his considerable knowledge of sixteenth-century Jewish culture in Europe to guide my efforts. Any errors in my representation of these characters' lives are mine, not his.

I also want to acknowledge the inspiration provided by two excellent books (in addition, of course, to one excellent Shakespeare play). The first is Trudi Alexy's *The Mezuzah in the Madonna's Foot*, which helped me understand something of the paradoxical historical conflicts and harmonies among Sephardic, Islamic, and Christian cultures in Spain (thanks, Laura Apelbaum, for bringing this book to my attention, among all your other kindnesses). The second is Joel Gross's *The Books of Rachel*, whose fictional account of a

Jewish girl's life in early seventeenth-century Venice has stayed with me for the more than two decades since I read it.

I thank also my husband, Tom Lucking; my friends Karen Remer, Audrey Davidson, and Miriam Bat-Ami, Amy Silver, and Michéle Sterlin; my agent, Carolyn French; and my editor, Allison McCabe, and copyeditor Sheila Moody, for their careful reading and helpful suggestions. Thanks, too, to Robert Felkel, Mercedes Tasende, James Shapiro, Tova Sacks, and Rabbi Harvey Spivak of the Congregation of Moses in Kalamazoo, Michigan, for helping refine my flawed Spanish and nonexistent Hebrew. And thanks to Chuck Bentley for a taste of Venice.

Finally, I'm grateful to my friends and neighbors Heather Addison and Jennifer Johnson for their enthusiasm about the book. It was they who gave me the confidence to show it to others.